Manipulations

Book One of the Fashion and Fiends Series

by Angel Ackerman

Angel R. Ackerman
angel.ackerman@yahoo.com

Published by Parisian Phoenix Publishing, Easton, Pennsylvania USA

Author Photo: Joan Zachary, joanzachary.com
Cover Design: Gayle F. Hendricks
Butterfly Photo: Lukas Gojda/Shutterstock

C O N N E C T with the author:
🔗 bit.ly/3s6R8Ln
▶ AngelAckerman
📷 angelackerman
🐦 creatively angel

DEDICATION:

This book is dedicated to all the friends and family who supported my efforts — including the Greater Lehigh Valley Writers Group — and specifically my husband, Darrell Parry, and also my dear friend Gayle F. Hendricks. These characters survived because of you.

BOOKS BY ANGEL ACKERMAN

The Fashion and Fiends series
Manipulations
Courting Apparitions, coming late November 2021
Recovery, anticipated early 2022
Road Trip, anticipated 2023
Absolution, anticipated 2023

INTRODUCTION

This novel entered my life 30 years ago. Of course, It started as entertainment for my cousin Amanda Smith and I one summer after I discovered vampires. The story was mildy awful, but I was sixteen. I spent the next decade trying to fix it.

Meanwhile, I got married, had a baby, and a newspaper career. The novel got shelved. But somehow, I joined the Greater Lehigh Valley Writers Group and people like Kathryn Craft, William Prystauk and Jonathan Maberry encouraged me to keep going.

Now you won't find any vampires.

I've surrounded myself with a great number of talented friends to make this book, and the small press launched with this book, happen: Gayle F. Hendricks, my publishing partner, graphic designer, and book designer; Darrell Parry, who did the final proof on this novel and pushed me to write during our 20-year marriage; Joan Zachary, who took my head shot; Darnell Davis, for his small business know-how; and people like Jan Kreiger, Rachel Thompson, Michel Watts, and Tiffani Velez who offered so much support.

I wrote this book because I am a woman who likes scary stories and rich storytelling. I like Stephen King, Dean Koontz and Orson Scott Card's *Lost Boys*, the creepiest and most dated horror novel I ever read. But I also like romance and good erotic scenes and humor. Linda Lael Miller. Judy Deveraux. And later — *The Devil Wears Prada* (if only Lauren Weisberger's later novels had the same energy). Toss in some dark Poppy Z. Brite and the mix gets better.

I wrote the book I wanted to read. And then I wrote more.

As I gained more life experience, my stories focused more on relationships and their complexities as well as the monsters. My monsters serve as metaphor for the human condition.

If you've read this far, let me add this.

My novels have many layers. Most of the places my characters go are settings I have visited. Étienne's renovated farmhouse is based on the house where I lived as a child. The town depicted there is my hometown.

The themes in this book transcend a scary story. This is a story of self-esteem and how one young woman's insecurities contributed to her becoming a victim of domestic violence. It also examines how we love each other — how do we express love and to whom? And who decides what love is appropriate? Who is the "perfect couple," young lovers Galen and Adelaide or the often sparring Etienne and Basilie? What makes love healthy and when does it turn dangerous?

Another note about this book refers to time. I write my stories in very specific historical periods. This book starts in August 2002. It has to begin there because the 1980s made Basilie rich, French conscription laws made Étienne who he is. I don't think Adelaide would be as fragile if she wasn't a part of Generation X (like me!). Eventually, the impact of French colonialism creeps into play, as does the war in Afghanistan (but not until later books). The universe these characters live in connects to a very specific time.

And ironically, one of the later stories relates to intersex identity, but I first explored these issues circa 2012, before we heard so much about transgender. Book three of this series looks at Muslim customs, African traditional practices (infibulation) and medical care for women.

Thank you for picking up this book. I hope you like it. The next in the series, *Courting Apparitions*, should be out before the end of November. The official publication date for this novel is September 11, not because of the Twin Towers, but because that is Darrell's birthday and he deserves that recognition. And the end of November? That's Gayle's birthday.

Let's use fiction to explore some of the complexity of our world. Join me —

Angel

🔗 bit.ly/3s6R8Ln

📷 AngelAckerman

📷 angelackerman

🐦 creatively angel

🌐 www.angelackerman.com

August 2002

CHAPTER ONE

L ughaidh gripped the crumpled *People* magazine page against the steering wheel as he stared across the parking lot. It had been too easy to track her. A supermodel should know better. He relaxed his fingers and the page drifted to reveal photographs of fashion designer Étienne d'Amille's renovated farmhouse, one particular photo and caption circled with a thick black marker. In it, Adelaide Pitney arranged pottery in a mustard-gold painted kitchen with, if Lughaidh could trust the photograph, Tiger's Eye countertops. The caption read:

"D'Amille's long-time muse helped him find many of the distinctive elements of the home, situated in Upper Mount Bethel Township on River Road."

That provided enough information. Lughaidh found Adelaide and waited for her to leave without the French boss. After a trip to a grocery store twelve miles away, she'd led him to this dumpy bar. Someone even partially famous should have been harder to track, but Adelaide Pitney didn't act like a celebrity. You'd think she'd be more careful. You'd think she'd travel with someone. You never know when someone might pop out of the bushes with a razor and cut that beautiful face.

Lughaidh reached for his cigarettes. The styrofoam cup where he stored his cigarette butts had gone from empty to full during this recent hunt. Snapping his thumb against his index finger, Lughaidh conjured a flame from his fingertip and lit his smoke. Fire could mar Adelaide's flawless skin. The flame on his finger died. Lughaidh inhaled and watched her, as he had for the last several days.

Adelaide sat in her powder blue convertible, the top down, her rock music assailing his ears screaming 'dazzled and doused in gin' about changing tastes in men. Her heart-shaped face pinned her cell phone to her ear, not that you could see the phone beneath that thick strawberry blond hair. Without raising the roof of the car, Adelaide emerged.

Her excessive height and endless legs still surprised him. In those heels, she was easily six-foot-plus. She lingered at her car door, the cell phone still attached to her shoulder. Her hair, perfectly cropped to the chin, swayed with her movements. A couple, foul with perspiration, staggered from a mud-spattered pickup and disappeared into the bar. Adelaide smashed her phone closed, muttering, and jammed it into a cylindrical purse with a triangular d'Amille logo.

Lughaidh opened the Viper's glove box. Papers fluttered across the passenger seat, not one of them a valid registration or insurance card. The disarray covered the ornate silver chalice he had no right to have. Lughaidh let the papers go. Instead, he reached into the pedestal of the chalice and plucked from within a small marble with blue swirls. He slipped it into his pocket. Its coolness penetrated the fabric of his pocket and left the sensation of wetness on his thigh. He set his hand against his leg to warm it.

He dug into the mess on his passenger seat. Lughaidh cast aside a European Union passport and business cards from phony companies before he opened a leather billfold with a dozen driver's licenses. Each had "his" photograph, doctored in Photoshop. He needed a less exotic moniker than the Lughaidh, selecting the name Galen Sorbach on a Pennsylvania class C drivers license. It exaggerated his height at five-foot-two, but it also claimed that he turned twenty-three this October. Twenty-three was a very long time ago.

Meanwhile, Adelaide had not moved. She eyed the bar's doors suspiciously. An unlabeled door fronted the parking lot, while the proper door, which no one used, loomed at the top of the hill. Lughaidh stepped out of the car. He wondered what kind of personality Galen should have, but he didn't have time to ponder. He had to get the girl. Neferkaba, the Spirit Guardian, had requested it. The girl had to be emptied to protect the balance of the universe.

Retrieving his wallet from the rear pocket of his jeans, Lughaidh added the license. A baby face like his, never touched by five-o'clock shadow, always got carded. Evoking Ambisagrus, Gaulish god of weather, Lughaidh crossed the parking lot as a breeze. A drunken jumble of women with bleached blonde hair, cheap denim, and tight tank tops stumbled toward a Firebird placing themselves directly in the path between Lughaidh and his quarry. The women made their way, arms tangled and bodies barely upright, as they exuded a dreary fog of intoxication that blurred the defining lines between them.

Lughaidh aborted his call to Ambisagrus, plopping himself before the drunks with their quasi-exposed tits. Adelaide jerked, dropping her keys. The women offered a collective gasp and their limbs twisted together as the one in the middle hit the ground.

"You dropped from the fucking sky," the one on the far left said.

At this point, she was the only one firmly standing in this alcohol-drowned chorus line. Adelaide approached them.

"Are you okay?" she asked.

The woman on the ground struggled to get to her feet. Her hands and knees bore scrape marks, fresh with traces of blood and puddles of yellow pus. Adelaide grabbed a crumpled napkin from her purse and placed it against the woman's palm.

"You're hurt," Adelaide said.

Adelaide wiped at the woman's hand, and as she did, the napkin turned the color of electrified dusk. The bleeding stopped. The wound had healed, not completely, but enough so the injury was forgotten. Adelaide had used her power, the same power used a few months ago on a larger healing, the one that attracted Neferkaba's ire, the one recorded in the marble.

"You'll be okay," Adelaide said.

Lughaidh retrieved Adelaide's keys. The strange floral-nature scent of magick hung in the air. The women stared.

"Are you sure you can drive?" Adelaide asked. "Maybe I could call someone..."

Don't get involved, Lughaidh thought. The last thing he needed was Adelaide protected by a bunch of drunk women. He needed to isolate her so he could fill the cup with Adelaide's water magick, that's how she healed others, and return the cup to Neferkaba. That meant the drunken women had to go home. Lughaidh imagined a kiss of fire, and it danced across the air. An orange imprint of lips fell against each of the women's temples and dissolved.

"You should go," Lughaidh said quietly.

In complete synchronicity, the women directed their gazes toward Lughaidh. With similar unification, they went to the Firebird and piled into it. The car peeled out. Lughaidh walked to Adelaide and curled her fingers, and their translucent white-tipped fingernails, around her keys. Her gigantic blue eyes welcomed him.

"I hope they get home okay," she said. "They seemed really drunk."

"They might get arrested," Lughaidh said. As soon as he said it, he paused. It was a stupid thing to say.

Adelaide smiled. In her gold sandals with five-inch, red-soled heels, she didn't fit in this rural hamlet. Neither did he. His body relaxed, despite his anxiousness over the job he had to do, the deception he had to pull, on her and on Kait. Adelaide's magick pulled him like a tide. Her water lulled his fire. Her lips, so pale and pink, drew him and begged him to kiss them, promising a sweetness like cotton candy.

The marble, with its enigmatic blue swirls, had showed him everything he needed to know. Neferkaba had ruled Adelaide dangerous. Kait should have dealt with her by now, but she hadn't, so Lughaidh would. Perhaps Neferkaba would anoint him fire guardian. That would make him Kait's equal.

Lughaidh stepped closer to Adelaide, her toned body casting a shadow over him. He peered into cleavage through the strategic keyhole in her halter. Her bulbous breasts stirred him and that pissed him off. He had work to do! Somehow her water-heavy sexuality had distracted him. Galen could not become a victim of her charms.

Adelaide rested her long fingers against her hips. Her manicured nails gleamed in the moonlight. A charm bracelet crossed her slender wrist. An Eiffel Tower, a ballet dancer, and a Star of David toppled across her hand. The metal striking metal chimed like a fairy call.

"You know which door is in?" she asked, "because I really need a beer."

She placed extra emphasis on the "really." Her smile offered simplicity like ice cream. Her gleaming eyes served as windows to her soul in fourteenth-century, cobalt stained glass. His mouth went dry. His words flipped across his tongue. A wailing electronic version of the James Bond theme interrupted them. Adelaide sighed. She opened her purse and snatched her phone.

« *Oui, chef*? » she answered.

Lughaidh's tongue loosened and his limbs warmed. She mumbled through a one-sided conversation with her boss, as the French 'chef' implied, while Lughaidh memorized the New York plates and the name of the Manhattan dealer on her Mercedes.

"I'm in Portland, Et... Portland," she said, "so no, I can't stop for Oreos."

She murmured more French and closed her phone.

"Guess I'll try that one," she said, pointing to the door facing the parking lot.

The phone returned to the purse. Adelaide pivoted. Those killer heels paraded away, offering a view of swaying hips, backside and bare spine. Prepared to launch his Galen persona, Lughaidh called upon Baile, god of blarney, with a whispered incantation. He jogged after her.

"Hey," Lughaidh called. "Wait!"

Her chin grazed her shoulder as she glanced back.

"I'd like to stay here," he said as he reached her.

His authority filled the gap between them, then boomeranged.

"So stay," she replied, turning the grimy doorknob.

"With you," he said.

She raised her eyebrows at him and mounted the stairs.

"Don't you want to stay?" he replied.

She didn't stop. Lughaidh followed. He definitely could not manipulate her will if he couldn't make eye contact. He caught himself clenching his fists so tightly that his knuckles popped in protest. The wood floor reverberated with Led Zeppelin. Billiard balls cracked. Smoke surrounded them. The man at the video poker machine froze. The man shooting at the pool table thrust against the cue ball with too much force. The ball jumped against the green felt and ultimately scratched. The women bristled.

Adelaide maintained her course and claimed an empty spot at the bar. She ordered a light draft. Some dollars exchanged hands and the bartender handed her the beer. A lip-pierced woman in dark clothes sunk her hands into a school bus kiddie backpack, slapping a magazine against the bar. She beckoned the bartender.

Adelaide sipped her beer gingerly, the foam barely touching her lips, leaving no lipstick on the rim. She stood there, one heel rocking against the rung of the barstool. Lughaidh leaned closer. Their eyes met. Sliding one arm onto the bar, Lughaidh extended his fingers toward her forehead and pressed into her flesh.

"Sit down," he snarled.

She rested the beer on its coaster. She placed her hand on his forehead and mimicked him.

"No, Mr. Leprechaun."

"Do I sound Irish?" he asked.

"Yeah," she said. "You do. A little."

"I'm not Irish."

She shrugged.

"Neither am I," she said.

Lughaidh craned his neck toward the window and when he couldn't find the moon scanned the room for a clock. He was running out of time. Lughnasadh would arrive in a few hours, as would Kait. If Kait noticed that he had stolen her cup... His fingers slipped into his pocket where he rolled the marble between his index fingers and thumb. He had to return the chalice and the marble before she discovered what he had done.

The bartender slapped a *Vogue* onto the damp bar. It featured a full-page d'Amille ad with Adelaide in a cropped, plaid box jacket, teal and brown with suede collar; a v-neck sweater in a similar blue; brown mini-skirt and thigh-high leather boots.

"That's you," the bartender said.

"Adelaide Pitney!" the pierced woman burst out.

Adelaide nodded.

"She wants you to autograph it," the bartender explained.

Adelaide grabbed a metallic pen from her purse and drew a giant N, then looped against it transforming one side into a P and the initial triangle into an A. She returned the magazine to the bartender. Her hands tightened on her glass, stroking the condensation.

"I can't even go to a hick bar without being recognized," she muttered.

"What do you expect? You're a supermodel," Lughaidh said.

"Very observant, little man," she quipped. "Is that why you're hanging around?"

"And you're rude," he responded.

Her shoulders and her chest rose and fell, but no breath escaped her lips. She silently stared at him. Levity flecked her irises as her lips crept into a sly smile.

"Sorry," she said. "You haven't hit on me. You haven't tried to grab my ass. And you didn't slither away after my leprechaun joke. You could be a nice guy."

"Maybe," he answered. "Maybe not."

"All the better," Adelaide replied. "I always fall for the wrong guys."

The women grumbled. The men, few discreet, feasted on the slit in her shirt as her torso slanted over the bar.

"I'm not thrilled with the atmosphere," she admitted, slipping a single under the coaster. "I'm going."

"Wait," Lughaidh called.

He brushed his fingers across her wrist, disturbing the charm bracelet. The metal made that soft cry again.

"It's your tits," Lughaidh said.

He clasped his lips. Her eyebrows lifted. How had that phrase escaped him?

"Want to take a walk?" he asked. If her water power had attracted Neferkaba's attention, then Lughaidh knew what kind of place would please her. He did his best to hide his discomfort with a quiet cough. "There's a bridge, a block away. It goes across the river. I thought..."

The blankness of her face and the stoniness in her eyes made her response clear. The thickening Irish accent tripped his tongue. He had to get home, but he couldn't risk failure.

"I thought we could..." Lughaidh didn't know what to say next. Would Baile fail him? He should have given a sacrifice. He had not properly planned this endeavor.

An unshaven man beside Lughaidh raised his cell phone, pushed a button and photographed Adelaide. Inspired, Lughaidh called Baile again.

"I'm a photographer," he said. "That's why I recognized you."

"Yeah, right, and here I thought it was my tits," she said, walking toward the door.

"I've never met a celebrity before," he continued.

He kept pace with her. Concentrate, he told himself.

"I need a job," Lughaidh blurted out. "I graduated in May with an art degree, but I'm stuck taking kids' portraits. I hate kids."

"I don't even know your name," she said.

"Galen Sorbach," he answered. He'd said the name out loud. It was his now. "If I had a photo of you in my portfolio..."

Galen had to sound young. He had to sound like Generation Y.

"That'd just be... awesome," he said.

Her eyes softened. Leaning on the pool table, she scrawled on a napkin. Adelaide gave it to him. Her hand chilled him, relaxed his muscles, and mashed his brain.

"Do you know where this is?" she asked.

Her voice punctured his reverie. He read the napkin. The farmhouse. Four miles away. He nodded.

"Would you like to meet my boss?" she asked.

"Now?" he replied.

She posed amid the men at the pool table, snatching a stick as its owner continued to chalk it. The billiard player dropped his jaw. She took her hand and pushed his chin where it belonged. The room silenced, even the jukebox.

"You could stay here," Adelaide said.

She stole the man's shot and the yellow billiard ball cracked against the side of the table and into the opposite corner pocket.

"But I'm more fun," she said.

Adelaide laid the stick on the edge of the pool table, her hand lingering on the wood as she left it, stroking it slowly, up and down.

"Lots more fun," she said.

She darted to the door. The bar resumed its clamor. The men gathered around the pool table, walloping the guy who had retrieved the pool stick. Galen pursued her.

By the time Galen reached the parking lot, she had slammed the Mercedes into gear and raced to the street. Another check of the moon confirmed that Kait should have arrived. Would she find out what he had done? Galen should go. He hadn't succeeded, and now he risked Kait's wrath for nothing. If he left now, Kait might never know that he planned to interfere with her official duties. He had no desire to meet Étienne d'Amille, no desire to take Adelaide's photograph. He would never isolate Adelaide at Étienne's house, or could he?

He had to take the chance. He had to prove his worth to Neferkaba. He rushed after Adelaide. She drove fast, but the Viper caught her within the first mile. Adelaide glanced into her rearview mirror and pushed her car harder. Galen shifted into fourth, amused. A CLK430 couldn't dust the Viper. He didn't even have to cheat.

Her blinker flicked on. Entering the driveway caused a tingle to rise from Galen's tailbone into his spine. Galen parked behind the Mercedes. He headed for the mammoth deck that sprawled to the magnolia tree. Adelaide got out of her car, wielding a plastic shopping bag and a dessert cookbook. She peered at the Viper.

"That's a helluva car for a recent college grad," she said. "You don't really need a job."

"I do," he insisted. "That's my dad's."

"My dad drives a Honda," she replied, "that I bought him four years ago." She trotted across the deck.

« *Mon petit chou*, » a voice said. "Have you it?"

A heavy accent mutated the English. Adelaide progressed through French doors, leaving Galen outside. At the breakfast bar between foyer and kitchen, Étienne d'Amille ironed napkins, each wedged between press cloths as he deftly creased it trifold. The man's shaggy, dirty blond curls consumed his face, each napkin taking mere seconds as the iron hissed. Galen recognized him from the magazine.

"I thought you said you never iron vintage fabrics," Adelaide said.

"These?" the fashion designer said, his accent transforming the 'th' into a 'z.' "From Williams Sonoma last week. I need the work, calms me."

Étienne kissed her cheeks and she his. Galen studied Étienne's nose. The media mocked him for its crookedness, and while it did seem more severe than in photographs, it wasn't as ridiculous as the caricatures claimed.

"Ironing calms you?" Adelaide said. "Not sex?"

He placed the iron upright on its stand.

"Without my wife, I iron," he replied.

Étienne embraced Adelaide, his hands supporting her elbows as she rested a hand on his shoulder. She had at least six inches over him in those heels. He adjusted a strand of her hair.

"You're French," Adelaide remarked. "If you need to calm yourself, have a glass of wine."

Adelaide removed a blue package from her grocery bag. Étienne grimaced. He sank his hand into his thick bangs, exposing three pronounced wrinkles on his forehead. He wore a thin gold band on his left ring finger and a plain gold watch on his wrist.

"*Qu'est-ce que c'est?* What is this?" he asked, shaking the blue bag.

"Starch," Adelaide replied.

"*Je pense pas.* The brand, all wrong."

Adelaide teetered on her platform heels. Her shoulders sunk like those of a scolded child. Étienne tiptoed toward the door, his attention switching from the starch to Galen lingering on his deck. Galen recoiled against Étienne's crispness, his pink-striped Oxford shirt and beige slacks pressed as perfectly as the napkins.

« *Qui est là?* »

Étienne poked his head into the door, prompting a rise from the hair on Galen's neck.

"Oh," Adelaide remarked, rushing between them. "Étienne, this is Galen Sorbach. He's a photographer. Galen, this is Étienne d'Amille, creative director for Chez d'Amille."

Étienne chuckled and reached for Galen. His broad hands sandwiched Galen's in unexpectedly soft skin. Étienne shook Galen's hand rapidly but tightly, and tugged Galen toward the house. Galen didn't move. He couldn't.

« *Entrez,* » Étienne said.

The key phrase uttered, Galen entered. He stayed by the oversized white chair in front of the gas fireplace. Étienne returned to his napkins. Adelaide kicked off her heels and swung them by the ankle straps. Étienne piled his completed linens on the bar.

"You take *les photos*," Étienne said, "and you are... *un bel homme, n'est-ce pas?*"

Étienne considered Galen handsome or so he had remarked. The men locked eyes, and Étienne lowered the iron. Adelaide opened the refrigerator.

Étienne's head tilted, quite obviously surveying Galen's feet. The man's gaze rose slowly. Adelaide closed the refrigerator door. She held a bottle of Perrier.

« *Oui, un bel homme... C'est dommage you are petit*, » Étienne said, "or you go front of the camera."

"I don't photograph," Galen said.

Adelaide unscrewed the water. It offered a mellow hiss.

« *Hein?* » Étienne said as he unplugged the iron.

"Do you think we could give him a chance? Give him work?" Adelaide asked.

Étienne's lips twisted.

"You want me to employ the boys you bring home?" Étienne said.

He wrapped the iron's cord. They stood silently, waiting. Finally, he spoke.

"I invite you to my *fête*."

"That's not a job," Galen replied.

"It is if you sell the photos to *People*," Adelaide said.

Étienne smiled unnaturally wide. He kissed Adelaide's cheeks. He carried his napkins toward the pantry. Adelaide gave Galen a long look, a look that devoured him.

"You prefer to be alone," Étienne said. "I count the champagne."

Étienne shook Galen's hand, ran into the pantry and disappeared. So had the moon outside the bay window. Adelaide trod barefoot across the slate floor. She propped her hand against Galen's shoulder. Her face came to his. Her perfume drowned him in vanilla and orchard mixed with her sweat and desire. Her lips tapped his, tentative and testing. Galen's body pushed against hers and his hands slipped under her halter. Her breasts rested in his hands. More tingling filled him, followed by a strange cooling.

« *Merde!* » Étienne bellowed from the basement.

Feet pummeled the stairs. Adelaide tore herself from Galen. He found himself empty-handed and falling against the overstuffed chair to catch his balance.

« *Le champagne!* » Étienne exclaimed, infesting the room with orange and maroon energy from his aura. « *Il y a dix-neuf!* » He counted on his fingers, twice. "Nineteen," he said. "I ask for twenty. *Je dois aller*. We go. *Allons-y*."

"Et, there's nothing we can do until morning," Adelaide said.

« *Non*, » he insisted. "*Maintenant*. First thing I go to that... that... *ordure*."

"In the morning, Et," Adelaide repeated.

"NOW!" Étienne screamed, trembling as his hand sank into his curls.

Étienne's heart rate throbbed. Its force struck Galen from across the room.

"Okay, Et," Adelaide said.

"We were about to do something," Galen said.

"Sorry," she murmured, avoiding eye contact.

Galen begged his patron deity, Lugh, to help him gain this girl's water powers, to prevent her from unskilled healing. Maybe he wanted sex first but that would facilitate his work.

"You need to stay," Galen commanded.

"I gotta go," she said, shrugging.

Étienne lifted Adelaide's purse. Étienne swiftly shook Galen's hand for the third time. They escorted Galen to the driveway where Adelaide gave Étienne her cars keys and they drove away. Galen found himself alone, balling his fist and kicking the lawn. He might not have the power of a guardian, but he should have enough power to control a pouty girl and a scatterbrained Frenchman.

He had nothing. He had failed to fill Kait's cup. Sex had been dangled before him and then refused. Étienne's power of suggestion obviously out-weighed his. Oh, no, Galen thought, this was not over. He would keep the Galen-the-aspiring-photographer persona and finish this.

Unless Kait found out.

CHAPTER TWO

As it tore onto Church Lane, the Viper decapitated day lilies and spewed gravel. The rawness of his failure reverberated through his mind as the car careened and skidded to a halt before the decommissioned church. Galen got out, pounded the concrete steps, and threw his arms upward, one palm open to the massive cross on the steeple. The other clung to Kait's cup. He inhaled, deeply. The fresh air soaked into his lungs and into his muscles, unknotting them. The cross quietly creaked, imperceptible to average human ears, as the wind threatened to bring it to the ground.

With a whisper to goddess Ethne to supervise his travels, Galen relaxed his body into a sheer film, leaving the cup to clunk down the stairs. His foggy essence passed through the church's heavy door into the vestibule. He materialized. His body shivered in response to a drastic chill, so unlike the heat of August outside. Unnatural stillness and musk greeted him, the signs of Kait's presence. He snapped his fingers to conjure a flame and reached for the candelabra. Before the candle could ignite, air whistled against his ear as talons and a robust paw swiped his face. He fumbled, dropped the candelabra, and fell.

Another blow sliced toward him. Galen rolled across the torn carpet narrowly missing hitting his head against the doorframe. With his hand now engulfed in fire from the spark he had called for the candles, he prepped a fist. He swung into the darkness. A feline snarl answered his offense. Green eyes flecked with gold hunted him. A slit in the center of each shrunk with the brightness from his burning fist.

The creature leapt onto him. Sinewy front limbs braced against his chest as its snout, covered with beige fur and tan leopard spots, loomed against his face. An orange mane fanned its head. It unlatched its mammoth jaw. Galen flinched. The creature had one paw on his shoulder and the other pushing his ribcage. His fist, flames gently licking his skin, pounded the feline's neck. Its eyes flashed. Its lips curled. It rose on its rear haunches.

"Kait!" he screamed, sensing her nearness. "Help me!"

The creature's mane transformed into wavy hair of orange and fire engine red. The animal visage stretched into Kait's freckled face and naturally flushed cheeks. The cat torso and haunches morphed into her lean, androgynous form. Galen staggered to his feet, quivering with leftover adrenaline and confusion.

"You shapeshift?" he said.

Her pale nudity glowed, the blue and silver droplets embedded in the skin of her back shimmering and swirling in fluid designs. She licked her hands and wiped her face, brushing her eyebrows with her knuckles. Galen rushed her, bending her preening arm until the pressure nearly dislocated her shoulder and elbow. He stood behind her, his breath against her ear. His lips pressed against the necklace that dangled a seashell and pearl into the hollow under her throat. The metallic flavor and the earthy and perspiring taste of her skin filled his mouth. She cackled and disappeared. Poof, gone. He smashed through the swinging doors into the sanctuary. As the doors crashed into the wall, it broke from the top hinge and groaned as it sagged. Kait snagged him and twisted her fingers into his hair.

"What were you doing with my cup?" she hissed, nipping the cartilage of his ear.

His elbow jabbed her ribcage with a bone-splintering crack. She reeled back as he staggered forward. Laughing, she countered with a hook to his jaw, the jolt tearing muscle in his neck. They exchanged a barrage of punches. She dodged more than he landed. Her nails shredded his shirt, leaving bleeding welts. He tossed her into a pew, on her back, her legs kicking. They twisted, flailed, pounced, and recoiled until they collapsed on the floor. Her toothpick legs laid over his, her golf ball breasts jiggling as she rose to her elbows.

"What you were doing with my cup?"

He sat up, cross-legged, and removed his tattered shirt.

"Why are you hiding in this church?" she asked.

Without answering, Galen walked to the pulpit and the giant stained glass window of Jesus surrounded by sheep. Jesus's outstretched arms reached for the congregation. Kait joined Galen.

"That wasn't water magick," he said.

"No. Earth," she answered. "And my cup?"

"I borrowed it."

"To go after Adelaide? As if I wouldn't know?"

They gathered at the altar, statues of their patron Celtic gods flaunting their presence before Christ. Kait aligned herself with The Morrigan, the three crones: Badb, goddess of battle; Macha, goddess of life; and Nemain, goddess of death. She smirked while standing before the altar, so Galen kept a mistrusting eye on her as he placed his hand upon the head of Lugh, god of fire riding a dragon. Slime coated his palm. Whipping his fingers from the statue, a condom hung from his hand.

Galen roared as he seized her tiny body, her soles hovering off the ground. A maroon cloud consumed his head. Her eyes danced with glee. He tackled her, their bodies slamming to the floor. He struck her, back and forth across the face, knuckles striking cheekbone. Her arm reached toward his back, stroking his spine, while Galen beat her. She closed her eyes and Galen's arms swung in slow-motion. Blood dotted her lips. Scratches peppered her face. A wave washed his anger from him. She patted his cheek.

"How dare you attack me when you took my cup."

"You hadn't done your job."

"And you, you thankless bastard, thought you would do it for me. Hiding in this church, as if I wouldn't find you."

He climbed to his feet and lingered before the Jesus window. Kait had arranged their sharpened athames, cauldrons, cups, and plates on this altar that once honored a God who didn't belong to them.

"Do that again and they'll be no more lovin' for you," she warned. "You're my brother, but I will let you die."

Kait chanted a consecration in archaic Gaelic. Galen joined her. Kait stripped him, her hands working rapidly, mechanical and utilitarian, until he stood naked. She kissed the edge of his pelvis. It stirred him.

"Male and female we approach you," they said in unison. "We honor and emulate you."

Kait lit a candle, whispering to the goddesses. Water splashed from her chalice into the libation dish. She filled her cauldron and added a pinch of coarse sea salt and her native soil. She grabbed her athame and extended the blade toward the heavens, its tip aimed at the moon.

"As your body sinks away from the dawn," she recited and paused.

She turned to Galen.

"Can we skip to the fun parts?" she asked.

Her wrist swung the knife.

"No," he replied. "I need the gods' blessing."

"Do you?" she asked.

He motioned for her to continue. She returned to her post, sighed, and held the athame lackluster with elbow loose.

"May I continue to mind your ways," she said, reciting the words without reverence.

He covered her arms with his, stiffening her pose.

"You're mocking the ritual," he said.

He released her. She sighed, again, and dipped her athame into the cauldron, tapping it to her forehead. Murky water stained her face. She extended her arm so the athame hit his temple.

"I can bless you, too," she said.

He slapped the knife away.

"That's not the way it goes!" he yelled.

She dipped the knife again and touched her feet.

"May I continue to follow your path," Kait said.

Galen exhaled and gave her space. She moistened the knife a final time and lowered it. Before she spoke, she turned again, the athame resting against her navel.

"We've been doing this for hundreds of years," she said.

His fingers spread and his arms shot out to choke her. She stepped away from him.

"And every time, we go through every detail like we're novices," Kait commented. "This is nonsense."

"Easy for you to say, you're immortal."

She rolled her eyes.

"Lughaidh... Hadrian... Galen... George... Whatever you call yourself these days. The harvest comes again. The world goes on. You go on. Never die. As long as you fuck me."

She stroked his face and pressed her lips against his.

"That's all you need," she said.

"Do it. The right way," he said.

She scowled and tossed her limbs like a child in the middle of a tantrum.

"You don't know how it works, so you need to do it step-by-step," she remarked. "It has nothing to do with the gods! I have blessed you. No one else."

She shoved the blade into the red candle's flame and stared at him. Galen reached for his athame.

"I approach you, great god," he said in Gaelic, the tongue of his teacher and Kait's mother, "consort of all that is female."

Galen lit a white candle from the red one.

"God of sun, of day, of all life."

He poured water into the libation dish.

"Drink," he continued.

"Because Lugh's been waiting for you to bring a glass of water," she interrupted.

He ignored her. He prepared to bless himself and his tools as she had. Galen ran his fingers through his soil. It rushed like warm water against a winter-bitten limb.

"Revive."

Galen's voice crossed his lips without his brain guiding.

"As you come forward to greet this day, allow me to greet it also."

The magickal energy of the sun consumed him with blinding, golden rays. His athame stung his hand as it conducted heat. His blood boiled. He drew a long, deep breath. He thought only of his breath and how it cooled his body.

He brought his left hand to the censor. The burning incense of sandalwood, frankincense, and cinnamon swallowed the room.

"You're blessed, humbled. Seen your glimpse of the sun. Time for the fun part," Kait said.

Kait placed her gleaming hot athame, as orange as her hair, into Galen's cauldron. The water hissed. Kait led the wet blade against her wrist and cut.

"You can't do my job," she said.

He laughed at her.

"I will be the fire guardian and I won't need your favors," Galen said.

"So that's your game?" she replied.

Kait leaned forward, dipped her finger against her wrist and smeared a few drops of her blood against his lips. Adrenaline pounded his system, making him laugh. Kait dropped her athame. His body stiffened, everything about him invulnerable and hard. Kait gave him a wry smile and grabbed his penis with her velvety hand. She toyed with him until his thighs quivered.

His senses screamed with the vibrancy of her blood. Galen peered through the church wall. The pink clouds preceding the sun cluttered the horizon. In the air, he noted the freshness of the creek, the sour carcass of a fallen bird, the pollen of the grass losing its potency with the approach of fall, the fumes from the cars on the highway, even the mixing smells of humans from the housing development across the woods. Kait's creamy juices from her unwashed body carried the mushroom scent of past ripe Camembert. He ached with hunger.

"Uniting our blood," he said in Gaelic with Kait, "our flesh and your spirits."

Kait clocked Galen's shoulders with the base of her palms, knocking him to the floor.

"The fun part," Kait said.

She cackled as they dropped, limbs on top of limbs. Galen landed with his back against the hard tile and Kait on top of him, thighs against thighs as she lowered her body to his. She snarled. Her hair lashed across him. Snatching her skull, Galen kissed her. He thrashed against her and threw her, her back against the floor and him on top. Kait kicked free and flipped him.

Kait straddled him. Her thighs pressed against his pelvis. Her body sucked his erection into her. It snapped every nerve. Galen rocked against her, with her wiry arms pinning him as her legs clenched his. Her strides taunted his body, caught in the seconds before his world would end as his life and his seed would spill into her. She slowed time, and literally trapped him for what seemed like forever in that agonizing moment the need for sexual release turns painful.

Pain and joy. Dark and light. The Morrigan and Lugh. Opposites, complements, pounding each other and building something. Combining energies to create something, adding something to the world... The Great Rite. No other magick proved as potent or primal as sex.

Kait rolled her body up and down, breasts jutting, taking him deeper inside of her. She plunged her tongue against his chest and licked him. Her hips swayed. She returned time to its normal speed and Galen feared it might happen. It might end. Now.

But then she exposed him and swallowed him, walls grasping tightly as she rode. Galen grabbed Kait by the waist, lifted her, and dropped her, head crashing against the floor. Wind stirred around them as he pinned her wrists to the floor and pushed her knees apart. She cursed in Gaelic. Her body arched into him. Her hips tilted. Kait smiled softly and kissed him. They rocked together. Her hands soothed him. Their bodies shuddered.

"The wheel of life has no hold on us," Galen said as he brushed the hair from her eyes.

"Man and woman, violence and blood, sex and life," she said.

They rolled across the floor together. Kait interlaced her fingers in his and peered deep into his eyes.

"Lughaidh, Adelaide's not merely an assignment. She's family."

She hopped to her feet. She pranced to the rear of the sanctuary and dressed in Galen's shredded shirt.

"You wouldn't understand," she added, "you're adopted."

CHAPTER THREE

Kait left as abruptly as she had arrived, disposing of Galen until her urges required him. To Kait, the harvest festival always meant fierce copulating, although in normal witchcraft that behavior would correspond with spring celebrations. Sex on Lughnasagh was her way of honoring him.

By August 2, she had deserted him. He spent most of the week that followed planning how he would corner Adelaide at Étienne's housewarming party, despite Kait's warnings. To busy his hands, Galen loosened the Jesus window. He carried the panes at a fifteen degree angle and rested them against the choir box. He built crates lined with Styrofoam. He loaded the panels and sealed the boxes. He had a small problem to solve. The sections would never fit in the Viper.

Upon nightfall, he hiked through the woods to the last remaining farm in the area. Emerging from stalks of corn that stood as tall as he did, Galen sneaked to the barn and found a rusted Ford pickup truck. At its advanced age, Galen could easily spark the engine with fire magick and not fry any delicate electronic components. He drove the truck to his borrowed church, where he loaded the crates into the bed. He headed for Canada with a fake American passport. He brought the glass to his studio in Montreal. Later he would restore it and sell it. Late nineteenth century American church glass wouldn't fetch much, but Galen liked the depiction of Jesus as shepherd. His low acquisition cost would protect his profit margin.

While in Montreal, he packed his tuxedo into a garment bag and tossed a few toiletries into a small suitcase. By the day of Étienne's party, Galen had returned to the basement of the church, where he dressed amid the forgotten chairs and tattered Sunday school workbooks. He dabbed on a sandalwood-based scent. He unwrapped his tuxedo from its dry cleaning wrapper.

Galen knew how to wear a formal suit: plain, black, satin stripe on the leg, jacket square and straight with narrow lapel, gold-rimmed black button covers, ebony and diamond cufflinks, and simple bow tie. A quality tuxedo never went out of style.

Galen didn't need a mirror to confirm he looked good in his tuxedo, lucky for him since he didn't cast a reflection. Neither did he appear in photographs. He existed outside of time. His relationship with Kait changed him.

Every time their bodies joined, he became more like her but they would never stand as equals. Neferkaba had granted Kait immortality for as long as she served as water guardian. What did Galen have? No connection to the mortal plane and he certainly didn't have access to the metaphysical one. His mission could change that.

First, Adelaide.

Then, Neferkaba.

If it worked, he could leave his sister Kait.

That became Galen's mantra as he drove to Mount Bethel. Adelaide, Neferkaba, Kait. Magick, power, freedom. When Galen arrived at the d'Amille country house, uniformed valets navigated high-end luxury and exotic cars. Galen had a small camera, fresh from the box, and spare film. He followed the path to the deck where a chamber orchestra played. People were everywhere. Each step immersed Galen in mirth, pride, and lust, a multitude of colorful auras exploding like a private fireworks display. He opened his hands, pulling energy into himself.

As he crossed toward the open doors, the temperature plummeted and everything blurred into slow motion, alerting him to Kait. She had crashed the party. He pushed onward up the stairs of the deck, bumping the party-goers against the railing. He shoved toward the entry, stopped by a wall of guests.

Heartbeats surrounded him like the ticking of a thousand clocks, slowed with Kait's distortion. He scanned everything, everyone, but did not find her. Then, a tiny patter caught his ear. He followed it into the kitchen.

Between the stove and the sink, a woman leaned, dressed in a cocktail-length speckled black dress. Several conservative gowns and suits crowded her, laughing at the right times and encouraging her to regale them. Their limbs hung close to their bodies, as if protecting themselves. When she pursued direct eye contact, even the men straightened and painted adulation across their faces.

Galen's breath synced with the tune of her heart, inhale, exhale, quick and through the nose. Then he noticed it again, the patter. The woman's heartbeat definitely cooperated with it. With perfect posture and a haughty angle of her chin, she peered at a sheepish young man. He vibrated with tension.

This fortyish woman had sallow cheeks painted lightly with rouge, mousy curly hair, and heavy smile lines. At the same time, her skin gleamed like a twenty-something's. Galen drew closer. Her low-cut dress had a crescent of glittery silk that matched the metallic ruffles ringing her hips. Galen stared at the diamonds on her neck, wondering if they ricocheted her pulse, creating two.

Then he remembered the second woman he had seen in Kait's marble. Adelaide had used her magick against this woman, without her permission. Here she stood. She stood with her feet arranged in third position like a ballet dancer. She had a natural smell unmasked by deodorant or fancy soap. Her fuming hormones confirmed his suspicion, as Galen detected the separate life asserting itself. Her diluted brown eyes tightened, meeting his. She stepped through her admirers straight to Galen. She forged a connection, eyes locking, trapping him, with nothing but her overstated but mundane confidence. Her sling back kitten heels clacked against the slate floor.

Adelaide didn't merely heal this woman. Somehow, Adelaide had gotten her pregnant.

"You don't look familiar," the woman said, her voice revealing a hint of New York accent. "I thought I knew everyone at my party."

Galen's hands loosened. He hadn't noticed twisting them into fists. The focused eye of the pregnant woman in the black cocktail dress wavered. Her step faltered. Her breathing quickened. She sucked her bottom lip into her mouth. Fierce triangles of color bombarded her, giving Galen a glimpse of confusion, fear, and joy. He couldn't read it fast enough. She sighed, shedding the cyclone around her. No one but Galen even perceived her weakness as her blood sugar crashed. Her body had no idea what to do, despite Adelaide's interference.

This would not be an easy pregnancy. Amateurs could only do so much.

Étienne slid between Galen and the pregnant woman. He gripped the hand of an apple-shaped woman in a green gown that tamed her bust and created the illusion of a waist. She batted her eyes, emitting a lusty pink aura.

"*Pardon, mon ange*. I see the dog, *une minute*," he said as he released her.

The pregnant woman exhaled sharply through her nostrils as Étienne planted his lips near the cheeks of the so-called angel, mock kissing her on each side before she flitted away. Étienne's gray vest, silver ascot, and black-and-gray-striped pants matched the metallic details of the pregnant woman's dress. He accepted champagne from a white-gloved waiter. Étienne went to shake Galen's hand, his grin lighting the room.

« *Bienvenue, mon ami*, » Étienne said.

"Étienne, he is a friend of yours?" the unsteady pregnant woman said. This time her voice carried a European singsong pattern.

Étienne leaned toward her. He angled for her lips, but she nudged away redirecting his effort to her cheek. Étienne placed her elbow in one hand, holding his champagne in the other. He pointed his flute at Galen.

"Know you my wife?" Étienne asked.

The woman placed one hand on her hip. If Galen couldn't sort the strange rainbow of her aura, he could read her stiff body language.

"Ex-wife," she replied.

Galen recalled the basic facts, gleaned from *People*. This was Basilie Saint-Ebène d'Amille, the wealthy financier. Étienne pulled Basilie's chin toward him and kissed her other cheek.

"Zélie, this is my new photographer," he said.

"Galen Sorbach," Galen said, introducing himself.

She presented Galen her hand, which he accepted, surprised at her firmness when she offered the same quick handshake Étienne did. Her lips parted as she met his eyes. She hesitated.

"Basilie d'Amille," she finally said, as if he didn't know.

"All the woman I have touched... and I live for her," Étienne said, draining his flute.

Basilie rolled her eyes.

"I must check with the caterer," she told them. "Excuse me."

She shook Galen's hand again. Étienne kissed her cheeks again.

« *A tout à l'heure*, » Étienne replied.

Basilie headed into the dining room.

« *Les femmes*, » he said. « *Je les adores.* »

Women, Galen translated, I adore them.

"You're divorced though, right?" Galen said.

« *Mon jeune ami*, » Étienne said. "I have papers... papers say we are *mariés*, others say *divorcés*."

Every pore on Étienne's body exuded alcohol. Étienne propped his elbow on Galen's shoulder, transferring his weight to Galen. Out of instinct, Galen's arm reared and almost punched Étienne, but he caught himself. No one usually touched him. Galen glared at the Frenchman and discovered Étienne's diamond cufflinks. This could be fun since the alcohol had influenced Étienne's circulatory system. Even so, Étienne's arteries stretched with effort. Galen smirked, noting that Étienne had a bit of a heart condition. In the next room, a dog yipped.

"Paper, *c'est rie*n. Nothing," Étienne said. « *Je crois pas les papiers.* »

As Étienne prattled, Galen searched the multitude. His attention switched between candidates until he spotted the surging haze around a woman with turquoise eyeliner and beady eyes. Galen beckoned her, surrounding her with a magickal tide that pulled toward him. The woman came, holding a chocolate truffle.

« *Très* Versace, Melody, » Étienne remarked.

Galen took Melody's hand, pressing his palm with hers. Cocaine coursed through her blood with unnatural intensity. She nibbled the chocolate, her tongue scooping blueberry filling from the shell. Galen drained the stimulant into his own body and transfused the energy through the diamond cufflink into Étienne's left arm. Galen trembled with the rush.

Within a fraction of a second, Étienne crumpled. His heartbeat accelerated beyond control. His blood vessels expanded, constricted, and expanded again to the point where his heart didn't take a beat to rest. Étienne's coronary arteries spasmed and the blood flow ceased. The man's heart simply stopped.

Well, shit, Galen thought. That's not what he meant to happen.

Throwing Étienne against the wall, Galen planted his palm over Étienne's heart, radiating a rich blue and calling on the waters from Aibheaog's sacred well. Étienne's heart sputtered. Setting his host on the floor, Galen waited.

Awkward silence surrounded them. The Frenchman's face had turned purple. Several partygoers had witnessed Étienne's episode. Galen slapped the man's cheeks and gazed into his lifeless grey eyes.

Shit, Galen thought again. Had he reacted too slowly?

Galen studied Étienne's pupils, digging for some sign of life. He touched Étienne's temple. Somewhere in Étienne's brain, something fired. The warmth of life met his fingers. There wasn't much there, but it was something.

Come on, Galen pleaded, come on.

Concern from the guests blanketed them. To misdirect their attention, Galen laughed. Because of the connection Galen had forged between them, Étienne mimicked him. The purple drained from Étienne's face, fading to a healthy pink and to his everyday beige. Galen promised Aibheaog a gift. The guests around them resumed their activities.

"I have... a funny..." Étienne paused, « *mal au coeur.* »

I bet you do, Galen thought, a funny heartache, indeed. That was too easy. There was no sport in it.

Étienne's hand rose to his chest. *Mon ange*, the angel in the green dress, motioned. Étienne smiled weakly in her direction.

"The woman... want something... *toujours*," Étienne said as he closed his eyes briefly.

"Too much to drink?" Galen asked.

« *Peut-être,* » Étienne replied. "*Excusez-moi, s'il vous plaît.* I made the commitment."

He scrambled to stand, stumbling to the point where Galen finally pulled him to his feet. Étienne shook Galen's hand again, limply this time. Étienne disappeared into the crowd. He reappeared lifting a ridiculously tiny black and white poodle, with tight curls and shaved snout. Galen took a photograph, his first... ever. As the flash snapped and the dog's snout appeared in the viewfinder, Galen remembered that he wasn't alone here. He had forgotten Kait. He no longer felt her, but he couldn't shake the sensation that she remained.

Galen swept the downstairs: the enclosed front porch, a den, and the ballroom with a Steinway grand. He raced through the dining room and tripped backwards into a south-facing atrium. Butterflies twirled around him. They blinded him. He blocked his face with his arms. More butterflies darted between the lush greenery, dotting the glass room with ocean blue, swirls of red and fuchsia, and orange. Galen lowered his arms. Mist sprayed him. A magnificent waterfall climbed beyond the second story.

Galen's stomach knotted. Time tensed. It started with the butterflies, their wings streaking as they flew. Among the people, eyes closed too long between blinks. Galen searched for the source of the distortion, for Kait. Something alien tugged at him. He followed the strange attraction, like chasing a pleasant smell. People blocked his path. He stopped and waited until the butterflies lost interest in him. He spotted Adelaide, a head taller than those around her. She watched him. Unlike the others, her eyelids blinked independently of the disrupted time. Her expression remained soft and natural while the others could have been wax. Peacock feathers adorned her up-do, with gold glitter around her lapis lazuli eyes, and lips that combined the two, a tiny pout in blue with gold glitter. Beyond her, a flash of red hair crossed the room. Galen lunged toward it, but Adelaide intercepted him.

With her haphazard dash Adelaide brushed against people, and when she did, they softened and smiled suddenly immune to Kait's trick. Adelaide's thigh-high, deep blue boot with stiletto heal separated the crowd, peeking from a slit in her gown. The miniscule, blue glass beads of her dress caught every nuance of the light. A wide peacock feather held her bodice together. It barely contained her cleavage, breasts lifted and bounding.

That's when something pounded Galen's skull. He pivoted. No one was there. No one had done anything. It had to be Kait. Finally, Galen glimpsed her. Leaves matted her hair. And boom... she had gone. Adelaide's blue silk glove slid along his arm evoking shivers across his shoulders. His body sagged toward Adelaide's touch.

"You came," she said.

An emerald pendant surrounded by diamonds dangled from a black velvet choker around her neck. Her fingers pressed against his sleeve, eliciting more shivers. She wore an emerald bracelet that matched the necklace.

"Not now," he barked. He had to find Kait before Kait ruined his plan.

He should go. Galen blamed the stones for detaining him. Emeralds attracted, usually money or lust.

"I... have to go," Galen replied.

"You want that strange girl," she whispered.

He disengaged. Adelaide tightened her grasp. Her emerald earrings sparkled. His gaze washed across her body, not exactly voluntarily. Galen imagined his hands full with Adelaide's breasts, her curves splayed before him to do what he wished. She rocked as she stood with him, disturbing the ornate train of peacock feathers that gradually fanned from her butt to the floor, doubling the width of her dress. Their motion filled the room with a scratchy swoosh.

"Please," she said quietly.

Galen's ears popped and crackled. Everyone resumed their former pace, milling, pawing at Adelaide. She beamed with each affection and distributed energy in return, something he couldn't label. It mesmerized him, holding him in his spot as if waiting for his turn to bathe in her light. Galen shook his head violently to free himself from the paralysis. He had to find Kait.

"I have work — " he began.

"You have pictures to take," Adelaide interrupted, her voice full of false bravado. "So you used me to get to Étienne. It's not the first time."

She lifted her hem and stepped into the dining room. Galen followed, surprised that Adelaide's path traced Kait's scent, reminiscent of harsh incense blended with summer rain. Adelaide sped up as she entered the hall. When Galen turned the corner in pursuit, Étienne seized his elbow. The wide-plank stairwell spanned before them, with Basilie's voice carrying to Galen's sensitive ears. She stopped Adelaide with nothing but a cold glance.

"This whole time," Basilie said, "you knew his every move toward her."

Oblivious, Étienne adroitly lifted a glass from a waiter's tray. The house quaked. A mushroom of magick dropped through the ceiling, brilliant color pelting Galen like hail. He faltered, the thickness of the magic unbalancing him. Étienne held him as Galen recovered.

"Too much to drink, *mon ami?*" Étienne asked.

The explosion had not phased the Frenchman. Pink fog filled the house, sticking to clothes and jewels. The rubies shined the brightest. The diamonds, now glowing pink, quivered and trapped the energy. Of course, the amethysts didn't falter. They never did. Galen surveyed the crowd. No one had noticed, or so it seemed. Étienne opened his arms wide, spinning.

"*C'est très beau, ce soir...* the night beautiful," he said.

Étienne ran off. Adelaide raised her hands as if pushing away the burst or perhaps in fear that Basilie would strike her. Galen took the stairs two at a time until he could not pass Adelaide's feathers. Basilie planted her hand firmly on Adelaide's shoulder. Adelaide withered.

"My husband bought her a poodle," Basilie said.

Adelaide nodded.

"Yes, Bas," she replied, curtly. "I picked it up in Baltimore."

"You hate dogs!"

"It's not a dog. It's a rat with curls."

"Why a puppy?"

"Her husband left her," Adelaide said. "Et wanted to cheer her up."

Adelaide looked nervously toward the second floor.

"Buying her a four thousand dollar tea cup poodle?!" Bas exclaimed.

Basilie groaned and left. Adelaide barreled to the top of the stairs, her feathers whirling.

"Adelaide," Galen called.

Adelaide zipped through the hall and rounded a corner. The pink fog laid so thick Galen could ball it in his hands. Galen chased her. Adelaide unlatched a heavy door with a creak. Inside, a magick-drenched Kait bewildered Adelaide with an impish smile.

"Thanks for the aspirin," Kait said with a wink. "I found everything fine."

Kait kissed Galen's cheek.

"Good luck, tiger," she whispered in Gaelic. "It's watching."

Kait had wrapped herself in a purple dress, tied with a huge bow at the waist. Galen clawed his fingers into her hair, but Kait wrenched from him and disappeared, only the magick residue lingering. Adelaide mounted the stairs behind the door.

"You might as well join me," Adelaide said.

Galen did. Once they reached the top, Adelaide waved him into a living area, still hidden by the energy left behind by whatever had happened. Adelaide went into a small kitchen at the opposite end. Galen lowered himself onto a blue-and-white striped sofa as fog cleared, revealing a wrought iron coffee table. A white horse stood on its glass surface, at its side a crowned blonde warrioress with spear.

"Queen Medb?" Galen whispered.

The image faded. Medb ruled Connacht, but she also talked to fairies. Kait had called Medb? More fog dissipated, revealing a rigidly poised tan-and-black tabby perched on the arm of the couch. He extended his hand toward it, wondering if it would disappear like Medb and her horse. The cat glared at him with yellow-green eyes. It raised a white-socked paw and curled its lip, showing a clean fang.

"Do you have a cat?" Galen asked Adelaide.

"Yes," she answered from across the room. "Oh my God, you're not allergic, are you? Because she's locked in the bedroom."

"You sure?" Galen replied.

He carefully rose from the couch. The cat snarled. He meandered to the kitchen.

"I had to," Adelaide said. "Look at me. I'm a giant bird, a problem if cat meets couture."

Disarray and the aroma of cocoa ruled the tiny kitchen, with pots and pans overturned on dishtowels and wooden spoons soaking inside a double boiler. Adelaide peeled off her gloves. She opened a can of Fancy Feast while the tabby screeched.

"Did you let her out?" she inquired.

He shook his head.

"This is a weird place for an apartment. Is this servants' quarters?" Galen asked.

"No. It's mine."

"Your own place?" he asked. "In your divorced boss's house?"

She set the cat food on the floor. Adelaide stepped around the small bar separating the kitchen from the living room. The cat deserted its meal.

"This is a perk. Et keeps me close at hand," she answered. "I've worked for him forever. He can be... demanding."

She sat on the sofa, carefully arranging her feathers. Galen lowered himself beside her. The cat returned to the arm and monitored them. Galen avoided the cat's stare, turning to the dirty mugs, paperback novels, napkins, and pens littering the table.

"Étienne's a rough boss. Parties, a flat like this," Galen quipped.

"It's complicated," Adelaide said. "I love my job for all the wrong reasons: glamour, celebrity, money, sometimes the clothes."

"Only sometimes?" he remarked.

"I'm from Chicago," she answered. "When there's a foot of snow, I want to wear a flannel and sweatpants."

"You?"

Adelaide nodded.

"I'm not the girl in the pictures," she said.

The cat stretched a paw toward Galen. It hissed.

"Zut!" Adelaide yelled.

Bending her beaded and feathered torso across him, Adelaide swatted the cat's nose. The peacock feather on her chest tickled his cheek. Her cleavage smothered him. Her perfume assailed him, sweet but tangy.

"Sorry, she gets moody," Adelaide explained. "Hence the name."

"Damn," he translated.

"As in 'that darn cat!' Like the movie."

"I don't know it. The movie."

She eased toward the other side of the couch.

"It's before our time," Adelaide replied.

Her hand rested on his thigh, too close to his groin, and her face studied his.

"Galen?" she said, as her hip sunk into the cushion beside him.

Her voice sounded distant. She lowered her lips to his. Their mouths collided, sharing the flavor of her champagne. He grabbed her arms. Jerking away, breathless, Adelaide brushed his hands off her.

"Don't bruise me," she warned. "Étienne..."

The cat growled. Adelaide shot it a forceful stare. It laid down.

"Are you always this..." Galen wasn't sure what to say. "Forward?"

"Étienne says it's a problem I need to work on."

Galen's abdomen tightened. His heart whispered her name between beats. She stroked his face, her eyes lost. Galen drew his hand from her ear to her emerald pendant and to her bracelet. She kissed him, light and teasing. Her mouth danced across his face and took his earlobe. His inner fire flared. He tasted her fingers and kissed her palm.

Suddenly, the couch beneath him shook. A presence pushed between them. Adelaide's cat flung itself at his face. Galen reared. The cat spun like a whirling dervish, screaming heinously as it sunk its claws into anything that would take damage. Galen's face streamed with blood.

"Son of a bitch!" Galen yelled.

Antiquated Gaelic profanities flooded the air. Adelaide dove for the cat. It attacked her.

"Zut! *Zut alors*! Stop!" she screamed.

Galen let the beast latch onto his arm. It hung from its teeth and nails, kicking wildly. Galen scruffed the cat's neck, ripping it free. He hurled it against the wall. It landed on the narrow ledge beside the stairs and withdrew spitting. Adelaide rose from the couch, ready to follow, but instead surveyed Galen and their wounds.

"Your face," Adelaide gasped. "It's bleeding."

"No shit," he returned. "My tux is ruined."

With trembling hands, she petted the vintage fabric. Her pupils dilated and refocused.

"Savile Row," she said. "1913."

Galen's mouth dropped. How did she know? He bought this bespoke suit in London, on Savile Row, in that exact year.

CHAPTER FOUR

I n the farmhouse's cool basement, Étienne fondled his 1921 Château d'Yquem Sauternes, brushing off the dust and turning the bottle. His hand traced the letters on the label and could imagine the sweetness of the wine, even though he knew he wouldn't open it for several years. Nothing compared to a good woman or a quality wine. Since he no longer collected lovers, he shifted to fine vintages, almost as enjoyable a hobby.

Étienne had accompanied three waiters in stiff white jackets *à la cave* for champagne. He repeatedly adjusted their ties. Above them, partygoers circulated, feet heavy on the two hundred-year-old wood floor. Two waiters retrieved a crate from Epernay, though Étienne hadn't been choosy. Most *'Ricains* didn't know French champagne from New York sparkling wine.

Étienne head swished as he followed. The third waiter, stationed behind him, raised a hand as if expecting him to fall. Étienne laughed and dashed up the remaining stairs. At the top, a fourth waiter refilled Étienne's flute. As he sipped the bubbly, Étienne approached familiar footfalls, sure they belonged to his *petit chou*, his little cabbage. He paused near his wife and a tall man with salt-and-pepper hair and a receding hairline. Étienne placed his arm around Zélie's waist. He moved a hand into the hair cascading past her shoulders, tumbling in tight curls. He pinched one. The spiral crackled under his touch, crisp with the hairspray from the stylist. He sniffed it.

L'ananas... The English challenged him... Pineapple! Pineapple and Chanel No. 5. The combination always signaled a celebration.

"I'm sure your wife is here, Bob," Zélie said.

Her words sounded as crisp as her hair. The sentence slid off her tongue with ease, her English enunciation perfect. He couldn't have said it, not like that, not even when sober. Yet she was as French as he was and she could. Zélie flinched, swatting at his hand. He lowered his head toward her bare shoulder. His lips brushed her flesh.

"Étienne, stop it," she commanded.

Adelaide burst into the room, apologizing as she knocked into several guests. Her head jerked. Her gown shed feathers. In her clumsy distress, his cabbage's lips puckered. Her eyes pleaded. Her cheeks and jaw hung with anxiousness. Even so, she remained the most beautiful fixture in the room.

Étienne patted Zélie's bottom and ventured toward his muse. The men faded like pillars into the background, so empty of color compared to the vibrant, florid gowns of the women. Plunging necklines, halters perking what nature had dropped, waistlines that rose or sank, hems that showed or hid legs, and the fit, the young girls mostly, wrapped tight in the hips and belly, not an ounce of misplaced flesh. Having spent his lifetime sewing and his adolescence exploring the opposite sex, Étienne could assess a woman completely by her clothes. He retrieved Adelaide's lost feathers as she wove deeper into the room. Blood streaked her arm.

"*Mon petit chou, qu'est-ce que c'est passé?* What has happened?" he asked, hating the blemishes on that perfect skin. He reached for her but she wouldn't stand still.

"Have you seen Galen?" she replied.

« *Non,* » Étienne said. « *Les bras?* »

"It's nothing," she said. "My arms are fine, Et."

"Not fine," he replied. "Not good at all, *pas de tout.*"

"Are you sure? About Galen?" Adelaide asked.

He made that clucking noise she disliked, a sound learned from his grandmother. He reached for her again, but she dodged.

"*Chef,* I'm fine," Adelaide said. "My cat... Galen got the worst of it."

« I will find something to care for that, my cabbage, » Étienne said in French.

Étienne didn't care if Galen had scars.

"I've got to keep looking for him," Adelaide said.

Adelaide went into the kitchen. Étienne swerved toward the stairs. He recognized a dress. One of his. It had a droop in the bodice. Without even thinking about the woman inside it, he pinched the fabric at the waist. The woman wearing it turned, gentle eyes now piercing, ready to chastise whoever would seize her like that. Discovering him, her façade softened. She blushed.

« *Madame,* » he said since he could not remember her name. "You have lost the weight."

He might forget names, but he never forgot a body whether he dressed or undressed it.

"Not even five pounds, Étienne. Nothing significant," the woman replied.

"The dress, *bien-aimée*, old. Two years, *n'est-ce pas?* If you must wear, we fix," he kissed her hand and continued on his path.

He climbed the stairs. Outside the bathroom, a line of women stood with cosmetic cases unhinged in their hands, evening bags swinging from their elbows. Étienne darted from woman to woman, kissing the air about each woman's knuckles until he arrived at his bedroom. The master suite opened into a workshop with a long sewing table. Étienne didn't turn on the lights.

A few steps in, a stout figure in a top hat jumped toward him with a boomerang blade about to decapitate him. He clutched his chest as pain bombarded him. He looked again expecting Oddjob the villain in the shadows. Instead, Zélie's headless dress form wore Étienne's top hat. Perhaps he had seen *Goldfinger* too many times. It was his favorite James Bond movie.

He sighed longingly at the bed and crossed the room. He sat. He bent to untie his shoelaces but couldn't because his arms wouldn't move with his coattails so tight. Étienne stood. He crouched to take the laces in his fingers. He undid one of his Balmorals, but completely knotted the other. Like a strike of lightning he remembered why he had come up; his *petit chou*, though she was too old for the nickname of 'little cabbage,' needed a bandage.

He rushed to the master bathroom, opened the mirrored medicine cabinet, and rifled the contents. Étienne tossed aside Zélie's prescription vitamins, cotton swabs, his two orange bottles of pills, three tubes of lipstick, before locating Looney Tunes bandages and antibacterial ointment. Who bought these Band-Aids? Adelaide. Had to be. Étienne clucked again.

The references to Pépé and Penelope had gone stale. Slipping the necessary items into his jacket pocket, he returned to the hall and the bathroom line, his hand brushing dangerously close to the bosoms waiting there. When his fingertips almost touched the exposed mound of one breast, the owner tittered, stumbling in her glimmering Jimmy Choos.

« *S'il te plait*, » Étienne said. "Do not swoon. *C'est urgent.*"

Her smile, even as she cast her eyes downward, brightened her young face. Étienne couldn't help from smiling in response. His fingertips brushed her hand, he offered a kiss on each cheek, actually touching flesh, and continued to the ballroom. Zélie met him at the stairs, as did a waiter with champagne.

"Have you seen Nancy Cornwall?" Zélie inquired.

"Who?"

"Bob's wife."

Étienne didn't remember Bob, but he could find any man a companion. He kissed his beloved's cheek. He drained the wine and gave her the glass.

"Do you know what Bob likes in a woman?" Étienne asked.

"He's so boring, got to be a tit man," Zélie whispered.

"Aren't we all?" Étienne said.

He slipped one hand partially inside the bodice of her gown, his fingers in the warmth of her cleavage. Zélie pressed her hand against the back of his neck. Her fingers maneuvered beneath the curled tufts until they nestled against his skin. His body shivered. His pelvis leaned against her hip, and he closed his eyes to kiss her. As his lids fluttered shut, he glimpsed Adelaide. His eyes flew open. He patted the Band-Aids in his pocket.

« *Pardon*, » he told his wife. "I must…"

Étienne ran after Adelaide. He caught his petit chou by the grand piano, an art-carved Steinway in rosewood. Her eyes darted, almost as disconcerting as the mismatched eyes in the Picasso print above the mantel.

"Galen's not here, anywhere," Adelaide said. « *Pas de tout*. »

That meant no one captured Adelaide's fragile beauty on film.

"Perhaps he left, *chouchou*," Étienne said.

Étienne took her bloody arm into his left hand. His right hand held the box and the ointment. Unable to open the first aid cream, Étienne gave Adelaide the bandages. He uncapped the bacitracin with his teeth. But what if he swallowed the cap? As if reading his mind, Adelaide transferred the bandages to her other hand. He spit the cap into her now empty palm. He plopped gel onto her wounds.

"This isn't necessary," she insisted.

He brushed the hair from his face, smearing ointment in his bangs. He tilted her arm, checking for more scratches. Étienne pointed the tube toward her. She capped it.

"*Chef*, you're drunk," she said.

"*Mais non, bientôt j'espère*… soon," he said.

Étienne remembered Bob Cornwall's need for a mistress.

« *Pardon*, » he said.

He almost kissed her cheeks again but instead grabbed them between his palms and kissed her lips. Étienne scanned the ballroom. He stepped to the piano, plucking a chocolate truffle between his fingers. He popped it into his mouth. The thin outer coating cracked, revealing a chocolate center with blueberry and Chambord. As he chewed, Étienne checked Zélie's den, though no one had discovered her hideaway. He mingled his way through the ballroom and across the dining room.

"Did you try *des chocolats?*" he asked everyone.

So many women… He paused at the *hors d'oeuvres*. Étienne's fingers guided a cracker into the crab dip. He skipped the caviar. Before he stabbed *escargot*, a hand clamped his shoulder.

"Étienne," a voice boomed.

Étienne turned slowly. A waiter passed him another champagne flute, for which he exchanged his appetizer plate. Étienne found himself face-to-face with Charles Sabatine. The two men met at the Ferrari dealership shortly after Étienne's arrival in the United States. Two years ago next month. He knew because his visa would expire.

« *Charlot*, » Étienne replied, using the French diminutive.

He pulled Charlie closer and planted a kiss on his cheeks.

"Hey, I heard something that screamed your name," Charlie said.

« *Mais non*, » Étienne replied. "My wife is still fuming about the '67."

"This is business, not a homeless yellow Ferrari," Charlie said. "A racing team needs a sponsor for the Grand Prix."

"The Grand Prix?"

"Yup. Let me get Ben, his brother heads the team."

"He's here?" Étienne asked.

"Everybody's here, Étienne," Charlie said.

"You really should talk to John Clowes," Étienne said. "He is my guy... how do you say *relations publique?*"

"Public relations? John Clothes?" Charlie replied.

Étienne nodded. Charlie steered him through the guests, stopping by a brown-haired man with a thick beard. He reminded Étienne of Didier, his *premier* in Paris who ran the dressmaking workshop.

"Ben... this is Étienne," Charlie said.

They shook hands. The three men slunk into Zélie's office where Étienne signed a check. As he scrawled his name, Étienne remembered his quest to find Robert Cornwall's wife. Étienne did not know Nancy, or, more importantly, what she had worn. He went to the porch where people lounged on his white-wicker furniture. Two women sat on a love seat with blue paisley cushions. One had a short torso, medium build, brown hair, brown eyes, and a plain black linen dress with a velvet collar. The other was tall, thin, with shining blond hair, bright red lipstick, and a red dress that arranged her buxom figure with boldness too vulgar for his work.

« *Excusez-moi, s'il vous plait, les femmes...* »

Étienne offered his hand to the blond. She snickered but took it, standing. He slipped his arm around her elbow and set his hand on hers.

"Have you tried the chocolates?"

The blond shook her head. They traipsed to the other end of the house, where Zélie stood near the man with the receding hairline. Étienne tapped his wife on the shoulder. Zélie opened the circle so he and his selection could enter. Everyone stared.

"I found her," Étienne said.

"Found whom, *chéri?*" Zélie asked.

"*C'est elle, ouias?* For Bob."

He bowed. The blond giggled.

« We are looking for his wife. That is not Nancy, » Zélie hissed in French.

« Perhaps she would be. Ask her, » Étienne said. "Would you be Nancy?"

The blond shrugged. "I could be Nancy."

"Take her," Étienne said, pushing the girl to Bob. "She is pretty, *non?*"

« Étienne! » Zélie snapped.

Étienne leaned closer to Bob.

"You like?" he asked. « *C'est bien.* »

He pointed to the girl's *décolletage*. Bob's facial expression did not change. Étienne sighed. He patted the girl's hand.

"*Pardon, mon lapin*, but he does not like. *Quel dommage.* They have money but no hair," Étienne said.

« Étienne! » Zélie repeated.

« *Peut-être il préfère les garçons,* » Étienne said. "I could find... the people from the fashion..."

Zélie snapped his name again. Adelaide appeared. Zélie took her by the elbow.

« Can you keep an eye on him? He's lewdly drunk, » Zélie whispered in her native tongue. « He's offering Bob lovers. »

Étienne leaned on the bar where the waiters kept clean glasses. He raised his thumb and forefinger into the air and a young man ran over and filled two flutes. Étienne kept one and gave the other to the girl. Adelaide monitored him closely, sternness across her face.

"Do you speak French, *ma coqueluche?*" Étienne asked the rejected girl as they walked.

"No, but it's beautiful."

« *Oui. Très beau, comme ça, vous avez du monde au balcon, des gros, beaux nichons.* »

"What does that mean?" she asked.

"Your eyes calm me like the sea," Étienne replied. That sounded good.

They returned to the porch. Étienne kissed her hand. He lifted his fingers and contemplated gliding them over her exposed assets. Adelaide cleared her throat. He turned.

"You are full of shit," Adelaide said.

« *Comment?* » he said, nursing his champagne.

"'Eyes like the sea...' You said she had big tits," Adelaide said.

"Big, beautiful tits," he corrected her. Étienne laughed. "*Ne t'inquiète pas, mon petit chou. You have beautiful tits, too. Pas mes favoris...*"

Beyond Adelaide, a middle-aged woman smudged with dirt staggered into the dining room. Zélie and Bob Cornwall rushed toward her.

"Et, let's go outside. You need air."

The dirt-smudged woman wore nothing but a demi-bra and lace-edged bikini panties. Zélie leaned to a waiter who headed for the stairs.

"Do you think I should..." he said, edging toward the commotion.

Adelaide grabbed him by the arm.

"No, you've insulted the Cornwalls enough," she said.

Étienne grabbed a bottle. He skimmed the label and curled a finger toward a nearby waiter. The waiter responded. Étienne whispered into his ear.

"Go to the cave," he directed the young man, "and find — "

"Et, what are you doing?" Adelaide's voice boomed.

As they talked, someone draped the mysterious guest with the robe Zélie's mother sent for Christmas.

« *Rien,* » he replied. "*Je veut* ... a good bottle of wine."

"We don't need a good bottle of wine. The champagne is fine."

He offered a Gallic shrug. The waiter resumed filling flutes.

"Have you tried the chocolates?" Étienne asked Adelaide.

"*Chef,* I made them," she said.

"Where is my head?" he asked. « *Mais oui. Magnifique.* »

They walked outside where the musicians played. According to his watch, the one Zélie had given him on a whimsical trip to Monaco during their courting days, it was one a.m. Adelaide steered him to a table, but he veered. He asked the conductor to play "Orange Colored Sky." The band complied. Adelaide waved her champagne flute with the music. Étienne shuffled his feet in fancy flourishes as he crossed the deck. He took Adelaide's drink, set it on the table so he could pull her into his arms. He adored the vanilla and orchid notes of her perfume marketed by the man he hoped would sponsor him for the *haute couture syndicat.*

"You have eat the chocolates, *n'est-ce pas?*"

"I wouldn't," Adelaide said. "Not with the show so close."

The blue of her dress made her eyes explode with color. The guests gravitated toward them. Étienne wound his arm around Adelaide's slender waist. Étienne could transform any woman into a creature this perfect, like he had molded Adelaide from an awkward teenager.

The upbeat tempo of the song made it difficult to dance, but he loved guiding Adelaide's lithe body into wicked spins (when did she detach her feathers?) with the rapid beat of the piano and the ascending saxophones. She laughed and tossed her head. She followed his lead, gliding smoothly with him. When the chorus hit, he sent them into circles. It ended too soon. He clung to her, partially because of dizziness but also to admire her and listen to the gentle rhythm of her breath. She slid her hand from his shoulder, interlacing their fingers.

Meanwhile, Zélie bid everyone farewell. Étienne stepped in that direction, furious that Zélie would sneak his guests away, but Adelaide stopped him. She returned to her champagne and her chair.

"How can you be this drunk and still dance like Fred Astaire?" Adelaide said.

Too drunk for English, he answered her in French. « You forget. I have been dancing since I was nine. »

He sat beside her. The orchestra played more Nat King Cole, "Those Lazy-Hazy-Crazy Days of Summer," if he had the adjectives in the right order. Étienne clapped. Adelaide unzipped her boots.

"Her sister," Étienne said, staring toward Zélie, "needed a partner. I wanted to play football. Our football. Not yours."

Adelaide stretched her legs across his lap. His attention went to them. The weight of the beads pulled the dress away from her thighs. Her garters poked from beneath the fabric. Zélie never wore garters, no matter how much Étienne begged. He rested his hand on Adelaide's ankle.

Zélie crossed the deck. She paused by the orchestra, said something to the conductor, and he nodded. She progressed to Étienne and Adelaide, dropping a gold box. Adelaide put her feet on the ground as Zélie pulled a chair to Étienne, wrapping her arms around his neck.

"That was a first," Zélie said. "Nancy Cornwall was so drunk she couldn't even remember how she lost her clothes. But then, look at you, Étienne. The waiters had a bet. They had a pool to see how much you could drink."

"*Combien?* How much?" he replied.

"You surpassed it an hour ago," Zélie said.

"*Qui a gagné?* The winner?" Étienne asked.

« *Moi,* » Zélie said. « *Mais oui.* »

"And who after?" he said.

Adelaide raised her hand.

"Between finishing this house and the *haute couture* show, you've been working all summer," Zélie said. "That is not you."

Zélie opened the box, revealing a chocolate truffle and a peanut butter, banana, and rice krispie candy coated with white chocolate. Zélie brought it to her lips. She purred as she ate.

"If the staff at Godiva tasted these, they would hang their heads in shame," Zélie said.

She tipped the box to Adelaide. Adelaide shook her head. Étienne reached into the carton and gave the truffle to Adelaide.

« *Vas-y,* » he directed her. "Eat."

Adelaide tentatively brought it to her lips. She nibbled a shaving of chocolate, and ecstasy rippled across her face. The band stopped. Zélie dragged Étienne to his feet. She folded against him as she always did. Their chests came together. Her mouth brushed his cheek. The musicians launched into "Unforgettable." Her hand reached up his back. She hummed quietly with the music, the same way she always had, as her head cuddled against his shoulder with her hair against his neck. Suddenly, she looked him straight in the eye as Nat King Cole would have sung the line: "thinks that I am unforgettable, too."

"I cannot believe Nancy Cornwall was so drunk—"

Étienne held his fingers to her lips.

« *Chut,* » he whispered. "Let me enjoy you."

He brought his lips to hers to quiet her, and they danced, tenderly tasting each other. In the final measures of the song, Étienne stepped away, twirled her to the end of his arm, then pulled her back, and dipped her across his thigh where he kissed her, this time long and thorough.

The black silk sash had fallen, covering her breasts. Her creamy skin set off beautifully the strand of black pearls he had given her. He liked how the pendant sparkled, though now it hung upside-down making a cloverleaf instead of a heart. He squeezed her hand and roamed her body with his eyes. His outlined her jaw and her cheekbone with his index finger.

"Étienne, let me up, *chéri,*" she said, interrupting his visual consumption.

"I was just — "

"I know exactly what you're doing," Zélie said. "Let me up."

He sighed and spun her out.

"I better take him up," Zélie said to Adelaide. "Can you see to everything?"

Adelaide nodded. She held a half-empty glass. Her other hand clutched the truffle, still only half-eaten.

"And Adelaide, don't forget, the jewels go back to Cartier on Monday," Zélie said.

Adelaide nodded. She fingered the emerald bracelet. Her glow had faded. Her lipstick streaked her lips, blue where it clung and pink where it faded.

"No no, for her I will buy," Étienne said before switching to French. « My little cabbage looks lovely in emeralds. »

Zélie scowled. Étienne kissed Adelaide's lips.

« *Bonne nuit, mon chou,* » he bid her.

"Your Oxfords are untied," Adelaide said. "Be careful."

Étienne looked to his feet. He didn't have Oxfords. They were Balmorals. Zélie gave Adelaide *bises* on her cheeks. Adelaide returned them.

"Sleep well," Zélie bid her.

"You, too," Adelaide said.

After he kissed Adelaide's cheeks one final time, Étienne's feet sunk into the deck and refused to budge. Zélie tucked herself under his arm to support him. Once in the bedroom, Zélie deposited him on the bed.

« Work on getting undressed, » she instructed him.

He nodded. She walked toward the master bath.

« Zélie, I would rather undress you, » he said.

« No doubt, » her voice returned.

He bent to take off his shoes. One shoe had a knot in it, so he tugged it until it flew free and landed somewhere several meters from the bed. He removed the other easily. Étienne pinched the first button of his vest between his fingers to undo it, but the thickness of his fingers interfered. Zélie returned, handing him his toothbrush and an empty cup. She lowered herself into a wing-backed chair where she slid off her shoes. She tossed them over his head, aiming for the walk-in closet. He brushed his teeth.

« Don't eat the toothpaste, » she said. « Spit into the cup. »

He did. She took the cup to the bathroom. She brushed her teeth. He struggled with more buttons, wondering if his *petite main* made the button-holes too small. Zélie ran water, opened the cabinet door, and shook a bottle of pills.

« *Chéri*, did you take your blood pressure pill? »

« *Non,* » Étienne replied.

« That's probably good, » she said.

Zélie brought him a large glass of water and a white pill. He had managed to undo one button, but his finger stuck in the buttonhole.

« Open your mouth, » she told him.

Étienne did. She set the pill on his tongue. He jerked his head and spit the pill into his hand. Was she trying to kill him? He couldn't possibly take that now. It might cause heart failure.

« Étienne, it's an aspirin. »

She gave him the water. He swallowed the aspirin while she unbuttoned his vest. He dropped the empty glass.

« I'm glad one of us is sober, » Zélie replied.

« You didn't drink a thing. Not a single drop of champagne, » he observed.

She pushed the vest down his arms and unfastened his ascot.

« But, why, my love? You know you yell less when you drink, » he said as she roughly unfurled the ascot. « Are you angry? »

She rested her fingers behind his neck, buried in his hair, curls twisted around them. He closed his eyes. When he did, he slumped backwards, but Zélie caught him by his collar.

«No, I'm not angry, » Zélie said, her voice quiet.

Her fingers tickled. She offered a weighty sigh.

« Étienne, I have something important to say. Tomorrow. »

« You're returning to France, » he guessed.

« No, » she said, tousling his hair. « You're in no shape to discuss it now. »

The light from the bathroom, though far away, permeated the room enough to flatter the bottom-heavy hourglass of Zélie's figure. Her dress appeared black, the straps sparkled, and her skin glowed. She had put her jewelry away. She reached for the discarded glass. As she bent, Étienne planted his hands on her hips. Her torso moved, changing the line of her dress. Her breasts came near him. Étienne fell into her. Silk lined his cheeks. His hands met on her back, her warmth permeating the fabric. His body came alive as he smelled her buttery depth, punctuated with bursts of neroli, ylang-ylang and the artificial notes that made Chanel perfumes famous.

« Étienne, *chéri*. »

Bracing against her, he rose. He went for her shoulder straps. Lowering them one at a time, he followed each with kisses as it dropped. The supple texture of her skin against his lips caused his body to collapse against her, his weight about to guide her to the mattress when she shoved him upright.

« Étienne! If you intend to land on the bed, we need to turn around. »

He glanced up. She was right. He would have knocked them to the floor. *Oups.* He ran his fingers down her sides and locked his lips against the top of her breast. She exhaled rapidly, almost choking on her breath, which meant he was getting to her. Good, because she got to him. He sucked on her and did not release until he needed to breathe.

« I have had my fill, my love. This does not change what I will do to you, » he said.

She unbuttoned his shirt, placing a cool hand against the blond curls inside his undershirt. She hadn't spent the hot summer evening in a jacket and tie. His body twitched. Even his toes cramped. He kissed her. She responded, her tongue penetrating him.

« I disagree, » she said, « because you are always more patient with what I will do to you. »

The shirt fell to the ground. She helped him with the undershirt. His fingers wandered to her side seam where he unzipped her gown. The dress joined the shirt. Zélie wore control-top pantyhose and panties. She reached for his fly. He touched the restricted curve of her belly.

« Why do you wear these? » he asked. « I make the perfect dress to highlight your waist and your hips and you flatten yourself. »

« I don't know, *chéri*. Makes me think I can compete with the girls. »

« They need to compete with you, » he said.

His pants fell, and he dropped to the bed. She lowered herself across his lap, her knees against the mattress. They kissed again, her lips cool against his, their bodies meeting as he grabbed her hips and guided her against his erection, up and down, while her pantyhose and his boxers teased them both.

Standing, holding her around the waist and backside, Étienne threw Zélie against the bed. He peeled her nude. He licked her leg, from the ankle, to the knee, into her inner thigh. His hand pressed against the outside of her panties, flinging the moist fabric to the floor. After twenty years with her, he could imagine it all as she lay in the rich silver moonlight, and it frenzied him.

He kissed her again, quickly, nibbling at her lip. He had memorized every texture of her skin and he wanted to taste it all tonight. He knew the pitiful whimpers she would make when he teased her, and the red splotches on her chest that would appear at the height of their love-making. She ran her fingers down his back. He closed his hand against her breast and lowered his head to the other. Her nipple grew taut. He licked around it. Zélie made the noise he liked, the quick, high-pitched moan. She thrust her hips against him.

She put her hands to his cheeks and drew his face to hers. She kissed him. He pressed against her, continuing their kisses as his fingers danced across her. He removed his underwear, and, standing beside the bed, gently pushed her legs apart.

His fingers gripped her thighs and slipped under her until he had one side of her bottom firmly in hand. His other hand explored a breast, while he nibbled her ear and darted from her neck to her collarbone leaving a path of kisses and licks.

« Étienne, » she muttered. « Now, darling. »

He nudged her, her legs slid over his hips. He leaned, and her body tilted toward his as he thrust deep into her. She hummed. They immediately fell into a rhythm, their rhythm, as their bodies reverted to the conditioning of decades together. He brought himself against her, retreated and reentered. He kissed her lips again. Her interior cradled him. He paused, something clouded his head and he wasn't sure whether her influence had cleared his intoxication or worsened it. Her hips rocked against him. Étienne swallowed hard as she pulled him deeper.

« Zélie... » he whispered.

Étienne groaned. His knees buckled, shattering the proximately of their finish. He should lie down. Étienne withdrew, hoping the break would preserve his consciousness. Air swept between their parted bodies. Zélie shivered.

« I love you, » he told her.

« My God, Étienne... You know I love you, too. »

He climbed into bed with her, lowered his hips to hers, and drove into her those last few times. Her body bucked and trembled against his, her noises increased as her nails tore into his shoulders. He shifted his weight. His ecstasy barreled unavoidably through him and reduced his stiffness to room temperature butter.

His hands brushed against her as he kissed his way down her torso. He rested his mouth between her legs and used his tongue to dance across her crying folds. A few pointed licks direct to the clitoris, some wide strokes across the entire area, Étienne tasted her until she released into a scream. He curled along side of her and rested his head on her shoulder. There he could hear her heart racing and her pants as she recovered. Unable to escape the effects of the alcohol, Étienne passed out.

CHAPTER FIVE

É tienne tossed and turned until he could no longer resist the inevitable. *Il me faut pisser.* Ignoring his headache and dreading the sunshine, he opened one eye. The dull pain in his temple did not increase. Étienne opened the other eye. On his arm, he found his watch. He hadn't taken it off. His eyes focused on the tiny numbers. The face read just before nine.

What time did he go to bed? He couldn't recall. He remembered a woman with a red dress and large breasts that could suffocate a man, and comments *en français* about them. The nearly bald man... *Ça alors*, did he write a check to *Charlot*? Dancing... Adelaide's feet in his lap... a bet amongst the staff... but he didn't remember coming to bed.

Zélie hid under the covers. Tendrils of hair spilled over the beige pillow-case. Clothes lay in a disheveled heap. Étienne yawned. He grabbed a water glass from the carpet. The aspirin... removing her dress... Maybe he did remember. He twirled the glass in his hand. He gazed at the woman-sized lump in the bed. *Mais oui*, he remembered. That was good. He chuckled.

He backtracked to the closet for boxers and a tee-shirt. He and Zélie hadn't even officially moved into this house and he'd filled the shelves with shoes. His Manhattan sublet didn't have storage space. Étienne left the closet and rounded the corner. In the master bathroom, he relieved himself and washed his hands.

Étienne ran wet fingers through his hair but no amount of attention changed its disarray. He dipped his head under the brass faucet. That worsened his headache. He opened the medicine cabinet, grabbing the orange-tinted bottle with the childproof cap, and popped it. He tapped his atenolol into his palm and swallowed it.

Knowing he would never fall asleep again, Étienne stumbled downstairs. Might as well make coffee. He headed into the kitchen where he grabbed the carafe, shoving it into the kitchen sink. He knew he would brew better coffee with the press and grinder, but he couldn't, not with his head throbbing. By the time he got coffee started, he figured he'd gather breakfast. He put a salt shaker by the coffee maker.

Étienne staggered to the pantry and grabbed two *bâtards* from the bread basket. He asked the baker to do a late batch before he left Manhattan, since he didn't relish the idea of spending the weekend without decent bread. He reached for his cutting board and a bread knife and sliced each loaf in half. He arranged them on a platter. He checked the coffee, still gurgling.

Wincing at the sunlight on its black face, Étienne opened the *frigo* and selected the strawberry preserves and the *coing* jam. He spooned each into a little bowl. Taking the jams and the bread to a silver tray, he added real triple-cream butter imported from home. The headache blinded him temporarily, so he waited. When it had passed, Étienne removed the carafe from the coffee pot and stuck a mug under the streaming fluid. When he had half a cup, he replaced the carafe.

Today, he drank his coffee black. He didn't drink much coffee. He added salt. He prayed his brain would revive with the caffeine. Before Zélie woke, he had to remember what happened with *Charlot*.

Adelaide wandered into the kitchen, hair in her face, body barely covered by an eyelet baby doll. She shuffled toward the coffee pot. Her arms hung loosely at her side. Zut rolled on the floor by the refrigerator.

« *Ça va?* » he asked.

Adelaide grunted.

"Do you dress like that in the house of your father?" he inquired.

Adelaide poured a huge mug of coffee and leaned against the counter.

"Like church?" she replied. "No. I add heels and red lipstick for church."

"Not Mass," Étienne said. "Your father. Home."

"I don't sleep in my parent's house. I sleep with you. I mean, here, not with you," she said. "Besides, you made this."

He shook his head. "And they say I have the bad English. No need to wear this at me."

"For you," she corrected him. "You've seen me in less. God, am I hung-over. You?"

Étienne handed her the salt. She dumped some in her mug.

"My head has bad...no, headache," he said winning a small battle in an endless fight with English grammar.

He poured cream into a small pitcher and placed it in the microwave. While Adelaide sipped her coffee, he poured a mug for Zélie. He added sugar. Zélie liked her *café au lait* sweet.

"Yum," she said. "You bought this coffee in Barbès, didn't you?"

He nodded.

« *Je voudrais te parler* — » he began.

« *Chef*, it's Sunday and I'm hung over. English, please. »

"We should speak," he repeated.

"Thank you," she said, shaking her hair from her face.

"I try in your ugly language. I think," he continued. "This thing... *ce parrainage...*"

Her hair did not hide the way her face wrinkled as she deciphered his meaning.

"Taneisha..." he clarified.

The microwave dinged and Étienne brought the milk to the platter. Now, the orange juice...

"The mentoring? The experience for the kids at the fashion charter school?" she said. "They are going to love spending a week in your office."

"I not know... *pas une bonne idée* ... you invite *ados* from such neighborhoods."

"It's still a couple weeks away," she assured him. "I'll take care of it. It'll be fun."

Étienne retrieved their cloth napkins from the drawer in the hutch, folding them nicely onto the platter.

"Where's the bananas and Orangina?" Adelaide asked.

Two aspirin, two bananas, and an Orangina remained Étienne's classic hangover remedy.

"I forgot some Orangina."

"You can't forget the Orangina," she replied.

He shrugged and carried his tray upstairs, leaving Adelaide to finish the coffee. That would be her breakfast. In the bedroom, Zélie snuggled under the sheets. Étienne set the tray on the bureau. He crept toward her and pulled the sheet, his lips kissing her bare spine.

"Zélie," he whispered.

Her hand groped for the sheet.

"Zélie," he repeated. « Food. »

« I don't care, » she whined. « Get out of here. »

He ran his hand along her torso.

« Go away, » she said, her face in the pillow. « Get out and give me peace. »

Zélie's hand found the sheet and covered her body again. He tugged the sheet down again, this time drawing a trail with his lips all the way to her butt. His kissed that, too. She swatted at him. His mouth followed her spine up to her neck, where he lingered.

« I made you coffee, and brought juice, and a *bâtard*. »

« I like a bastard in bed for breakfast, » she said, referencing the less polite definition of the word '*bâtard*.'

Étienne smiled.

« Are you questioning my parentage? » he asked.

Zélie sat up and motioned for the tray. He gave it to her. She drained the juice.

« Happy wedding anniversary, » he said.

Zélie blended the cream into her coffee.

« You celebrate, » she said.

Why wouldn't he? Though technically divorced, they spent most of their time together. She had dreamt up the divorce. She had already filed when she left him. She probably wouldn't have told him if he hadn't had to meet with the social worker. French law at the time mandated such a visit to determine if both parties agreed to the separation. He never agreed. He had no choice.

He figured if he played along she would come back. Although he had never cheated or mistreated her, she could ruin him. With the ready-to-wear business in its infancy, he worried he would lose clients if the divorce turned ugly. *Après tout*, her mother was his biggest fan.

« Here you are, naked in my bed, » Étienne said.

She stifled a laugh.

« Your bed? » she said.

He nodded.

« I chose this bed, » she said.

« You put it in my house, » he replied.

« You built the house for me, » she said.

« I did, » Étienne conceded.

For nine years they had lived like this, the eccentric *Madame et Monsieur* d'Amille. The tabloids and gossip magazines like *Paris-Match* adored their flashy parties, society appearances, public spats, and separate homes. It's why every social event he hosted required security.

Every columnist had a theory. Étienne didn't. He knew what Zélie claimed, but he didn't believe her. But that wasn't his concern today. Étienne returned the tray to the bureau. He pounced onto the bed, surrounding Zélie with his arms. Zélie giggled, a girlish sound that didn't match her personality. He kissed her forehead, the bridge of her nose, and ended with his lips against hers. Zélie pushed him.

« Étienne, wait. I can't be distracted. »

« Why not? You think you're going to stare at that stock ticker on the television news... »

His hands scooped her breasts, their weight burying his hands against her rib cage. He kissed her collarbone, and his tongue raced toward his fingers.

« Éti... »

It was a whimper more than a protest. Étienne forgot his headache. He caressed her belly.

« Étienne, I'm serious. »

She shoved him. Gently, but still a shove. He searched her eyes for some indication of how serious. The look gave Étienne flashbacks of Sister Mary-Theresa, who claimed he'd rot in Purgatory for his liaisons and his pranks. His blood went cold.

« Remember when I went to the doctor? » she said.

His chest constricted. His headache returned. His heart pounded. A pain, like the intense burn last night, stifled his breath. Was she sick? She wouldn't look so solemn over nothing. She couldn't be sick.

« Are you ill? If you are ill... »

« Étienne. »

He wiggled the fingers on his left hand. Something definitely pinched and it jumped throughout his arm. He couldn't breathe.

« A heart attack, » he said. « The thought of something happening to you, it kills me. »

« You are not having a heart attack, Étienne, » she replied, her lack of concern disconcerting. « You do this to yourself. I'm not sick. »

She tucked his curls behind his oversized ears and rubbed his stubbly cheeks.

« Saying this is hard, » Zélie said. « You'd think by now... Everything we've been through... »

Étienne placed his hand on hers. He pulled a deep breath into his lungs and the pain disappeared.

« Basilie, » he said, using her full name to prove his earnestness. « I'm here. Forever. »

« I'm pregnant. »

« Don't make jokes, » he immediately replied. « I'm ready. »

« I'm not joking. »

« That's not possible. »

She offered an odd smile, lips tight. « It's true. »

« It can't be. »

Étienne breath careened from his control again. Where was the air? His heart rate quadrupled. Zélie took his hands. He restrained himself from ripping free and clutching his burning chest.

« My God, look at you, you're red as a tomato. You're going to hyper-ventilate. Breathe. Easy, through the nose, » she instructed him. « Are you over-reacting or do you need your nitroglycerin? I never know. »

His breathing settled, though his heart wanted to leap from his chest. He closed his eyes.

« It passed, » he said. « You're pregnant, again? »

"Seven weeks, » she said in a small voice.

« That's why you're so tired and you got sick at that restaurant and the special vitamins, » he said. « Seven weeks? When exactly was that? »

Tears wet his eyes.

« Late June or early July, » she told him.

« I was in Paris, » he said.

« Yes, » she responded. « It had to be either when you left or the day I flew in. »

"Zélie, the day you came to Paris we made love in the Aston Martin. »

She laughed heartily.

« It is safe, yes, having a baby, at our ages? » he said.

Her age, he wanted to say. But he didn't. Yet he knew that she'd infer it. She would celebrate her forty-fifth birthday this fall. He was almost two years younger.

« We have access to the best medical care in the world. »

« And last time... » Étienne replied, but paused, interrupted by memories of their bed swimming in blood and the chemical-laced antiseptic smell of the hospital.

She touched her forehead to his.

« Étienne, I can't handle it if you worry. »

« I can't help it, » he replied.

« The doctors say there's no explanation for it, » Zélie said. « I even talked to my sister. Somehow my uterus has recovered. Even she said it shouldn't be possible after... you know... »

He did know. He knew exactly what she went through last time. Queasiness overtook him. He had wanted a baby. They had wanted a baby. They had wanted many babies. But now, after everything, they had resigned themselves to the idea that it wouldn't happen.

Zélie rose from the bed. Etienne rolled to his side of the mattress, reached to the night stand and opened his father's sewing kit. He retrieved the brass thimble from its pouch. He spun it on his finger.

« I don't have an answer, Étienne. I don't know how this happened or why. It's damn frightening if you want me to tell the truth. »

« Yes, it is, » he admitted. « I feel better to hear you say that. »

Even Zélie's sister Jacquelyn, the obstetrician, said she would never conceive again after what happened more than fifteen years ago. It offered a strange finality at the time, and the relief that the difficult pregnancies would end. After that, witnessing Zélie's pain and the complications... She never even said goodbye. He had to. So, as much as they wanted a family, he never wanted to live through that again. Ever. He'd bet his life that Zélie couldn't survive it again, emotionally or physically. And here they were. His heart thumped.

« Nothing can happen to you, » he said. « When they say recovered... »

She slipped her bathrobe onto her arms.

« Even Jacquelyn says there's no reason I can't have a healthy pregnancy, » she answered.

« I don't believe that, » he said.

« But it's okay, Étienne? You want this baby? »

More than anything, he thought to himself.

« We have to be careful, Zélie. That's all. Very careful. »

CHAPTER SIX

Twenty-four hours later on the cusp of his work week, unable to stop obsessing about Zélie's news, Étienne sat alone on a guest room balcony overlooking the atrium and admiring the butterflies. He had selected them as frivolous beauty to highlight the lushness of his atrium, but now he considered their short lives with sadness. The breeders warned him that the bright-colored creatures live three to four weeks. Ephemeral beauty, temporary life. He closed his eyes and fought tears. He couldn't help but dwell on Zélie's pregnancy.

Hall and Oates' "Rich Girl" belted from his phone, his cabbage's idea of a practical joke. Adelaide had personalized Zélie's ringtone, and Étienne lacked the technical prowess to delete it. He checked his watch. He hadn't expected to hear from his wife this early. He wiped his tears onto the cuff of his shirt, as if she could see them via the phone.

"I'm out of my breakfast meeting," Zélie said in English.

The meeting involved a hostile corporate takeover. He didn't remember if she was helping avoid one or stage one.

« *Coucou, aussi, chérie,* » he answered hoping to switch her to French.

« *Bonjour, mon prince charmant.* I received the oddest text message from the bank. Did you write a large check during the weekend? »

He answered rapidly, in French, without pausing between words. « It could be. I think I gave a friend of *Charlot's* $500,000 to sponsor a Grand Prix racing team. »

« It could be? You think? » her voice reached amazing shrillness. « You write a check for half a million dollars to Charlie and you're not sure? Charlie of all people! »

« A Grand Prix racing team. Isn't that fun? »

« Fun? Étienne, how do you know Charlie didn't take you for half a mill? »

« I don't, » he admitted. At least they had settled into French now.

« Half a million, » she grumbled.

« I think that was a down payment, » Étienne continued.

« A down payment? They'll get more? » Her voice escalated. « For a car? »

« With my name on it," he said. « Good exposure. »

« So many well-dressed women are European auto racing enthusiasts. By the blood of Christ, Étienne. For that amount, they should let you drive it. »

« Do you think they would? » he asked.

« I can't believe you did this without consulting me, » she said.

« It's my money, » he answered.

« Your money... Oh, bedbugs, » she muttered. « I've got to go. I had hoped the bank made a mistake. I see now they didn't. »

Zélie hung up. She took that well, Étienne thought. He speed-dialed the main office in Paris. The six-hour time difference sometimes served as an advantage. The New York employees would roll into the office as the Parisians finished their day. Soon, his French employees would embark on their August *vacances*, if they hadn't already. With the *prêt-à-porter* show in October, Didier led Étienne's dressmaking hands on runway samples. Étienne definitely needed to talk to Didier, professionally and personally. The two had served in the army together, and Didier's help in Étienne's father's tailoring shop had saved the d'Amille family's livelihood.

Sabine answered the phone. As she paged the *atelier*, Étienne unfolded the red blouse from Didier's urgent package. The sloppy trimming left stray strings, which he might have forgiven, if he hadn't noticed other oddities like the "Made in the U.S.A." label. He didn't have American manufacturers. This shirt, clearly marked an American size six, looked like a shrunken eight.

« Hello, Étienne. You've seen the blouse, » Didier rattled in French. « They shipped like that. »

« These shipped? Where? »

« Yes, » Didier said. « Dozens. I told her she made the patterns too small. I thought she'd scrapped them, but apparently she downsized and shipped. »

« She? Since when do I have American factories for ready-to-wear?"

« She didn't tell you about the factories? »

« Who didn't tell me about factories? »

« Adelaide, Étienne. Adelaide has factories in Pennsylvania. That came from a shipment to Bergdorf Goodman. »

Étienne inhaled rapidly as his chest tightened. The pain overwhelmed him.

« Adelaide ... shipped this," he choked on the word 'blouse' and skipped it, « to Bergdorf ... Goodman? Oh, dear God."

As his lungs burned, Étienne told himself to relax. It helped, but not much. Not now. Not holiday. Holiday had such a brief retail window. This might make d'Amille ready-to-wear miss the Christmas season. One blouse couldn't ruin an entire collection, could it? This wouldn't help his footing in America. Manufacturing defects ... He might need nitro.

« I will find Adelaide, » Étienne said.

He hung up. Who authorized this? Why would Adelaide deliberately mis-label garments? Étienne dialed Adelaide's cellular. First, his wife leaves him here with no transportation. Now this. Étienne paced from the balcony into the spare bedroom and to the hall, one hand squeezing his father's sewing kit in his pocket. Étienne banged on Adelaide's door. Her phone blared the James Bond theme.

"You have reached Adelaide Pitney..." the recording told him.

Étienne hit redial. He continued banging. James Bond played. His heart throbbed, but he didn't have any more pain. The song stopped. Adelaide answered, without a greeting.

"*Chef,* what do you want?" she whined. "Why aren't you in New York?"

« *Bonjour, aussi, mon petit chou.* »

She said nothing.

"Coffee downstairs in twenty minutes," he said.

"Étienne," she drew out his name, screeching. "You promised I could have today off."

"We have a problem."

"What problem? I promised Taneisha I'd take her to the open house at school," she said.

"Get dressed," Étienne commanded. "You may go to New York for your *protégé. Il te faut me dire...* How did an American factory send blouses to Bergdorf Goodman the wrong size?"

"Oh," Adelaide said.

She hung up. Étienne headed downstairs, the offending shirt clenched tightly in his hand. After a hunt for his briefcase, he scattered the most recent quarterly report across the dining room table. Adelaide arrived, her hair in a ponytail and her face mildly painted. She wore mint green pants. The blouse was Spring 1999: short-sleeved, shawl collar, white, tiny gold buttons on the sleeves and the breast pocket.

"Why didn't you go to the city with Bas?" she asked.

"She left early."

"And didn't take you?" Adelaide remarked. "So I'm stuck being your chauffeur."

"Find coffee," he said. "I am having a crisis."

"You're always having a crisis," she answered. "You're French. It's part of your national identity. If it's not a protest, it's a riot, and if it's not a riot, it's a full-blown crisis."

As she went to the kitchen, he whispered, "You are a monster until that first cup of coffee."

"I heard that," she yelled.

Adelaide returned with her mug.

« Why do I know nothing about American factories? » he replied in frantic French.

"I thought you knew. It started six months ago," Adelaide squeaked. "You told me to find subcontractors to manufacture, but not Mexico or Indonesia or anyplace else that might tarnish your image."

Étienne raised his hand to stop her.

"Inferior, *mon chou*," he said, shoving the blouse at her.

She snatched it. Étienne flipped through the report unable to find factories. She seized the papers from his hands and opened directly to the page that listed the mills' operational costs.

"You're unobservant," she replied.

« *Il y en a deux.* » he said. "You made two factories?"

Adelaide gulped coffee. Her body relaxed. She always reacted to the process of drinking coffee before the caffeine entered her system. Étienne pointed to the problems with the blouse. He pinched the tag between his fingers as he emphasized that this was nowhere near a six.

"I read the specs wrong," she admitted. "I cut the patterns a half-inch too small. You know I suck at numbers. I downsized everything to compensate."

"But it's too big," he replied. "You should have started over. Didn't you do a size run?"

She shrugged.

"No, you forgot," Étienne said. "We recall them. We must. Quality first. What else is going on? Show me the factory."

"That came from Roseto," Adelaide said. "It's not too far."

"Take me," Étienne directed. « *Maintenant.* »

He gathered his papers and shoved them haphazardly into his briefcase. Adelaide slammed her way through the dining room. Étienne followed her. She picked up her little d'Amille bag and led him from the house. Adelaide paused near her sporty Quartz Blue CLK430.

"I never asked for this, Étienne," she said.

"Did I?" he replied. "*Mon chou,* it is nine and a half on a Monday. I have not had a vacation since the damn American office opened. Let me make the clothes and you do what you do best."

"What would that be, Étienne?"

Étienne threw up his hands in exasperation.

"*Je sais pas.* I don't know!" he exploded. "Adelaide, to the car."

Adelaide's bottom lip quivered. Her d'Amille bag tumbled to the driveway. She twisted her hand under her nose and turned her face to hide.

"Go to the car," he said again.

"It's 'get in' the car,'" she snapped.

"Get in the car," he replied.

"I need a minute," she said staidly. "Do you want to drive?"

He yanked the door.

« *Non,* » Étienne said, sliding into the cabin. "*Ta bagnole* ... Too slow."

Adelaide retrieved her purse. She pulled free a compact. She opened it. She patted a tissue against her cheek. Her shoulders rose and fell with a hearty sigh. She got into the car.

"Sorry. It's not an S-series like Bas's. Maybe my next raise," she remarked.

"German piece of shit," he muttered.

Adelaide whipped the car into reverse and then drive. She tested Mercedes' claims that the car could accelerate from zero to one hundred kilometers in six-and-a-half seconds.

"Why am I here?" she asked. "I was happy doing P.R. in Paris! I liked working with Alain and Solange. I didn't ask to come to New York. You brought me because I'm American."

She had the top down. Her speed and the wind, despite the car's aero-dynamics, interrupted their conversation.

"And Et, congratulations," she said. "How can you be so mad after such big news? I know she told you."

A shiver rose from his shoulders into his skull.

« *Comment?* You know? » he responded.

"Bas told me."

Étienne fixed his eyes on the water as they drove down River Road. He couldn't look at his cabbage. Zélie never told anyone about her previous pregnancies, until the last one. She hid them. They had never told anyone. Zélie had told Jacqueline, years later, because she wanted a second opinion. But now Zélie told Adelaide? It didn't make sense. Why? How? Wait a minute, when? When had Zélie spoken with Adelaide?

"When?" Étienne asked. "When did Zélie tell you?"

Adelaide merged onto Rte. 611 south. Her speed dropped to join the traffic.

"Last week," she answered so low that he struggled to hear.

"She told me yesterday," he said.

"I guess she needed to get it off her chest. I offered to get you, but she left."

"You do not tell me, *mon petit chou?*"

"Wasn't my news. She was upset, Et. Everything's okay, right?"

He studied Adelaide's face. She seemed so sophisticated now, with her sunglasses, hair cropped to her shoulders, and gold bracelets on her wrists.

'Everything's okay, right?' Her words echoed. What could he say? Helplessness overcame him. He and Zélie hadn't questioned their fertility, not even after the miscarriage. The doubt and the real pain came years later with Christian. The closest he ever came to a child. The doctors called it a miscarriage, despite the induced labor and... the body. He could only pray that if this pregnancy would not bear fruit, it would end quickly. 'Everything's okay, right?' He had to answer Adelaide.

"For now," Étienne finally said. "Stay quiet, please."

Memories of Paris, the *Place des Vosges* apartment, and petit Christian... He gazed to Adelaide and remembered their meeting thirteen years ago. She might have made Étienne and his wife whole again. They had met her not that much after... A year, about. Ready-to-wear, bringing a child into their lives (technically an employee), but it couldn't repair their marriage.

Adelaide's discovery happened at JFK airport. Adelaide's hair hid her face as she kicked the floor with her plastic flip-flops. The long, thick tresses swept in wonderfully pale red waves from shoulders to waist. Adding that to her blue eyes, ruby cheeks, long legs, and athletic build, Étienne instantly imagined her in the multiple shades of purple of his debut line. He needed her. Her hair would make the perfect foil.

That was thirteen years ago. Thirteen years ago Air France Flight #93 for Charles de Gaulle had left without him. Thirteen years ago, Étienne d'Amille introduced himself, or more accurately Zélie introduced him, to a man named Gerald Pitney. Gerald had two daughters: Janine, age ten, and Adelaide, almost twelve. Étienne's heart fell. He knew the girl's age fit industry standards, but he didn't want to expose a young girl to the fashion world.

2002. The same girl drove him to a factory he never knew existed. He gazed at the town: turn-of-the-century architecture in disrepair, grimy vacant storefronts, a burnt-out frame, a quaint library, so different from Europe. Adelaide navigated the car through narrow streets. A line of children in gold and brown plaid pullovers and jumpers walked from the church toward a brick school. Adelaide pulled into a parking lot and jerked her emergency brake.

Étienne hadn't noticed the square cement block building with the fresh coat of white paint. He spotted his logo on the door. He stepped out. Uneasiness settled in his gut. He pressed forward. Inside the door, he stopped by a sliding glass window to the secretary's office. Muffled mechanical sounds permeated the space.

"Can I help you?" the lady at the desk asked.

Adelaide entered.

"Adelaide!" the woman exclaimed.

"Paloma, this is Étienne. Étienne, this is Paloma."

Paloma ran into the hallway.

"We didn't expect you to come," Paloma said. "Hello, who was it? Étienne? »

Étienne brought Paloma's hands into his own, layered them together, and pulled the woman toward him as he kissed her cheeks.

« *Bonjour, Madame. Enchanté,* » he replied.

Recognition flashed onto Paloma's face.

"Oh, my God! Wait... Étienne? As in Étienne d'Amille, the name on the label?" Paloma said.

Paloma didn't untangle herself from Étienne's grasp. Étienne smiled at her, not too much, merely playful.

"Just like you described him," she observed.

"Cosmopolitan? Debonair?" he asked.

"Incorrigible flirt," Adelaide replied.

"Let me get Rocco," Paloma said, disappearing.

"Rocco's their boss," Adelaide told Étienne.

Étienne walked the narrow hall as the sewing machines pounded. Their intensity grew and fell as operators changed their pace. The thin door did not block the rapid-fire hammering. Paloma returned with a thick-chinned fellow dressed in khakis and a Henley.

"Adelaide," the man said, sandwiching her hand between his.

A friendly gesture, Étienne thought, raising an eyebrow, too friendly.

"Mr. d'Amille," the man said, mangling Étienne's name.

Rocco offered his hand. Étienne extended his hand politely. Setting his briefcase on the small table in the entryway, Étienne retrieved the blouse and emphasized the flaws. The chubby Italian paled.

"We're starting over," Adelaide said.

"More than half the order already shipped, another ten dozen are ready to ship, and there's twenty dozen on the floor," Rocco said.

« *Quatre-vingts*? Eighty dozen? » Étienne blurted.

The tight feeling resumed in Étienne's chest. His head swirled.

« *Mon Dieu.* »

Every single holiday blouse intended for the North American market, Étienne realized. He confirmed it on the paperwork. Étienne reached for his nitroglycerin tablets.

"Adelaide, you should not have," Étienne said.

"I wanted to be consistent," she said.

"Stop it," Étienne demanded. "Stop the sewing."

Étienne barged into the cutting room. Two men hunched over yards of layered satin, with size markers matching the blouse Didier had sent.

"Stop!" Étienne yelled.

Behind the cutters, several young women inspected finished blouses in the light. He progressed to the sewing floor, scanning for the floor supervisor. Rows of women at noisy machines throttled through garments. A tucked head joined shoulders. Another figure sewed collars. Others sewed cuffs, others stay-stitched linings to front facings.

"Stop!" Étienne yelled again.

The floor supervisor carried bundles from bin to bin. Étienne glimpsed two styles of his long-sleeved blouse. One style had a scooped collar and faced sleeves and the other a classic line with French cuffs and a jabot collar. He had sewn the samples. Twenty dozen floated across the room. He took the floor supervisor by the elbow.

"Stop the workers," Étienne commanded.

Adelaide caught up with him and confirmed the orders.

"We'll have to send everyone home until we work this out," she said.

Étienne stormed to the Mercedes. Adelaide followed a few minutes later and placed her calendar and her purse in the backseat. She started the car without a word. She reached for the shifter. He covered her hand with his.

"You meant well," Étienne said, "but that mistake probably cost me $200,000."

She didn't look at him.

"I'm sorry," Adelaide said.

"You did good," he said, "until you... *tu as dépassé les limites.*"

"Yeah, I overstepped my bounds," Adelaide replied, "and I made a bad call that cost $200,000. Ouch."

She faced him.

"I hired you because you were beautiful. Then, you were charming. Then, you were smart."

"But now?" she asked.

"You almost lead my business," Étienne said, "but you have the things to learn."

Before Étienne got any further, Shirley Bassey interrupted with a boisterous chorus of "New York, New York." Adelaide motioned to her cell phone. He knew it was the Manhattan office, thanks to her neurotic ring tones. She answered. Étienne lifted a plush Spiderman from the dash. Adelaide grabbed his fingers and scowled. He replaced it.

"Yeah, he's here," she said. "No, I won't put him on, John, not until you calm down."

Étienne opened her compact disc case. Adelaide slapped his hand.

"John, it can wait," she said.

Étienne read the first CD, *Placebo*. Why did that sound familiar?

"John, I've got to go," she said.

She snapped the phone shut and threw it.

"Must you touch everything?" she asked.

He shrugged.

"That was John. Some ordeal about the New York shows. Oh, I almost forgot. Some guy called about a d'Amille logo for a race car. What's that?"

Étienne welcomed that news.

"A race car, *chic*! Zélie feared I pissed half a million."

"What?" she said.

"*Charlot* had a friend who knew about a Grand Prix race car — "

"You sponsored a race car?"

He nodded.

"Cool," she said. "I'm sorry about the blouses. It won't happen again. I won't make any decisions involving numbers without double-checking with someone. And I'll do two size runs on everything. I could pay you back... at $100 a week, it would take... Two hundred weeks, which is like four years."

"I do not have *le coup mathématique* but I believe it is two thousand weeks or *quarante* ... forty years, » Étienne replied.

"That's a mortgage!" she exclaimed. "Maybe I could take you to lunch."

Her attitude did not help. It wasn't about money per se, but responsibility.

"'Lemme buy you a cheeseburger. The sky's the limit. Up to seven dollars... and eighty-four cents.'"

Étienne groaned. "Not *Spiderman encore*. You owe a couple hundred thousand. You take me to the nice place."

He sunk his hand in his hair.

"I will. Seriously. There's a place with awesome egg and pepper sandwiches in Pen Argyl."

"*Mon petit chou*, take me to the city. I have a mess to sort," Étienne said.

"Et, my people are on it," Adelaide said. "You need nourishment. Eggs are perfect — "

"Your people?" he interrupted. "You do not have people. I have people." His stomach rumbled.

"Regardless," she said. "Paloma will track the shipped orders. Paris will send fabric. Didier sent corrected patterns. This will be over before you know it. Our job is done."

« *Pas de tout*, » Étienne said.

"What if we go see James Bond? Bas won't go. I have time."

He had to admit, he'd enjoy the new Bond film. He deserved an indulgence, *n'est-ce pas*? His tension melted with the prospect. Étienne drummed his fingers across his leg, combating his potential acquiescence.

"It's been ages since I've gone to the movies..." Adelaide said.

"*Tu me roule*... This idea is a trick," he said.

"I know. We've watched *Goldfinger* so much I have it memorized," she replied.

He shouldn't allow her to influence him like this. He wouldn't succumb to a bribe as simple as a movie, would he? No, he did have work. He had a company to oversee. Her mistake had cost him money, time, and reputation. A movie would not maneuver him from that. Would it? Adelaide cocked her head and flashed her sweet smile.

"How much do you really need to do today?" she asked. "Come on, Et. If anyone notices, we say we were stuck in traffic. A movie, two hours. Traffic."

Adelaide winked. She had a point. He had everything under control. This was a setback, but not insurmountable. He had squandered half a million on a race car...

She hummed the James Bond theme. What was $200,000? His company spent about that much at The Peninsula New York last year. His anger dissipated. He took her hand, their fingertips lightly touching.

"We go see James Bond. Our little secret," he said.

CHAPTER SEVEN

B y Friday, Étienne had orchestrated the solution to the Holiday blouse problem, met Zélie's American obstetrician, okayed the design for the race car, approved the set for the Spring 2003 show in October, and selected designs for the January couture show. Now, Étienne propped his elbows on the blotter and folded his hands as he waited for Adelaide's opinion on this very important dress. A couple hours and he could escape for the weekend. The more early he could leave this brownstone on 36th Street, the better. He wanted to wake tomorrow morning with the chirp of birds, not the pounding of sewing machines from the Koreans below his sub-let.

Adelaide held his sketch that someone had mounted to Bristol board with swatches from Becky, the fabric buyer. Through tortoise-shell glasses, Adelaide studied the garment as she gnawed on her pen. She had slipped one foot from her Tod's pumps, the seams at the toes of herringbone tights burrowed in the carpet. In the reception area that connected his office to Adelaide's, his secretary, Seema, chattered on the phone. His eyes surfed the black leather sofa, the coat rack, and Adelaide's d'Amille ads on the walls.

His typical sketches wouldn't leave him this raw. Paris crowds, photographers, even fashion editors didn't scare him. Étienne had experienced this business long enough to survive. As long as he had *couture* collectors like his mother-in-law, Marthe-Georgine Saint-Ebène, he would have a job. Even the whims of department store buyers didn't scare him. His wife, on the other hand, petrified him.

Étienne waited for Adelaide's reaction to Zélie's Christmas gown. Every year, Étienne made something for Marthe-Georgine's annual party, two somethings actually, one for mother and one for daughter. Adelaide stared at the storyboard. Étienne liked it. Dark green velvet flared like a robe from an empire waist, trailing over an ivory velvet underskirt with medieval flair. For the bodice, he would stitch embroidery in gold rayon.

« *Chef,* » she said, glancing over her reading glasses. "It's gorgeous."

There was hesitation in her voice.

« *Mais?* »

"Isn't it old-fashioned?" she replied.

Étienne chuckled. Seema knocked on the open door.

« *Ouias?* » he asked.

"There's a problem," the Indian woman said.

« *Ouias?* » Étienne repeated.

"Mr. LaForêt called. Payroll account for the mills is empty," Seema said.

"Shit," Adelaide exclaimed, jumping to her feet.

"Something about a transfer between accounts..." Seema continued.

Adelaide cursed in two languages.

"I forgot," Adelaide said. "I told Albert I'd take care of it."

Who let Adelaide take responsibility for a financial transaction? As much as Étienne adored her, Étienne had left strict orders that she shouldn't be left in charge of anything involving money. She whipped a white laptop from the suede d'Amille purse they nicknamed the 'utility bag.' Adelaide typed.

"I can't focus on the account numbers..." she said. "Seema, would you read them to me?"

Seema recited them slowly as Adelaide pounded keys.

"A couple bounced," Adelaide said.

Étienne drummed his fingers across the desk. Adelaide closed the computer.

"Thanks, Seema. I got it," Adelaide said.

Seema left.

« Sorry, *chef.* »

Adelaide removed her glasses and placed the machine in her bag. Lately, she lacked concentration on many of her duties. She had more ideas, like the upcoming fashion camp for urban high school students, than sense.

"What does not go, *mon chou?*"

"You mean 'What's wrong?'" she corrected him. "Nothing. Or my damn math-challengedness."

Silence. She frowned.

« *C'est tout?* » he asked her.

"Maybe there is something else," she said.

Adelaide pulled the chair closer to Étienne's massive desk.

"Et, in the last few months I've taken on responsibilities that I'm not..."

"What about it?"

"What am I? I mean, what's my job? I'm some miscellaneous taskmaster," she said. "I've been doing stuff I'm not suited for..."

Seema reappeared.

"Adelaide," Seema said. "You have a phone call from Galen Sorbach."

"Tell him I'm in a meeting," Adelaide said.

"For a good looking man, you should take it," Étienne said.

Étienne lifted the receiver and passed it to Adelaide. She refused it.

"We were talking," she protested.

"*J'attends*. It can wait," Étienne told her. "*En plus*, I need my photos."

The secretary returned to her desk. Étienne jiggled the phone and poised his finger over the blinking button. Adelaide's expression drooped.

"Don't you ever take me seriously?" she asked.

« *Toujours,* » he answered.

"That's why you call me a cabbage," she remarked.

"We finish," Étienne promised. "You have the stress. Talk to pretty boy."

"You talk to him," she replied. "I haven't talked to him since my cat attacked him. He must think I'm a nutcase — "

"Talk to him," Étienne said.

"We need to finish this," she insisted.

« *Plus tard,* » he said with finality.

He pressed the phone into her hand. She brought it to her ear. Étienne punched the button and started around the desk to give her privacy.

"Chez d'Amille," she said. "This is Adelaide."

Adelaide grabbed his wrist. She shook her head violently and mouthed the words, « *reste-la.* » He loved when she addressed him in French.

"Hello, Galen."

Étienne sat.

"You don't need to apologize. I'm the one who's sorry."

On his desk blotter, Étienne doodled.

"Really?" she said. "After the last disaster?"

The suspense was terrible. Étienne wanted to know what the handsome young man had said to his cabbage.

"Well, yeah... I guess... Sure... *Au revoir,*" Adelaide said.

She replaced the receiver. Étienne lowered his pencil.

"He wants to see me," she said.

She had her shoes off again and her brow furrowed.

"*Est-ce que* you do not like him?" Étienne asked.

"I like him," she said.

"*Alors, mon petit chou*, what is it?"

Adelaide crossed her arms.

"I tell myself not to sleep with them, and I cave," she said. "No one cares who I am, just what I look like or what my tits feel like."

Etienne snickered. "You make the bad choices. Avoid *les rock-stars* like *la lopette*, the girlish man. This one... he is not *célèbre*, but everyday. Try him."

Adelaide hid her face. "Brian's still prettier than me. He wasn't exactly gay. Trust me."

"What about *ce type* … that last guy? Before?" Étienne asked.

"The inker at Marvel?" she said. "David never missed a hockey game and had a few video game addictions. Normal guys aren't always the answer. Anyway, Galen invited me to dinner at the bar in Portland."

"What bar?" Étienne asked.

"There is only one," Adelaide said.

Silence engulfed them. She stared at Étienne with her sad face as if she expected him to offer some incredible wisdom. What did he know?

"The problem is not the sex," Étienne answered. "You could use *l'amour physique*, but do not give your heart. You lose you."

"From the man divorced for a decade," Adelaide quipped. "With a pregnant ex-wife."

Adelaide gathered her shoes and lifted her bag.

"Et?" she said. "Will you come?"

"You need the chaperone?"

Her eyes fell to the floor again. Étienne pushed a hand into his hair. Her foot scratched the back of her calf.

"There's something, Et. About that town, and him…"

"I will find you later, when Zélie comes."

She left. Étienne used the time to finish paperwork. Adelaide had created many problems this week. What had she meant about her job? Did she need a more concrete role in the company? Did she not see how much he valued her?

He jerked his tie from his throat, tossing it to the floor. Perhaps he should schedule American trunk shows. That would cure any doubts of d'Amille quality. He pulled a pair of pants from a pile of mending on the table beside the door. Étienne sat on his desk and crossed his leg, the pants across his thigh. That was how Papa had taught him to sew. The sewing kit came out from his pocket. He threaded his needle and he forgot about the worries of the day.

As he adjusted the thread bar anchoring his cuff, Zélie arrived from her Wall Street office. She wore her navy blue suit with the knee-length skirt, navy hose, and Giuseppe Zanotti pumps in warm beige with jeweled toes. Her blouse was white silk, the cut almost too low for business, with a lacy camisole and a gold locket.

« Bonsoir, ma femme, » he said.

« I've been thinking about you all day, darling, » she replied breathlessly.

He didn't know if he liked the tone in her voice. Zélie strutted toward the desk. Tufts of hair fell in her face. Her cheeks were flushed.

« The market was up, the market was down, » she said.

Étienne folded the pants and set them in his chair.

« How did the market close? » he asked.

Étienne stood in front of his desk. He hoped the stock market stayed down. A thriving day of trading excited his wife in more than one way.

« It closed up, way up," she said, reaching for him.

« Sacred God, » Étienne replied.

Her fingertips undid the button at his throat. Her breasts jiggled.

« Are we alone? » she asked.

Her nipple rubbed against the silk. He placed his palm against the fabric, her warmth permeating it. The nipple stiffened.

« I hope you didn't go to work like that, » Étienne said.

« No," she said, her hand dipping into her jacket pocket.

She dangled her bra from her fingers.

« I took it off it the car, » Zélie said.

« Zélie, I don't know what's gotten into you, but you're killing me, » Étienne said. « It's all you think about. It's all we do. »

« You're complaining? » she said.

« Zélie... I'm not the young man I used to be. »

"So, you are complaining. »

« I'm not complaining. I'm tired, » he said.

She laid her hand across the back of his neck and kissed him hard. His mind fogged.

« My cabbage asked me to check on her. She has a date, » he said.

« Adelaide's a big girl, Étienne. »

She kissed him again. Zélie knew how to get what she wanted. She finished unbuttoning his shirt.

« We could go to my house, » he said.

« I'm not going anywhere, » she replied.

She untucked his shirt and deftly removed his belt.

« Zélie... »

Zélie tossed the belt to the floor and pulled him toward the reception area. His dress shirt disappeared, leaving just his undershirt. She pushed him over the arm of the sofa. The leather wheezed. He propped himself on his elbows. She kicked off her pumps, tore off her hose, and crawled onto him. Falling against the cushions, he laughed.

« Zélie, you're a wild beast. »

Her shirt strained at the front placket, exposing the appliqué seam of the lace on her camisole. Under other circumstances, he would consider that a defect. She kissed him again, and, burying his preoccupation with the fan of her buttonholes, he touched her cheek. Her brown eyes burned golden. She pushed his pants and his underwear below his hips. He didn't know when she removed her jacket.

« Blame the hormones, » she said.

She centered herself over him and bunched her skirt to her waist. Étienne's eyes widened at her naked hip.

«Don't tell me you removed those in the car, » he said.

« No, » she said. « I've been planning this. »

She gently eased onto him and straightened her back. His eyes closed as she rocked softly against him. She'd consume him, pause fleetingly, and tense.

Then, she'd exhale, offer a small smile, and move again. He lost himself in her rhythms. She rested one hand against his chest as she glided and moaned. Étienne hoped he could hold out. She pressed her body against him. Her body quaked. His body soared into bliss as Zélie collapsed against him. She rested her cheek to his. Étienne hugged her. She climbed off him and adjusted her clothing. Étienne covered himself, slipped his belt into its loops, and retrieved his shirt.

« I will call for my car, » he said.

« Your car?" she said. « Mine's outside. »

« I don't like yours, » he said.

Étienne called for his '67 Ferrari 250GT. Zélie grimaced.

« That car rattles, » Zélie said.

« That is what a car should sound like. »

He walked around the office, extinguishing lights. Étienne wrapped his arm around Zélie's hip. They walked into the hall and down the stairs. Étienne set the alarm and locked the door. The valet pulled the canary yellow Ferrari behind the Mercedes. Étienne traded keys. The S600 disappeared as Zélie begrudgingly got into the Ferrari.

« Could you buy one car, » she showed him her thumb for emphasis, « with seatbelts? I shouldn't even be in this car. »

« I've been thinking about a new car, » he admitted.

He didn't mention the 1,000 horsepower Bugatti Veyron that had begun road trials.

« Let me guess, a V — »

His heart skipped a beat. His middle finger jumped off the gated shifter. Did she know he had expressed interest? It was a verbal commitment, over the phone...

« — Volvo? » she finished.

Sure the color had drained from his face, he turned toward her. Nestled against the black leather bucket seat, she had that tilt of her face, her pointed stare. She was definitely irritated.

« Would you drive a Volvo? » he asked.

« No, » she said, relaxing into the seat, « but I'd feel more secure if you did. »

Depressing the clutch, Étienne shifted into reverse, a specific and barely forceful move. The clutch felt heavy, but right. This was no cushy luxury car, like her Mercedes. He could spread out in her Mercedes. Not in this car. His legs canted toward the center to compensate for wide wheel wells. Even at 1.73 meters, he had to adjust the seat to sit comfortably. Étienne headed toward the tunnel.

The car resisted as he downshifted, the transmission begging for fifth. When Étienne cruised onto the highway, he worked the car into gear, relishing the familiar chink. Étienne pushed the throttle. The RPMs jumped. Zélie glared. Étienne raced into the passing lane and zigzagged by the other cars. Étienne jammed the accelerator.

« 160 kilometers is not necessary, » she said.

A white Porsche with maroon soft-top threatened him from behind.

« You'll get a ticket, » Zélie said.

The Porsche kept on the Ferrari's bumper. The speedometer approached 200 kilometers. He swerved into the right lane and cut the wheel to push in front of a clunky SUV. The Porsche mimicked the maneuver, trying to pass. Étienne wouldn't allow that.

« Étienne, I'm going to vomit, » she said.

He let off the gas. The Porsche dusted him. The driver flashed Étienne the middle finger.

« Your car has an electronic speed limiter, » he said.

« So idiots like you don't kill yourselves. Can we please practice responsible behavior? »

She set her hand over his on the shifter knob. Étienne settled his speed at 110 kilometers. He fell nicely into traffic. A boring seventy-five minutes later, the Ferrari coasted into Portland. The one traffic light in town stood at the bottom of a small hill, and Étienne caught it red or he probably could have made it the three blocks down Main Street with the engine in neutral. The bar sat on another knoll, sandwiched between an antique store and a Methodist church. Étienne parked next to Adelaide's convertible. He got out and opened Zélie's door.

« You're really going to check on her, » Zélie commented.

« I told her I would, » he replied.

« Let's do this so we can eat dinner. It's almost nine, » Zélie said.

They proceeded across the gravel, Étienne wincing with each dusty step. Her Zanotti pumps wouldn't show the dirt, but his Ferragamos would. Reaching for the grimy doorknob, Étienne noticed a strange pool, foamy and golden. He spun and seized Zélie's waist. Her foot narrowly avoided the puddle of fresh throw-up. She yelped and promptly turned green. Étienne tugged her into the doorway, unsure whether he should let her go first or if he should serve as a buffer. Zélie covered her mouth and nose with her hand as cigarette smoke accosted them.

Étienne climbed the stairs, clutching his wife's hand. The jukebox wailed some country singer's laments. When they crested the stairs, shaggy heads peered from the bar. Étienne progressed to the men's room, the door a simple opening in the cheap paneling. As they swam the sea of denim and cotton tee-shirts, one man in a greasy work uniform broke the monotony. They passed Adelaide, a pool stick against her hip as she prepped a shot, wearing Western-style perforated mules and a 1920s whipped brim Stetson. She struck the cue ball. It hit the yellow striped ball that fell into the corner pocket. Étienne patted Zélie's bottom.

« I shall return, » he said.

She nodded. The swinging doors of the bathroom resembled shutters. The lone light bulb above the stall didn't throw much light. Judging from the array of stains in the urinal, Étienne could accept that. He did what he needed to do. He pulled paper towels from the dispenser and used them to loosen the spigot on the sink. He washed his hands and returned as Adelaide cracked the billiard balls again. Galen stood too close to Adelaide, his eyes burning as Galen noted the d'Amille's arrival.

"What are you doing here?" Galen asked.

Galen closed his hands around a brown pack of cigarettes, retrieving one. "I... *Mon chou...*"

The red striped ball bounced against the purple solid one, but only the striped fell into the pocket. Adelaide straightened. She kissed Étienne's cheeks, left-right-left, and, seconds later, framed her next shot.

"*Merci, chef.* I'm glad you came," she said.

Étienne leaned against the table, his hand beside his cabbage's long-necked brown bottle of American lite beer. He swigged it. It tasted like donkey's piss. Galen arranged his shot. His cigarette hung from his mouth as he knocked the cue ball and landed not one but two solid balls into the far pocket.

Despite the air conditioners and the fan overhead, Galen's cigarette smoke moved against the wind and circled Étienne close to his body. The smoke twisted into fingers and slithered across Étienne's shirt. Étienne blinked, hard, attributing the hallucination to fatigue. But when he opened his eyes, the fingers still gripped his shirt and they now attached to a smoky arm. Its palm pushed against him, creeping along his rib cage. It stopped directly over his heart and its fingers drummed against his chest in the same rapid rhythm of Étienne's heartbeat.

Galen smashed his cigarette between the depressions of a Coors Light ashtray. The cheap metal made a faint clatter against the edge of the pool table. With no cigarette to fuel it, the smoke appendage disappeared.

Étienne's heartbeat didn't have a chance to settle because he suddenly realized that his wife was no longer with them. Étienne scanned the room, over his shoulder first, then toward the bar. He tried not to seem frantic, as she wouldn't have gone far. His hand ran along his thigh, relaxing when he hit the bulge of his car keys. Unless Zélie took Adelaide's car and abandoned him, she had not left the bar.

« My cabbage, where is Zélie? »

Adelaide missed her shot. The lonesome cue ball rolled into the pocket. Galen dipped his hand in to retrieve it. Adelaide motioned to the booths.

"Galen suggested getting her out of the smoke," she said.

Étienne rubbed his shirt where the smoky hand had touched him. Trembling, Étienne navigated through men on barstools. He found Zélie inside a tall wooden booth with a bag of unsalted pretzels. Her hand gripped a tall glass, heavily iced. Straw between her lips, she sucked its red contents to her mouth. Her other hand withdrew from the Snyder's bag and waved playfully.

« *Salut,* » she said.

"You look comfortable," he said in English. "What do you drink?"

"Cranberry juice," she said, sliding the glass away.

He lifted it, sipping from the rim. Its tartness assailed his tongue.

"Checking for vodka," he joked.

"Disappointed?" she replied. She tapped the paper placemat, conveniently printed with the menu. "Galen recommended the chicken fingers."

"We eat? *Ici?* Chicken fingers?" his mind reeled. « *Bâtonnets de poulet?* »

She nodded.

"You do not eat the chicken fingers," Étienne said. "You eat nothing with the fingers."

Zélie shrugged and returned to her juice and pretzels. Étienne sat beside her, interlacing his fingers as he set his hands on the table. She snuggled against him and tickled him. He squirmed. Her other hand settled into his lap, fingertips against his thigh, tickling him in a much less innocent manner. He moved away, but she followed, fingers taunting him.

« *Tiens-toi bien!* » he chastised her.

Turning toward the bar, Étienne considered a root beer. Zélie nibbled his shoulder as her fingers swiftly sunk against his groin. She was not herself, Étienne thought. His hands pushed against the table and his arms tensed as she caressed him, gliding her fingers against parts of him she didn't normally pay attention to in public.

"Zélie," he whimpered. Definitely not herself.

In his head, it sounded tougher. Her hand eased away. Étienne exhaled. It didn't really help. She had already managed to stir his interest. Zélie reached into her hair and removed the bobby pins holding her bun. She slowly freed her thick curls and combed them with her fingers. That was the drop that overflowed the vase. Étienne could now ignore the reaction in his pants. Chicken fingers, tickling him, letting her hair down...

Her hair expanded thirstily into the humidity. It twisted into her earrings and would ensnare anything in its path. That's how Étienne gave up his diamond stud. Her hair ripped it from his earlobe early in their marriage and neither of them ever found it. Étienne might overlook grabbing his *queue* in a redneck bar, but she never unleashed 'the beast' in public. No, the hair stayed up.

Adelaide, Galen's arm around her waist, veered toward the bar. Étienne joined them and asked for that root beer. Adelaide ordered another lite beer.

"As long as you're here, Adelaide might as well give you the photos," Galen said.

"They're in my car," Adelaide said.

The bartender, a leggy blond with bad teeth and cutoff jeans, handed them their drinks. Étienne passed her a ten. Adelaide left. Galen took her drink to the table. Zélie's chicken fingers arrived in a red plastic basket with a grease-stained liner. She ate two pieces of stringy chicken drowned in honey mustard by the time Adelaide returned with a gift bag overflowing with lavender tissue paper. She offered it to Zélie and presented Étienne with a manila envelope.

"Addy already picked one for *People*," Galen said.

Zélie wiped her hands on a thin paper napkin. She parted the tissue paper delicately, pulling from the folds a stuffed frog in a diaper.

« *Félicitations,* » Galen said.

No one made a sound. Zélie brought one hand into her lap. She swallowed, something only Étienne would notice. He covered her hand with his. Adelaide laughed, plucking the stuffed animal from Zélie.

"That is funny," she said. "Where on earth did you find it?"

Zélie's chest rose with calculated precision. Her eyes narrowed, forehead crinkling. Hair tumbled into her face as her stare, if it could have, sawed through Adelaide.

"You told him."

Zélie said it simply, with the slightest questioning evident in her intonation.

"No," Adelaide replied.

Adelaide's head snapped to Galen, whose face remained blank, then to Étienne before resting on Zélie's frigid expression.

"Did I do something wrong?" Galen asked.

Adelaide buried the frog in the bag. Zélie peered coldly toward Étienne. She raised her eyebrows.

« *Mais non*, » he said. « *Pas moi*. »

"You mentioned it at the party," Galen said to Adelaide.

"No, I didn't," Adelaide responded without hesitation.

Zélie pounded Étienne in the shoulder directing him out of the booth. She threw the gift bag against the bar and ran for the door. Étienne chased after her with Adelaide on their heels.

"Et, I didn't. I swear," Adelaide said.

The door slammed as Zélie exited.

"Do not explain to me," he said. "Tell Zélie."

Étienne pursued Zélie. As he walked quicker, so did she. If he lengthened his strides, she lengthened hers. She pulled the car handle, but it didn't budge. She pounded her fist on the Ferrari's roof. Étienne fumed inwardly, but did not speak. He unlocked the door and opened it, but he blocked her from getting in.

« I don't think — » Étienne uttered.

She shoved him, half-hearted, like she wanted to push harder but didn't have the strength.

« That cunt,» Zélie said. « And you believe her. You always believe her. »

She dropped herself into the vehicle and slammed the door. Étienne got inside.

« She takes it for granted, » Zélie continued. « She takes her youth, and her beauty, and her sexuality for granted! »

Her fingers curled into a fist. Étienne didn't know what to say. He shifted and peered at his wife. As the Ferrari left the parking lot, she slammed her hand into the dash.

« What did the car do? » he asked.

Tears streamed her face.

« Sorry, » she said.

« She doesn't understand, » he said.

« Sure, » Zélie said. « Adelaide's always innocent. You treat her like she's still twelve. Even though she's not. Innocent. Or twelve. »

Étienne floored the accelerator.

« Why do you always think she's plotting something? That she's after you? » he said.

« She's not after me. » Zélie muttered.

Étienne's hand slipped from the steering wheel. He quickly regained his grip, but the car had swerved over the double yellow line. The thickness of the night made it easy to spot the flashing lights behind him. He glanced at the speedometer.

« *Putain!* »

Étienne stopped in front of the grocery store. After passing a field sobriety test and receiving a speeding ticket, Étienne drove carefully home with his agitated wife who didn't say a word for the rest of the night, not even a 'thank you' when he cooked her crêpes with Nutella and bananas.

CHAPTER EIGHT

Kait sat cross-legged on Galen's sleeping bag in the basement of the church. She giggled. She wore an oversized tee-shirt, sleeves billowing over slender elbows and hem resting across her bare thighs. Her hands rested on her legs. She swayed like a snake looking for food, nostrils wiggling.

"I smell her," she said.

Galen remained twenty feet away. He placed his keys on the folding table he'd set up after he brought his stained glass tools from Montreal.

"Her perfume. It's like vanilla and nail polish remover," Kait said. "With cheap beer and cigarettes. Fun night?"

Galen walked closer. The rush of Adelaide's kisses cycled within him, their effect something he still didn't understand. Adelaide could paralyze him. She resisted his attempts to subdue her. How is that possible? Kait's presence held him by the guts, a raw, elemental power that drew him and terrified him.

"Her lipstick stains your lips," she said.

Kait pushed her hands in the air close to his body, a ritualistic dance he didn't recognize.

"Do you know who she is?" she asked. "You think you can do my job."

"She's a girl and not very bright," Galen replied.

"You haven't figured it out," Kait said, rising on her knees.

Galen sat beside her. Kait draped her arms over him and cuddled in the hollow between his neck and shoulder.

"What did you do at the party?" Galen said.

He seized her hand, focusing fire into her arm. She yanked away and slapped his face.

"Bankers are delicious," she whispered into his ear, "but fashion types are faggots."

"You stole a dress, left a woman in the bushes thinking she was drunk, and performed magick with a couple hundred people in the house."

"And I thought you didn't notice."

"What did you do?" he asked again. "You summoned a fairy."

Kait nodded her head, smirking. She pushed Galen's temple, her fingertips lifting his hair.

"You always did miss the obvious," she stated, her smile twisting.

Kait pushed him to the floor.

"Neferkaba wants Adelaide controlled. I can control her," Kait said. "You stay out of it."

Her nails grew longer. Her freckled face grew red. Hair appeared on her knuckles. Galen leaned against the bedpost. Kait reached for his neck with her beast-like hand. He fell to his knees. She dug her claws into his scalp. Her nails curved into black, speared talons. She stroked his jaw as she pulled him by the hair. A pronounced ridge lined her forehead.

A claw ran over his eyelid. It sent a quiver down his spine. Galen punched her, square across the jaw with a left hook and then a right hand against her nose. She recoiled. Kait wiped her nose with her hand, her fingers rich with blood. She reached for him but he jolted upright. He flung her across the room. She crashed into a miniature altar on the far side of the room. A Christian flag and a framed sketch of Jesus fell from it.

Kait propelled herself to her feet. Kait lunged at Galen, who had stood, ramming him in the stomach. They stumbled, Galen backward and Kait forward, and fell again to the sleeping bag. Galen latched into her hair. He snarled his fingers into the orange mane. He pushed her. Her feet flailed. Her arms scratched. Galen punched her in the face. She leapt. Her hands raked his chest, shredding his shirt. Her knee landed in his groin.

Galen rapidly sucked in breath. His torso stung, the impact of her knee reverberated. A black cloud expanded around him. Galen absorbed the dark energy into his chest. Combining this with adrenaline, he chanted for Branwen, goddess of the sea. He muttered the words quietly, building momentum, hoping Kait wouldn't understand.

"Branwen, come forth," Galen called when his energy mounted.

A pipe above their heads exploded, spraying water. Kait turned. Galen threw her. Like any good cat, she landed on her feet. She walked toward him, cautiously, growling from the depths of her throat. She pounced, sinking her talons into his wrists. Her eyes glowed green, yellow and black. Their bodies pressed together. They dropped to the floor again.

"Kait?"

Saliva gathered in the corners of her gaping mouth. Kait brushed her leg against Galen's thigh. She ran the bridge of her nose down his neck.

She kissed him. Galen's elbow twisted. In one mangled instant, a noise like ice crushing filled the room and blinding pain shot into Galen's hand. Instinctively, he closed his eyes and meditated against the sensation. That's when Kait climbed onto him. He wriggled against her. She gripped his wrist and crushed the bones she had broken. Screaming, he swung with his other arm. Kait captured his balled fist in midair.

He stopped resisting and she loosened her grip. She had blood under her nose, and on her shirt. A meek layer of humanity flashed behind Kait's eyes. She plucked an almond of gleaming white light from the air and stretched its glimmer to surround them. It sucked her body inside, and Galen, too. He threw his eyes open wide, the colors and images pelting him like hail. The haberdasher's shop on Savile Row, an American suburban kitchen as children rushed to catch the bus, an elephant hunt in Zimbabwe, satellites cluttering space... She navigated this storm, touching one of these glimpses, tossing him to the ground. He heaved as he hit.

He could barely keep his eyes open. Galen couldn't focus. Kait's head seemed round and older, her body rotund and dressed in heavy skirts and a corset. The rhythm of old Gaelic drifted in and out of his mind. He landed outside the thatch-roofed stone cottage where he had lived with her and her mother, the midwife Meadhbh. Meadhbh's face reminded him of Adelaide, something in the eyes or maybe the cheekbones.

Galen thought of Adelaide's soft smile at the billiards table and tumbled toward a dream. Her smile! It was her lips! Something about the shape of Adelaide's lips resurrected memories of Meadhbh. His head slumped. Kait continued to talk, but he didn't heed. She smacked him and Galen rolled with the impact. In his sleep, Adelaide lay beside him, gathering him in her arms. She slid her fingers underneath his shirt, one fingertip against his belly button. She stroked his hair. Adelaide spoke, but not with her own voice.

"Why did you kill me, Lughaidh?" the voice asked from Adelaide's mouth.

Checking Adelaide's face, Galen noticed something different in the eyes. He couldn't recall the color. She spoke with Meadhbh's voice and she looked with Meadhbh's eyes. She used the name Meadhbh had given him. He had never told Adelaide that name.

"Why did you kill me, Lughaidh?"

Galen shook his head. He hadn't killed her. Adelaide's red-blond hair darkened, became redder, richer, and thicker, and lengthened. The structure in her cheeks angled less, the bones less pronounced. The soft spot at the end of her nose moved. It sloped and pointed. Her mouth widened. Her lips darkened. She became Meadhbh, and at the same time, remained Adelaide.

"I didn't," Galen said, the words sticking. "I didn't."

"You let me die," she said.

He did. Galen had let his foster mother die. His fury at losing Kait to Neferkaba and his jealousy of Kait's guardian post had fueled a fire that he could not control. "You let me die," Meadhbh accused.

"No," Galen said. "I couldn't stop it. I wanted to. I did."

He reached for Meadhbh's hand.

"Why did you kill me, Lughaidh?" she asked again.

Meadhbh wore a chemise dyed woad blue, a corset of madder root red and a voluminous skirt of plum-red. She had the sleeves of her loose-fitting shirt pushed past her elbows.

"I taught you everything," Meadhbh said, "but you never learned control."

The sun came out from behind a cloud. Galen shielded his eyes. The sunlight washed across his legs and made them invisible.

"Be careful, Lughaidh," Meadhbh warned.

In Meadhbh's shadow, a crack split. Thousands of fairies shot from the crevice. They bombarded him. They swirled the air with vivid pink, blue and red. Galen hid his face with his arms. Kait appeared, latching on to his hand. She grabbed one of the fairy's colored orbs and dove into it, bringing him with her.

Galen woke on top of his sleeping bag alone. Pain from his swollen, misshapen wrist exacerbated the migraine hammering his sinuses. His fingers hung limply, pointing to the ground. Caked blood and scratches adorned his chest, reddish-brown and pink stripes against bronze flesh. He ached, but did not fear his wounds. He could suffer indefinitely and never die.

Galen rolled into the soggy carpet. Kait had disappeared. He could feel it in the stillness. With his good arm, he pushed himself to a seated position and lit a smashed kretek cigarette from his shirt pocket. He flicked the ashes toward the south, then to each of the other cardinal directions, using his cigarette as a cleansing offering. A natural, leafy smell with the sharp taint of clove washed over the room. The nicotine worsened his headache.

Galen dragged himself to his backpack of basic supplies, pulling out a blue candle and polished white pebbles. He arranged the stones on the floor in skeletal lines. He lit the candle, dripping blue wax across the rocks. He called for Aibheaog to bring the healing waters from her sacred well.

As the wax joined the marble pebbles, warmth cascaded from his shoulder into his arm and stopped at the elbow. Chanting and promising a gift of wine in a wooden bucket (similar to an unfulfilled promise after the incident with Étienne last week), Galen pleaded with the goddess. He needed her restorative waters. Dull warmth spread but did not reduce the swelling.

Galen pulled another cigarette from his pocket. His shoulder drooped, numb. He hoped the wrist would follow. He retrieved his homemade flint runes, haphazardly grabbed a book from the floor, and dumped the runes upon it. He arranged them carefully, almost as painstakingly as he had placed the marble pebbles. He lit another cigarette, this time guiding the ashes into a bowl where he drew a cross. Chanting the names of the runes, his fingertips circled the symbols.

Together, they spelled Kait's strengths. He bit his good wrist, baptizing the line with his blood. After another incantation and a breath blown across the blood, Galen plucked the first rune and tossed it into the bowl. He added another. He grabbed a third, but paused.

That should get her attention, he thought. Galen pawed for the bottle of rum he had with his other victuals. He unscrewed the lid with his teeth and gulped the liquid until it scalded his throat. As the alcohol made the world swirl, Galen collapsed onto his sleeping bag only to be woken by Kait, an animalistic crunch in her nose and an angle to her ears. She wore a plaid miniskirt. She kissed his forehead and rested her temple against his. Running her fingers down his neck, Kait leaned into his ear.

"You weakened me," she said. "That's dirty."

Galen glared at her.

"You want help healing that?" Kait said, pointing to his wrist.

He nodded. If he opened his mouth, he'd say something terrible. He lowered his head against her chest. If he pissed her off, he wouldn't get his wrist fixed. Kait ran her fingers through his hair. Reaching for his elbows, she lifted his arms. She knelt. Kait chanted and manipulated both wrists, but gently, as not to incite pain.

Galen recited the spell with her. Warmth returned to him. Blue light consumed them. Without the candle, without the stones, with nothing but her bare hands, the gods and goddesses came when Kait called. She dug her fingertips into Galen's tender flesh. Burning pain seared throughout his arm and hand, but, as quickly as they had caused the agony, her fingers sent numbness. Under that strange anesthesia, his splintered bones fused, expanding and contracting against the muscles and arteries. He absent-mindedly itched the skin. She slapped his hand.

"Sorry if it's uncomfortable," Kait said, "but I'm missing some of my strength."

Her fiercely-glowing blue hands massaged his swollen limb. Galen rotated his wrist and fanned his fingers. It cracked in a few places as he moved it, but no pain. She snatched his arm from the air as he tested it. Her nails penetrated the soft underside of his arm.

"Undo the spell," she commanded.

He handed her the bowl of runes. She accepted it and sent runes and ashes across his sleeping bag before she hurled the bowl. Spitting into her left hand, she prodded the spittle with her fingers until it grew into a golf ball-sized sphere. She pitched it at the runes, dousing them until they glistened. Powder and smoke puffed from them. She flopped onto her belly in the midst of it, inhaling. Her pleated skirt exposed her rear. She zoomed upright. The crunch in her nose flattened. Her ears rounded. Her face softened. She wound her arms above her head.

She jumped to the floor and burst into a jig. Her body glimmered as she moved, her bare feet swiping the floor. Her hand stroked his face. His nose brushed against her arm, and he noted a man's perspiration on her with the undertones of sex. He stroked Kait's side as she danced and thought of Adelaide's heart-shaped face as he aimed his mouth for Kait. Kait backhanded him.

"I think not," she said.

CHAPTER NINE

C hilled air exhausted from a vent near Adelaide's bed. Without opening her eyes, she nestled the ducky comforter over her arms and under her chin. The dream, a recurring favorite where she and Étienne toured the French wine regions, welcomed her without missing a beat. She resumed her role by purchasing *Duval-Leroy Champagne Rosé de Saignée* to accompany her famous strawberry truffles.

In the dream, Adelaide sipped the remaining sample in her glass while the salesman tallied her bill. The champagne's bubbles tickled her tongue. A drop splashed onto the tip of her nose. It didn't have the fruity notes of the wine but a fishy odor. She reached into her bag for a tissue. The salesman suddenly scoured her nose with a Brillo pad. Adelaide slapped the salesman, but he kept coming with that Brillo pad.

Enough of that nonsense, Adelaide decided as she opened her eyes, meeting the brightness of the country morning. After two years waking up in Gramercy, this Mount Bethel sunshine proved obtrusive. A yowl punctured her addled mind. A familiar weight leapt onto her chest. A huge cat head loomed. Zut licked Adelaide's nose. Her rough tongue explained the Brillo pad.

"What time is it, Zut?" she asked.

Zut licked Adelaide's cheek. The cat usually didn't bother her, unless she overslept. Adelaide ran to the window. Étienne's Ferrari remained in the driveway next to her Benz. The clock's red digits flashed 9:12 a.m. What day was it? She yawned. Well, if Étienne hadn't left then she couldn't be late for work. That was a good thing.

Then, she heard it: muffled electronic music from her dry-cleaning pile. When she got closer to the dirty clothes, she recognized "Jack and Diane." She dug toward yesterday's slacks and retrieved the ringing cellular.

"Hello," she said.

"Hey, Pumpkin," her dad replied. "How's my girl? You didn't answer the phone in your apartment. You get away for the weekend?"

"Yeah," Adelaide replied. "I had a date."

"Oh, no, Pumpkin. Who is it this time?"

"He's a photographer, Dad."

"Not another fruit..."

"Daddy!"

"I don't want to hear anymore. Whatever happened to Thad?"

"Tom, Dad."

"I liked him. He played rugby, didn't he?"

"Yeah, Dad. That was Tom."

"Never saw a rugby game. But he seemed..." her father's voice trailed.

"Manly, Dad?" she suggested. "Have you heard from Jay?"

"She likes it in Germany. She likes the school."

Of course Janine likes the school, Adelaide thought. Her sister, the Fulbright Scholar.

"Okay, Helen... Your mother wants to talk to you," Dad said.

Adelaide wondered if she needed to delve into her stash.

"Addy?" her mother said. "Hi, sweetie. You've met someone?"

"You don't ask about my job, my cat, or the new ad campaign. It's men."

"Tell me you didn't sleep with him," her mother said.

"I'm practically naked in that new ad, you know..."

"That's avoiding my question, Addy, which makes me think the worst."

Milky Way, her mind screamed, as she envisioned the brown and green wrapper. Étienne didn't have to know. She crept toward the kitchen.

"No," Adelaide replied. "I haven't slept with anybody, Mom."

"Well, I worry. A woman your age needs a good career or a good husband. You have no education, no serious job. You won't be young and beautiful forever. Your sister —"

"Mom, I am not my sister," Adelaide interrupted, inching to the refrigerator. "What I am is second-in-command in the New York off — "

"Are you going to church?"

"...ice," Adelaide finished. Of a major international fashion manufacturer, she wanted to add. But she didn't. No point.

"Your father and I tried very hard not to pressure you," her mother said.

Adelaide braced for the next onslaught. It was always men first, then religion. Having a Jewish father and a Christian mother complicated everything.

"You need something to ground you. Isn't there some voice telling you something?" her mother asked.

I want a Milky Way, Adelaide thought. She said nothing.

"I need to know that deep down you have substance..."

"I'm hanging up. I love you."

Adelaide tossed the cellular onto the counter. The cat jumped.

"I'm not stupid," Adelaide told Zut.

Men and God, she had no luck with either. Adelaide tiptoed to the freezer. Her arm snaked behind the eggplant cutlets. Her fingers clasped her candy. Her cell responded with Moby's James Bond theme. Not surrendering the chocolate, Adelaide slammed the freezer shut and grabbed the phone. How did he always know? Goddamn it, she could eat nothing! Unless it was a professional call... Her "no serious job" required an awful lot of attention.

« *Ouias, chef?* »

« *Coucou, mon chou. Ça va?* » Étienne asked.

"I'm good," she replied. "What's up?"

"Can I come?" Étienne asked.

Adelaide wanted this Milky Way (oddly, she had purchased this one in Paris) and coffee.

"If you have coffee," she retorted.

« *Mais oui*, » he answered.

"Then sure," Adelaide said.

She gazed at the Milky Way. Would the pleasure from a European Milky Way cancel out Étienne's ire? Since the recipe did not include caramel, she couldn't decide. Étienne unlatched the door. Zut raced to greet him. Adelaide hid the candy behind her back.

"*Mon chou*... We need to talk," he said.

The cat jumped onto the couch. When Étienne passed, Zut straightened from her haunches and aimed her front paws for the man's light blue shirt. The two stood face-to-face. Zut purred.

"*La minette méchante*, if I had the tuna I would tell you, absolutely first," Étienne said.

The cat leapt to the floor. Étienne walked to the breakfast bar and set the coffee on it. He leaned over the counter, his fingers brushing Adelaide's shoulder as his lips grazed one cheek. His nose passed hers as he planted a kiss on her other cheek, immersing her in the scent of his after-shave, the one that matched his summer cologne. Allure smelled amazing on him, fruity, floral but still spicy. She loved how Chanel fragrances harmoniously blended notes. She hoped her perfume would do the same.

Adelaide returned his *bises*. Sometimes they practiced this routine several times a day. Today, his polite greeting streamed through her, pooling below her abdomen and draining the steadiness from her legs. She shifted her body, Milky Way still hidden, turning as if to keep her bosom from view. The nightgown barely contained her breasts.

"You have what?" he replied, gesturing toward the hand behind her back.

« *Rien,* » she answered.

« *Du chocolat?* »

He extended his hand, silently asking for whatever she had. Adelaide bit her lip.

"*Donne-le-moi.* I do not need a model with ... *Comment dit? Les boutons.*"

"Pimples," she translated.

Adelaide reluctantly passed him the confection.

"I only wanted a bite," she whined.

Étienne sunk his hand into his hair.

"What's taken you? You ruin Holiday, make payroll empty, tell personal news to the stranger, and *maintenant chocolat.*"

She clutched his fingers, which had closed around her Milky Way.

"Ruined?" Adelaide whispered.

She'd ruined holiday? Really? She tumbled into a puddle of tears. Surely, she didn't bomb the season. Maybe she should have stayed in the suburbs and waitressed at a greasy luncheonette. Damn, she wished he hadn't taken the chocolate.

« *Merde,* » Étienne muttered. « I do not have time, mon chou. »

He placed the Milky Way in his pants pocket and wrapped his arms around her convulsing torso. She clamped her fingers onto his shirt, resting her cheek against his shoulder. He whispered sweet phrases in French, repetitions of « it's all right, » « please, don't cry, » and « What troubles my cabbage? » His hands rubbed her back, his warmth and his presence a tide pulling her in forbidden directions.

« *Qu'est-ce que c'est?* » he asked.

"Sorry," Adelaide said, relieved that she hadn't done her make-up. "I just talked to my mom and what you said..."

"*Moi?* What I say?"

"That I'm a stupid, pretty girl who ruins your business," she said. "You sound like Mom. She thinks my job is to give head."

"*Faire un pompier?* To who?" Étienne asked. "No one in my company... *En anglais* ... 'Gives head?' Not as business. *Mon chou,* look at me."

She raised her burning, tearstained eyes.

"You had a bad week. *C'est tout, chérie.* I am not going to toss you... *non,* fire you. You believe, yes? I must go. Mass starts in twenty minutes."

"Mass?" she said in disbelief.

Adelaide released him. He swung his bangs from his face and gave her a Gallic shrug.

"Zélie. She waits and she wants to go to Mass. To pray. It is like my mother. But I need to ask you it. Why did you tell him? Did you not think — "

"I didn't tell him!" she yelled.

He brought his fingers to her lips.

« *Chut,* » he said.

His touch rippled down her spine.

"Okay," he said, "but please... no more talk. Not even to Zélie."

He wrung his hands.

"Et, what's the big deal? Bas said you guys wanted a baby — "

« *Pas de temps,* » he interrupted, gripping her hands. "*S'il te plait,* promise no more talk."

"I promise," she said softly.

Étienne kissed her forehead and retreated to the stairwell. She turned to the cup of coffee and placed it into the microwave. Adelaide dropped a bagel in the toaster. As Étienne's and Basilie's footsteps descended, Adelaide's tears resumed. This time, no one held her. No one asked what was wrong. A craving welled in Adelaide, one that had followed her since Friday night, something that might distract her. She scolded herself. She wouldn't start that habit again, no matter how much she wanted it.

Why did she stay here? To torment herself? The bagel popped from the toaster. She couldn't blame Et for her excitable condition. She was an adult. She should be able to handle it. It didn't help that Galen had gone home early on Friday. She didn't have a chance to test Étienne's hypothesis that she needed *l'amour physique*. She smeared jelly onto her bagel. Butter had too many calories and too much fat.

She should work on her needlepoint. She had that half-finished cross-stitch for Marcy's birthday. If no one interrupted her, Adelaide might complete the project today. Then, for once in her life, she might give someone a birthday gift on time.

Her cellular offered its crackling rendition of "Space Oddity." It reminded Adelaide of David Bowie's "Janine," which her sister detested. So, of course, Adelaide adopted it as her ring tone.

"'Oh, my love, Janine, I'm helpless — ,'" Adelaide belted into the phone.

"Funny, chicken lips," her sister said. "This is an overseas call. Don't waste my money."

"Call collect. I don't care."

"Étienne probably pays the bill," Janine said.

"Don't start. Mom already gave me my weekly lecture on my lack of viable skills."

Adelaide dropped onto a bar stool at the counter and chomped into the bagel. She hadn't had bread in a month.

"Rough week?"

"Totally messed up a big blouse order because I read the specs wrong."

"So you screwed up a couple blouses."

"Eighty dozen."

"That sounds like a lot. Would it cheer you up if I told you about my genealogy project?"

"You are such a boring nerd," Adelaide replied.

"I found a branch of the Larkins in England and they look Irish. It's hard to tell, because the records... Some of the names got lost. I've traced Mom's family to a village in Cornwall... I'll e-mail it ..."

"So we might be Irish Catholic German Jews?" Adelaide joked.

She retrieved her coffee from the microwave.

"Nobody Catholic in our family," Janine said. "We were pagans, until the Protestants got us. Most families have baptism or wedding records. Not us."

Adelaide opened her iBook. She launched her e-mail.

"I got it," she said as the file downloaded.

They talked for a while with Adelaide deleting spam while her sister talked. When they ran out of conversation and said goodbye, Adelaide gave her email account her full attention. She eagerly clicked on a message from the perfume house. They would ship a sample of Bas's formula this week. This would go faster if Étienne had never transferred her from France. She and Bas had selected a primary note of lavender, with secondaries of mint and lemon, and a base of lily-of-the-valley and grass to replicate the French countryside. Not that Adelaide remembered what that smelled like anymore. When it arrived, Adelaide would have to hide the package from Étienne or it would ruin the surprise.

Next, came a video sent by her friend Liz. The subject line — "It's baaaaack!" — didn't look promising. It couldn't still exist, could it? Adelaide clicked. The familiar scene came to life on her computer: polka dots, the silver d'Amille logo, the pale beige carpet of the catwalk. Adelaide watched herself emerge from the wings in a straw hat, yellow polka-dot sundress and platform espadrilles.

October 1996, almost six years ago. The mold counts in Paris hit unusual highs and Addy took a prescription antihistamine on the morning of the Spring 1997 show. She shouldn't have. The music was Primitive Radio Gods' "Standing Outside a Phone Booth With Money in My Hand." She had sold Étienne on the song. It happened on Adelaide's third outfit. Even though Adelaide refused to watch the video, she knew by the music and the gasp of the audience, and finally the clatter. Adelaide did a face plant on the runway. She spurred the fashion show equivalent of a three-car pile-up. Adelaide's stomach churned painfully.

She slammed the laptop closed. Sparks oozed from the machine. Fuck, she thought. Usually she fried watches, not computers. She tentatively opened the device. The Mac sputtered and went silent. Adelaide pushed the power button. No chime greeted her. No lights lit. She slammed her head against the kitchen bar. How would she review the prototype for the new d'Amille web site? Bas had asked her to supervise it. One more reason for Bas to hate her.

Leaving the broken computer behind, Adelaide dressed and retrieved her cross-stitch. She placed her embroidery ring on the coffee table and selected her DVD of the BBC's *Pride and Prejudice* from the drawer under the television. She settled onto the couch with Zut.

Several friends called with invitations but then expressed disdain that Adelaide had fled the city. Apparently people only wanted to hang out with her in New York City, probably to "be seen" or to score celebrity perks. Mount Bethel did not offer the same excitement. Half-way through disc two (two hours and she hadn't had enough Colin Firth), she approached the end of her cross-stitch, pleased that a watering can with flowers had grown from the gray mass with colored blobs. Her phone rang with the default ringer. She didn't recognize the number.

"Hello?" she said.

"Hi, Adelaide?"

"Galen?"

Her heart thumped. She would have to find him a ring tone. Maybe TLC's "Ain't too Proud to Beg." No, that song was probably older than he was.

"Hi. I wanted to see you," he said.

"That's cool," she said.

He called. He wanted to see her again. She could use "Hot in Here" by Nelly.

"Would six work?" he asked.

"Okay," she said.

They worked out the details and he hung up. She dropped the phone and circled the living room. She should change. She should make her bed. Should she put fresh sheets on? She had to keep her wits about her. Would she end up sleeping with him? She shouldn't. Or should she? Et might say she should, but her mother, even her girlfriends would say no. How long had she really known him? Two weeks. But only one date.

Adelaide bit her nails. And she stopped herself. Because Étienne would kill her if he caught her with gnaw marks on her index finger. She headed for her closet. She knew the outfit she wanted: her scanty, dark-red beaded halter with wide-legged, low-riding black silk pants. She had stitched the halter. It took forever, and Didier had to help her.

She considered black stiletto sandals, but with Galen's lack of height she vetoed them. Instead, Adelaide slipped into her Gucci Malibu mid-heel pumps. She could kick them off seductively later. From her jewelry box, she retrieved her charm bracelet. Adelaide reached for her garnet and diamond earrings. She spritzed herself with perfume.

From the cabinet over the kitchen sink, Adelaide retrieved her Chambord (a habit she learned emulating the d'Amilles, though not as dangerous as green Chartreuse). She also got an imported German chocolate bar. Adelaide then locked her cat in the attic apartment.

In Étienne's kitchen, Adelaide retrieved the last two servings of white chocolate mousse from Étienne's fridge and garnished it with German chocolate. She drizzled brandy and plopped a fresh raspberry on top. She ignited the gas fireplace. Something swooshed and it wasn't the flame. The air fluttered. Adelaide turned. The tiny redhead from Étienne's party, the one who asked for an aspirin, stood on Étienne's counter. Adelaide jumped.

"A fire and air conditioning," the redhead remarked.

The woman soared to the floor. Her tiny body forced Adelaide toward the fireplace. The redhead slammed the heel of her hand into Adelaide's shoulder and used the other hand to immobilize Adelaide's wrist. Adelaide screamed. Frizzy red hair coated Adelaide's mouth as she wrestled with her petite foe, whose skull knocked Adelaide's jaw. Adelaide reached for the fireplace poker. The intruder's fingers tightened against Adelaide's right hand. Their palms met.

"Cacht," Adelaide said, not quite understanding why.

The name flashed into her mind with an image of a redheaded girl wading in a river, holding a crude tunic above her knees.

"What did you say?" the woman asked.

"Cacht," Adelaide repeated.

The woman tightened her hold on Adelaide's arm, pushing it farther into the fireplace. A strange shadow buzzed around Adelaide's head. The women's fingers crossed into the flames. Adelaide kicked her attacker, but it didn't affect the tiny woman.

"What are you doing?" Adelaide hollered.

The shadow resembled a huge fly and it dove around her head emitting blue and gold bolts.

"I'm showing you something, relax," Cacht said.

The heat intensified as Adelaide's fingers boiled with pain and her nails blackened and shriveled.

"Goddamn it, stop!" Adelaide screamed.

Gold bolts struck Cacht in the forehead. She flinched, but ignored them. Blue bolts shot down Adelaide's arm.

"Now do it," Cacht said.

"Do what?" Adelaide whimpered.

With her free hand, Adelaide reached the fireplace poker. Before she could lift it, Cacht ripped it from her hand without releasing Adelaide's shoulder or the hand in the fire.

"No," Cacht said. "I'm not trying to hurt you."

"Well, you are!"

"Put the fire out."

The women's bright green eyes bore into Adelaide, knocking the breath from her. The giant fly circled them.

"I can't, Cacht. You're crazy."

Cacht seized Adelaide's arms and shook her violently.

"My name is Kate," the fiery-spirited redhead said. "That's K-A-I-T, the Irish spelling. No one uses the name 'Cacht' anymore."

"But your name is Cacht," Adelaide said.

Kait's hold loosened. Adelaide jerked from her, stumbling into the kitchen. She cupped her injured hand against her chest. Her whole arm trembled with the sting. She knocked the spigot with her good hand. Adelaide laid her hand's red flesh in cold water. Kait followed her, her fingers streaking the shiny black refrigerator, then exploring the doo-dads on the counter. Adelaide's fingers slipped inside Étienne's knife drawer and caressed the handle of what Adelaide hoped was a fatally-sharp carving knife. She yanked it out, her resolve melting when she revealed the six-inch utility knife.

"You gonna cut me? Go ahead," Kait said.

Adelaide thrust the knife forward. Kait offered the pale insides of her wrists. Adelaide rested the blade against them, but could not cut.

"Go ahead," Kait said.

Kait pulled the knife from Adelaide's hand. She opened her own flesh, vertically down her arm. She tensed her lips while cutting, but she showed no real signs of pain. She removed the knife and waited for the blood to flow. She watched it, smiling, separating the two sides of the wound. Adelaide turned the other way.

"No!" Kait screamed. "Watch!"

Kait grabbed Adelaide's chin and pulled her head. Kait's hand on her uninjured arm gleamed with a strange blue, a similar blue to the bolts that came from the fly creature. She passed her hand over her laceration. The cut disappeared.

"Not that I would have bled to death," Kait said. "I have this."

She lifted the shell pendant hanging from her neck. Kait sat on the counter beside the sink and crossed her legs.

"Spare me the mundane bullshit," Kait said. "There's no way to play this that won't sound like trite drama."

Adelaide stared at this five-foot tall woman perched beside her.

"Look at your hand," Kait suggested in a chummy tone.

Adelaide stepped away. She would not move her eyes from this woman for a second.

"I really think you need to look," Kait said.

"No," Adelaide said in a sad attempt at a growl.

Kait laughed. It ricocheted off the kitchen ceiling and hit Adelaide in waves. Kait shoved the limb into her face. Fresh, white flesh gleamed on her hand, complete with sparkling fingernails. Adelaide poked it.

"What happened?" she asked.

"You healed it. It's what you do. You're a healer," Kait explained.

"Huh?" Adelaide responded.

This chick is nuts, Adelaide thought, flashing a nervous smile.

"I've been sent to neutralize your magic, but I can't. I can, but I don't want to. So my Louey thinks he will. Oh, wait, you call him Galen."

"What the Hell are you talking about?" Adelaide said.

"There's a whole level to this world that you know nothing about. Like this..."

Kait snapped her fingers, opened her palm, and blew air across her hand. A glittery cloud covered Adelaide. A dark creature with iridescent wings appeared beside Adelaide, over her shoulder. It had huge eyes and a sagging belly. Adelaide shrieked.

"He's a protector," Kait said.

Adelaide almost didn't hear her over her screams.

"Settle down, he won't hurt you," Kait continued. "I assigned this fairy to you, so he can keep you in balance. No more errant magic. Maybe Neferkaba will leave you alone."

Adelaide's eyes widened.

"That's a fairy?" she said.

Adelaide lost her breath and mimicked a maneuver she'd seen from Étienne a thousand times; she clutched her chest.

"That... is..."

She couldn't speak.

...not..."

"Do me a favor," Kait continued, ignoring Adelaide's distress. "Don't give Louey anything: not sex, not love, and certainly not power. It can't be taken, not by him. Protect your magic."

Protect my heart, now protect my magic, Adelaide thought.

"Speaking of... I gotta go," Kait said. "He's here. We'll meet again. I'm watching."

She hopped from the counter.

"No sex."

Kait turned, pivoted and raised a finger in warning.

"I mean it. None."

She disappeared as someone rapped gently on the French doors that led to the deck. Adelaide walked across the room. Her wide pant legs swished. Her heels tapped against the floor. She answered the door. Galen's hazel eyes assessed her.

"You okay?" he asked. "You look pale."

"A woman... from the party... She stopped by," Adelaide absorbed the darkness of the yard, unable to see far as her eyes scanned for Kait. "Never mind."

Adelaide returned to the fireplace. She surveyed her hand again.

"Someone was here? Just now?" Galen said tersely.

"One of Étienne's crazy friends, I guess — "

Galen lips thinned and his eyes burned.

"Redhead?" he interrupted. "Lots of freckles? Curly hair?

She nodded.

"My sister," he told her. "Kait."

Adelaide said nothing.

"If she did anything to you, you'd tell me," he said. "Right?"

Adelaide blushed. The glow of the fire highlighted the gold in his skin. And his hair, she loved that auburn color and that one curl that fell across his forehead. It reminded her of Superman comics. If only he looked like Tobey Maguire instead... Galen wore a lightweight plum sweater of gorgeous Irish wool and gray slacks.

"That color looks incredible on you," she said. "I love that purple. You look great."

"Thanks," he replied. "You do, too. Did she scare you?"

A voice in her head warned of danger.

"I don't want to talk about it," she said.

"I'll talk to her," he said. "I'm sorry. She's a tad... touched."

He handed her a bulbous stoneware canister with a cork lid.

"I made you tea," he said.

"Isn't it cold?"

He smiled. The way he moved his lips, their thin lines and the way they matched the color of his skin, it softened Adelaide. Did her hair look carefree? Did he notice that lip-gloss was her only make-up? Did she look slutty? Even in the low heels, she felt ridiculously tall. Not to mention she had to duck in the doorways.

"Tea leaves," he explained. "This blend is a calming tea, to relieve tension."

"Maybe I should have some now," Adelaide said.

"Are you tense?" he asked.

Galen slid his hand under her hair, directing her face toward his. His fingertips pressed against the base of her skull. His lips searched for hers.

Oh my God, I shouldn't have worn these shoes, she screamed inside her head. I must be a foot taller than he is. He's going to kiss me and I'm a freaking skyscraper.

Adelaide closed her eyes and followed his lead. His lips brushed hers, barely meeting them. He repeated the motion with more force. Adelaide no longer heard the crackle of the logs on the fire or the crickets outside the door. The only thing she wanted was him. She knew nothing about Galen, but here she stood, in his arms, or as much in his arms as she could be in these ridiculous shoes. The fever of his touch consumed her. Their mouths twisted in a frenzied melding.

"Protect your magic."

An icy sensation rushed into her body. It started at her toes, consuming her legs, then spine, and arms. Gooseflesh lined her arms. She pulled away and crossed the room where she put the tea on the counter. A hand fell onto her shoulder. She jumped.

"Addy?" he said. "You all right?"

"Yes, just cold," Adelaide replied, facing him.

Something urged her to get farther away.

"Let me get dessert," she said with her photogenic smile.

She couldn't shake this numinous feeling. Adelaide went to the refrigerator and brought out the chocolate mousse. In the past, she never took these episodes seriously. Nothing ever came of them. They were erroneous feelings of doom. She had an overactive imagination. But the crazy lady in the kitchen, that was very real. Adelaide got two spoons.

"White chocolate mousse," she said.

He took one mousse and one spoon.

"Let's share," he said. "I can feed you."

"I really shouldn't with the show."

Galen walked to the entry and pushed the oversized white chair toward the door. He sat on the floor in front of the fire. Adelaide poured Chambord and joined him.

"Stick out your tongue," Galen directed her.

With a raspberry between his thumb and forefinger, Galen dipped it into the mousse. He ran the fruit over her tongue. Adelaide closed her eyes. The sweetness filled her mouth until the bitter shavings of German chocolate struck her taste buds. Adelaide relaxed. It was going to be a good night. She'd bet her life on it.

CHAPTER TEN

The delirium from her successful date did not combat the arrival of a frantic Monday. At the unholy hour of 6:05 a.m., Adelaide found herself in the parking lot of the Portland Diner. She left her Benz running. She stretched her legs to the ground and as she closed the door, a scruffy mutt ran to her. She pulled her legs back into the car and slammed the door. It wasn't a big dog, but it was muscular and hairy and hungry-looking. It had grey patches on its snout and oversized paws, tufts of hair came out its ears and it breathed in an odd rhythm.

They stared at each other. Adelaide wasn't sure if it proved a threat and she couldn't tell what the dog was thinking. The scar near her armpit itched. She inched the door open again. The dog growled. Adelaide wondered if she could skip the coffee. She gauged the distance toward the diner, the door only open enough to expose her hand. The dog continued growling. Adelaide slammed her head against the steering wheel. The door closed. She dug through her purse for something the dog might want to eat. Nothing. Not even a miniature Milky Way.

She had to get into the diner. She slowly opened the door for the third time. She extended her leg. The dog sniffed her toes. Sweat doused Adelaide's forehead and dampened her armpits. The dog licked her big toe, exposed by her five hundred dollar Prada thong sandals. The dog retreated, still looking at her with a cock-eyed expression. Adelaide shook so badly she couldn't pull herself out of the driver's seat. The dog left. Adelaide waited a few minutes and walked calmly toward the diner.

Once inside, she asked the smoking waitress for a large cup of coffee to go. Everyone — which at this hour meant two burly truck-drivers, an old man with no teeth, and two giggling high school girls — stared at her. And not in a good way. Not in that "Oh my God, she's gorgeous" way. Nope. Adelaide picked up a spoon to check her distorted reflection. She had bags under her eyes, straggly hair, and, as Étienne feared, a pimple smack dab in the center of her forehead.

She hadn't washed her hair and blow-dried it into perfect waves. She opted for extra sleep. When she set her eyeliner pencil against her face, she'd smudged more than she got into place. The lipstick only made it worse. Without her traditional cosmetic routine, the muted tones of Woodland Rose seemed garish. The pink clashed with her hair somehow. She had scrubbed the make-up off her face, but reapplied the lipstick since her lips felt exposed.

The waitress lowered her cigarette and grabbed a half-empty coffeepot. She filled a thirty-two-ounce Styrofoam cup. As the liquid poured from the carafe, it thickened like mud and landed in Adelaide's cup. She shuddered.

"How do you take it?" the waitress asked as she put the carafe on the burner and hit the orange switch to make a fresh pot.

Adelaide tasted it and grimaced. Certainly not black, she thought.

"Give me two creamers and dump sugar in."

She wouldn't make it to the city if she didn't drink this coffee. This coffee needed sugar. But, could she forego it? After all, Étienne had a bikini with her name on it. She grabbed the sugar shaker.

Her hand gripped the cup as she rose from the stool, her thighs tearing from the vinyl with a slurp. Why had she worn shorts? They were short shorts, too. The fitted white dress shirt and the narrow black sequined belt didn't dress them up the way she intended. She forced herself to stand straight and hold her head high and steady.

"Dollar fifty," said the tall man behind the glass case of candy bars and breath mints.

Adelaide passed him two singles. He gave her two quarters. She glanced out the window, double-checking for the dog. Returning to her car, she drank as much of the coffee as she could in one chug to fortify herself against the Monday morning traffic into Manhattan. She pawed for the compact discs on the passenger seat. She opened the case, flipped through the albums, and decided Cake might keep her alert.

She couldn't blame Galen for her stupor. He had left at ten, knowing she had to drive in this morning. She had given him the abridged version of her life story, as summarized by the charms on her bracelet. She prattled about dance lessons, tormenting her sister, and visits to Paris. She omitted the parts about bad dating choices, getting stoned in five-star hotel rooms with groupies, and using supermodel status to score favors from celebrities. Ah, to be eighteen again...

And her parents worried that she hadn't matured. Her last boyfriend had no connection to fashion, music, professional sports or Los Angeles. And she didn't subscribe to the 3C diet: cocaine, cigarettes, and champagne. In the back of the Benz, Zut scratched at her cat carrier reminding Adelaide to move her ass. Adelaide sighed and drank more coffee. She put the convertible's top down. No reason not to since she hadn't fixed her hair. She buckled her seatbelt and drove. She merged onto route 80 east on auto-pilot.

Last night, Galen kept putting his hand on her knee. She liked it, but at the same time it alerted her "spider sense," electrifying the hairs on her arms. She couldn't relax after he left, so she read a romance novel. The consummation of that relationship, as fake as it read, did not improve her mood. She worried about the strange visit from Galen's sister. Some of the comments made sense, but Adelaide couldn't believe them, could she? And if she did, what could she do about it?

She made a cup of Galen's tea. It smelled like catnip, which may have explained why the cat kept sticking her head in it. By the end of the cup, Adelaide's legs had liquefied and her arms hung heavily. Zut settled drowsily on the pillow beside her. Adelaide crawled into bed but her dreams didn't allow her any rest.

Adelaide dreamt that Galen came into her bedroom. Even now, the next morning, her hands trembled when she thought of it. His fingers ran along her neck. He rested his hand over her heart, her lace teddy the only barrier between them. His mouth latched onto hers. He slipped his tongue across her lips. His hand caressed her breast. Galen's spicy scent, like cigarettes and cinnamon, circled her. He removed her lingerie. His lips kissed her breast higher and higher until his mouth rested above her heart, pushing against her pulse.

Even now, in bright morning light, sunrise bursting from the horizon ahead of her, in the crisp breeze of the speeding convertible, reality did nothing to hide the blossoming passion as Adelaide remembered the dream. Driving her car, singing aout a "Long Line of Cars" without even realizing it, Adelaide shifted her weight to release the heat where her crotch seam amplified her pseudo-memory. She couldn't remember anything else. She had woken, naked, next to a sleeping cat. She had gotten out of bed to grab her teddy.

But now was not the time to think about it. She had to focus. In the orange glow of the emergency lights in the Lincoln Tunnel, she shook her head. Driving in Manhattan required concentration. Six months ago, the mere prospect of driving through lower midtown would have reduced her to nervous tears. And that's before she bought a brand new Benz convertible. Heck, a year ago, she didn't even know lower midtown from Gramercy. Now, she navigated the traffic while barely conscious. She wasn't sure this was a change for the better.

Adelaide dropped the cat at her apartment and rushed to work. She stopped at the corner bakery for another cup of coffee and a vibrant white donut overflowing with the reddest jelly she'd ever seen.

Her work colleagues gasped as she stumbled through the hall. Most of them gaped at the doughnut. The rest couldn't believe she hadn't "done" her face and her clothes. She went right into the miniscule room she called her office.

It didn't even have space for a desk, only a small drawing table. Adelaide put on her glasses and read her messages. So tired... She couldn't even open the envelope from the music label. Why would a music label send her a letter? She folded one arm and leaned her head on it.

« *Mon petit chou*, » a sing-song voice said as silky digits stroked her hand. "Wake up."

"Galen?" she said.

A snicker.

"Et?" she said, half-asleep.

He sucked breath through his teeth.

« *Le bouton!* » he exclaimed. "It is as I said!"

She blinked. In her hands, she clutched an envelope and a cup of coffee. Adelaide saw a door and... Seema's desk? She turned to the window and the gloomy skyline. She focused on the pink memos.

"I'm at work," she said.

Étienne loomed over her.

"Your body is," Étienne replied. "Maybe not in the spirit. Go home?"

"No, I'm fine," she said.

Étienne tugged the napkin with her doughnut.

"What has passed?" Étienne asked.

"I didn't sleep well."

"And the doughnut?"

She slid the doughnut farther away.

"Forty-five minutes, *chef*. I'll have everything together, I promise."

"*Nom de Dieu!* I did not see..."

Étienne seized her hand on the napkin and pulled her upright by the arm. His hands gestured toward her body.

"What do you wear? Le *mini-short*? For the office? Where is the hair and the face?"

"Et, *chef*. Don't start. I almost called out ugly today."

"You should have," he responded.

Étienne headed toward the door. Adelaide gulped the final icy dregs of coffee. She gobbled half her doughnut. Étienne ducked into her office and snatched the rest. He smashed it, tossing it into her garbage can. She sunk toward her drawing table.

"Et *mon chou*... Put on the make-up and find the clothes, *s'il te plaît*."

He disappeared. She picked up the telephone and dialed the first number on her messages.

"Is Mr. Gerard available?" Adelaide said. "This is Adelaide Pitney from Chez d'Amille."

The other person on the phone said the expected "Hold, please. I'll see if he's in."

"Thank you," Adelaide replied.

Philip Gerard served as principal buyer for Marshall Fields, a family-owned department store chain in the Midwest. Gerard's message that he wanted ready-to-wear in the store had reached her via the American client relations department (consisting of Heather and Monica). Étienne reserved final approval on new venues, but first, they had to meet Adelaide's standards. The American buyers had ended up in her jurisdiction, with American manufacturers, event planning, *haute couture* scheduling, brainstorming ideas for the d'Amille web presence, and even designing. Impressive for someone with "no real job."

"This is Philip Gerard," a voice said.

"Mr. Gerard, this is Adelaide Pitney from Chez d'Amille. We met in March at the collections."

Within minutes, Adelaide agreed to fly him to Paris for the upcoming show, and in return he would host a trunk show in Chicago, if she would attend, probably in mid-September. That gave John time for publicity. She returned several other calls. Seema tiptoed in and hung a suit on the hook inside her door. A not so subtle hint from her boss. The other staff members shuffled toward the conference room. She closed the door and changed clothes. She checked the jacket pocket and sure enough, Étienne had included earrings, tasteful gold hoops. She put them in.

Adelaide checked the clock on her cell phone. Just enough time, she decided. She reached into her top desk drawer and pulled out her spare cosmetics bag. Once she masked the zit and got the rest of her face together, Adelaide grabbed a legal pad, pen, and the manila folder labeled Spring 2003 RTW. A month until the show. She also seized the letter from the record execs, knowing this could be very cool. She dashed into the conference room, a mere five minutes late, which was at least five minutes early on French time.

The conference room separated Adelaide's office from Étienne's. And Étienne was already there. Shit. Étienne sat with John Clowes, the North American marketing director; Heather Smith and Monica Perry; Becky Isaaks, the fabric buyer; Joey Schaffer, the event coordinator; and Seema Gupta who would scribble the conversation into shorthand. A shoebox rested on the table the vacant chair adjacent to Étienne. Adelaide peeled up the lid, dumping onto the table 'the' espadrilles from her runway accident.

A chuckle came from the phone. If laughs could have a French accent, this one did. So the bastard had conference-called into the meeting... He barely spoke English, why would he call into a New York staff meeting? It was five p.m. in Paris, you think the man would go home. It was the middle of August. Shouldn't he run to the south of France like everyone else?

« *Très drôle, Didier,* » Adelaide said.

Étienne adjusted his tie and shot off questions. Well, maybe not questions. He yelled out fragments and expected answers. With the first word, 'production,' he looked at Adelaide. The Pennsylvania mills had completed half the redo orders for Holiday, and the recall on the defectives had reached the appropriate retailers. Plus, Paris had at least a third of the samples for the show ready. Didier cut in (in French) to say that he had shipped dresses to New York, because, he explained, Adelaide had 'thickened.'

"I'm not a soup," Adelaide replied. "I did Milan last season. No one complained."

"Not to you," Didier rebutted.

"You make the clothes. I'll fit into them. I've got weeks — »

"You have not lost some weight in years," Didier said in uncharacteristically clear English. He must have been practicing that line.

"Ladies, please," Étienne commanded.

Adelaide bristled. Didier didn't even protest. Étienne blurted 'guest list.' Joey offered a sweet smile, never a good sign. Étienne ran his fingers through his hair and tossed his head.

"Nicole Kidman is a maybe, rumors of Liv Tyler, Ben Affleck might stop by if J.-Lo is interested, and that old chick from Murphy Brown... Candace Bergen. That's all I got."

"I invited Candace Bergen," Adelaide said. "She's elegant."

Étienne sighed. "Can't we ever get anyone I know?"

"Is Sophia Loren still alive?" Joey asked.

Adelaide pinched the bridge of her nose.

"*Ouias, ça c'est une femme.* And Catherine Deneuve. Who is Jay Low?" Étienne shrugged. "And the editors?"

"Paris has the list," John said. "Meanwhile, I've confirmed a shoot for January's *Elle*."

"*Janvier?*" Étienne replied. "So slow a month."

"*Harper's Bazaar* is considering a shoot for March with Adelaide," John said.

« *Très bien. Satisfaisant,* » Étienne said.

"They want to interview her. I'm working on the clothes," John continued.

"No clothes?" Étienne asked. "They want talking? *Mon petit chou?*"

Adelaide leaned her elbows on the table. Her lips pressed against her thumbs as her eyes pierced the shoebox on the table. How dare John mention this in a strategy meeting without consulting her! She had never done an interview. Étienne would never allow it.

« *Très bien,* » Étienne responded. "I like. We do."

Her hands fell to the table.

"But I don't talk to the media," Adelaide whined.

Étienne always had shielded her from the "fashion journalists." What an oxymoron. Now Étienne planned to deliver her to the horde? No matter, she thought. She had a counter-attack, thanks to that letter from the rock publicist.

"I have an opportunity, too, a better one," Adelaide said. "They want me in a music video."

« *Le vidéo-clip?* » Étienne said. « *Certainement pas. Non.* »

"It's my favorite group. And my favorite song," she pleaded. "You can dress me."

« *Non.* »

"You don't own me," she remarked.

« If you check your contract, » he returned in French. Étienne always switched to French if he needed to act like an authoritarian prick. « I have the right to govern your public appearances. No one takes your photograph without my permission. Except your mother. Maybe. »

Everyone around the table froze. They didn't speak French. They didn't have too. They understood that Étienne completely took her down a peg. He exhaled and turned to Becky.

"*Maintenant, on continue.* Fabric.

Becky clutched a single sheet of paper. She cleared her throat.

"We're in good shape," Becky said.

The bantering lasted about an hour, as Étienne assessed their readiness for the fall show. When Étienne dismissed them, Adelaide lunged to intercept John, but Étienne grabbed her.

« *Attends,* » Étienne said. "I need you."

"Can't it wait?" she asked testily.

Étienne shook his head.

"Sit," Étienne commanded.

He busied himself stacking the reports from the others. Adelaide shot John a cold, penetrating stare.

"Sorry," John muttered as he scooted past her.

Adelaide slouched into her high-backed chair. She rocked side-to-side, while tapping her gel pen against her tablet.

« Don't be impatient, » Étienne said in French. « You know my expectations for this office while I am in Paris? »

« No wild parties. No boys spending the night. No champagne on my expense account. »

« I am serious, » he said.

« You heard them, » she said. « Everything is under control. And I'm fat. »

Adelaide rested her head against the chair.

« The interview? » Étienne asked.

« You want me to do it? I mean, *Harper's Bazaar*? At least it's not *Cosmo*. » She rolled her eyes.

« I want the world to my see my beautiful girl as the talented business woman she is, » Étienne said. « Sell us to young executives. Too many people of your generation see us as outdated, a label their mothers would wear. »

« I'm too old, » she replied.

« That's absurd. Old and fat, » Étienne scoffed. "You're twenty-four. Didier? Jealous. He cannot appreciate a beautiful woman. That's too bad. You will always be beautiful. You're one of those women who has a gift. »

Her lips slipped into a hint smile. He usually had that effect on her.

« Without you, I never would have left Paris, » Étienne said. « Zélie started it, but your face, that special something you bring to your pictures, that's what made my clothes sing »

« I bet the folks at *Harper's Bazaar* speak French. You give the interview. »

Adelaide pulled her legs into her lap, quasi-lotus position. She closed her eyes.

« I need you to do this, » he said.

He ran his hand along her calf.

« I'm not special, » she said.

« I think you are, absolutely, » Étienne said.

Even though she hadn't smoked in seven years, Adelaide longed for a cigarette.

« Promise me you'll do it, » he said.

« I guess, » Adelaide answered. « Because you asked me to. Don't expect wit and charm. I'm a pretty face not an eloquent speaker. »

« It's a change, » Étienne said. « I understand this. There are many changes underway now. We're all facing challenges. »

Adelaide opened her eyes. Was something seriously wrong with the business?

« I want to tell them, » Étienne said.

« Tell who? What? » she asked.

He would call *Harper's Bazaar*?

« My family. About the baby, » he answered.

« So tell them »

« We never have before, » Étienne said. « They never knew how badly we suffered — »

« Et, I wouldn't worry, » Adelaide interrupted.

Her eyes fell closed again. Talking about something so personal made anxiousness build in her stomach as if she expected Bas to be sitting outside the door eavesdropping.

« I hear the rumors. Everyone, especially Zélie's father, has suggested that I was impotent, » Étienne paused. « Nobody knows about her miscarriages. I've told my grandmother the slightest pieces because I couldn't face it alone, and Zélie wouldn't... »

Étienne paced the room. His footsteps stopped, so Adelaide opened her eyes as he gazed into the street below.

« I hesitate because people will think we had some sort of treatments. It's the fashion, but we didn't. I am here in New York because my wife could not produce a child. She won't admit it, but she gave me a business instead. »

Adelaide closed her eyes.

« And now, » Étienne prattled, « after the doctors have said it would never happen... »

Adelaide jerked open her eyes. She didn't remember when or how Étienne ended the conversation. The nib of his pen scratched paper as she regained focus on him in the chair across from her. Oh, man, how much did she miss? Did he notice? She swallowed a yawn.

« *Va mieux?* » he whispered. "You fell asleep."

He noticed.

"Did I? Oh, Étienne, I'm sorry," Adelaide said.

Étienne shrugged. He kept sketching. She allowed herself to yawn.

"What time is it?" she asked.

"Almost four."

"I slept all afternoon!"

Adelaide stretched her legs to the floor.

"*Et tu as marmonnée...* You said things, like my name."

He signed whatever he was sketching, folded it, and handed it to her.

"Go home," he said. "I do not pay six-figure salary for sleeping."

"No," she replied. "I get that for being pretty."

"And I have not wasted a single franc," he said.

With that, Étienne left. Adelaide turned the white paper in her hands, revealing her portrait. She stared at it, admiring the softness of her face. She left the conference room. In her office, she carefully placed the drawing in her bag, with her laptop and the hidden package from the perfume house.

Once she reached her apartment, Adelaide dropped her purse on the hall table. First she opened the box from the perfume house and held the sample to her nose. The grassy, floral notes blended well with the lemony tones but the spiciness came on a tad too strong. She placed it in the pouch with her lipstick. She'd have to ask Bas.

Adelaide retrieved the portrait and traversed her living room. Zut greeted her with a routine of figure-eights. Adelaide selected a photo album nestled on the bookshelf and from the rear of it, she withdrew Étienne's previous works. The new one laid on top of one of her and Bas in Central Park. Adelaide traced the pen lines with her finger. She lifted the album to the shelf. Then, she abruptly clutched it to her chest instead.

CHAPTER ELEVEN

A few days went by without incident. No calls from Galen. No further harassment from Étienne. And she couldn't find anything she had fucked up. Until today. She tried on her clothes. It wasn't time for her fitting but she had to know if Didier was right. So she did it. The answer made her turn to alcohol for comfort, not that alcohol would help her weight.

The chemical smell of the public restroom's azure toilet water twisted Adelaide's stomach. Maybe that last bean burrito swimming in hot sauce and those extra margaritas weren't a good idea for several reasons. She tripped as she walked toward the metal stall. Luckily, Liz caught her elbow. Steady, old Liz in her black Armani suit. She patted Liz on the back. My girlfriend wears Armani instead of d'Amille, Adelaide thought.

In celebration of Liz's recent promotion at Lancôme, they met after work for a movie (Hugh Grant!). The girls had convinced Adelaide to invite Galen to *El Sombrero de José*, or whatever they called this place. As Adelaide finished her business on the toilet, the red stains on the toilet paper explained why her guts hurt and why everything pissed her off. And it even explained why she was so fucking fat.

"Liz," Adelaide called. "Do you have a tampon?"

The magnetic closures on Liz's purse opened and snapped. A hand passed a cardboard cylinder under the partition.

"Thanks," Adelaide said.

When Adelaide emerged, Liz had set her purse in the last dry area by the sink. Adelaide wiped the excess water and soap with unbleached paper towels.

"You would love this," Liz said, throwing her long brown hair over her shoulder as she gave Adelaide a tube of coral pink lip color.

Adelaide looked at the hue and returned it. She applied a fresh coat of her matte-finish ruddy pastel. Liz hefted a sigh.

"Woodland Rose, again," Liz said.

"I like Woodland Rose," Adelaide replied.

"There should be a statute of limitations on cosmetics," Liz said as she unhinged her compact. "Change your colors every two years or face a serious make-over."

Adelaide rubbed her lips together.

« Étienne picked this in... I think Fall '94, » she said.

"Eight years?" Liz said. "Will he fire you for changing your lipstick?"

Adelaide dropped the tube into her purse.

"He doesn't own your face," Liz said, closing her bag.

"He thinks he does," Adelaide said. "He recently told me I need his permission if my mother wants to take a picture of me."

"I hate the way he controls you. I don't understand why people go crazy over that man."

"That sounds sleazy," Adelaide replied.

"Isn't he?"

"No," Adelaide answered. "Which you'd know if you'd come for a suit."

Adelaide pushed her purse strap onto her shoulder.

"So Étienne can feel me up?" Liz remarked. "I don't think so."

"Et isn't like that."

"Addy, he's touched your tits more than any boyfriend you've ever had."

"That's totally inappropriate, Liz."

"Don't play cool and aloof. It's disgusting the way you live for that man. You said you were going to quit."

"I said I wanted to quit," Adelaide said.

"Jump his bones and get it over with, that might fix all this weird office tension."

"That would never happen."

"Interesting choice of words," Liz retorted.

Liz led them into the dim dining room. Someone new had joined their table. A dark head of hair bobbed between Marcy and their other friends. There was also a fresh pitcher of margaritas. Adelaide ruled out more. She couldn't handle the calories. The newcomer was Galen. A thrill passed through her when she confirmed it, but at the same time, she grew paranoid. He turned his head and smiled at her, but the gesture seemed frigid and forced.

Marcy smiled, sipping her drink, while Liz slipped into the booth next to Sara, who was nibbling *fluantes*. Galen embraced Adelaide, and she stuck her fingers in his belt loops. Their lips met in an innocent kiss. She pushed her hair behind her ears. Her stomach fluttered, and she couldn't blame the cramps. They sat, with Galen on the inside. Adelaide poured herself another margarita. Casey, previously the token male in the group, took the pitcher from her, offered her chips and salsa, and 'accidentally' touched her breast while placing the bowl in front of her. Galen maintained a disconnected stare.

Liz immediately launched the potential boyfriend inquisition. Galen accepted the questions without fanfare. What do you do? Where are you from? Who's your favorite NFL team? (Just as rapidly Galen answered, "photographer," "I have a place in Pennsylvania," and "That's professional football, right?") Giggling ensued, but Adelaide didn't care. Galen had gathered her fingers into his palm. She stopped listening. She fixated on their hands, his flesh against hers. She heard a whisper. She heard it again, not quite audible. She heard it a third time and this time deciphered it.

"Danger."

Adelaide glanced over her shoulder. The couple behind them shoveled food into their mouths. No one sat beside them. They had smothered the table with their bags (several d'Amilles and Liz's Louis Vuitton — what a label whore, Adelaide thought) and Casey's guitar.

"Danger."

It grew louder. She looked around again.

"Did you hear that?" she asked, interrupting Liz.

No one reacted at first.

"Hear what?" Galen said.

"I heard whispering," she said.

Galen shook his head. Everyone else shrugged. Conversation resumed. Galen's fingers seared hers, heat soaking through her skin and burning the tissue underneath. She heard the danger warning again, extremely piercing, as pain stabbed every bone in her hand. Slowly, the pressure released as his fingers slid away. The pain settled into a consistent ache. Adelaide grabbed a fork. The room went absolutely silent, no longer full of Latin music from the stereo, nor voices from other diners, nor the rhythmic clang of silverware against plates. She couldn't move the hand Galen had pinned to the table.

His hand, near hers, shriveled. The bronze skin flaked, white scales blowing into the air. Muscle dried and peeled away from the bones. Finally, the bones crumbled into dust, a bit at a time, fingers first, then knuckles. She blinked, hard, and the hand appeared normal. The heat sinking into her hand increased and shot into her wrist and arm.

Clutching the fork, Adelaide raised her elbow, stealthily, as she turned the utensil toward Galen's hand. She slammed the fork toward him, but his fingers detained her. The fork crashed to the table. Adelaide shrieked. The restaurant went still. Even the wait staff paused with plates half way between their trays and patrons.

"Addy, your hand is blue."

"Did you just try to stab him?"

She couldn't sort the voices.

"You burned me," she shouted.

Galen released her hand.

"Your hand is blue," Liz repeated.

Marcy nodded. Sure enough, Adelaide's hand had turned purple-blue. Adelaide poked the bruised-looking flesh.

"What happened?" Adelaide asked. "Why did I..."

"Maybe I should take you home," Galen said.

Adelaide remembered Kait's warning and the whisper of "danger."

"Addy, you need looking after," Casey said.

"Just like a man," Adelaide quipped. "I can take care of myself."

"Armed solely with a fork, apparently," Sara added.

Galen grabbed Adelaide roughly by the arms. Adelaide massaged her hand, but it didn't get warmer.

"Addy, we should go," Galen said.

Why was her hand so freaking cold?

"Unnatural to be alive," the whispering voice spoke again.

She didn't even ask anyone if they heard it, because they didn't. Adelaide prodded her hand but she couldn't get the blue to fade. She couldn't make it turn white or pink or red. She pinched the skin and sighed. Galen touched her arm again.

"Stay away."

It echoed through her head in a whisper. She hadn't opened her mouth but she recognized her voice. Her friends gaped with wide eyes. She had said it. Why can't I be normal? Adelaide fought tears. It had started again.

"Tell him you saw the tower in his eyes," the voice prompted.

Galen retrieved his wallet. Adelaide placed her hands on her face, her frigid hand against a reddened cheek. Her cheek absorbed her fingers' coldness, but her fingers didn't accept heat.

"Tell him," the whisper commanded.

Go away, Adelaide thought. He's not dead. He's sitting right here. How can Louey, no, Galen, be dead? Louey? Dear God! Where did that voice come from? Was it the gargoyle-looking fairy thing? Did Kait tell the truth? Did Galen want her magic? Did she have magic?

"Tell him," the whisper insisted.

It sounded small, a childish voice speaking through tin cans.

"Tell him you saw the tower in his eyes."

She swallowed. A lump caught in her throat so she reached for her margarita.

"Louey..."

He turned, wide-eyed. Why did she call him 'Louey?' That's what Kait had called him. She gulped the cocktail.

"I..."

It didn't even make sense. How could she tell him? Something goaded her.

"I... see the tower... in your eyes," Adelaide said.

His normally serene hazel eyes filled with red burning with fire like the inside of an opal.

"What did you say?" Galen said.

Galen shackled his fingers around her wrist, twisting, putting tension on her elbow. The joint nearly popped.

"Ow," she exclaimed.

He released her. Liz and Marcy hadn't seen it. Sara ignored it and played in her purse. Casey flashed the only look of concern.

"I see the tower in your eyes," she repeated.

"You don't know what you're saying."

Galen smiled and his posture dominated the table, like the moon blocking the sun in an eclipse. We had too many margaritas, Adelaide decided. Except, she didn't feel like she had thought it. She felt like someone told her to think it. Galen wanted them to forget. She stood. Run, her 'spider sense' said. Hide.

"I better go. I'm sorry," Adelaide said.

"Let me walk with you or at least get you a cab," Galen said. "Something's bothering you."

His nails on her shoulder dug through her shirt and into her flesh.

"It's nothing," she insisted.

He probably thought she was crazy. She did. His grasp tightened. She winced.

"Weird things just happen to me," Adelaide said. "It's not you. I'm okay."

She lied. She wasn't okay. And it was him.

"Do you know what the tower is?" he asked.

She shook her head in exaggerated motions while she clung to her purse.

"Were you in the city September 11?" Galen continued.

Adelaide nodded. This display between them mesmerized her friends.

"The tower is a tarot card," Galen said.

He took her hand and squeezed it, hard, too hard.

"Think of September 11th. The tower means catastrophe, a large burning building with people falling out."

She nodded. The Twin Towers. She'd never forget. Even now, a year lapsed, the hole in the skyline opened fear inside her. She couldn't understand how Basilie could work on Wall Street when she'd been so close to what happened that day.

"It's the strongest card in the tarot," Galen said. "You didn't know that, did you?"

Adelaide wanted to take her shoes off. She wanted a cigarette. Why had she said that to Galen? Why didn't she keep quiet?

"Let me walk you home," Galen said. "Maybe you can tell me what's happening."

Galen circled his arm around her waist. It stung. He walked with her, his hand resting on the top of her hip and his body close, his other arm on her shoulder as if she were a marionette. Galen didn't want to comfort her. He wanted to keep her in line. She knew this, but she didn't have the strength to protest. They left the restaurant and he kissed her on the sidewalk. His kiss compelled her toward him. She couldn't stop herself. It unnerved her, made her raw. It wasn't a nice kiss, his lips against hers tightly, his teeth knocking hers. It was a threatening kiss.

A man with a stocky Rottweiler drew close. The dog tugged at the leash, his tongue dangling from a mouth framed with pointy white teeth. Adelaide leapt closer to Galen's side. The dog rubbed her leg and her body tensed. Galen stepped to the curb and flagged a cab, or he appeared to. A taxi zipped to the sidewalk before his hand rose. The dog and owner had reached the corner, but Adelaide stared. Galen addressed the cab driver, announcing "thirty" before he stopped. She hadn't told him where she lived, or had she? Had he almost given her address?

"32nd and Third," Adelaide said.

This man had evil in him, she said to herself, or maybe the voice told her. When she looked at him, she saw only veins of black shadow. He pushed her into the taxi. When they arrived, Galen paid the driver. She reached for her door, but Galen stopped her. He dragged her from the car via his side. He pushed a hand in the pocket of his not-quite flannel shirt. The texture resembled suede, but the weight resembled cotton or linen, probably a micro-fiber. Adelaide tittered. He could kill me, and I'm analyzing his wardrobe, she thought.

Galen lit a cigarette. Adelaide entered the lobby hoping Galen would stay outside smoking. She gathered her bills and catalogs from the mailbox. Galen followed, nonchalantly smoking his cigarette as he hovered, the aroma of cloves and tobacco the only signal to his presence. At her door, Adelaide put her key in the first lock. She stopped, left the key dangling, and turned. Galen glared. She could taste that cigarette.

"Can I have a drag?" she asked.

Galen shrugged. He handed it to her.

"I didn't know you smoked."

Adelaide set the cigarette to her lips and inhaled deeply.

"Any model who says she doesn't smoke is lying," Adelaide said.

She felt the faint, familiar pinch in her nerves. God, nothing could compare.

"I quit," she added as she inhaled again. "Et didn't like it."

"Keep it," Galen said. "You need it more than I do."

She unlocked the second and third locks.

"I haven't had a clove cigarette in ten years," Adelaide said.

She glanced for somewhere to put the butt. Galen remained on the threshold.

"Can I come in?" he replied.

"I guess," she said. "Is something stopping you?"

Galen tentatively moved forward. He closed the door.

"Only your desires," he answered. "Desires are powerful."

Zut dashed into the hall and stopped at Adelaide's feet. The cat hissed, arching her back with hairs upright and tail doubled in size. Adelaide grabbed the cat by her belly. Zut kicked, screeching. Adelaide tossed Zut into the bedroom, slamming the door. The cat clawed desperately. Adelaide walked away, wishing she had another cigarette. She pivoted. Alone in the hall, Adelaide stared at her closed bedroom door. She shivered and wondered if the cat knew something. Zut yowled so loudly the neighbors might call the super or the cops.

In the living room, Galen sat on her couch. Adelaide turned on National Public Radio to drown out the cat. She went into the kitchen and grabbed a coffee-stained mug. She joined Galen in the living room. The mug became a makeshift ashtray on the cross-stitch runner decorating her coffee table. Adelaide stayed on the edge of the couch, her elbows on her knees and her hands folded.

"You seem jumpy," Galen said, flicking his ashes into the mug. "Can I make you tea?"

"No, thanks," she answered. "I'm home. You can go."

"Your attitude, I don't understand. A week ago you liked me. Now — "

"Galen, please. It was the dog. I don't like dogs."

"You tried to stab me before the dog."

NPR droned about politics.

"I do crazy shit sometimes," she said.

"Do you want me to go?" he asked.

She couldn't shake her uneasiness. But, honestly, the man had done nothing.

"Tonight has you disturbed," Galen said. "Do you want to talk about it?"

"No," she answered, wringing her hands. "I could put a CD on."

"Kait said something."

Adelaide didn't know if she should answer him.

"She said you want my magic, because she won't take it," Adelaide blurted out. "That Nefa-someone thinks I can't keep my healing powers."

"You believe her?"

Adelaide shrugged. "I don't know. Do you believe in magic?"

Galen reached for her hand. "I do. I can help you understand. Tell me everything."

He doesn't really care, the tiny voice warned.

Adelaide didn't listen. She told Galen about the whispers she had heard recently and when he didn't say anything she continued. Kait said she had healing powers, but she'd never healed anyone. Broken electronics, sure, but not healing. She told him about the weird visions. She had never told anyone about them.

"Sometimes, I think something has happened, like a premonition, but after the fact. Like I'll sit down and know that an old woman sat in the chair before me," she said. "Crazy, huh?"

"No," he answered. "It's called psychometry."

"Psycho-what? It means I'm crazy, doesn't it?"

Galen smiled, in a twisted way her feel stupid, like she should know something she didn't.

"Psychometry," he repeated. "You read the psychic vibrations people leave on objects."

"I do?"

He passed her a pocket watch.

"Take it," Galen instructed her. "Listen to it."

The gold watch had ornate engraving. The face displayed Roman numerals. She closed her fingers around it.

"It's a watch," she said. "It can't talk."

Cold, grooved metal, nothing more.

"You're not trying," Galen said gruffly.

Galen transferred the watch from her left hand to her right. Instantaneously, hands wrapped around her throat, choking her. An old man's eyes haunted her. Pained, faded eyes and a white beard... She couldn't breathe. No, he couldn't breathe. He wouldn't let go of the watch. He clutched it, fingers tight on its eighteen karat gold surface. She hurled the watch across the room.

"Someone choked him, for that watch. They killed him over a watch, Galen," Adelaide screamed. "Why do you have it? Throw it away! Oh, God. That old man loved that watch."

Though she had dropped the timepiece, the details haunted her.

"His wife gave it to him. They were married for fifty years. To buy it, she scrimped on the grocery budget, gave up haircuts, darned socks," Adelaide said.

She dropped to her knees, slammed her head against the coffee table, and wept.

"It was a watch," she whispered. "She died of cancer. He couldn't afford the medical bills. The bank foreclosed on the house. He moved into a dumpy apartment by the el train. The watch, it was all he had."

She wept more. Galen touched her back.

"She had Lou Gehrig's disease," Galen corrected her. "Other than that, you're right."

His other hand rubbed her shoulder.

"Sorry," he said. "I didn't think you could really do it."

"Those things really happened?" she asked.

Galen nodded. Zut scratched at the bedroom door. Adelaide crawled to Galen's side. She laid her head against his shoulder as she curled against him. Psychometry. She had waited her entire life for an explanation.

"Give yourself to me," Galen whispered.

You're a man, she thought. I always do.

He kissed her hungrily, and she responded reflexively. She kissed him, desperate to maintain his interest since he had given her answers. But the kiss didn't affect her. It left her nervous and empty.

"Playing with fire," the voice whispered.

She pulled back.

"'With great power comes great responsibility,'" Adelaide said, quoting the famous Spiderman line.

Galen placed his hand softly against her forehead.

"It's your time of the moon. That's why your powers have heightened," he said.

"My what?" she replied.

Heat poured across her temple. Her eyes fluttered closed.

"Adelaide," he said. "You have to give me something."

Tension melted from her face.

"I'm going to make love to you," he said.

Something sharp struck her ear. Adelaide flung open her eyes. Galen's fingertips massaged her forehead. His face registered disappointment.

"You didn't touch..." she said as she pointed to her ear.

He snarled and lowered his hand.

"You said something about making love to me," she said.

"No, I didn't."

"Yes, you did."

Galen approached her again. His hand touched her forehead. Her eyes closed.

"Would you give yourself to me?" he asked.

The voice in her head screamed no. She had just gotten her period, and Kait had warned her: no sex.

"Kiss me, Addy."

She did. The cat threw herself against the bedroom door. Galen pulled her closer. Her muscles relaxed. She almost toppled, but Galen caught her. A strange buzz reverberated through Adelaide's head. Something tapped the back of her skull. Adelaide opened her eyes. Galen struggled with her buttons.

He removed her blouse and her bra. His hand unfastened the side zipper of her pants. She didn't help. Nor did she resist. She felt no need to do either. He lifted her and spread her on her back across the sofa. He pushed off her slacks, his hands under her, as he kissed her navel. The slight touch of his lips streamed into her body, swirling her chest and groin in fire. Before she could react, he brought their mouths together as bodies met, her bare bosom against the smooth flesh of his chest. She didn't remember anyone taking off her panties, or his shirt, or his pants, but apparently, someone had. She was naked.

His lips broke from her, as his hands and mouth danced along, pulling heat across her abdomen. His mouth rested on her thighs. She stretched her hands over her head as his fingers stroked her legs. She thanked Mother Nature for not thwarting this with her period. His fingers split the inner lips of her body.

She swayed with his current, buoyed by his sensations rippling throughout her. Their bodies twisted on the couch, a shallow thrust stoking her. His gentle, flickering rhythm washed across her, pooling its intensity, until he extinguished it. Just gone. The air around her suddenly grew cold and dry.

"I need a cigarette," Adelaide said.

They shared one. She wrapped herself in a hand-knit blanket that had fallen to the floor. Galen already had his clothes. She hadn't seen him dress. Zut barreled into the living room. Adelaide gazed into the hall. Her bedroom door remained shut.

Galen approached the door. Zut followed him, growling. Adelaide got up, her legs shaky. Her body recoiled from each step sending miniature waves of arousal through her. Galen kissed her. Everything overwhelmed her again. Her heart skipped, her belly ached, and she was wet with desire. The cat screeched.

"I better go," Galen said.

He left and she locked the door behind him. She stood there wrapped in an afghan. As she stood there, her mind clouded. He had made love to her, right? She didn't remember him removing or replacing his clothes. Galen looked as fresh and perfect as he had earlier. How could that be? But, she couldn't ignore the sensations racking her body. Just standing here brought her body to the verge of orgasm.

Adelaide headed for the bathroom and a shower, a cold one. Blood lined her thighs, an unexpectedly heavy amount of it for having gotten her period in the last few minutes. While going about the ordinary motions of bathing — adjust the water temperature, lather the hair, put soap on the washcloth — Adelaide reflected on the sex.

Even in the midst of their coupling, they hadn't experienced any of the awkwardness that comes with a new partner. Something always happened. He moves in too soon, he gets up too late. You lose interest or he loses interest. His body pushes too hard against you. His size is too big or too small. You can't stop thinking about the dishes you left in the sink or the hole in your underwear.

"Now you've done it," an unfamiliar voice said.

Adelaide peered from behind the shower curtain. Zut watched her. Adelaide placed her head under the full stream of the shower. That romp was just what she had needed to relieve her stress from work. It was stress, right? Because the cat didn't talk to her. Couldn't be.

CHAPTER TWELVE

The wind whipped through the oak trees. Despite their steady green, Galen heard dryness in their crinkle, one sign of the approaching equinox. The last hints of lemon thyme hit his nostrils. The trees, creek, bullfrogs, and even the petals of the impatiens, every sliver of breathing, organic material, pulsed for acres. The energy sent sparks across the darkness, igniting embers within him. Each blade of grass held a stitch of the universe together.

Galen spun toward the church, aware of the slow and calculating presence of Kait. He ignored it, tracing the richness of the night into the woods where he climbed the highest boulder. Ironically, the locals called it witch's rock. Galen extended his arms in a Y. He stared at the sky, thanking Sheila-na-gig, goddess of birth and death, for leading him into Adelaide's vulva. He chanted to the absent moon.

From his pocket, Galen retrieved Adelaide's crudely embroidered table-cloth. He gently peeled the layers, sharing her scent with the woods. He arranged her saturated tampon on the rock and kept the stained doily.

The new moon provided a clean slate. The new moon stripped away inhibitions leaving pure emotions. Whereas creatures tended to act crazy on the full moon, the new moon inspired simplicity. The new moon made it easy to fool Adelaide.

Galen scurried from the rock. When he reached the church, he found Kait in the kitchen on a long-legged stool, her ankles and feet twisted around the legs. Hunched over the island, she laid tarot cards on black silk. She collected them into a pile.

"You took something from her," Kait said.

She shuffled the oversized cards, her small fingers more miniature against the deck. She drummed her fingers on the pile before each round. Galen didn't answer.

"Blood," Kait said.

The strap of Kait's black tank top tumbled down her arm. She suddenly stopped shuffling and placed the deck on her open palm. The cards levitated.

"Touch," she directed him.

Galen tapped the stack. Kait closed her eyes and leaned back.

"You are strong. You subdued her," Kait said.

"The moon had weakened her," Galen said.

The cards fell against Kait's palm. She shuffled them again.

"What did you do?" Kait said.

She cut the deck into three sections and reordered it. Kait placed the first card. Her hand blocked his view of it. She moved her hand. The Devil and his slaves, how apropos. Kait lifted the corner of the next card but didn't display it. She left it on the deck.

"You fucked her," she said.

"Certainly not," he said.

When male and female come together in the Great Rite, the joining yields new magick and there was nothing he wanted to create with her. He didn't plan to cooperate with her. He planned to consume her in the name of Neferkaba.

"She thinks you fucked her," Kait said.

She set the deck on the table, beside the upturned card. Her bare knees mounted the island, sliding toward him. She wrapped her legs around his waist and roped her arms around his neck. She wore the plaid miniskirt.

"Lughaidh," she said. "Be done with this game. You have made no real progress. Give it up. Neferkaba has no interest in you. You could not over-power her in her sleep. She resists you when she's awake. Her blood won't help you. That's powerful magick."

"You'll see," Galen said.

He patted his pocket. Kait planted her hands on her thighs.

"What if you had slept with her?" Kait asked. "What if you had climbed on top of her and gave it to her?"

Kait offered Galen a deep moan followed by rapid panting. Then, she screamed a series of "ohs." She hopped off the island, undid his fly, and dropped to her knees. The pleasurable part happened quickly: Kait's mouth around the rim of his penis, her movements transporting him where tension and bliss blurred. Her head moved to his thigh, her lips warm against his flesh. He tangled his fingers playfully into her hair, and she bit him fero-ciously on the leg. Using her curls as a grip, Galen pried her head from his body and struck her cheek repeatedly with his knee. Blood ran down his leg.

Kait grabbed his waistband, now hanging on his calves, and snapped it to the floor. Galen's ankles twisted and he tumbled, knocking into her. Kait fell and her head bounced on the industrial white linoleum. Galen somersaulted over her, hitting his left shoulder on the cabinets. Kait, laughing heartily, braced her hands against her belly. She laughed so hard that she stopped making noise.

"What's so funny?" Galen asked.

"You," she replied. "Look at you with your goodies exposed and your pants falling off."

He stood and covered himself. Galen offered Kait a hand. She took it. She placed her other hand on his elbow and pulled herself up. Kait snickered and dissipated.

Galen wandered to the tarot cards where he studied the image of The Devil, chains shackled to a naked woman and man. The position of the card, as first and central in the layout, represented him. The card had two meanings, and both fit, sexual misconduct or bondage to bad habits. Galen lit a cigarette.

He turned the next card, The Lovers, and placed it in the air position at the top of his star. The lower right point, corresponding with fire, received The High Priestess. He laid the left point, for water, in his case The Fool; the right point, earth, The Magician; and finally, the lower left, spirit, The Tower.

Romance ruled his intellect but not his emotions. He didn't give regard to emotions. He measured his passions and acted as if participating in ritual, never feeling. He bent the rules of the universe to suit his needs. The Tower represented his corrupted soul or perhaps impending doom, odd card considering Adelaide's proclamation: "I see The Tower in your eyes."

Galen collected the cards, their large size comfortable in his palm. He put his cigarette on the counter beside him, ashes falling on the smooth wooden surface. Galen shuffled. The act of holding the tarot, absorbing its energy and redirecting it, shuffling and cutting the deck quieted him. Galen thought of Adelaide.

The cards grew heavy, one end of the deck pressed into his flesh. He cut the deck, at first only once, but then again. He reordered the deck in his right hand. Electricity surrounded the cards as Galen arranged them in four neat horizontal rows of four cards.

One by one, the familiar archetypes appeared. Seventy-eight cards in the deck, and every time he read for himself he saw the major arcana, the archetypes. The minor arcana, the remaining fifty-six cards, depicted the everyday struggles of life to which he had grown immune.

He finished the first row and paused. The Fool. The Empress. The Lovers. The Sun.

That row rarely changed. That row depicted the beginning, the past. He was The Fool who knew everything but nothing, ran forward but never looked back or ahead. Guided by The Empress, Meadhbh Bean Mhic Crabháin, Kait's mother. He could still see her striped black and white hair pulled into a bun. Meadhbh had raised him and instructed him in the secrets of botany, healing and the magick of the ancient Celts. These were Meadhbh's cards.

Meadhbh, the village witch, taught him about magick, gods and goddesses, powers of plants; and how to use cards for divination, to scry with flame, to heal, and to offer thanks. People would walk for days to have her heal their maladies. A French Huguenot couple had lost their daughter to a fever that their eldest son now had. They had traveled with him and his brother from the south of England. Meadhbh healed the boy and the family stayed while he recovered. Their infant son was three months older than Meadhbh's daughter, Cacht. When it came time for the family to return to England, and escape the Irish climate, they offered the baby as payment. Or so Meadhbh had told him. He knew better than to believe her, but he didn't have any other story.

That was the family legend of how Galen became the son of a witch, and that was why he didn't have the same innate abilities that Cacht possessed. His Kait... The Lovers. Powerful magick required male and female representations, and so Meadhbh taught them to cast together. He had the fire magick. Cacht had water. The perfect complements.

And then The Sun, card of hope and possibility... Galen had apprenticed himself to a stained glass craftsman at age twelve. His steady hands and his knowledge of rudimentary mathematics had impressed the master. Galen left the cottage every morning at dawn and returned after supper. A skill like stained glassmaking would bring Galen stature in the village and replace the ambient fear of the witch's hut. Galen intended to hand-fast with Kait.

But that never happened, Galen thought, as he slapped the next row onto the table.

Death. The World. The Tower. The Star.

It was always the same, he thought as he read the cards. The past never changed, like the law of threefold, offering no forgiveness.

He had not meant for Meadhbh to die. How could they have known that Kait disappeared to join the ranks of immortal elemental guardians? If they had known that Kait was safe, maybe the anguish and the anger never would have festered into the inferno that consumed their home. His frustration at the lack of clues, when combined with the rumors consuming the village, Galen could not control the fire that exploded from within him. The heat struck Meadhbh with such force that her face melted.

She died instantaneously, or so he hoped.

It wasn't his fault.

It was hers. Kait's. For leaving.

CHAPTER THIRTEEN

ross-legged on her bed, Adelaide fed CDs into her new laptop as her mother prattled on the phone. While iTunes imported Avril Lavigne, Adelaide put Alanis Morrissette into the jewel case. Her mother talked about "Karen... You remember Karen Goldberg" whom she ran into at the supermarket.

"She was your best friend in high school," her mother said.

"Until she lost a three-year battle with acne and I ended up on the cover of *Vogue*."

"She's married with two kids," her mother continued.

"I told her to go to the dermatologist but she didn't," Adelaide said mindlessly.

"She married Jimmy Fields. Did you know Jimmy?"

"Yeah, Mom. I know Jimmy," Adelaide said.

She wouldn't tell her mom how well she knew Jimmy. She'd gone down on him. She'd wanted more, but chickened out. Not because she was a virgin, because she wasn't, but because that had happened in Paris that spring. Even at fifteen, she had her doubts that an American boy could measure up. Probably one of the better decisions she'd ever made. *Vive la France.*

"Adelaide, are you still there?" her mom asked.

A shadow crossed her balcony. Adelaide squinted, stretched over the laptop, uncertain if she really saw what she thought she saw. She held the cell phone an arm's distance from her face.

"Mom, I gotta go," she said, snapping the phone closed.

Kait tapped on the sliding glass doors.

"Can I come in?" Kait asked, a misshapen tank top falling off her shoulders. Adelaide slid the door open.

"You can't come in unless I invite you? What are you? A vampire?"

"No. I was being polite. Galen has limitations. I do what I want. We need to talk."

"I have nothing to say to you," she said. "Galen said you're crazy."

"Maybe I am," Kait said, "but I have a job to do, and he's nothing but a rogue mage. He'll be next on Neferkaba's naughty list."

The cat raced toward them. Kait crouched on the floor, whistled a cat noise, and rubbed Zut's cheeks as if the two knew each other. Kait sat on the bed. The cat jumped into her lap.

"That's my cat," Adelaide remarked. Zut never befriended anyone, except maybe Étienne.

"Funny thing about familiars," Kait said, while scratching the cat's ears. "They know danger. They know power. They know when to fight. Something you could use to learn."

"Familiar? Familiar what?" Adelaide said. "Didn't you say you had to tell me something? Why should I listen to you? What have you done but scare me? Galen taught me about psychometry instead of threatening me — "

Kait leapt to her feet and seized Adelaide's throat with one slender hand.

"Is that what you think?" Kait yelled. "That I'm the enemy? I'm the one who wants your power passed to the next generation, not returned generically to the universe."

Kait tightened her grip and lifted Adelaide from the floor. A pale blue haze bubbled from Adelaide's body. Adelaide choked and gasped. Kait hovered a foot off the ground. Adelaide wanted to scream, but no sound came from her throat. Her lungs burned.

Kait threw Adelaide to her bed. Adelaide collapsed on her back, struggling to regain air. The cat jumped to her side, licking her cheeks. Adelaide sat up, propped on her elbows.

"You gave to him," Kait snapped. "The blood."

"What blood?" Adelaide asked.

Adelaide needed a weapon. She ran to her mirror, fingering her hairbrushes, tangled necklaces, watches, and hairpieces. She put a metal nail file and manicure scissors in her pocket. Kait slid her fingers into Adelaide's pocket. She withdrew the scissors, then the file. She tossed them to the floor.

"I'm not going to hurt you," Kait said. "If I really wanted it, you'd be dead. Have you learned nothing?"

"Why are you here?" Adelaide asked.

"I had two choices: to take your excess water magic or to kill you."

"You did neither. Why?"

"You're the last one with our magic. Now, I have a third option."

"Which is?"

This girl was crazy and stalking her. Adelaide should have called the cops after the last time, but she didn't.

"You're shaking," Kait said as she took Adelaide's right hand, upended it, and stroked it, repeatedly brushing her fingers from Adelaide's wrist, across her palm, and to her fingertips. Calm sunk into Adelaide's body and the trembling ceased. "I'm going to make you a real witch."

"A what?"

"I'll teach you to control your magic."

Kait placed her hands on Adelaide's hips and turned her toward the mirror. Adelaide's reflection stood alone. Two circles of breath fogged the glass.

"Are you sure you're not a vampire?" she asked.

Adelaide faced Kait.

"There are no such thing as vampires," Kait remarked. "I don't exist in your reality. I'm outside it. That's why I have no reflection. I can manipulate your reality and so can Galen. You can't trust us. Look in the mirror."

Adelaide obeyed. The reflection in the mirror portrayed Galen's bronze skin, smoky eyes, and auburn hair. His lips parted and words tumbled into Adelaide's ear in Kait's voice.

"It doesn't take much," she said. "Especially when it's what you want."

She whipped around. It was Kait.

"That's how he got your blood," Kait said. "He made you think he was fucking you."

"Made me think..." Adelaide gazed into the mirror again. She could find no reflection other than her own. "Did he tell you that?"

"He didn't have to. I know him, and I know you, better than you realize."

Adelaide lit a cigarette, trembling fingers setting it to her lips for a hearty drag.

"You tell me, Adelaide," Kait said. "What happened that night?"

"I don't know."

"Focus. Clear the fog."

"I can't remember," Adelaide protested.

The volume of margaritas she consumed that night didn't help. That was the night she hallucinated Galen's hand as a skeleton and stabbed him with a fork. Then there was the comment about the tower in his eyes. At her apartment, they talked. They practiced psychometry. They made love on the couch, but it hadn't felt right especially she could have sworn that he never removed his clothes. So, now Kait wanted to know what did he do, and she had no idea. Really, no idea.

Adelaide smashed her cigarette into the ashtray. How could she do this? How could she figure it out. She only had one supernatural talent that she could control. She'd use it. The psychometry. Adelaide rushed into the living room with Kait at her heels. She dumped her body onto the couch. She shoved her right hand deep into the cushions. Kait clapped.

"That shows ingenuity," Kait said. "I was beginning to think you were hopeless."

Adelaide closed her eyes. She emptied her mind, hoping to block what she remembered, so she wouldn't impose her memories over those imprinted on the couch. The resulting vision slammed into her mind, sending her head into the couch like G-force during an airplane's take-off. She relived it. Galen stripped her clothes. He caressed her and kissed her. So far it was exactly what she remembered. She blushed.

Things started happening that she didn't remember. Galen removed the cross-stitch runner from the coffee table. He folded it and placed it beside Adelaide's thigh. He parted her legs, reached toward her, and.... Oh my God! He pulled her tampon from her body. Fighting a heaving stomach, Adelaide turned to Kait.

"The tampon," Adelaide finished.

"Your menstrual blood, which he offered to the gods and kept for his own magic," Kait explained. "You lack a masculine ground, and he has a part of your feminine power. It makes you vulnerable, but only until your next cycle."

"What does that mean?" she asked, confused.

The whole conversation reminded Adelaide of math class. She understood, but it was way too complicated to use.

"His fire becomes electricity, your blood the conductor. Your water follows the blood. He'll manipulate you into giving your magic."

"I don't know. I'm not into magic, maybe he should have it," Adelaide said.

"No!" Kait screamed. "It has survived generations and it defines what we are. That's why I'm going to teach you. You're all woman. First, you need a meditation to call your masculine energies. It will keep your feminine power from leaking."

Kait cracked her knuckles.

"I leak?" Adelaide repeated.

"That's why Neferkaba needs you contained. Think of something masculine," Kait instructed.

Adelaide closed her eyes. What counted as masculine? Like, boys? Kait brushed her hand across Adelaide's temple. Adelaide decided on a neck tie, very masculine. She thought of a pastel floral tie, like Et would wear in March. As she imagined it, she caught a whiff of Chanel Allure.

"Something masculine," Kait said, "not clothing."

"You can read my mind?" Adelaide said.

Kait wiggled her fingers and replaced them on Adelaide's forehead. Adelaide emptied her mind. Blackness fell and the ties disappeared. This time she pictured Étienne himself.

"Again, interesting choice," Kait said. "He's very balanced. No magic, but extremely balanced. Normally, I would suggest the sun, or air, or metal, fire, a sword, but that might be too subtle. Nope. Let's do the obvious. Think great, big penis."

Colin, a model, with a beautiful specimen of manhood. She had seen it backstage. But, Colin was gay. So, did that count? Instead, she thought of

Brad. Brad didn't have Colin's aesthetic value, but he had size. Or Simon? Simon was the best if you didn't include —

"Just pick one!" Kait screamed.

Adelaide visualized a throbbing, erect penis.

"Thank you," Kait said. "Now, hold that thought. When you get emotional, remember that."

"That's it? A big penis?" Adelaide asked.

"No, that's not it," Kait said, "but meditation is one step toward reining yourself in."

"Oh."

"Do you have any beer?" Kait asked.

"A couple Blue Moons," Adelaide answered.

"Get them," Kait directed. "And cake, if you have it."

Cake? Seriously? Adelaide went into the kitchen. She carried the necks of the beers in the fingers of one hand, then picked a pack of Twinkies. When did she buy those? She set the bounty on the coffee table.

"I didn't even notice that doily was missing," Adelaide said.

"Which brings me to my real challenge," Kait said.

Kait rose from the sofa.

"I need to teach you to see through his glamour. See things for what they really are."

"Can you do that?" Adelaide asked.

"I doubt it. But, hold your own against me, he won't have a chance," Kait said. "It's harder for a woman to block a woman. Too similar. Plus, I'm a stronger witch than Galen."

Kait went to Adelaide's door and threw Adelaide's purse at her as she darted through the hall, into the elevator. Once the elevator descended, Kait ran from it across the lobby to the street, tugging Adelaide down the sidewalk. Kait cackled as they approached Park Avenue South. She ran north to 33rd Street and dashed into the subway station. Kait shot past the turnstile which didn't even wiggle. Adelaide rummaged for her MetroCard.

Items cascaded from Adelaide's purse: comb, gum wrappers, condom, lipstick. She didn't bother retrieving them because Kait had walked away. Finally, she whipped free the orange and blue paper card.

"Here it is," she yelled as she swiped it.

Kait hopped onto the six train. Adelaide pursued. Could this day get any weirder? She jumped onto the train as it started to roll. Holding the pole, she stood breathless and white-knuckled before Kait. Kait smirked. She crossed her arms, her crazy red hair blocking the graffiti behind her. People surrounded them: white people, black people, Asian people; families, teenagers with MP3 players, even a filthy toothless lady with a winter hat. Kait tilted her head.

"Where are we going?" Adelaide whispered.

"Here," Kait replied.

A wiry black teen with baggy jeans (one leg cuffed, one leg down) and a bandana in his belt loop passed them. Kait's expression softened.

"They think they're so tough," she said, "but they're babies. Some are killers, yes, but babies."

"Why are we on the subway?" Adelaide asked.

"Because it's dynamic, crowded, and uncontrolled," Kait said. "Close your eyes."

"On the subway?"

"Do it," Kait said. "I'm the biggest threat here. Close your damn eyes."

She did. It intensified the smells and the sounds and the motion of the train, especially the metallic screeching.

"Whenever you don't trust your senses," Kait whispered, "close your eyes. Deception tends to be two-dimensional. You see, therefore you believe. If you close your eyes, you rely on other senses. You listen, smell, and taste. These are harder to replicate."

Kait's fingers touched Adelaide's forehead.

"Mind magic usually involves the forehead. Only blood magic is stronger. Guard who touches your forehead," Kait said. "If someone kisses your forehead, they love you deeply. Lips are about passion, temples about the mind."

The air shifted. The train paused. The doors opened. People got off and on. The train resumed.

"Open your eyes," Kait directed her.

She did. Across the train sat a large and muscular red Doberman Pinscher with alert eyes and soft, droopy ears, like her great-grandmother's dog, Zora. During summer, she and the dog would run in Oma's yard in Dabendorf. Oma loved red Dobermans. A phantom pain spread through Adelaide's arm emanating from her scar.

"You're losing focus," Kait said.

"There's a dog on the subway," she replied.

"Is there?" Kait asked.

Adelaide hated dogs. Oma's dog had turned on six-year-old Adelaide in Oma's basement while she and Janine stirred sauerkraut. Sure, Adelaide had swatted her sister with a wooden spoon but who expected the dog to bite her? Zora tore a substantial chunk from Adelaide's arm, creating the small scar near her armpit.

"Pay attention," Kait demanded. "Is there a dog?"

The dog on the subway whimpered. Its tongue wagged in tandem with the its raspy panting. It scratched its face with its rear leg.

"Is there a dog?" Kait repeated.

Adelaide closed her eyes, once again falling into the rhythm of the subway. The car clattered as it navigated the tunnels. People surrounded her, she could smell their scents ranging from sweet to sweat. She could sense their closeness via their heat and chatter. Staleness filled the subway car. In the middle of it, she could not find the panting of the dog or the click of its nails on the floor. She opened her eyes. No dog.

The night trudged on, hour after hour, exercise after exercise, as Adelaide grew exhausted and confused. Fact, fiction, she didn't know anymore. She curled into a fetal position across two seats. Kait paced the train, her fingers twirling across her chin. Adelaide's eyelids lowered. After so much time in the tunnels, the roaring, screeching and rocking of the car lulled her. As she drifted into a light slumber, the car jolted, the screeching intensified to ear-splitting levels and Adelaide rolled from her berth.

Glass showered into the cabin from the windows, the rear of the car fish-tailing and slamming into a steel support pillar. The pillar folded and crashed into the roof of the car, splitting the metal in half. Adelaide scrambled to get to her feet, but she couldn't. Other passengers climbed over her. Kait lay on the floor beside her, a thin trail of blood trailing from her ear. The pillar, suspended above them, suddenly tumbled down and knocked one man like a windsock in a breeze, before it soared further toward the floor.

Adelaide rose to her knees. The car twisted sideways. She sledded under a row of chairs, landing against the wall. The pillar landed and crushed the closest chair, pinning her leg inside its knotted metal. Black smoke surrounded her, as more metallic screeching soared toward them. Through the now open roof, Adelaide glimpsed the express train roaring their way. Their car had crossed the median between the local and the express tracks.

Adelaide grabbed the legs of the chairs, bracing, hoping the chairs would shield her. The engine of the express collided with and cut into their car, creating an accordion of walls. People flew everywhere. The wheels of the express pinched a businessman's head and kept rolling, stopping mere inches from Adelaide's sarcophagus. Blood spattered from every angle. Flames shot from the gored cabin. Adelaide hugged her own shoulders as her abdomen heaved, food rocketing up her esophagus and out her mouth as Kait dropped from nowhere. Adelaide showered her with vomit. Kait peeled off her soiled clothing.

"What's the problem?" Kait asked, now nude and oddly gleaming in the intermittent light of the tunnel.

Sweat covered Adelaide's face. Kait had a sparkling tattoo of water drops across her back.

"Accident," she told Kait.

"Close your eyes," Kait instructed her.

Adelaide did as told. When she did, the train rocked in its familiar lull.

"We're moving," Adelaide said.

She opened her eyes. The train had windows. The blood and the wounded bodies disappeared. The cabin had a roof. She squeezed her thigh, a solid, pain-free leg.

"It felt so real," Adelaide said. Then, she noticed Kait's freckled white nudity. "You're naked!"

"You puked on me. That was real. Unfortunately. Why did you panic?"

"I was hurt and scared. The train... It burned. And my leg... I think it was broken."

"You're a healer," Kait said. "You have water. Put the fire out. Heal your damn wounds. Emotions interfere, don't let them. Remember your penis."

A naked woman on the New York subway telling another woman to remember her penis... Kait scanned the passengers. She strode to a homeless man with a pink baseball cap and pressed her palm against his temple.

"Sleep," she said.

The man toppled to the side, dropping the brown paper sack in his lap. Kait overturned it. Several old pieces of silverware, a 20 oz. bottle of Coke, a half-eaten Big Mac in a cardboard carton, and a ratty sweater littered the floor. Kait crouched in the middle of the mess, slipping her arms into the sweater and then lobbing it over her head. She sat in an empty seat beside Adelaide. Kait turned solemn. Her eyes ebbed with calmness.

"Have you ever healed anyone on purpose?" Kait asked.

"Not that I know of," Adelaide answered.

She slid farther away from Kait, hoping to escape the garlic smell of the 'new' sweater.

"You sure? I'm getting something from you, like you never recovered from a big job," the witch explained. "When amateurs perform magic, they don't always cleanse themselves properly and it leaves a residue... I wouldn't think you could do it by accident. I know why Neferkaba wants your magic. You don't? You have no idea what you did?"

Kait escorted her home and gave Adelaide a beer and a Twinkie. Adelaide refused the cake. It was too close to October. Kait muttered in a strange language and brought her an orange.

"Will you eat this?" Kait inquired.

Adelaide, sipping her beer, nodded.

"Always replenish," Kait explained.

Adelaide peeled it.

"Tell me honestly. Do I have a chance?" Adelaide asked between sections of orange.

"Only if you think you do."

CHAPTER FOURTEEN

Adelaide did not share Étienne's *laissez faire* attitude regarding sleep. While they could carouse until the wee hours, especially together, Étienne could pull himself together with a two-hour nap. Adelaide couldn't drag herself from bed after eight hours sleep without a pot of coffee.

Luckily, last night's adventure with Kait did not involve excessive alcohol, only emotional trauma. Technically Adelaide had to go to work, but Basilie's semi-annual shoe purge would consume the day. That lowered Adelaide's thinking quota. In the cluttered closet of her Manhattan apartment, Adelaide counted fifty-two pairs of upscale designer shoes before she finally stopped. Except for her favorites, most pairs remained in the shoeboxes. All from Étienne.

Étienne loved shoes and bought them for everyone. Bas limited her closet to thirty pairs. To control the population, they donated shoes to the domestic violence shelter twice a year during Étienne's business trips. Adelaide selected ten pairs. She brought the shoeboxes to the office and dropped them in the hall. Seema offered her electric blue Manolo Blahniks.

"Seema, you love these shoes," Adelaide said. "They match that fabulous Versace dress."

"That dress was my roommate's. She moved back to India. With the dress."

"Those shoes are six-months-old, Seema. You could make a killing on eBay."

"I can't," she said. "Could you sell a gift from Étienne on eBay?"

Adelaide accepted them. Seema tied the shoeboxes together. Basilie would add more shoes to the company's official donation of ready-to-wear suits. Adelaide poured a third cup of coffee and emerged from the galley kitchen, as Basilie pounded down the hall in beige, open-toed sandals with suede fringe, multi-colored beads, and moderate heels. She wore them with an off-white skirt and single-breasted jacket with thin lapels, cropped below her natural waist with a gentle flare toward her hips. Adelaide gulped coffee. Basilie's blouse came from neither *couture* nor *prêt-à-porter*, Étienne made the shimmering V-neck from the weave Adelaide ordered for May's resort collection. It blended gold metallic fibers with beige silk, not quite day and not quite evening. Basilie paused by the kitchen door. She glanced to the shoeboxes and then to Adelaide. Adelaide stared at Basilie's feet and her throat went dry. Adelaide drank more coffee.

"Did Et leave before organizing your closet?" she asked.

Basilie's brow furrowed.

"I can dress myself," Basilie replied.

"I didn't mean... It's just... Didn't Étienne buy you the gold Valentino sandals? The strappy ones?"

"He might have," Basilie replied.

"They would look great with that outfit."

"Metallic shoes for the office?" Basilie questioned.

"Maybe not," Adelaide answered. "They just..."

Adelaide bit her tongue. Wearing those heels from the Ungaro spring couture show with a conservative outfit bordered on absurd. Basilie carted shoeboxes to her Benz sedan. Adelaide left her "J'[heart] Paris" coffee mug on the counter and assisted. In Basilie's double-parked car, the open trunk revealed a *tableau* of shoeboxes: Fendi, Chloe, Dolce & Gabbana, Miu Miu, Jimmy Choos, Yves Saint Laurent...

"This gets more painful every time. How many today?" Adelaide asked.

"I culled nine. The man has a compulsion."

"Add mine and that's fifteen grand in shoes," Adelaide remarked.

Basilie peered quizzically as she closed the trunk.

"I'm impressed. That's right."

"What do you mean?" Adelaide asked.

"You did the math," Basilie said. "Correctly. In your head."

Basilie pressed her key fob. She and Adelaide got into the cabin, where quiet jazz vocals serenaded them.

"You look rough," Basilie said. "Late night?"

As usual, Adelaide thought, Basilie didn't mince words.

"Yeah," she admitted. "A friend stopped in from out-of-town."

"A man?"

"Not a man."

Basilie grunted. Adelaide directed her eyes to the cityscape outside the window and held her breath. It was the best way to keep her tongue in check.

"I suppose you told your guest about my condition," Basilie remarked.

Adelaide exhaled. "I didn't tell anyone. I didn't tell Galen."

"Do you think I'm stupid, Adelaide?" Basilie said.

"No. You just think I am. After all, you can do higher math in your head and you speak like eight languages," Adelaide quipped.

"Six, if you count Japanese and Arabic, which I never mastered," Basilie answered. "Someone is lying to me, Adelaide. And I don't think it's Étienne. »

"Maybe Galen figured it out," Adelaide said. "Some people are intuitive."

An awkward pause.

"I have to say something, something that would sound nicer in French," Basilie said.

"Most things sound better in French," Adelaide muttered.

"I'll say it in English. I don't want you to misunderstand. I've tried to like you, but I can't. Do you know why?"

Nothing in Basilie's voice indicated malice, but she sounded grim. Adelaide said nothing.

"I worry. Your relationships especially. I think you want to emulate or impress Étienne."

"What's to emulate?" His... the proper phrase for philandering man-slut escaped Adelaide. ...free-spirited youth? "I don't think that's the way it is."

"Then what way is it? He's been gone a week. I haven't heard from him, but you have."

Basilie used her business voice. Normally, Basilie acted natural around her. Today, Basilie spoke with distance, treating her like an employee.

"God, yes. Several times a..."

Adelaide realized her mistake too late.

"...day."

They arrived at the shelter. Basilie turned off the car. She slipped one leg outside when Addy stopped her, a hand to her arm. Basilie's eyes raked icily across Adelaide.

"It's about the Holiday blouses," Adelaide said. "This is my warning."

Adelaide laced her hands.

"He couldn't do it himself," Adelaide sputtered.

"No, Adelaide. It's not the blouse," Basilie said, disgusted, "but even I know to do a size run. Étienne would never fire you. No matter what you screw up."

Basilie got out of the car. So, it wasn't about the blouse. It wasn't? Et hadn't asked Bas to reprimand her? That's what 'Then what way is it?' meant. Étienne couldn't treat her like an employee, their intimacy got in the way.

"Oh my God," Adelaide said.

Adelaide went to the trunk. Did Bas think ... that she and Et ... No. Bas would never think they were lovers. That would be dumb. Adelaide took a pile of shoeboxes. Étienne would never. Besides, wow, how wrong would that be? Especially now, with a baby! And everything else ... Well, that was a long time ago. Did Étienne suspect something? Because Adelaide had worked very hard to make sure he never suspected what happened when Bas left him.

Adelaide and Basilie stacked the shoes in the hallway and returned to the car for the rest. Adelaide pulled Basilie aside.

"Do you think I'm sleeping with him?"

"I don't think you'd be aggressive or stupid enough to initiate it, but I also know you wouldn't say no," Basilie replied. "It's a problem you have."

Basilie sped into the building, her out-of-place Ungaro heels echoing. A woman with the brownest, smoothest skin meandered by in a cranberry ready-to-wear d'Amille suit and Marc Jacobs pumps. Basilie nearly trampled the African American woman's companions, a preschool-aged boy and a toddler girl with beaded cornrows. Basilie froze.

"I got the job," the woman told the receptionist.

"That's great," the receptionist answered.

"Once I save up security, I think I can get a place. My momma said she'd baby-sit..."

The little girl had the brightest brown eyes and her brother the sweetest smile. They craned their necks toward the mysterious stranger who nearly mowed into them. Basilie didn't move.

"I had the money for a cab, but I took the train. So I can take the kids for ice cream."

Basilie fished in her purse. She cleared her throat softly. The mother in the red suit turned.

"Excuse me," Basilie said as she retrieved a business card.

The boy dropped a Matchbox oil tanker. Adelaide returned it.

"I'd like to help," Basilie said.

She presented the woman with the business card.

"I'm Basilie d'Amille, and I'm involved with the shelter."

The woman studied the card.

"d'Amille," the woman repeated. "That sounds familiar."

"You're wearing a d'Amille suit," the receptionist said.

"No way," the woman replied. "I got my job because of this suit."

"My husband's ready-to-wear line," Bas said. "If you find an apartment, I'll finance the security."

Befuddlement overtook the woman's face.

"She's for real," the receptionist said. "If Mrs. d'Amille tells you she'll do it, it's done."

"I don't need any crazy interest rates..."

"Five percent," Basilie said. "Maybe less. Call my cell. I'm never at my desk."

Bas progressed to the counter. She opened her checkbook.

"I doubled the usual amount," Basilie said. "So, it's ten thousand. I'll start a security deposit fund. I'm sure more women could use help. Have the director call me?"

"Of course, Ms. d'Amille," the receptionist said.

"Adelaide, I'm ready for lunch."

With that, Basilie slid everything into her purse and walked out. Adelaide waved to everyone then followed. Basilie collapsed into her car, pale and ghostly. Adelaide got into her seat and waited for orders. That's what they all did. The mastiff who liked to lead the pack as alpha dog, that's what Étienne said about Bas ... But now Basilie didn't give orders. The two of them sat. The stark expression on Basilie's face didn't lift. Adelaide wondered if she should call someone. Who? Étienne was overseas.

"Do you need a snack, Bas?" Adelaide finally said. "I might have a Milky Way..."

"No," she said so quietly Adelaide could barely hear.

Basilie had tears in her eyes. Her hands gripped the steering wheel.

"You're crying," Adelaide remarked.

"No, I'm not," Bas said, wiping her eyes with her hand.

Adelaide dug in her purse for a tissue.

"Maybe you should do the next delivery," Basilie said.

"Why?" Adelaide asked.

"It's not fair," Basilie whimpered.

"What's not fair, Bas? Did you get a parking ticket or something?"

Basilie laughed. "No, I didn't get a ticket."

Her purse open on her lap, Adelaide thrust one hand into the mess.

"Is it me?" Adelaide asked.

"No, not this time," Basilie said. "I don't want to sound like an ungrateful bitch. Let it go."

The hair on Adelaide's neck bristled with eerie *déjà vu*.

"You can tell me, Bas. I know you're an ungrateful bitch," Adelaide joked.

Luckily, Basilie laughed. That saved Adelaide a cab ride to the office.

"I can be," Bas admitted.

Basilie's hand slipped across her waistband and brushed her the fabric across her abdomen. The answer slapped Adelaide in the face. Their previous visit to the shelter, in July, before the couture show in Paris, had also upset Basilie. She had used those same words. 'I don't want to sound ungrateful.' Had Basilie offered that woman a security deposit and given a larger-than-usual check to the shelter because of gratitude? For what?

"I thought I dealt with this," Basilie had said after the last visit when she and Adelaide stopped at the park, where children played tag.

Adelaide remembered the giggles and the pitch of their voices as they screamed 'You're it.'

"I have everything: money, career, power... I made the *Forbes* list last year. The 100 Most Powerful Women," Basilie had said. "I have apartments in Paris and New York. I have a devoted lover and a wardrobe envied by celebrities."

"You do," Adelaide agreed.

Basilie pinched the end of her braid.

"Why am I jealous of poor women, running from abusive relationships, simply because they have children?"

That day in July, Adelaide studied Basilie's profile: chiseled nose, pointy chin, fullness of her cheek, and sadness in her small eyes that bordered on vulnerability.

"You?" Adelaide said. "You wanted a baby?"

"Hard to believe?"

"Yeah," Adelaide scoffed, immediately regretting it. "Does Étienne know?"

"We wanted a big family."

"I thought... your career, his business... no time," Adelaide said.

"The opposite. That's why Chez d'Amille means so much to me."

One of the children had nearly tripped over Adelaide's foot as they dashed across the park.

"If it meant that much to you, with your resources, you had options — "

"Don't," Basilie interrupted. "Once that might have been true. But after everything, I couldn't take any more. It wasn't meant to be. Listen to me. Blame hormones. The change of life approaches. Then I won't have the monthly reminders of my failure."

Two months had passed since that day. Adelaide glanced at Basilie, inside the cushy Benz, clutching the steering wheel. Adelaide should say something, but what do you say when the woman who wanted a baby was upset about her pregnancy?

"If anything happens to me," Bas said. "You must keep the business together. Étienne will fall apart and Didier, John, Sabine, and Jérôme will bicker. Keep Étienne focused — "

"Whoa!" Adelaide hollered. "Nothing will happen. You're just pregnant."

"Pregnancy does not agree with me. Don't let Étienne give up. He'll want to."

"You're talking nonsense. It's hormones."

"No, it's not, Adelaide. Promise you won't sleep with him."

"Bas, you're losing it. I think I liked it better when you were angry."

"Promise. I can't have your business acumen clouded by sex. If you ended up in Étienne's bed, you would be useless at the office. If something happened to me... He'd come to you."

Adelaide shivered, despite the New York heat.

"Stop it," she replied. "You wanted a baby. You're having a baby."

Adelaide remembered the exercises she did with Kait the previous night and Kait's comments about her having done a big job that attracted Nefa-whoever's attention. In July, Adelaide had hugged Basilie, as the children played tag and Basilie blamed her mood on peri-menopause. Adelaide had meant the hug as a gesture of comfort, but had she given Basilie the ability to get pregnant? She must have used her magic to heal Basilie.

In the Benz, with Ella Fitzgerald singing 'It's Delovely,' Adelaide stroked Basilie's fingers. Adelaide closed her eyes. A tiny, rapid-fire noise thundered in her head. She snapped her hand from Basilie's lap. The noise echoed, gradually fading. As Ella's voice replaced it, Adelaide repeated the odd noise's rhythm to herself. It was almost like... She pressed her hand against her own chest. Her heartbeat hammered. As she removed her hand, the sound stopped. Adelaide stared at her palm. Adelaide brought her right hand to Basilie's.

Their fingers met. Darkness blinded her as static blocked her senses. Nothing focused. But then, she had never done this before. Until a few days ago, she had never tried to read anything, not on purpose. There was a pink peanut, a fleshy mass and that rapid-fire noise. The center of the peanut pulsed with it. Adelaide inhaled rapidly. It was a heartbeat! And that pink lima bean was the baby! It somersaulted, revealing its black marble-like eyes and its fingers, pudgy and curled together. It turned again, this time showing her its profile, a wedge of tomato with a spine under its skin, and pinholes for ears! Oh my God, she thought, it's Étienne's baby, his son!

Bewildered, Adelaide tugged her hand from Basilie's lap and recited the alphabet to herself before she spoke. Basilie must have conceived after their last visit to the shelter, perhaps when they met Étienne in Paris. Had Adelaide caused it?

"Don't be afraid, Bas," Adelaide said, with certainty. "You're going to have a healthy, gorgeous baby boy."

Basilie laughed, cutting the nervous energy.

"You sound like my doctor," she said. "A boy, *eh bien*. Let's go get lunch. I need a harvest salad with walnuts and blue cheese."

"As long as I can get a burger," Adelaide said. "I am starved for meat."

CHAPTER FIFTEEN

delaide flopped onto the sofa in her Manhattan apartment, opening her phone with a flick of her wrist and scrolled the missed calls menu. Not that she missed a single one of Étienne's phone calls. She simply chose not to answer. And this was why: four missed calls, 5:42 p.m., 5:29 p.m., 5:17 p.m., and 5:05 p.m. The received calls menu displayed a similar pattern and, as Étienne would say, *c'est la goutte d'eau qui fait déborder le vase.* It was the drop of water that overflowed the vase.

Now, at quarter-to-six, Adelaide did the unthinkable. She turned off her cell. She tossed it onto the coffee table, grabbed a throw pillow, and shoved it under her head. Her hand grabbed the remote and turned on the television, not even registering what inane sit-com came on. Zut leapt onto the couch. The cat's lean body rubbed against Adelaide's torso as she licked Adelaide's nose. Adelaide giggled and scratched the animal's cheeks. The cat pushed her whiskers forward, purring louder than the television.

Adelaide weighed whether to make dinner, order out, or trade a meal for a shot of whiskey. Her landline rang. Adelaide stared at it. No one ever called her New York number. Except her parents. And they only called on Sunday. Étienne wouldn't. Would he? She answered.

"Did you turn your cell off?" her sister greeted pointedly.

"Jay," Adelaide replied with a sigh of relief. "It's the middle of the night in Germany."

"Tell me you have your laptop."

"Don't I always?"

"Yes, and you usually have your cell. Can I email you this paper?"

"A paper? What kind of paper?"

"French composition. The professor hates me, because I'm American. And my written French sucks. It's on *The Little Prince*."

"I have that here in my apartment. I love that story."

"I know, that's why you have to bail me out. Read it. Call me back."

Haphazardly flinging files from her suede bag, Adelaide's fingers brushed the vial tucked into the lipstick compartment. She gingerly removed the unfinished d'Amille fragrance. She and Basilie agreed it needed more lemon in the secondary notes before they could unveil it to Étienne. She replaced the perfume and grabbed her laptop. She returned to the couch, unplugged the phone, and snapped the cord into the modem port. She lamented that her apartment did not have wireless like her office and Étienne's house in Pennsylvania.

Before she flipped open the monitor, Adelaide took a deep breath and pushed her finger into the soil of her new elephant ear plant. Did she ever feel stupid... Kait said it would prevent her overflowing water from conducting electricity. If her water magic conducted electricity, did that mean... She poised her finger above the power button. She imagined a little zap, a pretty lightning bolt. The Mac chimed. Adelaide peered at her index finger. She continued staring until the d'Amille logo loaded onto her computer desktop.

Adelaide dug into her sister's awful book report, fixing Jay's backwards accent marks. She dialed her cell while she typed one-handed.

"Did you even read the book?" Adelaide asked.

"Addy, it's about a homesick boy. I read enough."

"Jay, the author was a pilot, right? He repeatedly leaves his wife alone, and he feels guilty, but she's demanding, like the rose. He likes adventure, time alone, but he knows, if anything happens to his rose, he'll be responsible."

"It says that?"

"Did you get to the fox?" Adelaide asked.

"No," Janine admitted.

"It's important. Do you have your pencil ready? *'Tu deviens responsable pour toujours de ce que tu as apprivoisé.'* "

"You become responsible always for that which you have... What's *apprivoisé*?"

"Tamed," Adelaide said.

"And why do you know this?"

"I read it in high school."

"And Saint Exupéry's wife? Who told you that?"

"Basilie."

"Figures," Jay remarked. "Thanks, sissy."

"No problem. Next time, finish the damn book."

After hanging up, Adelaide scanned the missed call menu again. Janine was the most recent, but Galen had also called. Could she handle him? Could she remember the defenses Kait taught her? The thought chilled her. She needed practice. She also needed to confirm what happened with Basilie. Had she healed her boss's wife? Adelaide paced the apartment, reminding herself not to bite her nails. She considered heading to the corner store for a pack of smokes but talked herself out of it.

She went into the kitchen, fed the cat, and sliced carrot sticks. She dipped them in hummus, nibbling as she formulated a plan. She fingered the opal pendant she had purchased on Kait's suggestion. Opals promoted intuition. She gripped the stone and closed her eyes, praying to some random entity for guidance. As her hands rubbed the opal, her vision clouded.

An hour later, she woke in her bed beneath her comforter wearing silk pajamas. Adelaide touched her face. She had removed her makeup. She checked her ears. She had the opal earrings. She dozed again, only to jerk from sleep because she sensed presence in her room. She leapt to her feet.

"Galen? I know you're there. You've been watching me all night."

Galen stepped from the shadows.

"You really shouldn't be here," Adelaide added.

The cat hopped to the floor.

"You didn't return my calls," he said.

Adelaide shook her head.

"What does it matter? You were watching me the whole time," she said.

He walked toward her.

"What's going on?" Galen asked.

"You didn't make love to me," she replied.

"I didn't?" he said.

He circled her, his eyes trained on the cat.

"You took my blood," Adelaide said.

"Did you need it?"

"That's not the point."

Adelaide remained stony-faced. Galen sat on her bed, his back to her, shoulders hunched. She planted her feet on the floor and balled her hands into fists even though they hung loosely at her sides. She thought about her giant penis and willed herself to stand strong.

"You're out of balance, and you're dangerous," she said.

"So are you."

"I won't let you hurt me."

Galen turned.

"I didn't hurt you."

Penises, penises, penises... God, why had her mind gone blank? Big, small, long, stout, erect, at rest... Galen approached her. Her breathing quickened with his steps.

"So much you can't explain," he said. "You're confused."

He took her hand. His other hand brushed the hair from her face.

"It's Basilie," Galen said in a sickeningly sweet tone. "Did you do something? Did you hurt the baby, Adelaide?"

"You've always known, about her, about me. You're not a photographer," she said.

"Does it matter?" he asked.

"Yes, goddamnit!"

Everything created a whirlpool in her head. She couldn't trust either of these supernatural freaks, but she wanted information... assistance... reassurance. The tears bubbled in her eyes but she refused to succumb. She reminded herself what Uncle Ben told Peter in *Spiderman*: 'With great power came great responsibility.' Zut leaned against Adelaide's ankle, docile but vigilant.

"Galen... I need to know... Did I get Basilie pregnant?"

"Usually that requires a man — "

"Galen, I'm serious," she said. "Did I make that baby? Kait implied it, but I was too stupid to understand. Let's say Bas was infertile or something, and I touched her, when we were talking about babies and families. Could I have fixed her?"

"You don't know how," he replied.

He lied. She could have. She didn't know how to do any of this magic, but she did it.

"Besides," he remarked, "you didn't have permission."

"Permission?"

"When you do magic without permission," his voice dropped to a menacing whisper. "It backfires. Either on you or the recipient. Hence my question. Did you hurt that baby?"

She reached into his pocket, pulled out his cigarettes, removed one from the pack, and held it for him to light. He did. She smoked it rapidly as she strolled the bedroom, heart jumping.

"Did you invite something into her womb?" Galen asked.

Adelaide's hands shook so badly the cigarette fell to the floor and smoldered in the carpet.

"Invite something?" she repeated. "Like a monster?"

Galen shrugged. Adelaide's knees gave out. She barely made it to the bed. Galen picked up the burning cigarette, puffed on it, and returned it to her.

"Oh, God," she said. "If anything happens to her..."

Then she remembered the tiny pink lima bean.

"No," she said, passing the cigarette to Galen. "It's a human. It's Étienne's baby."

"Just because it's human doesn't mean it can't be evil," he said.

"Evil?" she said.

Adelaide dropped onto her back, her hands gripping her head. Soft footfalls entered her bedroom. Adelaide lifted her head. Kait, clad in the tattered garlic-smelling sweater, handed her a drawstring sack as she glared at Galen.

"What are you doing here?" Kait said.

"Kait," Adelaide whispered.

Kait slithered across the bed and sunk her fingers into Adelaide's hair. She pulled Adelaide's body against her, cradling the model's leggy body against her chest as if an infant.

"*Abair liom a stòr*," the witch muttered.

Somehow, Adelaide understood the Irish. "Tell me, darling."

"I got Bas pregnant."

"You understand now, good. That's the next step."

Galen stood near the window, thumbing Adelaide's battered copy of *Le Petit Prince*.

"Galen says I needed permission, or it will backfire. He thinks Étienne's baby is evil. That's why Nefa-whoever sent you."

Kait flashed Galen a nasty look. Even though it wasn't directed at her, the heat burned her as it traveled.

"Neferkaba," Kait said.

Adelaide finally allowed herself to cry. Kait passed her a tissue.

"Shhhhh, *ciùin*," Kait said, rubbing Adelaide's forehead. "Anyone who's been around you as long as Basilie will know, subconsciously, what you are and what you do. She knew you had a gift like I have a gift for you."

Kait put the bag in Adelaide's hands.

"It's your native soil," she explained. "Keep it under your pillow to maintain your energy."

Kait arranged Adelaide into a sitting position.

"Don't let him manipulate you, Adelaide. I'll be watching," she said to Galen as they stood side-by-side by the door.

"Don't leave..." Adelaide said.

Kait walked through the glass and disappeared.

"...me," Adelaide finished.

Adelaide crawled to Galen. He rotated his thumb across his fingertips in a circular motion, his hand burning red. His thumb pulled at his fingers, an orange glow between them.

"What's that?" asked Adelaide.

She vacillated between fear and awe.

"I would like to give you something, too," he explained.

It mutated into an orb of pulsing red and orange.

"Fire," he said. "My primary element."

"Giving is bad," Adelaide said. "Kait said so."

"To assimilate power, feminine must be given and masculine taken."

"Oh," she replied, nonchalantly as if what he had said made sense. "Fire is masculine? Because you're a man?"

"No," he said. "Fire and air are masculine, because they are. I have yet to meet a straight man with innate water or earth magic."

"That explains Didier. I think he's fire and water."

Galen smiled. His globe had doubled.

"Each element has distinct powers," he said. "Look at Basilie, she needed you."

"Why?"

"She's rooted in earth but can't reproduce. Her passion, her connection to money," Galen said. "She's burning. She lost her water. It's why she both resists and needs Étienne."

"He's balanced, but no magic. Kait said so."

Galen chuckled.

"His personality is his magic," he said. "When's his birthday?"

"March 14," Adelaide answered.

"Pisces, the fish, a water sign. Bas surrounds herself with water."

Adelaide rolled to her back. She alternated her glance between the ceiling and Galen's hands. The globe, as big as a tennis ball, levitated in Galen's palm.

"Give me your left hand," he commanded.

He pressed the ball into her palm. She gazed at the speckled shapes within the sphere.

"Pull it in," Galen instructed.

She closed her fingers. It seared her. She almost dropped it.

"Through your hand," he said.

"I don't have an orifice in my hand," Adelaide snapped.

The ball flared, flames lapping her cheek.

"You absorb energy all over your body."

"Absorb... like a lotion? Soak into the skin? She imagined the sphere melting into her hand, into her flesh, and joining her natural powers. Slowly, in tandem with her breath, the sphere lowered. The closer it got to her hand, the more its pulse beat in the same rhythm as hers until the ball dissolved. Her heart ruptured. She reached for Galen, but crashed onto her face as pain roared through her veins.

"*The Little Prince*," he said. "You are responsible, forever, for what you have tamed."

I'm dying and he's reciting a children's story. Adelaide closed her eyes. One second her heart felt huge and puffy and the next it exploded. The pain settled. She opened her eyes. Her dark apartment, the faint remnants of diffused light behind her neighbors' shades, her cat's eyes. Even from across the room, Zut's purr roared. Everything had clarity. She ran to the sliding glass door and took a deep breath of Manhattan air from her balcony. She promptly choked. Galen slipped his arms around her waist, leaning his head against her arm.

"I knew you'd get it," he whispered.

Adelaide shot her arm across the balcony. Fire shot from the underside of her wrist striking the other side of 32nd Street.

"Just like Spiderman," she said. "Without the web."

She raised one fingernail to Galen's cheek. Adelaide kissed him. It ignited her body with desire unlike anything else. It flickered and ached like lust, but filled her from head to toe. Her eternal fatigue had lifted, leaving behind freshness. She grabbed the discarded paperback and opened it. She could read without her glasses!

"You won't keep it," he warned.

"What can I do with it?" she asked.

Adelaide took his clove cigarettes. She mimicked his pinching motions and shot a flame from her finger. She stuck the cigarette against it and set it in Galen's mouth. She lit another.

"Power is dangerous without knowledge," Galen said.

She rubbed her cheek against his. He squeezed her hand.

"This won't last," he said.

She couldn't label it. It stripped her doubts, worry, and inhibitions. She didn't care what anyone thought, not Étienne, not Bas, not her parents, nor her friends. Her fingers stung. She stood, smoking her cigarette, staring across the Manhattan skyline. So many things she wanted to do. She climbed onto the railing of the balcony, holding out her arms and leaning forward. Galen grabbed her.

"What are you doing?" he asked.

"I'm going to fly," she said.

"No, you're not," he said.

"I'm a healer," she replied. "If I hurt myself, I can fix it."

"Not if you're dead."

She considered that. She scurried down. But one thing no one could stop her from doing, if she had one chance to prove herself... Maybe capture Étienne's attention enough to show design potential, one of those devilish ideas she knew she shouldn't do. The crystal and diamond dress from July's *haute couture* show. It sparkled with crystals and diamonds that Étienne had sewn onto the two-piece dress, bustier and skirt. Her fire and its intensity blended into her mind until she imagined the gown, awash with blue feathers, her eyes in animal motifs.

"I have to get to the office," she said.

She raced into her apartment, through the bedroom, and into the living room. She retrieved the perfume, tapping it onto her wrists and behind her ears. Galen appeared next to her.

"Lavender," he said. "It's too sweet."

"It's not done," Adelaide said. "It needs something. Maybe more lemon."

"Nutmeg?" Galen suggested.

She grabbed her keys. Galen stopped her.

"You're in pajamas," he pointed out.

"I don't want to change," she said. "Do you have your camera?"

"No," Galen answered. "But I'm not a photogr — "

"We have a digital. You can use that. You're the closest thing I have to a photographer," she said. "I have the best idea. I'll call John. We're going to need feathers — "

"Adelaide, it's one o'clock in the morning."

"This is my chance. I'm going to blow Étienne out of the water."

CHAPTER SIXTEEN

É tienne stepped from the cab and paid the driver, discovering an out-of-date 200-franc note in his wallet with one crinkled American fifty and a handful of Euros. He bundled a bouquet of dark-edged peach roses into his arms, lifted his garment bag onto his shoulder, and crossed the street. *Depuis la jaune chignole ... en anglais*, he chided himself. As the yellow clunker turned onto Seventh Avenue, homesickness bore into his chest with heaviness. In Paris, he wouldn't be embarrassed to take a taxi from the airport. Taxi companies maintained fleets of white C-series Mercedes. He sighed. Zélie would have called it his overstated, pity-the-Frenchman sigh.

Groggy calls of hello came as he entered the building. Tracking galloping stilettos, Étienne poked his head into the workroom on the first floor. John sat on a folding chair, his head propped in his hands and his eyes weary. Galen stood beside him, with the office's digital camera. Feathers, in combinations of gray-blue, salmon and deep green, covered the floor. Joey slumped in a windowsill.

In the middle of them, Adelaide danced, each hand gripping feathers. She wore the bustier from July's *haute couture* wedding dress, pink *peau de soie* silk with 50,000 Swarovski crystals and diamonds. Garters held off-white stockings, which he traced to Frisoni pumps and back up to diamond-studded underwear. Adelaide danced, half-naked, oblivious, plugged into her iPod. John acknowledged Étienne first.

"She's been like this for hours," John explained. "She called us in the middle of the night."

The two men shook hands. Galen offered his hand, also. Adelaide turned. She had lined her eyes with brown, juxtaposed against pearly white eye shadow that fanned to her ears.

"Did we... *engageons*... hire... *mis à pied*... laid-off make-up artists from the *Cats?*" Étienne asked, stumbling over the language.

John chuckled. Galen smiled. Etienne nodded, his joke successful. Arms full of parcels, Étienne stood dumbfounded, studying her make-up. Humor aside, Adelaide had captured the haunting gaze of a cat. She ran to him, handfuls of feathers in her grasp, seizing his shoulders and kissing his cheeks. She nearly knocked his flowers and luggage to the floor. John took them from him. She flashed Étienne a broad smile and handed him one bunch of feathers. Her newly freed hand reached between her breasts and ended the screaming rock music in her earphones.

« *Chef, bienvenue. Tu m'est manquée,* » she greeted. "Exactly the man I needed." She smelled like lavender, but spicier.

"*C'est pourquoi* you not arrive *à l'aéroport*," he said.

"I was busy," she said. "You have to see the photos. I did some sketches."

Storyboards covered the walls. Bolts of fabric leaned against the wall. She drew the feathers across his jawline invoking an involuntary quiver from his inner thighs.

"I have an idea for the next campaign, an emerge from softness, wake from a dream, lose yourself kind of thing," Adelaide said.

Étienne looked to John and then to Galen. They shrugged. Adelaide pulled him across the room to a pile of feathers that had to stand twenty-five centimeters thick.

"You're in here," she said, "and it has to look like you're naked."

« *Nu? Dans les plumes?* » Naked. In the feathers. His shock made it impossible to utter the phrases in English. This didn't feel like an ad campaign. This could be considered seduction.

"You see, I'm the cat that ate you. That would be a killer campaign. Take your clothes off."

She ran the bundle of feathers down his ribs. He couldn't feel it through his shirt, but the light whoosh did something as disconcerting as his reaction to the earlier brush to his face. Perhaps he could blame fatigue from the red-eye flight, or maybe it was the presence of certain stimuli, such as breasts, feathers, thigh-highs and killer heels. Either way, Adelaide's flirtatious behavior spurred an involuntary response that was inappropriate for a business setting. The feathers fluttered from her fingers as she quickly unbuttoned his shirt.

"*Mon chou*, I cannot... now... this..."

His hand reached for her to stop her.

"It's okay, Et," she said in the sweetest of whispers. She pushed his hand to his side. The shirt fell. She seized his undershirt and whipped that over his head. "I know what the feathers do to you. I won't touch you. I promise. Now get your pants off."

He did as she asked and, in only his boxer shorts, buried himself in the mass of feathers. Their soft ends tickled his flesh and finished what her earlier teasing had started. The feathers barely hid his erection. He should have kept his clothes on. Adelaide crawled toward him on her hands and knees, facing the camera as Galen crouched low. She crept over him, her body slanted, her belly brushing across his abdomen. Joey dropped more feathers. Galen shot a few frames and showed them to John in the digital display.

"She's right," John said, "with some adjustments to the lighting in Photoshop, that's an incredible picture. I'll send it to graphics."

Adelaide rushed to the men around the camera. Étienne hid in the feathers camouflaging his erection. It happened with the blustery disorientation of a car crash. This didn't happen to him. This was Adelaide. These girls never appealed to him in that way. Even parades of them, nearly naked, didn't do this to him. Why would Adelaide? Joey knelt closer. A little too close.

"Do you need something, boss?" he asked. "A glass of water or some kind of assistance?"

"Cold water. Very cold."

Joey offered Étienne a hand. Étienne gathered his clothes.

"Cold water. Sure."

Joey smiled. "If you need anything else..."

"I am going to dress myself now."

Sometimes Étienne hated his job. Joey scurried away. Étienne promptly put on his pants. The thought of what Joey might have been thinking certainly helped lessen Étienne's condition. He went to Adelaide, patted her shoulder, and took his flowers and his garment bag.

"Put that bustier away. Shoot done, *mon chou*."

Étienne continued into the hall. He ducked into everyone's offices delivering roses. Adelaide was dancing in $100,000 lingerie instead of meeting his plane. Zélie could have met him at the airport. She knew when his jet would land. She left him there and didn't answer her phone. He called Adelaide in desperation and she suggested the cab. And what happened in the studio... How dare she make him uncomfortable like that and demand his nakedness!

Étienne met Seema at the photocopier. He gave her three roses. He bisoued her twice, but didn't actually touch her face. That would be too familiar. He clung to her arms a tad longer than proper. She had the same tantalizing scent as Adelaide. On her, it smelled less sweet. He detected lily-of-the-valley or maybe mint.

"You look..." he said, admiring the red and pink blend of her dress that accentuated her light brown skin. « *Magnifique.* »

"Thank you, sir. I hope you don't mind. The dress is Gucci."

« *Oui, je sais,* » Étienne replied. "Tom Ford. And the perfume is new... *captivante*."

Étienne released her and entered his office, tugging at the open door so he could hang his garment bag. On the hook, Étienne found a tuxedo, pressed and wrapped in plastic. Adelaide appeared still in the bustier. He gave her the remaining half-dozen roses, then leaned into her cheek for another kiss.

« *Est-ce que mon imagination ou...* »

He sniffed her ear.

"Every woman here has a smell of *Chartreuse*?"

"Do you like it?" Adelaide asked.

« *Chartreuse?* » Étienne repeated. "*Oui*. Very much. You drink? Now?"

Adelaide giggled. "No."

Étienne gestured to the formalwear on the door, first pointing, then turning his palm, until finally he brushed his curls from his face.

« *Le smoking,* » he muttered.

"Is it the wrong tux?" Adelaide asked.

He had forgotten something, an event. Did he miss it? Is this why Zélie hadn't met him?

"Montgomery Carter's anniversary," Adelaide said. "Tonight."

Étienne buried his hands in his hair.

"On a Tuesday? *C'est mardi, n'est-ce pas?*" he asked.

Adelaide nodded.

« *Merde,* » Étienne said. « *Quels raseurs!* »

"They're not so bad," Adelaide said.

He walked to his desk, leafing through messages. He noticed a newspaper with a prominent black-and-white photo. In the photograph, Adelaide played basketball with that girl she mentored and other *ados noirs-Américains.*

« *Qu'est-ce que c'est?* » he asked.

"I delivered the new uniforms and they invited me for a pick-up game."

"The press sees you, *comme ça?*"

He sat at his desk.

"It's good for the all-American image," Adelaide said. "Plus, that's a three-point shot I executed beautifully."

She dribbled an imaginary basketball and launched it into the air.

"*Sacré bleu. Les habits de sports?* They look large, and the shapeless, *mon chou.*"

"That's what you wear for basketball, Et," Adelaide said.

"*Mon Dieu*, what if you make yourself bad," he said, waving the clipping.

"You mean hurt myself. And I didn't. Besides, I don't bruise easily."

An unnatural silence fell between them, as if Adelaide had something else to say but stopped herself.

"I gave up basketball in high school because of you," she added, "but I belonged on the team, not running cross country. Remember, I'm five-foot eleven."

His mouth fell open. She plopped into the chair by his desk.

"Sorry," Adelaide said. "Maybe I did show off."

"How is Zélie?" Étienne asked, desperate to change the topic.

"So you never called her," Adelaide said.

He shook his head. He had meant to call, but there was so much to do. He had checked the samples. He met a few models and the directors at the *syndicat des couturiers.* He might get an early show this time, possibly Monday morning. That news required a round of drinks. Everyone knew editors attended the evening shows. No one went to morning ones. Plus, the "better" the designer, the later in the week he showed.

His mother, grandmother and brother wanted to see him. He arranged dinner at his favorite quiet café, the one harboring a talented young chef who made un-sauced langoustines melt on the tongue with nothing but secret spices. Over Chef Jules's delicate honeyed fruit salad, Étienne told Edmond, Edmond's wife Anne-Nicole, Maman, and Mémère about the baby. Something in his mother's eyes said she had suspected their troubled past, but she said nothing. His 93-year-old grandmother, Mémère, ordered a very expensive bottle of champagne.

"So, she's mad," Adelaide continued.

Zélie te fout en rogne, or as Americans would say, she was pissed off.

"This is why I have divorced..." Étienne said, leaning back in his chair. "Seema must call for the flowers. I visit Godiva. Have you had lunch?"

"I haven't had breakfast. It's 9:15."

« *C'est vrai,* » Étienne responded. "I am on Paris time. And I have a dinner party?"

Adelaide nodded.

« *Mon Dieu,* » Étienne said.

"Take a nap. You'll be good," Adelaide said. "As for Bas, that's another story."

"Speaking of tales of love... you and Galen... *ensemble?*" Étienne asked.

"In a way," Adelaide replied.

"You slept with him, *n'est-ce pas?*"

"I take the fifth," she said.

Étienne waved.

"*Je suis français...* I do not care about your Declaration of Independence."

"Constitution, Et."

He gestured again.

"*Bah!* Two hundred years old... you can use a new one."

Adelaide started for the door. Étienne rushed past her and retrieved a slender orange box with a brown ribbon from his garment bag. Adelaide accepted it.

"Hermès?"

« *Ouvres-la.* »

Easing the lid, Adelaide parted the tissue paper. She unfolded the pink silk carefully, revealing a whimsical red heart with flourishes. Adelaide draped it into position and tied the scarf with a perfect square knot.

"It's beautiful," she said.

She beamed. He stroked her cheek.

"What did you bring Bas?" she asked.

She toyed with the hem of the scarf and retied it. Étienne raised his eyebrows. Adelaide rolled her eyes and slouched like a seven-year-old.

"Nothing?" she said.

"Zélie looks terrible in pink."

"That's not the point," Adelaide said. "Et, she's your wife. Or she was. That's the point."

Oh yes, the infamous point, Étienne thought. Zélie usually had a list of points, which he forgot and violated regularly. He could hear her, her voice elevated and her words sharp: "The point is, Étienne, that you didn't even call me to let me know that your plane landed safely."

This required vanilla truffles and maybe roses, alstroemeria, lisianthus, Gerbera daisies, iris, lilies, freesia, or delphinium. If he ever gave up clothes, he could be a florist.

"You'll take the E train to your friends at Godiva. I'd keep walking up Fifth Avenue to your other friend's house," Adelaide suggested.

"Tiffany's? Is it that bad?" he asked.

She shrugged.

« Keep the scarf... » Étienne brought his finger to his lips, indicating a secret.

Adelaide removed the scarf. Étienne looked to the tuxedo. He scratched his head.

"Did you get a shirt laundered?" he asked.

"No," she replied. "And I didn't lay out your underwear."

She left. He searched for the Spring 2003 storyboards. He grabbed the quarterly report with up-to-date sales figures on Fall 2002. He pictured each sample destined for the runway and sorted the storyboards again.

He perched the top one against his mail tray and sighed, perhaps not over-stated, but a hearty sigh. This sketch paired a billowy sleeved, empire-waisted dress with a single-breasted vest. Adelaide had softened this collection. Would that make it sell here? But he would maintain his foothold in Europe, *non*? She had paired his conservative pinstripes with sheer, draping blouses. For the vests, jackets, skirts, and pants, they had toyed with colors: gray, pink, pale blue, and lavender. The sheer items came in white or beige with satin ribbon accents.

He needed lunch. He had errands to do. Étienne took the garment bag and the tuxedo. He stepped into the outer office.

On the sofa, Adelaide slept, iPod blaring, still wearing the *haute couture* crystal and diamond bustier. She lay on her back, one leg bent against the couch and the other on the floor. Arms similarly splayed, she had one across her thigh and the other between the cushions. Étienne threw up his arms, the garment bag sailing toward Seema. John walked into the room and noting Seema's impending danger, dove toward her, intercepting the garment bag as Seema ducked.

"There are more kind ways to kill me," Étienne screamed.

"What is it?" John asked, regaining his balance.

Seema's eyes darted. Étienne's finger stretched toward Adelaide.

« *Elle dort,* » Étienne said.

John's and Seema's eyes chased Étienne's finger.

"She's not allowed to sleep?" John asked.

"In that!" Étienne yelled. "Remove it. Before it wrinkles. To press the stones must come off. My fingers ached for days with the sewing done. *Pas encore, jamais.*"

"She's naked under that," John pointed out.

« *Je sais pas,* » Étienne replied. "We have seen her naked. *C'est mon petit chou.*"

Étienne knelt beside Adelaide. He stopped the iPod and removed her ear buds. Placing his hand against her leg, he shook her gently.

« *Chérie, mon chou...* »

She groaned. The hand across her leg moved toward the couch, planting itself firmly against the cushion as she shifted her weight.

« *Debout les morts,* » he said.

Her eyelids fluttered. Her eyes rolled, but she did not respond. Her body rippled, as a strange breath crossed her lips. Her arm tensed against the sofa. Her chest heaved. Her mouth opened. Her body repeated the motions again.

« *Mon petit chou, ça va?* » Étienne said.

He turned to his staff.

« *Une attaque?* Seizure? » he asked.

John shrugged. Adelaide's body arched. Her breathing intensified. Adelaide moaned. Her toes pointed. She gasped, as her hips raised and lowered against the couch.

« *Mon chou?* » Étienne's voice seared to a falsetto.

She panted. Her muscles twitched. Étienne didn't know if she could breathe. He grabbed her shoulders, seizing her head as he jumped onto the couch. His knee slammed between her legs. Her body went limp in his arms. As he lifted her, her eyes opened. Étienne had one arm around her waist, the other against the back of her skull. She dropped her iPod. Her mouth fell open as their eyes connected. She cried his name.

« *Ça va, chou?* » he said, his heart hammering.

Adelaide shook her head, rapidly. He dropped his hands.

"Et? What's going on? Why are you... on me?"

She squirmed from below him, separating their torsos, and covered her heaving bosom with her hand. He leaned away, acutely aware of how his thighs brushed hers. He settled beside her on the couch. She rubbed her eyes. Adelaide peered at John and Seema, then at Étienne. Étienne watched her from the corner of his eye with his hands clasped in his own lap.

"It is not... what it looks like," he muttered.

She nodded. "That's good. Because I'm half-naked, you were on top of me, and there were plenty of witnesses."

Adelaide offered the flat tones of an uneasy chuckle.

"I thought you had some sickness. What happened to you?" Étienne asked.

"Let's just say I know what happens on this couch after hours," Adelaide responded.

He flipped his bangs from his face and scratched his ear as he contemplated her remark. Étienne kissed her temple.

« *Il me faut aller,* » he said.

She nodded again. He patted her shoulder. He moved in to *bisou* her but decided against it. What did she know happened after hours? John excused himself. Étienne gathered his tuxedo and his garment bag a second time.

"Remove the bustier," Étienne reminded her as he left.

Once outside the building, he flagged a cab and headed for his apartment. Étienne leased a third-floor furnished walk-up in the garment district on West 35th near Jacob Javitz Convention Center, above a sewing machine repair shop and beside the bakery that baked his bread. He stopped in. The bakers asked about his trip.

In his apartment, he switched on the television and he fixed steak *tartare.* He debated whether or not to call Zélie. Would it make matters better or worse? He sat on the couch with the remote. He kicked off his shoes. Étienne checked his watch, half-past noon. He had risen at five a.m. Paris time, but he didn't think he could sleep. He closed his eyes and listened to the announcer. Where was a good soccer game when you needed one? When he got comfortable, the doorbell rang. He shut off the television. When he opened the door, Adelaide handed him a cup of coffee. He sipped it. He *bisou*ed her.

She had changed from the jewel-encrusted bustier to a sleeveless sheath with a single-breasted, two-button jacket, no vent, with a princess seam in the back, in a yellow shade resembling a not-quite ripe pear. He read his watch. It was nearly four. Étienne closed the door.

« *Merci,* » he said, jostling the coffee cup.

"It's half decaf. Et," she said. "About what happened this morning — "

He rose his hand.

"*Désolé, mon chou.* It looked... he said. "I may have... *envahir ton espace vital.*"

She shifted her weight uneasily.

"It's okay. It was just weird. Opening my eyes with you on me like that."

« *Navré,* » he said.

"I know," Adelaide answered. "If you need anything else..."

He shook his head. Another round of kisses and out he ushered her. Étienne retrieved a starched, white shirt and his diamond cufflinks. He attempted to comb his hair, tied his bow tie, and slipped his Louis Vuitton billfold into his pocket. He checked his reflection. *Pas mal.*

At the corner market, Étienne bought a dozen long-stemmed red roses. He didn't want to overdo it. He left his apartment early and flagged a cab.

"Upper West Side, Broadway and 73rd."

Étienne paused before entering the Ansonia. He gathered his strength as gazed up the round turret of the former Beaux Arts hotel. He nodded to the doorman and winked at the concierge. Zélie raved about her fancy apartment with the homey French touches, and the deal she got, more than 2,000 square feet for three million. He cringed at her pride. She had learned bad habits from the 'Ricains. A well-behaved Frenchwoman would never boast of such matters. *Ça alors*, he did not marry une *Française correcte.*

He entered the elevator alone. Étienne exhaled as the elevator climbed, two... three... Étienne's knees trembled ever so slightly, a reminder that he had wronged his wife. He never did it on purpose. The elevator door opened. He headed for Zélie's apartment. Étienne rang her bell twice before Zélie opened the door. She had one earring, a gold loop bedecked with polished amber. She wore an iridescent brown strapless gown, square across the chest.

She held the bolero jacket. He made it five years ago for a charity benefit. She smiled faintly.

"That's an old gown," he said.

Her smile faded. She retreated into the hallway, striding toward her bedroom. Étienne closed her apartment door.

"You didn't pick me up at the airport," he said.

Zélie pivoted. She parted her lips, but froze, instead reaching for the flowers. Beyond her shoulder, a new frame glittered between the courtyard windows. This hallway contained her favorite art pieces. The rest hung on the curved wall outside her living room.

He went to the new painting. His palm covered his mouth as his fingers touched his nose. Étienne instantly recognized the blue, green, and white strokes composing the girl in the white dress. He adored the peace within her pale face as she studied the nearby bird.

"*Young Woman with Sparrow*," Étienne said.

"Yes," Zélie replied.

"Is it real?" he asked.

Her dress rustled. The air moved. Something tapped the herringbone floor.

"That's it," Zélie said.

Étienne spun. She had thrown the roses. Zélie put her finger against his chest.

« Is it real? » she yelled in French. « Of course it's real, you fool. We have wanted this painting for a long time. »

Zélie ran down the hall, crying by the end. Étienne ran his fingers through his hair. He peered to the Berthe Morisot painting. When he was a humble tailor, Morisot, if not impressionism in general, had united them. And this oil painting... the serenity of this specific painting was the look he had found in Adelaide. Étienne followed his wife's sobs.

Étienne brushed his jacket across his hip as he crossed through the *porte-fenêtre* into the circular living room with Zélie's collection of perfectly matched Victorian chairs upholstered with the same microscopic burgundy floral. Zélie lay dramatically across a telephone bench. She hid her face beneath crossed arms. Étienne touched her back. She did not stop crying.

« *Qu'est-ce que c'est, mon amour?* » he asked.

He retrieved a red hanky from his pocket and knelt. He delicately dabbed the moisture from her cheeks and eyes. Her mascara left ashen stains on her face.

« Étienne, when did loving you get so hard? » she asked.

Étienne leaned into his heels. He flipped the hair from his face. He couldn't speak, because loving her had remained the easiest thing he'd ever done. She reached for the hanky.

« You don't need me, » she said. « You never did. That's why you didn't call »

Étienne let out a relieved half-sigh. If this was his offense, he could reassure her.

« I have always needed you, » he said.

« I'm old, fat, stubborn, and demanding," Zélie said.

« I love you, » Étienne said.

He placed his left hand in her lap. His wedding band stood out against the shiny fabric of her dress.

« You never did stop wearing it, » Zélie said, setting her finger against it.

He pulled her face to his. Her lips tasted salty as he kissed her, but even so, it felt good to hold her. She did not smell like Chanel No. 5. She had the same scent as the women in the office. On her, it smelled like an incredible blend of lavender, grass, and maybe pine, anise and vanilla. It filled him with excitement, until he remembered the dinner party. Étienne broke the kiss. Zélie ran her hands through his hair.

« Zélie, you are stuck with me. You are my wife, » Étienne said.

« No, I'm not, » she reminded him.

Her denial, and its intensity, stung like a slap in the face.

« Yes, you are, » Étienne said. « Why else would you keep my name? »

Zélie stood. She offered her hand to help him off the floor. He took it and rose. Zélie put on her jacket.

« Étienne, you're wrong, » she said, her voice elevated. « One day you'll realize it. I don't want to be your wife. My father was right. You're nothing but a womanizing jerk. If you had any idea how sick and how tired I've been. I'm too old for this. »

She adjusted the lapel of her jacket and marched away. Womanizing jerk? That he could ignore, but he repeated the other words to himself.

« I don't want to be your wife. My father was right. »

That hurt. Zélie brimmed with fire. Commanding in presence, brilliant, yet harboring this dainty girl who would lie against his body for hours, and she would say these terrible statements when she couldn't mean them, could she?

« Let's go, » she said.« Call for the car. »

« *Certainement pas,* » Étienne said.

She shot him her evil glare, but he didn't care. He needed to think. He sat on the bench.

« I am sorry if the baby makes you sick or tired or crazy, but how do I know if you only show me this false face? I have seen it all, Zélie. But you hide, »

Her eyes darted across the room. She didn't want to be late.

« This is not the time for a *tête-à-tête*, Étienne. »

« You have upset me, » Étienne said.

« You're upset? » Zélie retorted. « You flirt with every woman you see. You take them to lunch, buy them gifts. You lavish attention on the clients — »

« I do it to make them feel beautiful. For the business, Zélie! » Étienne hollered. « You had your violin and your ballet lessons and your nanny. I helped my mother iron your father's shirts! I learned to tat lace while you were at dinner parties. Your mother pinched my cheeks and patted my head as I helped my father pin her dress. My father offered me as your sister's dancing partner as if I were nothing more than a pet. My whole life that business has owned me! »

He looked into the fireplace. He couldn't see her and stay angry.

« I treat you like a real person, not like one of the rich women I dress, » he said. « You expected me to change, divorced me when I didn't. It does not matter. I can never stop loving you. I've tried. Every time you throw me out. »

Zélie walked to him.

« I'm sorry," she said. She pulled his shoulder and made him meet her eyes. « You're not entirely right. I never wanted you to change. »

The gray from her cheeks had spread to her jaw.

« Go fix your make-up," Étienne said, "and I'll call for the car. »

Étienne clutched his cellular. She paused in the doorway, giving him a cock-eyed look.

« And Étienne, » she said. « I won't throw you out tonight. »

She walked away. He didn't dial right away. He waited, thinking. Then he called for the car and retrieved the roses. He gazed at the million-dollar Morisot and, for the first time, recognized sadness in the girl's expression.

CHAPTER SEVENTEEN

Montgomery Carter lived in a sprawling courtyard estate in Oceanside with his latest trophy wife whose name Étienne did not bother to remember. Étienne hated Montgomery Carter, a man who had invested exorbitant amounts of money via Zélie's capable hands. Étienne also hated Long Island. With each wrong turn he orchestrated, like almost missing the Triborough Bridge and later heading for 678 North instead of South, Zélie corrected him. They listened to Debussy, which normally would calm him, but Étienne couldn't let go. Zélie didn't seem any more at ease. She fiddled with buttons, changed the music, and continuously fidgeted.

Étienne pulled into Monty's massive drive. The main house featured a spire and rooster weather vane above a triangular facade with a porthole window. A balcony over the entrance further competed for attention as the focal point.

« This house is probably 700 square meters, » he said to Zélie as the valet attended to the BMW 7-series in front of them. « Who does Carter think he is? King Louis the XIV? »

« Yes, Étienne. He thought, 'I want to build Versailles on Long Island,' » Zélie responded.

Étienne handed the S600's keys to the valet. He took his wife by the elbow and escorted her into the Carter home.

« Try not to flirt, » she added sharply.

The women at these parties received so little attention from these camels that if he even made eye contact, they'd flock to him the entire night. He did nothing but offer a few compliments. He understood their status, their emotional need. Étienne filled a role similar to trophy wife. At these parties, his purpose was to look good in a tuxedo. Their divorce didn't harm her reputation. These rich men had to ponder if they could end up in her bed.

These men shared a pivotal trait with Zélie: devotion to money. Zélie loved money. Her father had imparted to her that money could buy every-thing. Everyone needed a benefactor, according to Jean-Jacques Saint-Ebène, and with that came control. Every time they attended one of these parties, Étienne had to endure the boot-licking whores, *putains qui faisant de la lèche*, more appropriately translated as ass-kissers. He couldn't decide which image he liked better. Étienne walked behind her, giving her space for her disciples. They gushed over her gown, her jewelry, her eye shadow. Étienne fought the urge to chug his sparkling white wine.

Even with astronomical financial assets, these *putains* couldn't distinguish sparkling wine from champagne. This wine came from California. At least they hadn't bought local. He shuddered at the thought of upstate New York wineries bastardizing champagne.

Zélie looked stunning. Her laugh lines enhanced her character. Her hair, up at the sides, roamed down her back. Étienne's eyes fell to the curve of her breasts and to her waist. *Mon Dieu*, he loved the flare and drape of that gown.

Zélie talked to everyone. He talked to no one. They nodded politely. He returned the gesture. He overheard conversations, Dow Jones this, NASDAQ that. Étienne amused himself with the shimmer of Zélie's gown as it changed from light brown to gold. A white-jacketed waiter passed with miniature hot dogs in puff pastry. Étienne sighed, *'Ricains sots.*

A tall man with salt and pepper hair headed for Étienne. The man's tuxedo seemed dusty and frayed. Étienne stepped near Zélie, brushing his hand against her arm and bringing his body closer to her. The newcomer greeted Zélie then shot Étienne a condescending glance. Étienne straight-ened. What did this cow's hide want?

"Étienne," Zélie said, falsely sweet, "you remember Robert Cornwall."

Despite her normally flawless English, she spoke with a distinctly French pronunciation, transforming Robert into Ro-'bear.' Étienne raced through his memory, seeking names he never intended to recall.

"From our party," Zélie continued in the unnatural tone.

Bob from the bank, Étienne realized. Étienne extended his hand. Wasn't Mrs. Cornwall the one who emerged from the bushes drunk and nearly naked?

"You work with Zélie," he said. "Third in the firm for making money."

Zélie smiled. That meant Étienne got the facts right. Bob accepted Étienne's hand. Bob shook softly.

"Number two left the office. That leaves Basilie as my challenger," Bob said.

"She is your... boss, *n'est-ce pas*? She makes more money and she has the large title, no?" Étienne replied.

Zélie snapped her neck to face him with piercing eyes. Bob turned red.

"My wife attended your last show," Bob said. "She likes your work."

He must have threatened Bob, Étienne thought. Rich men always mentioned Étienne's occupation when uncomfortable.

"Is she here?" Étienne asked. "What is she wearing? La Perla *encore?*"

Zélie nudged him. She scolded him with her eyes. He shrugged. He didn't ask Nancy Carter strip to her underwear in his yard. Did Bob expect him to feel inferior because he worked as a tailor? What made banking and trading so noble? The navy blue suits they wore?

Bob called his wife. Zélie pinched Étienne's arm. The dig of her nails served as a warning. Nancy wore her silver-gray hair in waves. Her red dress draped around large breasts, easily twice Zélie's. The dress hung loosely around the middle, adding dimension to her waist and flat abdomen, a flattering gown for a firm woman.

"Vivienne Westwood," Étienne cited the designer.

Bob shrugged. The husbands never knew names.

« *Ravissante,* » Étienne said. "But..."

Zélie pinched him and he ignored her.

"...off-the-rack. *Madame is... très belle, à damner un saint.* With remarkable physical assets," Étienne paused.

Spotting a waiter, Étienne accepted more sparkling wine.

"I could do wonderful things to her," he stopped purposefully, angled his head, and gazed at Bob's wife.

Bob's eyes burned.

"Let me have her," Étienne continued, despite the constant sting in his wrist from Zélie's nails. "I will make a new woman."

Zélie jerked his arm.

« *Pardon,* » he told Bob.

The slant of Zélie's posture, the speed of her footsteps, and her squashed facial expression told Étienne what would come. Zélie dragged Étienne into an alcove. She whispered forcefully in French as she dug through her clutch. Étienne knew the game. He offered her his hanky.

« What was that? » she asked in their native tongue. « If you had stopped at ‹remarkable physical assets,› I could have let it go. »

She licked the edge of the handkerchief and dabbed at his lapel. Zélie used this for cover. She would pretend to clean his suit. It happened at every party. People must think him sloppy.

« But no, you go for the innuendo, » Zélie said. « 'I could do wonderful things to her' 'Let me have her.' Étienne, you disgust me. »

He brought his hand to hers.

« Did I misuse the English — »

« Don't even try the stupid Frenchman defense with me, Étienne, » Zélie interrupted. "You know exactly what you said. »

« He started it, » Étienne said.

« That's adult. He did not, » she replied. « Be good. For me. »

« Okay, for you. »

She kissed his cheek. Instinctively, he checked her lipstick. He leaned toward her face, about to kiss her perfectly painted smile, when tinkering bells punctured the glamour. They walked toward the dining room. The room smelled of hot grease, meaty and fleshy, smoky like bacon. There was an animal mounted on a metal frame in the fireplace: a pig carcass, an apple in its mouth, and slices of pineapple adhered to its skin.

« *Mon Dieu*, » he said.

« Étienne, » Zélie warned, reading his mind. "Not another word."

« That's a pig, » Étienne pointed out *en français*.

She read the place settings.

« They are roasting a pig in their fireplace, in August. Have these Americans no sense? »

« Étienne, » she said. « Don't. »

Zélie found their seats. He pulled out her chair.

"A pig on a metal stick! For a black tie party!" he ranted.

Zélie adjusted her skirt and Étienne pushed her chair to the table.

"You call that a 'spit,'" she clarified.

"All the pig," he said as he joined her at the table. "You do not show all the beast. *Tratata! Ma foi!* It's a pig."

Zélie lifted the menu card from her plate. She rested her finger against the line listing the plat principal.

"I believe it's Hawaiian roasted pig," she said.

"I wear my black tie, *queue à pie*," he said, gesturing toward his tails, "eating hors d'oeuvres from silver trays, with Nambé porcelain and they serve..."

« Étienne, please, don't. »

« Ham! » Étienne yelled in French.

Murmurs flooded the room.

"You had to yell «*jambon*, »" Zélie said. "Other people in this room speak French."

"They think I like the ham," he replied.

The staff brought the first course, bitter greens and mandarin orange slices with lime vinaigrette. Zélie took one bite, hid a sour expression behind her lace-lined napkin, and replaced her fork. A pumpkin soup arrived for the second course. Who serves pumpkin in August? Étienne scoffed. Eventually, some disproportional American caterer in a white outfit and a puffy hat entered the room with a large carving knife.

"I suppose he thinks he's a chef," Étienne said.

"I suppose," Zélie replied dryly.

Everyone received pig with a slice of pineapple, cherry, and curve of kale. Étienne held a knife in his left hand and his fork in his right. The clank of utensils filled the room.

"Good ham," Étienne said.

Étienne stole Zélie's cherry from her plate. A barrage of waiters cleared the table and poured the white dessert wine. Waiters delivered a dense cheesecake with apples and caramel. Étienne slivered his, barely pulling cheesecake onto his fork. He made his dessert last. Zélie wolfed hers and poked his.

"My wedding vows said nothing about sharing desserts," Étienne remarked.

"Maybe that's why you're divorced."

He stabbed a generous bit of cake. He brought it to Zélie's lips. She eagerly consumed it, whimpering. She smiled slyly. She dotted her lips with her napkin. When their hosts invited everyone into the study for coffee and after-dinner cocktails, Zélie apologized to Mrs. Carter.

"We must go, Melinda," Zélie told her. "Étienne returned from Paris today..."

"Of course," Mrs. Carter replied.

Étienne didn't recall the name Melinda, nor did he remember Montgomery's current wife as young and blond. Maybe he confused her with the last one. Étienne took Mrs. Carter's hand, kissed her cheeks, and said softly, "*Merci* for an evening *joyeux*. The Hawaiian roasted pig... *très bien, Madame.* »

Mrs. Carter placed her hand on his back.

"It was our pleasure," she said. "Sorry you can't stay."

Outside, a valet left Étienne and Zélie at the landing of the huge staircase. Étienne smiled at his wife, her hands gripping her elbows. Étienne couldn't resist her. His lips touched hers. Her mouth yielding under his made him forget everything else. She stopped him.

"Not now, Étienne," she said. "I refuse to fall victim to your charm."

"You prefer your anger," he said.

Zélie twisted toward the approaching Mercedes. They got in. She avoided eye contact.

"I can't believe you commented on the pig," Zélie said.

"I had to do something," he replied, "to redeem myself, if only to you."

Étienne loosened his tie after a few kilometers. Zélie nestled against the window. A stray curl wove across her face.

"I told my family," he said. "You can imagine Mémère's... excitement."

Zélie laughed. "Yes, I can."

"Did you tell your family?"

"No," she said.

He didn't know whether to push the topic. He waited. Finally, he decided to broach it.

"Why not?" Étienne asked.

"I'm not ready," she answered. "I haven't quite adjusted to the idea myself."

He continued down Grand Central Parkway. Traffic was quiet.

« Étienne, I don't know if I want to have a baby with you. »

"How can you say that?"

"You're late for everything, easily swayed by your own desires, and you don't even call your wife."

"I thought I don't have a wife," Étienne replied.

"You don't," she corrected herself.

" 'Easily swayed by my own desires'? I can sway you with those desires — "s

"Not now, Étienne," she interrupted. "Your adeptness with women's hearts, and bodies, will not serve you here."

"Zélie, say that like you mean it in your apartment later."

Her chin jutted forward as she gnashed her teeth.

"I do not wish to fight, my love," Étienne said gently.

Zélie reclined her seat a few degrees, kicked off her shoes, and curled her feet by the gearshift. Étienne tickled her toes.

"I have a confession," she said.

He waited for a torturously long time.

"I almost had an abortion."

Étienne depressed the clutch and shifted into fourth, but the car slammed to a halt in the slow lane, vibrating oddly. Horns blared around them. He swerved onto the shoulder.

"You just hit the brakes and shifted into neutral. The car's an automatic," Zélie pointed out.

"An abortion?" he said, as he turned his blinker on. "Did the doctor suggest it?"

Étienne placed the transmission in drive and merged onto the highway.

"No," she answered. "I was scared. I'm still terrified."

This time, he pulled to the shoulder on purpose.

"Zélie, if anything happens to you — »

"Don't," she interrupted him.

They sat silently.

"What stopped you?" he asked.

"Father Patrick... and the fact that... Étienne, I want this baby."

"I do, too," he told her, "but you are more important. You know that, yes?"

"Of course," she answered, nearly inaudible, without looking at him.

He returned to the road and focused on the traffic. As the kilometers droned by, he wanted to say something more but couldn't. She didn't talk. She hummed to the Mendelssohn, as she normally did. It sounded like Joshua Bell, one of her favorites. The disc changer switched to another musician. Norah Jones followed and Zélie sang softly with her. When the car stopped at her building, she turned to him.

"You're coming up, *n'est-ce pas?*" she asked.

"I'm easily swayed by physical pleasure," he warned.

"I know," she said.

She looked twenty years younger beneath the streetlights, eyes twinkling and smile playful. He followed her to her apartment. She unlocked the door and reset the alarm. Étienne folded his tuxedo jacket over his arm.

"Your alarm code remains my birthday," he said.

She nodded.

"I could take you for everything," he remarked.

"You did," she replied dryly, "a long time ago."

Étienne hung his jacket in the hall closet and lost himself in the new painting.

"Hold me?" Zélie asked.

Étienne wanted nothing more. His arms circled her waist. She rested her head against his shoulder and slipped her palms onto his shoulder blades. He leaned his cheek into her hair, reveling in its coarse yet soft texture and the light pineapple scent from her hair. He swayed, leading her in a dance where only they could hear the music.

He wouldn't change any of it, not a second.

"Would hot chocolate help?" he asked.

Zélie raised her head and pecked his lips.

"You know how I feel about your hot chocolate."

Give Étienne bittersweet chocolate, enough sugar to make it smooth, and farm-fresh whole milk and he could bend any woman's will.

"I'll bring some," Étienne said. "Remove that dress."

She departed. He slipped into the kitchen. He lit the gas and set a saucepan of milk to simmer. Stirring with a wooden spoon, Étienne dissolved the sugar. He grabbed two gold-rimmed bowls, their original wedding dishes. He traced the edge with his index finger. Étienne sighed. He reached behind the coffee beans to where Zélie kept her favorite Swiss chocolate. He unwrapped it and stole a nibble. He removed the milk from the heat and sprinkled in broken bits of chocolate as he stirred. When he liked the consistency, Étienne ladled it into the bowls.

Étienne untucked his shirt and lowered his suspenders. He brought the bowls to Zélie's bedroom. He joined her on the queen-sized bed. Draping chiffon dangled from heavy carved orchid hooks. Zélie accepted the chocolate and sipped, reclining on pillows. The *portes-fenêtres* looked east to Amsterdam Avenue at 73rd Street toward Central Park. Zélie wore an ivory-colored summer nightgown with lace on the straps and at the hem. He'd made her the same nightgown for more than twenty years. It suited her and it didn't hide much. Exhausted physically and emotionally, Étienne didn't care.

« *Chéri,* » she said, between drinks. "We can't live like this."

He didn't respond. He couldn't. He drank his chocolate.

"Do you realize why I took this job in New York?"

Étienne shrugged.

"Paris held too many memories," Zélie said. "I never forgave myself for divorcing you."

They drank hot chocolate. Étienne removed his shoes and socks.

"I thought fame and fortune would change you," Zélie said.

"Did it?" he asked.

She smiled and shook her head.

"Your success changed me. I am jealous," she said. "Jealous of how the world loves you. Everything I did for your company and I am the invisible *Madame d'Amille*."

Étienne finished his chocolate and rested against the pillows. His mind drifted. He worried he wouldn't have the energy to brush his teeth. He stripped to his boxers.

"People worship you, Étienne," she said. "You treat them with that same magic you used for me. I thought I was special — "

"You are," he interrupted her. "How can you doubt it?"

"Because you tantalize every woman you meet if not with poodle — "

"Not the blasted puppy again..."

"Goddamn it, Étienne. Every day you seduce a bastion of women."

"Zélie, I bought her a poodle. I did not sleep with her," he said.

"I'm not talking about who you fuck or where your dick ends up!"

Wouldn't that be the same place? He bit his tongue, literally. One wrong word and she'd expel him. His eyes struggled to stay open. He had slept three hours out of the last twenty-four.

"Étienne, I think we need marital counseling."

Étienne finally laughed, mostly from fatigue and partially from disbelief. *Merde*, he thought, he couldn't have a serious discussion now.

"Shouldn't we get married first?" he replied.

CHAPTER EIGHTEEN

To avoid any more discussion in his jet-lagged state, Étienne agreed to visit Zélie's therapist. *Et voila!* A few days later and here he was, surrounded by mahogany paneling in Dr. Millicent Ungerstat-Miller's office. Étienne crossed his arms and focused on the so-called doctor in the straight-backed chair. He surveyed the room again, to avoid Dr. Ungerstat-Miller's analytical, bespectacled stare. The office windows, if she hadn't positioned Étienne in the darkest corner, probably offered a reasonably impressive view of Greenwich Village. Étienne couldn't believe he had agreed to this.

The day had started well. He had a solid sleep last night, ate a civilized breakfast with Zélie, and continued preparations for October's show. John promised d'Amille fashions in American *Marie Claire* and *Vanity Fair*. Then, *Vanity Fair* called to interview him. The magazine had named him and Zélie to the Best Dressed Couples list. Adelaide appeared with a bottle of spiced wine, a gift from Galen. She suggested they trash it, but Étienne couldn't resist a taste.

"It has no label and the cork isn't sealed," she protested.

Étienne shrugged and drank a partial glass. It had an extremely earthy bouquet, and the spices had more zest than the typical cloves, nutmeg, cinnamon or mace. Zélie arrived for lunch and Adelaide left. The two women did not speak, other than Zélie stating perfunctory thanks when Adelaide said she would alert Seema to their "private meeting," which over the years had morphed into code for quickie sex. That was how Zélie made sure he went to the shrink. Zélie devoured him, shared his cab, and walked him to the door.

Dr. Ungerstat-Miller looked studious, her thick brown hair weighed nicely against her Manhattan wardrobe of black-on-black. She had the right diplomas on the walls and a politically-correct hyphenated name. Before he settled in his chair, Étienne decided that he hated her.

"Basilie told me you didn't want to come," she said.

"I do not like *la psychothérapie*," Étienne replied.

"Then why are you here?"

"My wife persuaded me," he answered.

"You mean your ex-wife."

Étienne didn't respond.

"You are divorced, Étienne."

"I am *Catholique*. I do not divorce," Étienne replied.

"Basilie said you never married in the Church."

« *Une bagatelle..* »

He didn't know if she spoke French. Frankly, he didn't care.

"Basilie tells me that your father died unexpectedly," the doctor said, "when you were in the army. In Africa."

« *C'est vrai, oui.* »

Dr. Ungerstat-Miller cast him an odd glance, as if enticing him to say more. He didn't. Perhaps she wanted to hear that he resented his mother and grandmother for not providing for themselves or that he harbored negativity toward his brother for not helping. His mother could have provided for herself. No one could starch a shirt like Maman. And Mémère had taught Étienne how to make a woman's dress.

"I wanted the business," Étienne said.

The doctor scribbled on a spiral-bound pad.

"Do you like your career?"

« *Mais oui,* » he answered. "The body is a canvas très compliqué. With clients like Madame Saint-Ebène, I love it."

"Madame Saint-Ebène, Basilie's mother."

« *Oui.* »

The doctor asked more questions about the business. The doctor scratched on her tablet.

"Do you think Basilie is jealous of the models?"

Étienne groaned, tossing his hair from his face.

"She says I flirt with the clients, not the girls. No, she is not jealous of the girls."

"Why not?" Dr. Ungerstat-Miller asked. "Everyone knows the detrimental effect of the fashion industry on the modern woman's body image."

"I did not do it. *Pas moi*. Professionals like you talk of the... the lack of..." Étienne carved an hourglass shape with his hands. "American designers made the waif. Not Europeans. *Pas les Français*. Some designers consider the art first, the woman second. It is a business for the gay men, *n'est-ce pas?*"

"Are you homosexual, Étienne?" she asked.

Étienne's arms returned to his chest, his eyes narrowed as he leaned forward in his chair. He reminded himself it was not polite to break the shrink's nose with a psychology textbook.

« *Non,* » he said. Étienne smiled and chuckled. "Some hope."

"I can't help you if you continue to joke, Étienne"

He would relish the opportunity to send this woman waltzing.

"I don't need help."

"Basilie told me you brought a man home from the army."

"Didier? He knows the sewing. I needed help for the business," Étienne explained.

"And he's homosexual."

"Most of my employees are."

Silence.

"What did you do in the army?"

"Drove a car. Shot things in the desert. Smoked. Drank," he said. "Do you know the *khat?*"

"Pussy?" she said in a tone less than professional, as if taken aback.

"No, the leaf. You chew."

"Were there women?"

"Whores? In the desert? The government provided a few. Do you know what they do to girls in that region of Africa?"

"Female genital mutilation?"

He nodded. "I think that is the English. My service made me realize many things, even before my father is died."

"That women weren't playthings?"

He couldn't respond. It sounded too much like Zélie.

"Tell me about Adelaide Pitney."

Étienne thrust his hand into his hair. Here it comes. No longer talking of 'the girls,' or the men, now the discussion turns to Adelaide.

"What to say? She is the face of my house."

"Would you consider Adelaide attractive, Étienne?"

"Faces... *moches*... the ugly face... don't sell clothes."

"Do you find Adelaide attractive, sexually?" the woman asked.

The recent photo shoot popped into his mind. Her fingers unbuttoning his shirt. The feathers against his bare skin. Her looming there, her body brushing his.

"She is the child," he answered.

"Not anymore, Étienne."

Their time was running out, Dr. Ungerstat-Miller told him. She closed her notebook and asked him if he usually projected so much hostility. Étienne laughed. No one had ever referred to him as hostile.

"Doctor, I want my wife happy."

"I don't doubt that, Étienne," she said. "Did you ever ask what would make her happy?"

"Zélie? No problem telling people what she wants," he replied.

"So what do you think Basilie wants from you? Why did you come?"

He reflected on the question. It wasn't one he could answer easily. When Étienne left the doctor's office, his head spun. Had Zélie said he had been a bad husband? What did the doctor mean by those questions about Adelaide? He needed to drive. He called for the Ferrari. He almost hailed a cab, but decided to walk. It would help clear his head.

Étienne sighed. Why did the doctor care about his father? His sexuality? Had Zélie suggested these as problems? He cringed. A shadow blocked his path. Étienne escaped his thoughts in time to avoid striking a scrawny tree.

Why did he agree to this? Why? Because he needed her to trust him. He needed to open up to her. They had to talk about their past, those poor babies, because with this new pregnancy they couldn't ignore it any longer. Fifteen years was long enough.

The first time, the first miscarriage, that was nothing. Étienne knew Zélie hadn't felt well. She rubbed her back repetitively, knuckles gouging the flesh near her spine. She wrapped herself in a blanket as she leaned into the windowsill. The tears came next. When she dropped the blanket, tiny polka-dots of blood spotted her pants. They called the doctor, and Zélie insisted on washing. Étienne spent the rest of the day waiting: first for her, then the doctor, for the rapid heartbeat which never came, and the worst, for Zélie's body to expel the leftover "products of conception." Their first apartment never regained its happy atmosphere.

That was twenty years ago, maybe less. Étienne had reached the garage. He didn't offer his normal array of handshakes. The valets, one buffing off the last remnants of wax from the Ferrari's fender and the other presenting the keys, accepted their tips while Étienne did nothing. They lingered, perhaps too long, probably expecting an off-color joke or hoping for an out-of-season handbag for their girlfriends.

He slammed the door of his Ferrari and turned the key. He closed his eyes to squash the memories. On his 28th birthday, the next time it happened, Étienne woke when a hand squeezed his shoulder. Zélie said nothing, but her nails tore his skin. Her grip tightened. The bright sun washed into the palatial windows of their new *Place des Vosges* apartment. Blood drenched the sheets and Zélie knotted her body, failing to pull herself from the mess, as her knuckles dug desperately into her back. No polka-dots this time, not at 19 weeks.

Inside the Ferrari, fifteen years later, Étienne covered his face with both hands, pushing his palms against his eyes. Recite the primary movements in art history. Translate Paul Personne lyrics from French into English. Remember what happened on your desk at noon. Go to Djibouti, but don't let yourself relive 1987. Étienne exhaled. If only he could forget his son Christian.

He took out his phone. Zélie hadn't mentioned her plans, so he left her a message regarding his whereabouts. He headed to Pennsylvania, replaying recent events in his head as he drove.

"My father was right."

"I don't want to be your wife."

"So, what do you think Basilie wants from you?"

"But do you find Adelaide attractive, sexually?"

Étienne exited Route 80 near Hackettstown, N.J. His nerves couldn't tolerate the traffic. His concentration faltered. Where did his marriage go wrong? Étienne accelerated. He could not control Zélie. With everything he had given her, how could she really think she had to compete with clients or models? And did she worry he would pursue Adelaide?

A summer rain cascaded as the sun shined. The large droplets crashed into his windshield. The tires of the Ferrari slid on the wet blacktop, but Étienne downshifted to compensate.

Did Zélie need reassurance? Was it really about puppies? He would call her, cook, carve time from his schedule, anything. He needed her. She had to trust him and depend on him, especially with the pregnancy. The windshield wipers scraped the glass. He pulled the car into the tollbooth, lowered his window, and handed the officer a wrinkled dollar.

"Crazy weather," the toll collector said in a boisterous voice that competed with the thunder. "Heavy rain's coming."

Deep gray clouds swallowed the sunshine. Lightning divided the purple and black clouds. The river reflected jagged bolts on rippling waves.

"If you're heading down River Road, be careful. It floods," the toll collector said.

« *Merci.* »

Étienne raised his window and merged to the exit. The clouds dumped more rain. Étienne turned on his headlights and turned under the bridge toward River Road. Étienne eased the car over the railroad tracks. As he shifted and accelerated into the straight-away, Étienne thought less about the storm and more about Zélie.

The therapist had implied so many issues. Did Zélie consider other women a threat? Did she think he lusted after the models, or teenaged girls, or Adelaide? The speedometer climbed as he passed the electric plant. The rain fell harder. Étienne drove faster. The road curved. The tires slid. Thunder cracked and lightning fragmented the sky. Rain bombarded the windshield. Étienne couldn't see. Thunder boomed. Lightning streaked the sky and illuminated the wilted corn.

With every blast, a new vision of Étienne's wife haunted him. The road turned. Étienne placed his hand on the shifter as he turned the steering wheel. Lightning snapped again, startling Étienne, and the car jerked.

Headlights approached. He gripped the steering wheel steadily, praying he wouldn't slip into the oncoming lane. If he slammed on the brakes, the tires would lock and hydroplane. His car zoomed toward the yellow line as his headlights caught gold nuances on the opposing car. Étienne assessed the car's front end.

The shape of the headlights and the grill belonged to a Mercedes. In mere seconds, he knew by the length of the sedan that his Ferrari would pummel his wife's Mercedes. Zélie must have come searching for him. No one else in this area drove an S-series sedan. Hands fumbling across the steering wheel, Étienne forced his car the opposite direction. The back end spun, so he downshifted, and the car thrashed into the cornfield. At least he had avoided Zélie.

I am a stupid, careless son-of-bitch, he thought.

His car penetrated the narrow strip of wildflowers between the road and river. Étienne tapped the gas pedal lightly to give the car more power against the mud. The car heaved, but the back tires stumbled over the remnants of an old stone row. Étienne bumped the accelerator again. The deluge of rain intensified as the car broke free.

A looming black shape appeared directly in front of him. Metal crunched as the car abruptly stopped, throwing Étienne into the windshield. The engine squealed and went silent. Étienne's rib had wedged into the steering wheel. He took a deep breath, but the pain that ripped into his lungs made him stop. He could not extract his head from the spider web in the windshield, so he leaned into it instead. Glass ground into his flesh.

His right hand pushed between his chest and the steering wheel. The pain in his chest soared with each movement of his fingers so he directed his hand to his temple, gliding over tender flesh wet with blood. Dizziness made the cracks in the windshield shift in and out of focus. The rearview mirror dangled in front of him. He tilted it and honed in on the blood coating his face and the glittering of the glass embedded in his skin. His right eye wouldn't open, and the eyelid drooped. The mirror tumbled to the floor.

His chest ached. His stomach throbbed. His heart fluttered with confusion. Étienne had to get out of this car. Had he hit something? Had something hit him? Had he hit Zélie? He hadn't. He had avoided her. He knew that much.

Étienne lifted his left hand, and piercing pain shot up his arm. Étienne fell against the seat. *Quel emmerdement*, he thought. The storm continued, but softer and distant. The air possessed a pale violet tint. The rain tapered. It seemed darker than it had a moment ago. Had he passed out? Étienne gazed out the fragmented windshield. A tree trunk stood where his hood should be. The accident had removed the car's left fender, replacing it with a large tree.

Putain, j'ai bousillé ma bagnole, he thought.

Where was his phone? It wasn't on the passenger seat where he normally tossed it. It must have fallen. Étienne carefully worked his upper body across the cabin. Pain racked him, made him stop a few times to rest. Don't be a sissy, he scolded himself. With his right hand, he searched the floor by the passenger seat and found the phone, barely within his grasp.

He stretched, pain stabbing his chest, but somehow he got it. He hit the power button, but the phone didn't turn on. The battery had separated. He moaned. His throat constricted. His breath would not come, and the struggle for air amplified the pain in his lungs. His hand swept across the floor, until finally he discovered the battery under the passenger seat.

He propped the phone against the steering wheel and snapped the battery into place. It took several attempts one-handed. He paused. Étienne adjusted the phone to dial with his thumb. He scanned the recent calls for Adelaide's number. The phone dialed, promptly beeped twice, and ended the call. He tried again. Same thing. He smacked the phone against the steering wheel. He had no reception.

The metal of the car hugged him closely. He had to get out. This was not the time for claustrophobia.

« Hail, Mary, full of grace, the Lord is with thee, » he prayed. « Blessed art thou amongst women... »

Étienne put the cellular in his shirt pocket. He moved, thinking he would propel himself somehow by his feet. When he shifted his left leg, more unbelievable pain coursed through him. His knee burned with a fire unlike anything in memory.

« *Aielle!* »

Étienne crossed himself and continued praying. How did he get into these situations? Étienne looked at his left arm. It rested limply across his thigh. Any time the arm even tensed, the pain from his hand screamed. Blood covered his legs. He couldn't tell where exactly it came from, but obviously the accident had smashed his legs.

With every attempt to move, sweat poured from Étienne's body. The front of the car, now the middle, had him trapped. If he fell to the right, could he use his good arm to pull himself? He flopped over the gearshift, taking a heavy poke in the ribs. His limbs and chest shrieked with the pain of the sudden movement, knocking his breath from him. Étienne, c'était très stupide.

Étienne vowed on his father's immortal soul, if he got out of this one, he would buy a sensible car, maybe that Volvo. Something with seatbelts. And he would go to Mass. Like a real Catholic. Although he had recently gone to Mass, maybe that was the problem.

« Our Father who art in Heaven... » Étienne prayed.

He latched onto the passenger door handle and threw himself. The gearshift continued to probe his torso and the pain in his ribs escalated, pain bringing the contents of his stomach into his mouth. He spit it out, and it ran down his shirt. Étienne settled back in the driver's seat. The air grew colder. Darkness swallowed him. The rain didn't seem as heavy, though steady. The pitter-patter of the drops against the car offered the only relaxing aspect of the whole situation.

Étienne retrieved the phone. Maybe he could find a signal if he waved the phone. The cellular displayed one reception point. It always showed one point. He needed two. Why did he have this damn phone if it didn't work in an emergency? He extended his right arm toward the back of the car and hit send, silence as it dialed, then beep... beep... disconnect. He repeated the process to the back left, the back right, left front, right front. Nothing. Étienne leaned forward until his head pushed against the patterns in the glass. He called Adelaide's number again. Static filled the connection but it rang. He hoped it would hold.

"Hello?"

It was Adelaide.

« *Mon chou?* »

"Et? Is that you? I can barely hear you."

« *C'est moi.* »

"Where are you? Bas called two hours ago..."

"Zélie? *Dieu merci.* She... safe? *Où est-tu?*"

"The house, your house," she said.

"*Au Pennsylvanie?* Thanks *dieu.*"

"Et?" she shouted. "I can't hear you."

She was less than five kilometers away. She could help.

"Et?"

"*J'ai besoin...* Help me, *chouchou.* I hit... "

The English jumbled.

« *J'ai bousillé...* »

"*Chef,* are you hurt?"

« *Ouias!* »

"Étienne, you had an accident? That's it? Galen, call 9-1-1. Talk to me. Et?"

"*Pas anglais,* » he whispered.

Her English didn't make sense anymore. Relief filled him. He could go to sleep. The pain and dizziness and rain could go.

"Étienne!" she yelled.

Adelaide would take care of everything. She always did.

"Étienne, we called the police..."

The pain didn't bother him anymore. He would close his eyes and wait...

CHAPTER NINETEEN

Adelaide screamed into her cell, compensating for the bad connection. She yelled because she knew the accident had left Étienne in pain. Her hands shook as she clutched the phone. She repeated Étienne's name as she scrawled Basilie's number on Galen's napkin.

"Call her," Adelaide demanded.

Galen ignored her request. She snatched his phone and dialed 9-1-1. Adelaide wanted to hear Étienne's voice again, but he did not respond. She refused to hang up the phone. Adelaide scanned the room for her purse.

Étienne must have left the city after his appointment. This wasn't a fender bender or he would have called earlier. Basilie called two hours ago, expecting him to be here. Étienne hated Manhattan. He thought it dark, grungy, and smelly. He hated the skyscrapers impeding the view of the sky. He hated the modern architecture of squares and glass. He especially hated the uniformity of the people.

Adelaide knew when Basilie called that Étienne's appointment had upset him. That was also why she hadn't worried. He drove for hours under such circumstances. She scanned the living room frantically for her car keys. Then she found them, in her hand. Galen stood by the window. She returned his phone.

"What's going on?" he remarked. "Did he drink the wine?"

He reached for her keys. Adelaide pulled away. He seized her wrist, prying her fingers.

"Let go of me," she snarled.

"There's nothing you can do. You called the ambulance. We were in the middle of something," Galen said. "Let Basilie take care of this."

"Excuse me?" she said. "This is Étienne we're talking about."

"No," Galen replied. "We were talking about your magic. That's more important."

Galen squeezed her wrists so hard, her bones couldn't move.

"Nothing is more important than Étienne."

With a frantic twist spurred by adrenalin, Adelaide freed her wrist.

"This is why you were supposed to drink the wine," Galen said.

"You drugged it!" she screamed into Galen's face. "What did you do?"

"He wasn't supposed to drink it!" he screamed back.

She dashed downstairs, through the hall, and down the other stairwell. Galen chased her. She raced from the house. She ran to her Benz and jammed the key in the ignition, but he jumped into the car beside her.

"Why are you even here?" she screamed.

"I'm trying to tell you!" he replied. "I laced the wine with hallucinogens, to guide you with your magic. I told you not to drink it until I got here."

"You didn't tell me it was drugged. You didn't say, 'Hey, this is dangerous.' You said, 'We'll open this later.'"

She floored the accelerator and zipped through the driveway in reverse. The clouds blocked the stars. The rain had ceased but dampness clung to them. She shifted into drive.

"The wine was for you," Galen said. "Did I tell you to share? How much did he drink?"

"A taste."

"The effects will be minimal."

Adelaide drove the speed limit, watching the road for debris, skid marks, or Étienne's car. She needed to find him, to know how badly he was hurt. The deep darkness terrified her, because it lessened her chance of finding him. The Benz's high beams spread into the road's shoulder.

"Do you see anything?" she asked Galen.

Adelaide focused on the road as her car traveled over a knoll. Like a projection against the stormy sky, Adelaide recognized a hazy image of yellow metal amid familiar wildflowers, the triangular lot near the railroad trestle and the river's rapids.

"He's around this next corner," Adelaide said.

The Benz continued toward the cornfield, the stalks like shadowy skeletons. Adelaide noticed a rut heading into the field. A police cruiser was parked on the opposite side of the road. She pulled alongside it. Red and blue lights flashed against the trees. Flares burned between the yellow stripes in the road.

"I told you. He's here," she said. "It looks like someone called the emergency squad. No thanks to you."

Galen gripped her arm as she tried to leave the car.

"You don't want to do this, Addy. When you're upset, your powers go haywire. Kait explained that to you. Neferkaba will kill you herself if you hurt anyone."

"I won't hurt him," she said. "I would never hurt him."

"You can't help it," he said.

Adelaide needed to go to Étienne. Étienne needed her. Adelaide stepped out of the car. She headed straight into the underbrush and the tall grass, toward the red beams. The mud trapped her shoes. As she moved, the quagmire sucked. A several hundred-year-old oak tree blocked her view. Adelaide's eye followed the tree to its base.

Shards of yellow metal littered the ground. The frame of the car had twisted around the tree, its trunk pressed against the driver's side door and the rest of the battered frame. The hood had crunched into the windshield. A tire sat near her. The front of the car was smashed into the engine compartment. Adelaide pieced together broken bits of car like a puzzle to recreate the accident: the left axle in a pile of plastic shards of headlight cover, the head-sized cracks in the windshield. She smelled the oil-and-gasoline mix of the aftermath.

"Oh my God," Adelaide cried.

The awful, mangled, and stunted abstraction of the car seemed like sick modern sculpture. Hair hung in the broken glass of the windshield. Adelaide fell. She didn't feel the coldness, wetness, or thickness of the mud, now against her pants' knees. It spattered her clothes. One bare foot and her knees sank in the muck. Adelaide pictured Étienne trapped in that broken car.

"Oh God," she said again.

Galen stood in the distance, his eyes bright across the dark distance. Adelaide managed to stand. Rain drizzled. Alone, she approached the open passenger door.

Adelaide's eyes narrowed. Basilie did this. The busted shell of the Ferrari mirrored the twisted status of their lives. Étienne offered Bas everything and it wasn't enough. To think Basilie had dragged him to counseling. Everything he did, Étienne did for Basilie. His world revolved around her. But Basilie didn't see it. Adelaide knew their problem. Bitch.

A police officer stood at the driver's side window with a flashlight. He moved to the back of the car. Once on the passenger side, the officer disappeared. After a few seconds, the flashlight beam flashed over Étienne. Adelaide had almost reached the car. The police officer mounted the flashlight on the dash, its light fixed on Étienne's face. A gash marred Étienne's forehead. Blood streamed profusely down one swollen-shut eye. The cop reached to support Étienne's head. The cop was a state trooper, who wore an angular hat with a plastic cover like a shower cap. He stared at Adelaide. The storm had soaked her clothes. She crossed her arms to hide how the shirt clung to her chest.

"Miss, this isn't the place for you," he said.

Étienne opened his good eye. Adelaide crouched, working past the cop and into the cabin as best she could.

"Lady, what are you doing?"

"I'm family," she said. "Is he okay?"

Étienne's lips parted. A whisper of a sentence escaped.

« *Les mains, desquelles sont au corps,* » he said. "*Aielle! Zut.* »

"Do you know what he's saying?" the officer asked.

"Nothing important," Adelaide replied.

Something tumultuous brewed within her. She could taste it, disgustingly sugary like cotton candy. It billowed and hiccoughed around her stomach. Effervescence tickled her insides. Her hands pulsed.

« *Chou? Dieu merci.* »

"You let me know if he says anything I need to know," the cop said.

Adelaide nodded. She forced herself farther into the car, but the trooper shook his head and tilted it, directing her away.

« *C'est moi, mon vieux,* » Adelaide said.

« *Ma femme ... Je l'ai vue,* » he paused every few words and winced as he inhaled. « *A-t-elle mal? Est-ce que je l'ai heurtée?* »

Adelaide puzzled over his questions. 'I saw my wife. Is she hurt? Did I hit her?'

« *Non, chef.* »

Basilie is in New York, she told him. The ambulance arrived, washing the scene with more red rotating lights. The cop looked away. When he did, the strangeness in Adelaide's body peaked. Blue light, like translucent mittens, lined Adelaide's hands. It trickled its sinewy wisps toward Étienne. Soon, it connected them. It struggled to reach his forehead. Adelaide turned her hands to facilitate contact. The cop watched the emergency squad. Adelaide didn't budge. The scratches in Étienne's head expelled glass as her blue light circled him. Adelaide gasped but suppressed the noise so the cop wouldn't notice. The flesh surrounding one cut on Étienne's temple wiggled into position and rejoined. The gargoyle fairy-thing appeared and slapped at her fingers. The swelling in Étienne's eyelid dwindled and his eye opened. Several men rushed toward the car, toting miscellaneous equipment. The chaos broke her concentration and the blue light dissipated.

"It's an up and over," one paramedic yelled.

A pear-shaped man switched places with the cop. His gloved hands took Étienne's head.

"He's all yours," the officer said.

The police officer turned to Adelaide.

"Come with me," he said.

"Étienne needs me."

"No," he said. "Come on. They're gonna cut him out. They're gonna strap him down. He's gonna scream like a girl. You don't want to see it. Especially if he's busted up as bad as it looks. He's lucky he's in the car and not on the ground. Or in that tree."

Behind her, Galen snickered. Although he stood near the road, nowhere near them, she heard him. The scowling cop had one hand perched near his shoulder on the microphone of his radio. The other arm rested on his thick black belt.

"Your friend has got to learn to drive like a normal person. He can't be coming down here with his fancy sports car, and his New York plates..."

A fire engine parked by the ambulance. More men and more equipment headed for Étienne's car. The officer walked toward his cruiser. He motioned for Adelaide to follow. She did. She heard metal cutting metal and willed herself not to look.

"He's going to lose his license," the cop said. "I gave him his last ticket. This will get him careless driving."

"You don't know he was speeding," she snapped.

"Oh, yes I do," the cop said. "I could make it reckless driving."

Adelaide kicked the ground with her remaining, ruined Prada T-strap slide. As the trooper predicted, Étienne wailed when the squad pulled him from the wreck. The blood-curdling bellow compelled Adelaide toward the sliced Ferrari. She couldn't stay away. The EMS guys strapped Étienne to a backboard. The firemen had gone. The rain drizzled. The pear-shaped man came to Adelaide as the other paramedics lifted Étienne into the ambulance.

"You his wife?" the man asked.

His gloves colored his hands a ghoulish tint. Adelaide shook her head.

"You family?" he asked.

She nodded.

"You speak his language? I need information," he said.

Adelaide nodded again. The pear-shaped man offered her his hand, helping her climb into the ambulance. Adelaide slid onto the bench. Another man tended an IV in Étienne's arm.

« *Chou?* »

"He keeps talking about his shoes," the guy across from her said.

"Not his shoes. It's my nickname," she explained.

"And 'zally.'"

"Zay Lee," she corrected him. "His wife."

The man kept looking at her.

"You look familiar," he said.

"Yeah. I'm a fashion model."

He laughed. The other man, beside her, fired off questions from the computer screen. He began with the easy ones, like name (which she had to spell, twice) and birthday (3/14/1959). He asked for Étienne's social security number. Adelaide looked at the guy blankly.

"He's not American. He doesn't have one."

"If he works in the country and doesn't have one, he's illegal."

Adelaide shrugged. Maybe he did, maybe he didn't. She told the man Étienne's next of kin (Basilie), medication (something for high blood pressure, a beta blocker), allergies (penicillin) and blood type (she had to ask Étienne and he clearly said « *oh, negatif* »). Adelaide wanted to touch him. An ache built as she fought the desire. She could fix him. She knew she could.

When they reached the hospital, after a preliminary examination, the nurse left Étienne and Adelaide in the emergency room promising that she would return to take Étienne for x-rays. The man in the ambulance had cleaned Étienne's cuts. Adelaide pushed Étienne's hair away from his face. His eyelids opened. She swallowed the lump in her throat and wished her heart rate would slow. Big penis, she thought, and immediately laughed at the ridiculousness of it. Étienne touched her fingers with his good arm.

« It will be done soon, » Étienne said in French.

Adelaide held her hand over his waist. The doctors thought Étienne had broken his hand and his wrist. How would he be able to sew? His leg looked bad. The staff told her his knee would probably require surgery. The paramedics thought he had flail chest, whatever that was, but no other signs of internal injuries or other trauma.

She moved her hand toward his foot without really thinking. Warmth flooded her. Blue light consumed her. Adelaide welcomed the blue light. The blue light was soft, calm, and warm. She understood the blue light. It healed. Her hand slowly crept near Étienne's ankle.

Something tugged at her earlobe. The gargoyle whispered, but she couldn't decipher the words. If she closed her eyes, she could see Étienne's bones in her mind. The leg looked like a simple break, clean, not even all the way through. Her hand progressed to his knee. The crushed knee absorbed the blue light. She conjured more. Inside the knee, Adelaide found dust, pulverized particles instead whole bone. She envisioned them as jigsaw puzzle pieces. They floated together seamlessly. The blue light faded. A chill enveloped her. Her stomach grew woozy. She had to sit, but, she knew. The knee was whole.

After a brief rest, she repeated more magic. The blue light soaked into his broken ribs. His body took her light, sapping her energy until, again, she could no longer stand. With each second of blue light, Étienne breathed easier so she made herself stay put. Fuck doctors, she would heal him. She needed to replenish. She needed more energy. She needed cake, beer, and a burger.

But Adelaide didn't have a chance. Even within the chaos of the emergency room, Adelaide could distinguish the pounding of chunky heels against the hospital floor. It was fast. Adelaide knew it well. It belonged to an angry Basilie. She emerged in the doorway.

"Where is the bastard?" she asked. "He certainly knows how to scare me."

Étienne had regained some color. Adelaide squeezed his good hand. Basilie stepped closer and winced a bit when she reached him. If Adelaide didn't know her so well, she never would have noticed.

"What's wrong with him?" she asked.

"Broken wrist, probably a broken leg, something with his chest," Adelaide answered.

"So I'm stuck here."

"You make it sound like an obligation," Adelaide said.

Basilie looked into Adelaide's face.

"You don't have to stay," Adelaide said, the words gaining volume. "I don't mind waiting, making sure he's alright. I came this far with him."

Basilie didn't say anything, just kept giving Adelaide this puzzled expression.

"You know, since he called me and I called you," Adelaide said.

Anger poured from Basilie toward Adelaide. Adelaide needed to step away.

"What's taken you?" Basilie asked.

Basilie mixed languages. In French, 'What's taken you?' roughly meant 'What's the matter with you?'

"If you don't want to be bothered," Adelaide said, "go get a cup of coffee or something. We don't need you."

"We?" Basilie repeated.

Basilie jutted her nose toward Adelaide's. Basilie's breath smelled like butter-rum Lifesavers.

"Étienne may consider you his little *protégé,*" Basilie said, "but don't you ever lump yourself with him like that."

The hair on Adelaide's arm prickled.

"This is your fault," Adelaide said. "He spends half his time chasing you and the other half running away."

Basilie's arm jerked from the elbow to strike Adelaide. But she didn't.

"Get out!" Basilie yelled.

Basilie's arm twitched.

"Go ahead, Bas. Hit me. It won't change anything," Adelaide said. "Take him back or leave him alone. I'm tired of the speeding tickets, the accidents, and listening to him cry over you. I've listened for ten years."

Electricity rippled through her. Her hand reached for Basilie, but when their arms met, the power of Adelaide's emotions fizzled and stalled.

"I am so sick of you!" Basilie screamed, losing her trademark cool. "I am sick of what he's done with you!"

"What he's done with me?" Adelaide repeated. "He doesn't do anything with me but treat me like his little doll. I'm not a person to him."

"You spend eight hours a day together, often more. He tells you everything, things he won't even tell me. He calls you, when he doesn't call me."

Adelaide flinched. Everything Basilie said was true.

"You eat lunch on the studio floor," Basilie said. "You help him pick the girls. He dresses you, and you can't deny that he puts his hands on you."

Adelaide didn't want to talk about Étienne's hands on her.

"You're so caught up with the glamour that you don't see how it all hinges on you, not me," Adelaide said.

"You're young and you're perfect," Basilie said. "How can I compete with that?"

"There's no competition, Bas," Adelaide sputtered. "You're the one he loves. He has no idea who I am. I've tried, Bas!"

A security guard asked them to quiet themselves.

"You've tried what, Adelaide?"

"I've tried to make him forget you."

With that, Basilie asked the security guard to escort Adelaide from the hospital.

CHAPTER TWENTY

Fairy godmother, as Adelaide had dubbed Kait, had brought her from the hospital to Étienne's weekend house. Now fairy godmother loomed at the bar, guarding Étienne's coffee pot. Adelaide wanted some, but Kait said caffeine would not help. Adelaide slumped in the poufy white chair, her feet toasty thanks to the small fire. She held her arms around her midsection, her stomach flip-flopping from Kait's teleportation.

"I want to die," Adelaide said.

"You're coming down."

Kait had found her curbside at the hospital. She didn't have a way home.

"It's my fault," Adelaide said. "I drove them apart."

"Bullshit," Kait said.

While Adelaide moped, Kait rummaged through the cupboards.

"You said it yourself," Adelaide said. "I'm all woman. I've always loved him, Kait. This magic, my feelings, it drove Basilie to divorce him."

Kait slammed the cupboard door.

"A thousand modern conveniences and do you think I can find a single fucking cookie?" Kait yelled.

Adelaide pointed to the hutch.

"Side door. On top of the silverware," Adelaide said.

The antique hutch squeaked as Kait opened the door.

"Silver silver?" she inquired.

Adelaide nodded. Kait snatched an unopened package of sandwich cookies.

"Oreos?" Kait asked.

Adelaide nodded as Kait stroked the box of silverware.

"Et loves them, but won't admit it. Too American," Adelaide replied. She scrunched her face as Kait kept rubbing the silverware case. "What are you doing?"

"Nothing," Kait replied, closing the door.

Kait shredded the Oreo wrapper and handed her four cookies.

"Eat," Kait directed. "Not exactly cakes and ale, but it will do."

"I really can't," Adelaide whined.

"Yes, you can."

Adelaide flipped the cookie across her fingers. She brought it to her lips. She sighed. She hadn't eaten Oreos in years. The chocolate and cream smothered her tongue in richness.

"You never sabotaged their marriage," Kait said. "That's your naiveté talking."

Adelaide peeled the lid from her next Oreo and sunk her tongue right into the cream.

"I would do anything for him, Kait. Anything."

"I don't doubt that."

"I healed him," she said. "His knee, they would have had to replace it. I fixed his ribs. And his eye... He might have lost that eye, but I can't tell her. Basilie can't know."

"Go to bed. You need sleep," Kait said. "Then we'll talk. Do I need to baby-sit?"

Adelaide shook her head.

"I'll be back," Kait said. "I can help you, but first you must sleep."

"Okay."

Kait disappeared. Adelaide finished her cookies. She trudged to her room, exhausted and worried. Adelaide checked her cell. No one had called. She chucked it onto the nightstand. She changed into a nightgown and fell asleep without even slipping beneath her comforter. She woke a couple hours later to find Galen by her bed. He had a silk-covered block in his hands. She scurried back toward the headboard and curled against her pillows.

"What the Hell are you doing here?"

"We have unfinished business."

"A normal person would call, on the telephone, in the morning."

"I was worried."

"Yet you didn't follow me to the hospital to give me a ride home," Adelaide remarked.

"You shouldn't have gone," Galen replied.

"He needed me."

"No," Galen said. "You needed him."

Galen put the box on her bed. He left the room. She ran her thumb over the fabric, soft with age. Each time her hands caressed the fabric, images sunk into her brain. They didn't make sense: Galen in a rage, a fire, a person blown backwards with the force of an explosion. She forced the ugly thoughts away.

When she did, warmer visions came. She 'met' a healer who had a gentle soul and an earnest smile. Adelaide couldn't label it, but they shared something, something distant... Galen returned with a saucer of milk that he set on the floor.

"You tried to heal him," Galen said.

Adelaide broke her aimless stare and repetitious stroking of the package.

"How would I do that?" she said, feigning ignorance.

"I watched you. I saw how your fairy had to keep it in, so Neferkaba wouldn't notice," he said. "You crossed the line. You're dangerous. Unstable."

"From the freak that keeps showing up in my house."

Galen met her eyes, his pupils condensing into tight dots that made her skin burn. A name popped into Adelaide's mind: Maeve. The face from her vision reappeared, smiling. Her smile cooled the uneasy heat generated by Galen's stare.

"Galen, who's Maeve?"

Galen unfurled the silk from the block.

"Don't touch things that aren't yours," he remarked.

He pressed the fabric flat. He lifted an oversized deck of cards decorated with Celtic knots.

"Tarot cards," Adelaide said.

"Meadhbh's. You really shouldn't use your powers to spy."

"Why do you have them?" she asked.

"She was more or less my mother."

"More or less?"

"My parents deserted me, probably because of my fire magic. I'm 400-years-old, Adelaide. You didn't blend in if you were different. Not in those days."

He lifted the massive deck in his boyish hands, shuffled them and fanned them with expert flourish. He cut the deck into thin sections, rapidly altering their sequence. He placed the deck on his open palm and reached for her hand. He positioned it above the deck.

"We were superstitious. We left milk for the fairies."

Adelaide stretched her fingers. Electricity snapped between them and the cards.

"Take them," Galen instructed.

She gripped the deck, its weight awkward. Meadhbh's face continued to smile on her.

"Shuffle," Galen said.

Adelaide couldn't do it with Galen's expertise. Her fingers didn't seem long enough. She shuffled them by cutting, again and again. Meadhbh nodded, gesturing for her to keep going.

"I want to know what's going on," Galen said. "How could you go to Étienne when I told you not to? You didn't drink the wine, but I have your blood. You should obey me."

Her hands froze.

"What was the wine supposed to do? Did it cause the accident?"

"Keep shuffling," he said.

He said the words harshly. She rearranged the cards more.

"How do I know when they're done?" Adelaide asked.

"You'll know," he said.

The cards' weight multiplied in her hands. Meadhbh thrust her hands into a stop signal.

"They're done," Adelaide said.

Galen accepted the cards. He tossed cards one-by-one. They fell so quickly she couldn't decipher the pictures.

"You're sensitive. You admired your parents. You're jealous of your sister."

Cards cascaded from his hands like petals in the breeze. One card showed a woman with a peaked hat on a throne. While the label looked French, Adelaide couldn't read it.

"It started around puberty," Galen said.

The next card depicted a young man holding a fish in a chalice.

"A young Étienne," Galen said. "A dreamer. You followed him because..."

The card featured a map with continents and oceans.

"He promised you the world," Galen said.

Galen continued flinging cards. Typical stuff, really, Galen recounted her modeling career and her temptations. Adelaide rested her chin in her palms.

"But then a storm came."

Basilie came home and tore out his heart, Adelaide thought.

"You were there that night," Galen said, "when she left him."

"I got home after. This isn't my future. This is the past."

"That's how the cards work," he threw another card. "You comforted Étienne."

The card displayed a man and women entwined, nude bodies washed by sunshine. There was no sunshine. Adelaide had found Étienne in the closet. She brought him Chartreuse and listened to him. She wanted to make it better. That's all she ever wanted for Étienne.

"It was a successful time for the business," Galen said.

Galen turned the next card. His forehead crinkled. Adelaide looked at the picture, a hairy beast man with horns.

"Adelaide, how old were you?"

"Fifteen," she answered.

"And what, exactly, was your relationship with Étienne? »

Her heart skipped several beats and crashed hard against her chest. What did Galen see? What did the flabby creature with the chained naked people mean? Fire consumed them and the woman covered her face in either shame or sadness. She recognized the French: *diable*, or devil. Was it Hell?

"What does that ugly thing mean?" she asked.

"You caused it," Galen said. "You were having an affair."

Her index finger wagged. A tide within her pulled her toward the floor. Her feet and her arms swam toward Galen, wishing to drown him. But she couldn't do anything.

"Étienne would never take advantage of me."

The river, outside the house, three stories below them, crashed against the bank with unusual fervor.

"I never said he took advantage of you," Galen said calmly. "You never slept with him?"

She hid her face. The current of the Delaware quieted.

"After she left," Galen muttered. "Of course."

"Étienne would never cheat," she said. "I won't listen to this."

She walked deliberately toward the bathroom. With those damn cards, Galen would figure the whole thing out. No one knew. No one. Not Étienne. Only her. Not even her friends. Her body quaked. She entered the bathroom. The faucet roared with water, startling her. She reached for the cold water knob. How had the water turned on? When she rotated the handle, it didn't move. It was off. Yet, water poured from it full-bore.

"Adelaide, come back," Galen commanded.

She turned. Her feet obeyed before she could revolt. The water in the bathroom ceased. Galen pushed her hair from her face. She jerked, but couldn't move.

"Tell me, Adelaide. What did you do?"

"She left," Adelaide said.

"Basilie," Galen clarified.

"Yes," she said.

Galen rubbed her forehead and directed his stare there, which she knew from Kait would lead him deep into her brain. His touch paralyzed her. She wanted to turn her head to the side, but couldn't.

"Go on," he said.

"I slept with him. Once. He doesn't know."

"How can he not know?" Galen asked.

"You've seen Étienne drunk. He gets frisky," Adelaide said. "He thought I was Bas. He thought it was break-up sex. He blacked out and doesn't remember."

Her foot dug circles in the carpet.

"Can I have a cigarette?" she asked meekly.

Galen prepared one.

"I don't buy it," he said. "A man knows his wife, Adelaide."

"He has no clue."

"How did you do it?" Galen asked. "A man knows his wife, her smell, her feel. You can't fake that, not the Great Rite. Especially not at fifteen. Show me," he said.

His free hand squeezed her chin and forced her to look him in the eye. Her mind disconnected.

"Adelaide."

Her muscles softened. Why resist, she wondered. She trusted Galen.

"How did you fool Étienne into believing you were Basilie?"

"It's none of your business, I shouldn't have said as much as I did."

He slapped her, the cold flesh of his palm pounded her cheek. He seized her head, his hands pressing against her ears and his gaze stared deep into her eyes.

"Tell me what I want to know," he demanded.

She chuckled. The side of her face stung and she couldn't bring herself to care anymore. So she told him. Adelaide told him what he wanted to know.

It happened March 12, 1993 after the ready-to-wear show. She had arrived at the apartment later than Étienne because she stopped for coffee and pastry, her normal routine when she could still eat pastry. She had a chocolate tart with hazelnut filling. The chocolate tasted bitter and the filling had the perfect blend of milk chocolate and sweetness. She'd never had another like it after that day —

"Addy, I don't care about the chocolate," Galen interrupted.

"But it's the chocolate I've been trying to replicate."

"Étienne, Adelaide. I want to know how you managed to have sex with him."

"I'm a bad girl, Galen. I never should have let it happen."

She sobbed.

"What happened when you got back to the apartment, Adelaide?"

"Well..."

She couldn't find him at first, so she assumed he and Bas went for drinks or got sidetracked in the car. The apartment had this heavy air in it, and small things seemed out-of-place, like Basilie's desk had no papers. She normally kept a ledger on the desk, with the checkbook and this expandable file folder for their receipts. There was no ledger.

"Adelaide!" Galen snapped. "I don't care about the ledger!"

"But, see, then I turned to go to my bedroom and finish packing. I had an afternoon flight from CDG the next day and the painting was gone. The Van Gogh."

"They had a Van Gogh?"

"Still do," Adelaide said. "It's a really ugly vase of yellow flowers. That's when I assumed they'd been robbed..."

The checkbook. The ledger. The painting. Obviously someone had stolen them. Adelaide recounted how she ran from room to room. No one had touched the kitchen. Her bedroom also escaped unscathed. When she reached the master bedroom, Basilie's closet door was open and the closet itself had nothing in it. Nothing. She climbed over the bed and scooted across the duvet cover on her knees.

In the middle of the empty closet, Étienne sat on the floor, his legs pulled to his chest, head to his knees, and arms locked across his calves with an Air France envelope crunched in his fingers. She swung her legs off the bed and dropped to the floor beside him asking what happened, if he'd seen the robbers, if he was hurt. The mop of dirty blond curls rose and revealed his empty expression.

« She left me, » he said.

He stammered and fumbled with his words and Adelaide blamed her poor French. Basilie had left him, two days before his birthday, on the day of the show, a day before they had planned a romantic weekend in Algiers.

« Algiers? » Galen interrupted.

« I guess they used to meet in Algiers during his conscription. Weird, I know. »

She continued her story. Fifteen-year-old Adelaide didn't know what to do. She laid her hand on his back and this insurmountable sense of despair knocked her backwards. She raided the liquor cupboard and handed him the Chartreuse bottle. She leaned against the closet door smoking cigarettes, which occasionally he shared, and he drank the entire bottle. He fell against the closet floor and stared at the vacant rod.

« I was the master of break-up sex, » Étienne said in a barely intelligible mish-mash.

He rolled over and placed his arms under his head as his legs curled into a fetal position.

« Amid the sorrow, the body needs a farewell. It loosens the pain of the heart. I wouldn't be here, » he said. « I'd be there. »

He pointed across his shoulder to the bed and then his arm veered toward the window, but she got the idea.

« Maybe you should go to bed, » she suggested.

« You are too young to understand, » Étienne said as she grabbed his hand and hoisted him to his feet. They stumbled backwards and nearly hit the footboard. Adelaide shoved him toward the mattress. « I can't let a woman go without tasting her one last time. »

Adelaide wondered if she understood this correctly. Between her French and his mumbling, he either said what she thought he said or maybe he said something about the blood of a baby bear. She knelt below him and untied his shoes.

« After I made love to her, I would bring her again with my mouth. »

This certainly isn't vocabulary they covered in French class, Adelaide thought.

He fought with the buttons of his collar. When she finished with his shoes and socks, Adelaide helped him. His hands turned to his pants. He struggled with those just as badly, but she didn't interfere. She processed what she had heard. If Basilie were here, right now, even knowing that she would leave him, he would want to fuck her and go down on her? Like, one last time? She filed that in "things I did not need to know about my boss."

« It would be desperate and beautiful and sad, and potentially violent, » Étienne babbled. « And I want it more than anything. »

Tears appeared silently and without fanfare. One tumbled to his jawline and clung near his chin. Another hung from the side of his nose. Without thinking, she kissed it. He laughed, but it was detached response. I wish I were Basilie, Adelaide thought.

Seemed like a better position to be in than hers. She would go home tomorrow, where her girlfriends would gossip about who was doing who in cars and on couches. The whole school gave her that look, thinking she went to Paris and drank champagne and had this incredible French lover, not that she ever implied that. Well, maybe the champagne part.

That scared off the nice guys, attracting the sleazeballs like Jimmy Fields who loved to grab her ass or pinch a tit in the hallway. Seriously, Adelaide wouldn't get a single earnest prom invitation unless she gave some signal that she was putting out.

And here's Étienne, pining over a woman who left him, wishing he could touch her one last time. If Adelaide could make Étienne believe she were Basilie, then maybe she could lose her virginity with Étienne and not some creep and not in the back of a Chevy.

"Whoa!" Galen interrupted. "You were a virgin."

"Why else would I want it, Galen?" she replied.

Once again, Adelaide returned to the story. In it, she went into the master bathroom and splashed water on her face. If she wanted to do this, she had no margin for error. She exhaled. Please, she asked some unnamed god, make him believe I'm Basilie. She slipped into the hall from the other door and returned to the bedroom. She paused in the doorway, straightened herself and mimicked Bas's footsteps.

"Zélie?"

« Étienne, » she said, mimicking the stern quality in Basilie's voice.

Believe I'm Basilie, Adelaide willed. Believe. I'm Basilie and I came back.

Thank goodness she hadn't turned on any lights. Perhaps the darkness would aid her. Étienne lifted himself awkwardly to his elbows. Adelaide sat on Basilie's side of the bed. Étienne seized her, set his mouth on hers, his taste complex and conflicting like the liquor, his tongue reaching into her, awakening a unfamiliar stir in her that made her gush.

« Come here, » he demanded.

Adelaide obeyed, walking to his side of the bed. His hands grabbed the hem of her shirt and pulled it toward her head, his lips dropping to her breasts. He gorged himself with her flesh while his hair tickled her chest. His hands slipped into the back of her waistband. His lips returned to hers. She responded to his kisses clumsily. He threw his legs to the floor.

He wore no pants. They had been discarded. He pulled her into his lap, forcing her legs to straddle his. Their bodies rubbed as his hands grabbed her hips, guiding her up and down against his erection, barely hidden beneath his boxers. She couldn't believe how hard he was, how clearly she felt him even through her jeans, and how these motions knocked her senseless, transforming her into a ball of fire.

Étienne threw her against the bed and flung her pants from her. He peeled her socks free, licked from her ankle to her knee and toward her inner thigh. She didn't know what to do, what to think, or what to expect as he deftly freed her from the flimsy panties she had worn for the show. The brief pressure of his hand made her tremble.

He kissed her again, then sucked one breast as his hand explored the other. His tongue danced across her flesh and traced the stiffness of her nipple. Her body bucked against him in some instinctive response, her hips arching toward his groin, her chest lifting toward his mouth and his hands. She wanted more. She wanted everything. She'd never felt so electrified or so lost.

Étienne's hands disappeared while he gave the nipple a tiny tug between his teeth. Adelaide moaned, and he broke from her chest. The bareness of his legs against hers revealed that he had removed his underwear. She panted, her heartbeat racing. Her virgin folds throbbed. Her nerves twitched with fear, in part with anticipation but also due to her deception.

His bare flesh rippled heat across her. It was too dark to see more than his slender shape backlit by the light under the door of the master bathroom. She wished she could see it. She'd never really seen a penis before and she was curious, how big was it? How long? Did it stick out? Did it stand up?

Étienne gripped her thighs and kissed her mouth again, his fingers squeezing around her thighs and under her bottom, until he had one butt cheek firmly in hand. He nibbled her ear and covered her in quick imprints from his tongue and lips across her neck and to her collarbone.

Still standing, he nudged his body between her knees and her legs slid over his hips. He leaned into her, and his body thrust into hers. She gasped, unprepared for how it burned when he filled her. Adelaide hadn't figured that something that normally fit inside a pair of pants could suddenly occupy so much room. She thought she might cry, but then he pulled away. He didn't exactly disengage, she felt something in there, but she had more space and it didn't seem so dry.

She exhaled. He returned to her, penetrating her as he had before but with less fire. He rocked and pushed against her in a place neither good nor bad. He moved faster, his body sticking to hers, and pounded into her so hard that her body skipped along the bed. She bit his shoulder against the pain of it.

His rhythm softened. His arm wound behind her back and pulled her up against him and into the bed at the same time. He claimed her earlobe between his lips and gently pressed into her, again and again. She became aware of a fleshiness inside her, and a certain ridge that if she angled her body it, it relieved the pressure and intensified it.

Little noises escaped his mouth and sailed into her ear. She wrapped her legs across the backs of his thighs and grabbed the flesh of his butt. She slammed against him harder. She had lost the ridge, so she wiggled and squirmed, desperately seeking it.

She didn't find it. She didn't have time. A wave started, rippling from the inside. Simultaneously, heat burst from the outside and exploded inward. A thousand silky fingers tickled her underneath her skin. Étienne groaned. His thickness inside her was reduced to something minimal and wet. He kissed her flesh, rapidly devouring every piece he could reach. He withdrew, and Adelaide shook, unfamiliar with the aftermath.

A man had been inside her.

Étienne kissed her knees. He licked her thighs and brought his tongue against her, parting her folds, tapping her still throbbing clit with it, and then bearing down long and wide. It blinded her with its intensity: the coolness of his tongue after the heat of his body, the direct stimulation, his mouth against areas that had never been touched before, let alone licked. She screamed, in a primal way, not sure if people could survive feeling like this or where it would lead. He continued his affections and she quivered with every one until she experienced something ten times more powerful than before.

Étienne laid his head against her shoulder, and with his breath moist against her breast, went to sleep. Adelaide waited for the strength to return to her muscles. Recovered, she crept into her own room and sneaked out the next morning before he left his bed.

A decade later, Adelaide told the story to Galen.

"Uther and Igraine," Galen said. "The oldest trick in the book."

"Huh?"

"Uther was King Arthur's father. Uther lusted after Igraine, the wife of a prominent duke. A war started. You don't know this story?"

She shook her head.

"I swear people were smarter when they were illiterate," Galen snipped. "Uther convinced Merlin to transform him into Igraine's husband, so that he could sleep with her."

"Did he?" Adelaide asked.

"He did, and Arthur was conceived. Igraine never knew the truth," Galen said. "You made yourself appear as Basilie."

CHAPTER TWENTY-ONE

Thank goodness Étienne was out of the hospital. He had gone to the week-end house to recuperate and Basilie hadn't barred Adelaide from there. She couldn't. Adelaide served as Étienne's professional proxy. So Adelaide gave up her life to tend to Étienne's. Like this second, ending the phone call and driving the car. Adelaide hated having to constantly rearrange her life like this. She closed the phone. She had rearranged her appointment with Taneisha again. Tossing the phone toward her purse, she nearly rear-ended a red Camaro. Adelaide rested her forehead against the steering wheel. The weekend had evaporated.

How could she have told Galen the truth? Would Galen tell Bas? Or worse, Étienne? Adelaide had scarcely eaten. Her stomach rebelled if she tried. Even Orangina tasted like chalk. She needed a cigarette.

Kait was right. She could only beat Galen if she believed she could. Right now she believed Galen would never manipulate her again. The tea, the wine, the cards. Adelaide knew she was stupid and it had to end.

In Étienne's driveway, with the rearview mirror as a guide, Adelaide applied her standard lipstick. She could use a Milky Way. She stepped out of the convertible. While she felt like a mess, she looked together. Her beige eyelet sundress blew against the car. Joey had tied the wide pink ribbon under her chest immaculately.

She retrieved the cat carrier. Zut snarled, mad from the car ride and madder yet that Adelaide had left her alone in the city all weekend. Adelaide set the carrier on the ground and reached for the remaining items: her iBook, new books in a plastic shopping bag, cigarettes, magazines, movies, and Oreos. With the laptop case on her shoulder, and bags dangling from her arm, she grabbed the cat.

Inside the kitchen, Basilie rinsed coffee mugs. Adelaide placed the carrier on the floor and released her frazzled pet. The cat pattered up the stairs. Adelaide dropped everything else in the white chair. Basilie took a dishtowel, dried the mugs, and organized them in a line.

"Bas? Everything okay?" Adelaide asked.

Basilie slowly turned. She wore a wide-striped blouse and the same pants from the hospital Friday night. Her hair lay flat, which meant she hadn't washed it. Basilie replaced the towel.

"Bas, did something happen?"

"No," Basilie said. "*Pardon*, I am late for work."

"It's Labor Day," Adelaide said.

"I don't stop for American holidays," she replied.

Basilie climbed the stairs. Adelaide fished her new carton of cigarettes from the Barnes and Noble bag. She dropped into the chair and lit one, sucking slowly on the first drags. The relentless headache that had plagued her since Saturday morning lingered. Cigarettes stopped the uncontrollable shaking. She had slept most of the weekend. Adelaide blew smoke at the ceiling.

"What are you doing?"

Adelaide jumped. Basilie had returned with her black crocodile briefcase, a 'vintage' d'Amille handbag, a hybrid of Hermès Birkin and Louis Vuitton Laguito.

"You're smoking again," Basilie observed.

Adelaide clasped the half-finished cigarette between her fingers.

"Not in my house," Basilie said.

Basilie walked by on her way out, corroding the air with sweaty body odor. Adelaide winced. Adelaide smashed her cigarette against the floor of the fireplace and threw the butt in the trash. From her bags, she retrieved a copy of *Bon Appétit* and the cookies. She headed for Étienne's bedroom. He was sewing Basilie's skirt, a needle in his right hand. The fabric almost hid the cast on his left wrist. His face displayed pansy-like swatches of purple and yellow. She had to remind herself that nothing bad happened when she healed Étienne, and Galen knowing that she had slept with Étienne didn't change anything.

« *Mon chou*, » he said, a smile brightening his face. « *Viens ici.* »

He patted a round stool between his chair and the dummy.

"Zélie ripped the kick pleat in her skirt again," he said. "*Mon Dieu*, you look *incroyable* but should you wear the sample near the show?"

"I thought you'd like it."

"Remove it before you eat, or drink, or anything," he said.

He looked pale. The bruise gash in his forehead appeared as a deep scratch. Étienne reached for her. She leaned into him and he kissed her cheeks, stubble scraping her.

"Didn't they include a shave in that hospital?" she joked.

"No *américaine* will touch this face," he replied.

"You'd let me do it."

He smiled. "Maybe. Do I smell some smoke?"

He continued his precise, effortless stitches. She offered Étienne the magazine and Oreos.

« *Merci*, » he said, crinkling the bright blue package. "No one remembers."

Étienne propped the needle between the fingers of his broken arm and accepted her gifts. He put the cookies on the floor. He gripped his side as he did, clutching the skirt against it.

"The doctors, they say I have bruised the ribs," he explained. "I should have them broken. With my concussion. That is the word, *oui?*"

He set the skirt on his lap.

"That is the word," Adelaide said, "when your brain bounces off your skull."

"The tests, they say that I had a heart attack — "

"Oh, God, Et, from the accident?" Adelaide interrupted.

If Galen's wine had unforeseen side effects...

"*Mais non. Je pense pas...* Recently, but not now. Wouldn't I know?"

"Maybe it was mild."

"The doctors said it was not mild."

"Oh," she answered. She gazed at her hand, wondering if the blue light had caused it.

"I do not see how one can have a heart attack and not know but..."

He laid the magazine on top of his sewing and paged past a spread of layer cakes.

"Zélie is angry with you," he said.

"Isn't she always?"

"You do smell of smoke," he said, not looking up from an article on fall entertaining.

Adelaide deflated. Her toes curled inside her shoe. She had hoped he wouldn't notice. She knew better. He finished the repair, executed a figure-eight knot, and tugged gently to break the thread. He turned the skirt right side out. His good arm reached behind the chair and returned with a hanger. She helped him hang the skirt and carried it to the closet. She placed it on the doorknob. Étienne tapped on the cast on his lower leg while his lips twisted.

"It itches," Étienne said.

"I can distract you. I brought paperwork, and the laptop. The fax machine is in my trunk," she said. "I also brought a James Bond movie."

"We shouldn't watch movies," he said.

"But we will, right? Come on, *chef*. It's noon. It's Monday. It's a holiday. No one has called," Adelaide said, showing him her cell.

Étienne took it and read the display.

"You missed a call from Galen," he said.

He rose awkwardly and hobbled to his bed.

"I've missed a lot of calls from Galen," she said, dropping the phone. "He's called my apartment, my cellular, and left three messages with Seema. He's a stalker. He wants my..."

Étienne motioned for her to sit beside him, patting his hand against the duvet cover, but she ignored it. She'd better stay right where she was. She didn't want to risk any backfiring magic. The same magic she almost told him about. As if it were a hair color or something.

"I'll get the work stuff..."

Adelaide went to the kitchen, poured a glass of iced tea and stacked her files on the bar. She fished out the big blue book, *Buckland's Complete Book of Witchcraft*, from her Barnes and Noble bag, smoking another cigarette while she scanned it. With the cigarette extinguished and a big swig of iced tea to mask her breath, Adelaide took everything upstairs. Her cat cuddled next to Étienne. Adelaide put on her glasses.

"My work?" Étienne asked.

She handed him a plastic bag of paperwork. He spread it across the bed. Adelaide opened the first chapter of Buckland's book. It covered the history of witchcraft. Adelaide glossed over rituals and sacred space, runes and candle magic, going skyclad (as if she didn't spend enough time naked), and covens. The basic premise seemed simple: a god and a goddess control the universe. Their activities mimic the life cycle. Nothing about a main guardian named Neferkaba and her underlings assigned to each element.

Zut squawked and stretched. Her wide eyes examined Adelaide. The cat spread her paw and picked at the hair between the tufted pads.

"Are you still mad?" Adelaide asked the cat.

Étienne looked up.

« *Non,* » he said.

"Of course I'm mad. You left me and you, spastic girl, didn't even make arrangements to have my box cleaned."

"You're never happy," Adelaide said.

"I'm not?" Étienne replied.

She looked to the cat. The cat offered a stabbing stare.

"Why should I be happy? How would you feel if..."

The cat's expression relaxed.

"Wait a minute... Did you hear me?"

Adelaide swallowed hard and leaned toward the animal.

"Zut..."

"After all these years, you finally understand?"

Adelaide needed another cigarette. She interlaced her fingers, squeezing her palms.

« *Mon chou, ça va?* » Étienne asked.

"Don't panic," the cat said as it raised a paw.

Adelaide leapt.

« *Chouchou?* » Étienne said.

"I need something. I'll be right back."

Adelaide went downstairs. The cat galloped after her. The cat poked her head between the slats of the railing. The animal's tail made S-patterns.

"Zut, stay," Adelaide said. "I need to think. Alone."

"Suit yourself," the cat said, turning toward Étienne's room. "Someone needs to watch the man. He likes his female companionship."

Adelaide continued into the ballroom. She opened the wooden doors of the primitive cabinet there, the lone piece of furniture other than the Steinway. Amid the bottles of top shelf liquor, Adelaide retrieved the Goldschlager bottle. She grabbed a triple shot glass. She filled it. She lifted it, took a deep breath, and swallowed the contents in two gulps. Now, she needed that cigarette. When she crossed the hall, she heard a dragging noise. It paused. Adelaide started walking again. The noise recommenced. A toilet flushed.

« *Mon chou?* » Étienne called.

"I'm here," Adelaide returned.

« *Ca va?* » he asked.

"Yes, *ça va,*" she replied. "I'll be up in a minute."

He retreated to the bedroom. Adelaide sighed. She slammed into the doorframe. She couldn't remember if had she eaten anything today. She lit a cigarette. She smoked and got the fax machine, carrying it to Étienne's room. She set it on his cutting table. Étienne had the blue witch book and Zut.

"Who is 'You're so Vain?'" Étienne asked, humming the song. "My Arlette?"

Her heart, and her stomach, sank.

"You didn't answer it," she replied.

Étienne shook his head.

"Galen," she explained. "Again."

Étienne held up the book.

"Do you want to talk?" he asked.

She shook her head. Then, she nodded. To top it off, she shrugged.

"You'll think I'm crazy," Adelaide said.

« *C'est moi, mon chou,* » he said. "You can say things freely."

"I feel things, Et. The other day at the office, when I fell asleep on the couch," she said. "It wasn't a seizure. My hand, on the couch, well, it showed me how you and Bas made love."

"Did Zélie tell you that? First her pregnancy and then intimate details — "

"No," Adelaide answered quickly. "Yuck."

"Then how do you know?"

"I told you, I feel things from things," she explained. "Like..."

She pointed to the black coil vase on Étienne's bureau, which held lavender roses and lilies that complemented the rich berry color of the room. Adelaide rushed to it, and planted her right hand against its base. Arousal swamped her, an aching need accompanied by darkness and tears. The potter cried as she pressed these coils together, wept as she shaped them and spun them into form. The potter dwelled in her memories, memories of the one who made her laugh, encouraged her art, and... Adelaide's legs quivered and she had to fight not to fall. An orgasm bore through with such strength it sucked the breath out of her and erased the images from her mind.

"Holy shit," Adelaide gasped.

Zut stretched across the thigh of Étienne's broken leg, her haunches resting on the bed, with her front paws crossed. Étienne peered vacantly.

"What are you doing?" he asked.

A face came into focus in Adelaide's vision. Dirty blond curls, crooked nose and that devilish smile could only belong to Étienne d'Amille. Something like thirty years ago but Étienne nonetheless.

"You dated her a long time," Adelaide said. "Monique."

"About six months," he answered.

The details came clearer.

"The last time you saw her, you went down on her in a ceramics studio, seriously down, on the day you left for the army," Adelaide told him. "You broke her heart, but she didn't want you to know so she made this, but she made it black. Like her heart."

"*Oh là là là là là.* How do you know that?"

"The vase. It told me. God, why does everything around you reek of sex?"

"That was a long time ago."

"November 1977."

"I left for Djibouti in October."

"She made the vase in November," Adelaide said.

"*C'est possible.*"

"I'm sorry," she said. "I'm so sorry. I have these powers, and I can't control them, and I can heal people but maybe I hurt them, too. My emotions, well, they're driving Basilie away. And the wine, it was meant for me and it had hallucinogens."

Étienne slipped her hair behind her ear with the fingertips under his cast.

"You couldn't drive Zélie away," he said.

"She hates me."

Adelaide closed her eyes. Étienne touched her arm. Adelaide jerked. Her chin moved and his cast bumped her jaw. The cat jumped onto the floor and scurried under the bed.

"Don't touch me," Adelaide said. "I can't risk losing control."

« You think you have powers? You think you can hurt me? How could you ever hurt me? » he had reverted to French. He could speak easier that way.

"I shouldn't have mentioned it. Here, let's sew."

Adelaide reached into her bag, withdrawing a small leather case, not much bigger than a wallet. His father's sewing kit. She lobbed it underhand toward him. Étienne caught it.

"You up to a fitting?" she asked.

"I have so many other things to do, here in my bed," he replied.

He winked. Adelaide trotted through the house. She retrieved a garment bag from her trunk. He'd have a conniption if he knew she'd laid it there. She brought the bag to him. Étienne unzipped the garment bag, separating the silver letters of his name.

He passed a pink silk/hemp mini-dress to Adelaide. He opened the leather case, needles and pins catching the sunlight. She rested the mini-dress on the chair and pulled off the eyelet sample. Adelaide shivered, suddenly aware of her nudity, wearing nothing more than lacy briefs and petal pink Louboutins. She'd spent a dozen years in a Calvin Klein G-string among strangers, but now, she worried what she'd see if she looked into Étienne's face. She pulled the dress against her chest, shielding herself as her fingers scrunched the fabric. She turned.

From his nest of pillows and shams, Étienne shuffled and sorted eight-by-ten photographs of Adelaide under the raised hood of Charlie's 1968 MGB. The Adelaide in the photographs, in a pleated, silk dress with pink ribbons and a tailored vest (the same 'mineral blue' of the car), posed with an oil can and a chunk of engine which hadn't really come from the car.

Here she stood, the real her, clutching a hemp dress, staring at him, so close to naked. His eyes never wavered from the glossies. His fingers — the ones not in a cast — threatened to touch the girl in the photographs. He arranged his favorites side-by-side, some slanting as they slipped from his lap. His hand moved from print to print. His lips parted. His hair fell into his face. Adelaide loosened her grip on the dress as Étienne discarded one photo. She shook the dress lightly, her exposed flesh jiggling. Étienne rejected another photo. She dropped the dress.

"Big penis," she whispered. "Big penis."

Étienne gazed across the bed, holding the last remaining print.

"Did you say something?" he asked.

"Big penis," she said even quieter than before.

"Where is the dress?" he replied.

He looked right at her. Étienne jostled the photograph.

"This is the one," he said.

Crouching, Adelaide scooped the dress from the floor and sprinted to the hall bathroom.

« *Mon chou?* » Étienne called. "Are you ill? Did you just say — "

"I didn't say anything," she hollered.

Adelaide took a deep breath. Big penis, big penis, big penis. As much as she loved him, Étienne didn't see her. She didn't exist. The only Adelaide Étienne knew was the girl in the photographs.

A headache made the light splotchy. Adelaide slipped her arms and her head into the dress. She fastened the side zipper and surveyed herself in the mirror, smoothing the A-line dress. She strode into the bedroom, each footstep poised for the catwalk. The girl in the pictures, the one Étienne liked.

She cocked her head, tossed her hair, and, as expected, delighted Étienne, who smiled and clapped and looked at her with sparkling eyes that turned blue thanks to the silver in his shirt. It was all about the girl in the photographs. Once she reached him, Étienne lifted one strap of her dress with his broken hand. His lips twisted in disapproval. Étienne tugged at the fabric on her left breast.

"Take it off," he commanded. "That dart. You look pointy."

"I do?" she replied, scrutinizing her boobs.

"Take it off. I need to fix it," he said.

"Can I borrow a shirt?"

"I spend my life making you clothes and you want my shirt?"

Étienne assisted her in pulling the garment over her head, bringing them face-to-face.

"In a half hour I'll have to put that on again, so why get dressed?"

« *Oui,* » he said, with a dramatic half-shrug.

In his closet, Adelaide selected a dress shirt with cornflower blue stripes. It draped across her with masculine meets feminine *déshabillé*, shoulders a tad too low, collar open, shirttails almost hiding her underwear. She kicked off her shoes, admiring her reflection in Étienne's mirror. Adelaide emerged, throwing her arms in the air as if spraying confetti.

« *Je pense,* » Étienne said from behind the deconstructed dart, "a high-waisted pencil skirt and that is *fantastique*. With a corset. Shirt *ouvert* but tucked."

Adelaide checked her cell, no new calls. Her stomach roared, nearly shaking the house.

"You want a late lunch?" she asked. "I haven't eaten and I could use some coffee."

"No cooking."

"Wouldn't think of it. I'd sooner make peanut butter and jelly."

"Not American bread," Étienne replied with a grimace.

She went to the kitchen, ignoring her cigarettes calling from the counter and concentrating on frozen entrees. She chose lasagna. Adelaide pushed the temperature button on the stove and hopped onto the counter, between the stove and sink, leaning her head against the cupboard. Galen barged into the entry and stood there. His black motorcycle boots braced the floor like a football player waiting for the ump to whistle.

"Knock much?" she snapped.

The oven beeped. As Adelaide jumped from the counter and inserted the lasagna's thick, ridged paper tray on the middle shelf, a beam of sunlight washed across the entry where Galen stood. When the sunlight hit him, Galen disappeared. Adelaide closed the oven door. She turned. Dark clouds rumbled from the south, the sunlight faded, and Galen reappeared.

"Did you turn invisible?" she asked.

"Where have you been?" he yelled.

"Right here," she replied. "I asked you a question. Is that some kind of trick?"

She planted her hands on her hips.

"I've called — "

"Yeah? And? Maybe I don't want to talk to you. I'm tired of your manipulations."

He jumped toward her, his feet never hitting ground the whole twenty feet. "What the hell is that outfit?" Galen barked.

"What does it matter to you?"

His hand slapped her neck and she recoiled, ducking and narrowly avoiding the hutch. Galen took her cigarettes.

"Why were you invisible?" she asked again. "How?"

She walked to the sink, maintaining surveillance. After her coerced revelation this weekend, she wasn't lowering her guard. If he could turn invisible, had he been watching her? His hand approached her. She slapped it.

"Give me the power. You feel how unstable it is. You could hurt them — "

"Is that what it will take to get you out of my life?" she screamed. "Maybe you should take it, if Kait would let you — "

He slammed his fist against the counter, inches from where she had laid her hand.

"I can't take it," he screamed. "It won't work unless you give it. Only Kait can take it!"

"I'm dangerous? I'm unstable?" she said, tilting her head to peer into this little man's angrily swirling hazel eyes.

Étienne called her. Her headache hit her full force. She had forgotten it for a while.

"Give me a cigarette," she demanded.

Galen tossed her the pack. She lit one. She trod carefully to the stairs.

"Galen's here, *chef*," she yelled. "I'll be up in a minute."

She could really use Excedrin. Adelaide returned to the kitchen. Galen cornered her by the stove. His face almost touched her cigarette. She pushed him.

"I need space," she said.

"With the emotions you have invested here, the magic will backfire," Galen warned.

"That's your answer for everything," she retorted. "You need permission. You need training. You can't have emotions. Or the magic will backfire."

Adelaide rolled her eyes.

"You can't control it, not with Étienne. You love him too much. Look at you. Half-naked in his goddamn shirt."

Swallowing smoke into her lungs, she exhaled at him. Galen grabbed her hair, twisting and pulling her neck. His nails dug into her scalp as his fingers wound into her locks. Adelaide dropped the cigarette.

"One day, I control you, the next you fight back," Galen said.

"That's the problem. You can't control me."

Adelaide threw a left hook into his jaw.

"Water puts out fire," Adelaide remarked.

Instead of loosening with the punch, his grip tightened. She stomped on his foot.

"This isn't rock-paper-scissors, Addy," he hissed. "I'm the expert. You're the novice."

Galen pulled her head lower. She kept her chin as high as she could. He pulled a small knife from his pocket. It had ornate Celtic knot metalwork across the hilt. He chanted in the strange language that Kait had referred to as old Gaelic.

One hand on the knife, one hand still in her hair, Galen used the blade to deepen the opening of Étienne's shirt at her neck, buttons tinkering across the floor. His arm twisted, his knuckles lurched upward, keeping the knife inside his tensed fingers as his blow connected with her eye and sent her reeling into the stove hood. A clump of her hair clung in the corner of the appliance. Galen picked it free and dropped it onto the counter beside him.

Galen pressed the knife in the flesh of her breast near her heart. He cut. Her screaming filled the kitchen. He tossed his little knife to the side and from somewhere grabbed a bowl, which he propped against her wound. She screamed again. Galen released her and used both hands to squeeze blood from her chest into his bowl.

Her heart pounded in fear that if she couldn't stop him, she'd die in Étienne's kitchen waiting for frozen lasagna to bake. She kicked Galen in the balls and seized his hand. Slapping it against the counter, she plunged his knife between his bones. He bellowed and tore away, except his hand remained cemented to the counter. The bowl with Adelaide's blood tumbled to the ground. Adelaide released the knife from Galen's hand and pivoted, tucking the knife into the soft spot above his sternum and between the collarbones.

"I won't give you shit," Adelaide said.

Her calmness disappeared. Authority overwhelmed her.

"Go ahead, get angry, Addy," Galen said.

She pushed the knife against his flesh, knowing she could kill him. A bead of blood swallowed the knife's tip. They wrestled, hands slapping while legs pushed. Adelaide had almost forced him from the stove when a gentle hiss, like air escaping a balloon, struck her ears. Galen slammed her against the oven door. She shoved, but she couldn't move him. A distinct pop filled the kitchen and heat seared her.

She jumped, dropping the bloody knife, stumbling into Galen's arms. The gas stove flared dramatically, lapping at the hood, blackening the front of the cupboards, initiating the excruciating chirp of the smoke alarm. Thunder crashed. The smell of singed fibers filled the room as Étienne's shirt burned. They fell to the floor.

« What the hell is going on down there? » Étienne screamed in French. « Shall I call eighteen? »

"It's 9-1-1 in the States, Et!"

« Do I need to call it? » he replied.

"See," Galen whispered to her. "I warned you. You're dangerous. You can't control it."

Lifting the bowl from the floor, Galen licked its walls. He jumped to his feet and wrapped his wounded arm around her waist, his hand low as not to graze her back, pulling her up. He extended his uninjured hand toward the fire. The fire immediately calmed.

"We're okay!" Adelaide called to Étienne.

"What happens next time?" he asked. "Maybe Basilie pisses you off, when you don't like the way she's treating Étienne..."

He butted the heel of his palm against her temple and her thoughts splintered like a kaleidoscope. Blue and gold glitter blinding her as it followed his hand toward him. A deluge of memory overwhelmed her: her in her cross country uniform, old boyfriends, struggling with state standardized testing in school, photo shoots, dinners with Basilie and Étienne, and high school graduation.

Adelaide couldn't fight. Tears trailed her face, hurting her bruised flesh. Her head throbbed. Her back ached. She couldn't stand anymore. Queasiness racked her head-to-toe, waves across her body. She fell to the floor. The cool tiles soothed her back. Galen crouched and crossed his hands on his knees.

"You can't handle magic," he said.

His eyes swirled with green and pink poison and her blood stained his mouth. He placed her hair from the counter in his pocket and headed out the door. When she believed he had gone, Adelaide pulled her battered body from the floor and ran to Étienne.

CHAPTER TWENTY-TWO

Under the cover of the storm, Galen sped from his battle with Adelaide. His good hand gripped the Viper's steering wheel as blood streamed from his stab wound, rivulets drying to his arm and onto the black leather seats. No pain — her blood blinded him from that, sizzling with the energy of approaching twilight. He simply looked at his hand and blue light worked the flesh, but the magick lessened the high in his system. The effort brought fatigue across his mind and a heaviness in his muscles. He let the hand go. It didn't matter how much blood he lost.

The car swerved across the gravel as he parked by the church. As he stepped from the Viper, three black cats strode from the bushes. They pattered to the kitchen door where they laid, flowing their bodies rump to rump, spiraling outward with their tails and limbs overlapping in a trinity knot. Galen blinked and shook his head. Three cats, definite knot. Then, something else flushed his body, slow and cool and old. The world paused as the cats' tails connected the symbol. He entered the church, welcomed by the rich scent of soil and a trail of muddy footprints across his kitchen floor.

Galen tracked them to the sanctuary, where Kait reached for the cross on the baptismal font. Her sleeveless lime green top exposed her white and freckled arms as she stretched.

"Still can't?" Galen asked.

"Maybe next century," Kait said. "I hate crosses. I hate Christians."

Her shoulders rolled, shoulder blades protruding from the thin shirt. Her head mechanically turned, her nose leading the effort, elfin nostrils flaring. In profile, the corners of her lips curled.

"Blood," she stated.

The nostrils flickered again. "Yours. And Adelaide's. What happened?"

She gazed toward the congealing would on his hand.

"Wench stabbed me," Galen replied.

Kait came closer, an artificial floral tainted her normal earthy smell. She licked her lips. He dropped into the front pew.

"Why are you here?" he asked pointedly. "This is where you disappear for a few years."

She backhanded his cheek. She propped one knee on his thigh and leaned into him.

"Keep on this path and Neferkaba will send a guardian after you."

"Then you'd be alone," he whispered.

"She won't give it to you," Kait continued. "I'll make sure."

Her knee pushed into his leg as she drew her other foot from the floor and stood on the pew beside him. Her nose crunched as she swiftly kicked him in the ribs. Kait took his wounded hand, licking it. Her mouth pulled away and her fingers remained.

"You need a healer," Kait said. "You can't do it. Not one hundred percent."

Numbness covered his hand.

"Let's play a game."

Galen opened his eyes.

"Just heal the hand, Kait," he said.

Galen reached his other hand to her neck.

"Stay away from Adelaide. The universe is safer that way," Kait said.

He lifted her body. Her fingernail poked into his wound. He howled. Kait shoved him against the bed, her body restraining his.

"Promise," she said.

She removed her finger. Her hand glowed blue.

"No," he said.

The blue faded. Her fingers squeezed his hand, mounting the pain slowly.

"Promise," she said.

"Never," Galen yelled, bucking against her.

Blood and skin spurted from reopened flesh.

"The fact you lived this long is a fluke, because I've guarded your sorry ass," she said. "You pursue this, I'm not bailing you out."

Kait left. During the next several days, Galen struggled against caffeine and chocolate cravings, slept a lot, and jumbled every number, even account numbers he had memorized decades earlier. He welcomed these discombobulated urges. They allowed him to slip into her mind. Her stubborn display of will on Monday had not prevented him from procuring fresh blood from her. By consuming it, he forged a connection into her mind.

On Saturday, he bandaged his wounded hand as best he could and headed for New York City. Adelaide had invited him to a party as her date before their recent episode. After one very important stop for the velvet blue box in his hand, he knocked on her apartment door. The door opened a crack. The face behind it had dark skin, bold eyes, and round cheeks. One dark iris in a sea of white surveyed him and closed the door again.

"Taneisha," Galen called, feigning a casual, friendly voice.

Taneisha's anger masked everything else behind the door. Galen couldn't even fathom how many people were in there.

"Addy, don't open it. One thing my daddy taught me from his time as a beat cop: always trust your gut," the girl said. "My gut says don't do this. Look at what he did to you!"

The door reopened a sliver, deadbolts chained, as a stripe of Adelaide's face peered.

"I want to talk," Galen explained.

"I'm busy," she said.

"Elizabeth's party," Galen replied. "You had asked —"

"Marcy's birthday party," she corrected him. "You're no longer invited."

"Because of the other day?"

"Yes," she curtly replied. "You hit me."

"You stabbed me," he said.

"You started it," she hissed.

"Close the door!" Taneisha yelled.

Coolness permeated into the hall.

"Addy, close the door," another voice hollered. It was Elizabeth.

"I brought this," Galen said.

He offered the jewelry box. Adelaide blinked. She closed the door.

"Don't you even think about it," Taneisha warned.

"If he wants to apologize — " Adelaide muttered.

"Addy, he can't bribe you with jewelry... Can he?" Elizabeth said.

"Addy, he assaulted you," Taneisha said.

"I'm sorry," Galen called.

"I can handle him," Adelaide responded.

Galen snickered.

"I've been worried," he said. "Has Kait cared for you?"

The locks unlatched. The door opened.

"I haven't seen Kait," Adelaide admitted, "and I don't require care."

Adelaide offered her palm. Galen dropped the Tiffany's box into her eager grasp.

"The color of that box is what got you in the door," she said.

She wore a retro-style 1960s pink dress. It had a high waist, belted and fastened with a rhinestone buckle. Taneisha guffawed. Adelaide pointed to the girl's bag.

"You should get going," Adelaide said. "You've got that paper due. Email it to me."

"Oh, like I'd trust your grammar," Taneisha said as she hefted her backpack.

"My grammar is fine, just don't ask for help with algebra."

Taneisha let herself out.

"Étienne would kill me for letting you in," Adelaide said, "but I can take care of myself."

"Famous last words," Elizabeth said, seizing her purse.

The thickness of Adelaide's foundation and powder turned her skin fake suntan orange. She wore lively pink lipstick.

"You're wearing too much make-up," Galen said.

"Without it, I look like a hooker who had a rough night," she replied.

Elizabeth stepped between them.

"If you're not calling the cops, can we go?" Elizabeth asked.

"Go ahead, Liz. I'll catch up," Adelaide answered.

Elizabeth stormed from the apartment.

"You caused quite the brouhaha," she said. "Everybody's upset."

Galen gestured to the blue parcel. Adelaide opened the multi-carat, ten-stone diamond earrings. At the post, they gleamed with whiteness until they became pink ice, which, coincidentally, matched her dress.

"No one has ever bought me anything like this," she admitted.

"Not even Étienne?"

Adelaide shifted her weight. "Okay, other than Étienne."

She grabbed a tiny purse that couldn't have contained more than her house keys.

"It doesn't matter," she said. "My 'spider sense' is tingling. What happened between us was way wrong. I won't forgive that."

Maroon balls of energy exploded from her. His arm twitched with the desire to throttle her. He could snap her in half. But she had to give the power first. She had to want him to take it. And for that he carefully had to deconstruct her world.

"I'm not asking you to," Galen replied. "Let's go to the party. It's a public gathering. Wear the earrings."

Galen steadied the box. He plucked the first earring. He looped it into her ear. On the way by, he kissed her cheek. He repeated the motion with the second earring. The maroon splotches in the space around her lightened.

"They look great," he said. "You look great."

"Thanks," she said.

He and Adelaide were alone. The lack of cat made him draw on preternatural perceptions. Galen checked under the furniture near him: the hall table, the coat rack, the chair near the kitchen door. He noticed a flash from the corner of his eye, then a flick of tail.

"Why don't we get out of here?" Adelaide suggested.

She didn't need to repeat herself. Galen crossed into the hall and waited for her to lock her apartment. They made their way to the curb. Once in a cab, they rode in silence. Galen placed his hand on her knee. She looked to his hand and raised her eyebrows.

"I'm sorry," he said.

As he shot his thoughts toward her mind, she turned away.

"That's not enough," she said.

She had placed bricks between them, perhaps not literally, but psychically.

"Don't look away," he said. "Please."

He tugged at his invisible connection to her. Their gaze met. He kissed her, very deliberately, as his hand continued up her thigh.

"You scare me," Adelaide said, when their mouths parted.

He swallowed, waiting. She didn't push him away, but she didn't encourage him either. He kissed her again. His hand glided along her leg.

I own you, he thought.

He kissed her again. This time, she melted against him without hesitation. He pulled his lips from hers. She retrieved a mirror from her purse and reapplied her lipstick. She sat there silently, meek perhaps. When they arrived, Adelaide guided him to Marcy's loft. Marcy frowned.

"Liz said you'd bring him," Marcy remarked.

Her hand brushed against the earrings.

"Spectacular," Marcy said.

"Thanks," Adelaide replied.

"Can I come in?" Galen asked.

"No," Marcy said.

Galen waited. Adelaide snapped her tongue against the roof of her mouth.

"Don't be such a jerk, Marcy," Adelaide said. "He's trying to apologize."

"Fine," she said. "Come in."

Marcy's fingers clung to Adelaide's elbow as they went inside her cavernous apartment. People swarmed the two models. Galen leaned into Adelaide's ear.

"I'll get you a drink."

He worked his way to the makeshift bar, sorting the influence of so many energies in such a confined space while deciphering the layout of the apartment. He recognized a few faces from Étienne's party, but not many. He found a bottle of red wine, sniffed it, and poured Adelaide a glass. He nipped his finger. This would solidify the connection. As he stirred the blood into the wine, a strong fiery presence crossed the room — straight for him. Basilie slammed his shoulder. Galen spun around. She snarled like a dog, her face nearly frothing.

"I don't think you realize what you've done," she said.

She stood dangerously close. The scarf around her neck brushed against his shirt. She wanted to intimidate him. She was taller than him, just as wide. She had a big presence, and anger to accompany it. The game had begun. The pawn leapt two spaces forward.

"I protect Étienne's business assets," she said. "Lay a hand on Adelaide again, I'll sue you."

"Are you threatening me?" he asked.

"Adelaide missed a job for Oscar de la Renta yesterday and so I'm warning you," Basilie responded. "Make sure nothing happens to prevent her from doing ready-to-wear."

"She stabbed me and set your kitchen on fire and you're defending her," Galen said.

He showed her the bandage. Basilie's eyes scanned the room, paused upon Adelaide, then she looked to Galen's hand.

"Do you know what your husband did with her?" Galen asked.

He emphasized the word 'husband.'

"What caused this fist fight?" Galen said. "Maybe you should ask. You might not be so quick to protect her."

Basilie's jaw shifted and locked.

"Excuse me," Galen said politely. "Adelaide is expecting a drink."

Galen meandered casually through the crowd. Adelaide held a shoe with white leather strap and thong, hemp sole, black tattoo appliqué, and a five-inch heel. She balanced it in her palm, her eyes rolling as it sat against her hand. Gazing to the barefoot crowd, Adelaide smiled.

"It's Jenny's," she said, "and the bitch paid half-price for these Guccis on eBay."

Jenny blushed. Galen grabbed Adelaide. Adelaide tossed Jenny her shoe.

"Addy, psychometry isn't a party game," he admonished her.

Basilie suddenly shot toward Étienne. Galen gave Adelaide the glass.

"I don't like red wine," Adelaide said.

"You'll like this one," he told her.

Galen pulled her to Basilie and Étienne. The gaggle of girls around Étienne dissipated. Basilie rattled in French. Her distressed tone carried, but not her words.

"They're at it again," Adelaide said.

She took a drink.

"Why do you suppose they're arguing now?" Adelaide asked.

Basilie jerked in a clumsy circle, starting toward them. She dragged Étienne awkwardly from his chair, as he attempted to keep pace without putting pressure on the broken leg.

"We may find out," Galen said.

Adelaide finished the wine. Like Adelaide earlier, Basilie kept lashing maroon spots, but her sapphire jewelry would temper them until they were merely inert wisps. Her intensity quadrupled with each glance at Galen until the sapphires sputtered on the angst.

"There's something going on," Basilie remarked. "Something happened between the three of you. And it wasn't business."

Adelaide turned to Galen, then Étienne, and then Basilie.

"No," Adelaide answered. "Nothing."

More, Galen thought, tapping their shared blood. He held his breath, waiting for his influence. Tell her why I'm jealous, he said telepathically.

"Galen thinks we're sleeping together," Adelaide blurted.

Adelaide paled and grabbed her throat. Étienne laughed so forcefully he bent at the waist and almost fell.

"So does all the world," Étienne said.

"Are you?" Basilie asked.

Galen hid a burgeoning smile.

"You need to ask this?" Étienne replied.

"We're not," Adelaide answered again.

"Zélie," Étienne said, his posture and face crumpling. "She is a child."

Étienne set his plastered hand against his wife's back.

"She hasn't been a child in years," Basilie said. "You cannot deny how you pander — "

"Zélie, how can you?" Étienne interrupted in a strangled whisper. "You consider this?"

Tears diluted Basilie's brown eyes.

"You cannot deny something between you," she said. "She always comes first. You bring her presents. You call her. When you are hurt, you tell her. You go to movies with her."

Adelaide stared at the floor. Her pink purse shook. Basilie's sapphires turned white with the effort of calming her.

"That does not mean we are lovers," Étienne replied. "I never, *chérie*. I would not —"

"Then, what happened?" Basilie asked, not letting Étienne finish. "Galen comes to your house. You are alone with her. Something makes him so angry they fight, and she stabs him. He punches her in the eye. Why?"

« *Je sais pas, ma femme,* » he replied.

The party-goers circled, leaving Marcy to navigate the group to reach the disturbance.

"Adelaide told me, Et," Galen said. "It's not a secret."

Adelaide's head snapped to attention. Her panic blanketed them, even Galen couldn't quiet his nerves. He placed one hand on Basilie's shoulder and the other on Adelaide's neck.

"Secret? *Lequel?*" Étienne asked.

Galen tightened his grasp on Adelaide's neck.

"Tell the truth," Galen said.

Adelaide's overwhelming feminine energy siphoned through the diamonds. The fairy stood dumbfounded, blinded by the glitter of those carats, as Galen blended her mysteries with his fire and trickled them through Basilie's flesh into her blood stream.

"Galen, no," Adelaide whined.

"I've spent years suspecting," Basilie said. "Do I need to say it?"

"Bas, please," Adelaide pleaded. "Don't."

"Have you slept with him?" Basilie asked.

« *Non!* » Étienne screamed. « *Mais qu'est-ce que tu fous?* »

Adelaide hid her face behind the little pink purse.

"You think I'm crazy, Étienne? Really?" Basilie said, her hand motioned toward Adelaide.

Basilie surveyed them: Galen, Adelaide, and finally Étienne. Her body stiffened as her heart rate and breathing intensified. She had accepted it without a single hint of proof. Stoniness and a masculine fortitude that must have come from the boardroom covered her face. Marcy thrust her hands on her hips.

"Tell the truth, Adelaide," Galen repeated. "Get it out. Basilie deserves to know."

"There is nothing to tell," Étienne insisted. "Tell her, *mon chou*. I never touched you."

"Did you sleep with him?" Basilie asked.

Silence followed for too long. Basilie balled her hand into her first.

"I did," Adelaide whispered.

Adelaide ducked. Basilie did not strike her, she brought the hand to her mouth and bit her knuckles.

« *Non!* » Étienne screamed. "That is wrong. *Mon chou, ce n'est pas vrai.* It is not true."

"It is, Et," Adelaide said, her voice barely audible over the rising murmurs. "You don't remember. It was the night she left. You were drunk."

"When she left? You had only fifteen!" Étienne exclaimed.

Adelaide cowered. Basilie slowly lowered her fist.

"It's my fault, Bas," Adelaide said. "Don't blame him. He didn't know what he was doing."

"He didn't know what he was doing?" Basilie commented. "If you told me you emptied his checking account, then I'd believe he didn't know what was happening. But sex? No."

"*Non. Jamais.* It did not happen," Étienne said. "I would have to remember."

"No?" Basilie said. "What were you drinking?"

"*Rien,*" he answered quickly.

"Nothing?" Basilie translated. "I blind-sided you with a divorce and you did what? Brushed your teeth and went to bed?"

"I drank Chartreuse," he said, "a lot."

"So you were drunk. What happens when you're really drunk, Étienne?" Basilie said. "On a psychotropic liquor, no less."

"I sleep," he said tentatively.

"Before that," she replied.

Étienne pushed the hair from his face.

"I want... I like... *à faire amour.* Zélie, I...no..."

"Your history speaks for itself," Basilie said.

"I'm sorry, *chef*," Adelaide said. "But..."

Adelaide stopped.

"Go on," Basilie prodded her. "*Vas-y, notre chou.* I need to hear it."

Adelaide shivered as Basilie used her nickname with such distaste. Basilie tugged on her braid. Étienne fell into a nearby chair.

"I helped him to bed after he had too much to drink and he starting talking about break-up sex," Adelaide said. "That you owed him that much, because he needed to share that pain..."

« *Sacré coeur,* » Étienne said.

Étienne buried his face in his hands. Make him believe, Galen prodded her. Adelaide leaned into his ear. With their link, Galen could hear her words despite the whispering.

« You said you liked to taste a woman, after you pleased her, so you both had something to remember, » Adelaide recounted in French, as if it would spare him some embarrassment.

Adelaide dropped to her knees in front of him. Basilie turned.

"I did what I did and I left," Adelaide said in English to everyone.

"You slept with him?" Marcy said. "Why didn't you ever tell me?"

"You came back to me, Zélie. I could not tell if it was real or a dream but..." Étienne said. "I never imagined..."

"That you were hallucinating?" Basilie snapped.

"You're ruining my party," Marcy interrupted.

Give him a detail that can't be denied, Galen commanded.

"I didn't want you to know, ever, but I couldn't avoid leaving something and you were too upset to notice," Adelaide said.

Galen had never seen a room so still and quiet.

"Yes, Adelaide?" Basilie said.

« There was... my blood... on the sheets, » Adelaide admitted *en français.*

Étienne buried his hands into his hair as his head fell between his knees.

« *Tu l'ai baisée,* » Basilie said, « *quand tu étais la vierge?* »

"Let's not be vulgar," Marcy said.

Galen didn't know Marcy spoke French, but he supposed models probably recognized the word 'fuck' in many languages. Virgin on the other hand, maybe not.

"You didn't know," Adelaide said, clinging to Étienne. "You thought I was her. Really."

It's time, Galen thought. He pointed at Basilie. Her hand slid across her back, thumb near her kidney, fingers pushing deeply toward her spine. She squealed, leaning backwards. Her body tensed as her face contorted. Then, Galen smelled it. As everyone else in the room watched her visage and the way she twisted, Galen smelled the blood. She began to hyperventilate as Étienne soared to his feet, kicking the prostrate Adelaide in the chest with his plastered leg and sending her across the hardwood floor.

"Zélie," he screamed.

He dove for her, but she forced him away.

« *Non, non, non, mon dieu, non...* » Étienne rambled.

Basilie collapsed to the floor, a tiny streak of blood on her ankle. Her head hit the wood, her hand still pushing that spot on her back. She tried to pull herself to her feet, but couldn't.

"Don't touch me," Basilie hollered. « *Ne me touche pas!* »

« *Mignon? Le petit bébé,* » Étienne whispered.

Étienne's broken hand reached for his chest. His whole body quaked as his good hand pulled a pill bottle from his pocket. Étienne set a nitroglycerin tablet on his tongue. Adelaide reached for Basilie. Basilie shot her the coldest look Galen had ever seen one mortal give another. Adelaide stumbled to the wall. Étienne crawled to his wife.

"Get away from me, Étienne," she said. "If this baby dies...*Tout est fini entre nous.*"

Adelaide sat alone against the wall, hands around her knees, emotionless and still. Galen offered her his hand. She took it. Her glassy eyes gazed into the throng of people.

"Do you believe me now?" he asked. "Magick really is dangerous. You're killing them."

Adelaide nodded.

CHAPTER TWENTY-THREE

É tienne got Zélie into a cab. How, he could not recall. She had conference-called her French and American obstetricians. Dr. Edison, the local physician, agreed to meet her in the emergency room. Zélie placed her BlackBerry into her purse, scowling. The nitroglycerin had fixed his angina, but nothing could repair the damage from tonight. Every few minutes, Basilie would push her body against the seat and close her eyes.

« It doesn't change anything, » he said in French.

« It changes everything, jackass. »

As the cab inched across the avenue, her face paled and she sucked her lip into her mouth.

« You're in pain. Let me hold you. »

« Étienne, I don't want you in this cab, so don't play with fire. »

He couldn't help but want her, arms aching to pull her close, even if he could only rest her head against the corner of his chest until they got to the hospital. She sobbed. Étienne reached his fingers to hers, their fingertips barely meeting. She didn't pull them away so he stroked her hand. He managed to keep that hand even as the clerk at the check-in station asked for their information, as they waited in the hard chairs with the flashing lights from the ambulance filtering passed the windows, even once the nurse in the blue scrubs escorted them between some curtains and asked the pre-admission questions that they'd heard before.

"Are you still bleeding, Mrs. d'Amille?" she asked.

This one almost said their name correctly, Étienne thought.

"I don't think so," Zélie answered, her fingers reversing their hold on Étienne's hand.

She crushed his fingers.

"How many times have you been pregnant?" the nurse asked.

Zélie looked at the nurse, then to Étienne, and back.

"Including this one?" she said.

"Yes," the nurse confirmed.

"Four," Zélie murmured.

"Four," the nurse repeated. "How many successful births, Mrs. d'Amille?"

"None," her voice dropped lower.

"Four?" Étienne repeated, unsure of what he had heard. « *Combien de grossesse? Quatre?* »

Zélie nodded. Étienne sunk his broken arm into his hair.

"But... there was two and this one... *cet mignon*," he said. "1984 and 1987."

Zélie shook her head. "Eighty-five."

His chest ached. He couldn't move his neck. The muscles closed around his throat. The sweat dripped from his forehead and his armpits.

"I need to get the doctor, and you two need a minute," the nurse said as she stepped toward the curtain.

"Doctor? What doctor?" Zélie asked.

"Our emergency room doctor," the nurse said.

"I'm waiting for my doctor," Zélie stated.

Étienne forced air through his nose and pushed past the tightness in his lungs.

"Mrs. d'Amille, we need a doctor now," the nurse insisted. "For your sake and the baby — "

"You and I both know if this is an inevitable miscarriage, then my cervix is already open and this baby's dead. I'm waiting for my doctor."

Zélie crossed her arms across her torso.

"Zélie..." Étienne said as the nurse rushed from the room. "You never told me... 1985?"

Her mouth moved and the corner of her eye twitched.

"I didn't want to worry you," she said.

"Do I have to tell you how idiotic that logic is?"

"Do you remember what happened after the first time?" she returned. "You went to Mass everyday for a month, and when you stopped... »

"I've never prayed so much in my life," Étienne said. "It had taken so long and I didn't understand how God could... It worked for Maman, but not for me."

"I wanted to protect you. Do you remember how you pressed the gown that Mémère made for me for my christening and you packed it into the smallest garment bag I'd ever seen..."

Her chest heaved and she cascaded into tears.

"... And I have never seen that gown since. My sisters and I all wore that gown."

"I have it safe," Étienne said.

"So, forgive me, but I wanted to spare you that pain..."

"What changed your mind?" he asked. "In '87."

"Going through it alone. It was bad with you by my side. It was hell alone."

The room spun as his weight fell upon his good foot. He staggered to the wall of cabinets and leaned against them, hand in his hair, eyes to the floor as the specks in the tile blurred into lines. The ache built in his chest, spread to his shoulder, and poked his lungs as they constricted, his breath breaking in minute spasms.

"I am here now."

"This shouldn't be happening to us," she said.

"What happens when we leave the hospital?"

« *Je sais pas, mon amour,* » she said. "I don't know."

Neither moved nor spoke. The cries of the old man in the cubicle next door personified the strangled agony in Étienne's gut, but unlike the other patient, Étienne stood in silence, choking on everything that had happened.

"Because you are ready to discard me, again," he finally verbalized.

A round face of a sunburned, balding man peeked around the curtains. He wore a white shirt, khaki trousers, and a stethoscope. He extended his palm to Zélie. She set her hand over it, pulling him closer and dropping a bise above his right cheek.

"Cal, this is Étienne," she said.

Étienne hobbled to them. He and Cal shook hands.

"Calvin Edison," he introduced himself. "I've been treating your... Basilie... since her arrival in New York. I'm sorry we had to meet like this."

As he rifled through her paperwork, Zélie finally exchanged her simple shift for a hospital gown. Étienne lifted the sky blue dress and folded it over the chair artfully so it would not wrinkle. The doctor asked her to lie back, and Zélie did, her eyes drawing Étienne toward her as her hand sought his. He took her fingers and tucked them into his palm, pressing them against his lips. Cal's eyes rested on the ceiling as he probed Zélie. She watched the doctor, and her fingers trembled. In a few seconds, Cal's hand reappeared as he whipped off a latex glove and tossed it into a garbage can.

"Great news," he said, as he and Étienne assisted Zélie into an upright position. "Your cervix is closed."

Zélie's fingers relaxed and she chuckled, her laughter chasing tension from the room. He noticed that he had begun smiling, though he had no idea why.

"What does that mean?" he asked.

"It means the baby's still in there," Zélie answered.

"So let's get you up to the perinatal ward and find us a heartbeat. I'd like to admit you."

"Chances are good, right?" she said.

"You've surprised me every other step of the way with this miracle baby," Cal replied. "We can't lose hope now."

A nurse transported Zélie to the perinatal ward. The staff gawked when Étienne limped by with his casts, but broken limbs or no, he would not be confined to a wheelchair. The doctor outlined his plans at the nurses' station, while Zélie arranged herself in bed. Cal, now in a white coat with his name embroidered on the pocket, came into the room. He dropped her chart into a holder on the bed and sat on the stool by her feet.

"We're going to skip Doppler and go right to the internal ultrasound if it's okay," he said.

Zélie nodded, and Étienne furrowed his brow as he looked between them. Doppler? Internal what? He covered his face with his hands as he processed the foreign English. When he lowered his hands, the doctor ripped open a small foil package. Étienne blinked, and as he leaned to ask Zélie if that was what he thought it was, the doctor took a condom and rolled it onto a slender and phallic plastic thingamajig attached to a computer monitor.

« *Mon Dieu,* » Étienne exclaimed.

Cal stuck it into Zélie, and Étienne gasped.

"Times have changed," Étienne muttered.

A fuzzy black-and-white image popped onto the screen, a long white line against a mottled white background, then other white lines and blobs. The doctor turned the device and Étienne noticed the long white line had other little lines. Near the top there was a small black space. In that space, a blob pulsed, and a racing thump permeated the static. Zélie clapped.

"That's the heartbeat," she said.

Cal nodded. He made some measurements, hit some keys, moved the device, and repeated the process. The whole time, Zélie and Étienne gazed at each other in awe, and shock, and relief. Étienne collapsed into the chair beside the bed. The doctor explained the upcoming tests, and that he'd check the results in the morning. He told Zélie to rest. But once he left, she didn't rest.

"We have to talk," she said.

And that's how Étienne spent his Sunday. By the time Monday came, he couldn't consider work an escape from his problems. One of his biggest problems had an office next to his. He stopped at Dean and DeLuca for coffee. It made him no less tired, only jittery. Étienne hobbled through his building. Adelaide and John gathered around a newspaper at Seema's desk.

"Do you think we can hide it?" Adelaide asked.

"Didier already heard," John replied.

Seema cleared her throat. Turning, Adelaide hid the newspaper behind her.

"Mr. d'Amille, good to see you," Seema said as she stacked pens in the pencil can.

Étienne didn't shake hands or shower kisses on anyone. Not even Adelaide. Not today. Her black eye gleamed purple and yellow.

« *Mademoiselle, à mon bureau,* » he told her.

She passed the newspaper to Seema.

« *T'apporte le journal,* » he added.

Reclaiming the paper, Adelaide walked toward Étienne's office. He closed the door. She laid the newspaper on his ink blotter.

"What can't I see?" he asked.

Adelaide opened the paper. Her hand covered the headline, but he recognized the headshot of the gossip columnist.

"Seems like his near-fatal car accident last week didn't provide a close enough call for fashion magnate Étienne d'Amille. At a party thrown by model Marcy Green, former supermodel Adelaide Pitney shocked everyone, including boyfriend neonate photographer Galen Sorbach, by admitting an affair with d'Amille before wealthy Basilie Saint-Ebène d'Amille divorced him. That's how a girl should lose her virginity."

Étienne closed the paper.

« *Espèce de salaud,* » he cursed.

Adelaide slouched. He almost reprimanded her bad posture, but didn't.

"Adelaide, why?" his voice pleaded.

"Do we have to go over this again?" she asked.

He etched every detail of her face into his memory. Instead of the awkwardly tall teenager, he noted the glow of her skin, the pout of her lips, the deliberateness behind her eyes, and he hated himself for never realizing how much of a woman she'd become.

"Et, I was fifteen. I'm sorry if it hurts, but I don't regret it," Adelaide said.

"Do you love me?" Étienne said.

"I would do anything for you," she answered. "I love you, but not like that. You were convenient."

"Convenient?" he repeated, disturbed.

"I had this," she said, gesturing down her torso, "...whatever it is. Boys were all over me. Photographers, designers, they wanted to screw me like the other girls, but they feared you."

"Who wanted... what...?" he asked. "Did you think I wanted to?"

"No, you'd never," she said emphatically. "Maybe that's why. I wanted to give, not be taken, especially the first time."

He sunk his hands in his hair. Give? Take? She hadn't come to France to leave innocence behind, *n'est-ce pas*? Étienne pushed his hair from his face. He blushed.

"*Mon chou*, you decided on that moment that you wanted me... »

Étienne couldn't say it in either tongue.

"To be the first," she said.

Adelaide reached for his arms. Her soft hands clung to him. Their eyes met.

"You okay?" she said.

She smiled. Étienne inhaled and exhaled.

"Why me?" he asked.

"You were cute. You're still cute even with the laugh lines," Adelaide shrugged. "I wanted a man, not a boy. Lots of reasons. Nothing has changed, *chef*. I know my place."

"You didn't know it then," he remarked.

He needed time. He needed to think.

"I will leave for Paris tonight," he said. "Please tell Seema telephone for the plane."

"You can't just leave," she blurted. "What about the camp — »

"I did not ask," he said. "It is Chez d'Amille, *n'est-ce pas*? My name. My business."

« *Oui, chef*, » Adelaide said.

She walked staidly to Seema's desk. Étienne dialed Zélie from his cell phone.

« Étienne, I am in the middle of a very important deal... »

She had gone to work? She left the hospital an hour ago...

« ...I will see you at dinner. I can't drop everything, » Zélie said.

« Darling, I'm going home. »

« What? » she replied. « Étienne, don't you dare leave. »

« Zélie, » he said. « I need to think. »

« I don't want you to go. I want you here with me. You can't walk away... »

He said goodbye and hung up. He could walk away. He needed to. Seema reported that the jet would be ready at six. Étienne thanked her. He called his brother.

« Étienne? How are you? »

« Hello, Edmond. I'm coming home. Can you pick me up at the airport tomorrow? » Étienne asked.

« It's Friday, » Edmond replied. « I have to work. Take the shuttle. »

« Can't you call out sick? Your only brother is flying in — »

« Which you do twice a month, » Edmond finished.

« I was wounded in a car accident, » he said.

« Étienne, I'm not going to lie to my boss. »

« It's not a lie. I have broken bones. Zélie almost had a miscarriage. My world is ending. »

« Oh, dear God, what did you do now? » Edmond asked.

« I can fill you in tomorrow. »

« I'll make you a deal, » Edmond said. « I'll drive you into Paris and then to Mother — »

« No, Edmond, » Étienne protested. "Not Maman! Besides, I have work at the office. »

« Take a taxi. Or call Claire. She'll do it. Wait, tomorrow? J.P.'s in town — »

« Geep?! Why didn't you tell me? » Étienne interrupted.

« We don't expect you to run home for the weekend. I think Evel might come, he needs parts for the race ... »

Étienne burst into a hearty laugh. Evel! He met the young motorcycle racer at LeMans. The blustery fellow insisted he would win the Tourist Trophy. So, Étienne sponsored him. His parents named him Emmanuel, but everyone on the circuit called him Evel. Étienne hadn't understood the nickname. That's because he didn't know Evel Kneavel, the motorcycle daredevil. Two years in New York City had certainly improved his knowledge of American culture. Someone knocked on his office door. Étienne bid his brother goodbye. Adelaide slipped into the room, followed by the scent of warm fish wafting from a white paper bag in her hand.

"I brought lunch," Adelaide said.

Étienne pushed his fingers into his hair. He leaned back into his chair. "That? *Voilà?*" Étienne remarked as he pointed. "Lunch? From a sack?"

She held up a cardboard drink carrier with two striped cups.

"I brought you a root beer," she muttered sheepishly.

He pulled his chair closer to his desk and lowered his eyes to the story-boards. Adelaide drew circles in the carpet with her Pucci sandal.

"I wish to be alone," he said.

Adelaide set the soda on the desk. She carefully unfolded the bag and retrieved a sandwich, a tuna melt on Russian rye. Adelaide motioned toward the empty seat.

"May I?" she asked.

"What did I say?" Étienne bluntly responded.

Adelaide tilted her head so her hair hid her face.

« *Mon chou*, » Étienne said. "You hurt me. You hurt my wife. In front of half the fashion community. You eat sandwiches? This is what I mean to you? You lie and give me a sandwich."

Her pout sunk into a frown.

"Would you rather go out someplace nice?" she asked.

"I do not want you here," he noticed his voice lurching into a yell. "I do not want to sit across a table from you and pretend it is nice. *Ce n'est pas vrai.* You did something wrong."

"Should I have told you sooner? So you could fire me, send me home? Then you could live happily ever after?"

"I may fire you *encore, mon chou*. You are selfish. I protected you, and you... did this."

"I was a child, Étienne. Please understand."

He stood, his arms braced against the desk.

"You know better," he told her. "Your parents taught better. I taught better. *Sors, s'il te plait.* Out! *Fiche-le-camp!*"

She left. The offending sandwich sat uneaten for most of the afternoon. The cheese solidified and the bread hardened. He took a bite and went for a napkin to wipe mayonnaise from his chin, but Étienne had wasted the napkins on his tears.

CHAPTER TWENTY-FOUR

The next morning, outside his Parisian office, Étienne stared at his father's thimble as it rested on the wrong finger. His brain hung on every inscribed syllable of the familiar message: Be faithful to love. When the heaviness in his face and heart matched the weight of the casts on his wrist and leg, he returned the thimble to his sewing kit and swung open the door.

Laurentine's bright smile greeted him as she rose fluidly from the reception desk, her linen box jacket dress holding perfect shape against her waist and her chest as she placed *les bises* on his cheeks. The peacock color popped from her post-*vacances* tan. At her neck, she had a double strand of choker pearls and a paisley scarf under her collar, matching the contrasting green trim on the suit but competing with the pearls.

Étienne returned her kisses, reached behind her neck and carefully unfastened the choker, struggling with the tiny clasp in the fingers of his broken arm. He loosened the scarf, shook it, and expertly folded the silk into a band. He wrapped it around her neck, looped it again, and tied a knot under her chin. He pushed it off-center and repeated the knot. He stepped back, surveyed her, and nodded.

« Who comes today, Laurentine? » he asked.

« Mme. Le Vagereuse at 10:15. »

« Then you are dressed well. She will buy anything reminiscent of Chanel. »

A clamor interrupted him. A chaotic meld of *café au lait*-colored lab coats, led by Didier, tumbled toward him from the hall. From beneath the lapel of his tweed blazer, Didier's tailor's tape lashed toward Étienne. Didier offered a hand to shake, exposing the pincushion on his wrist.

« Thank God, Étienne, » he said, overgrown facial hair not disguising his furled expression.

The remaining workshop hands — Marie-Thérèse, Odile, Jérôme, and Nathalie — filed by. Marie-Thérèse, Étienne's *petite main*, had embroidered the suede collar of her coat, a fine example of her handiwork. Étienne kissed her cheek, but only once, and she returned it. Odile, the youngest of the staff, had augmented the back of her coat with ruffles. She received a tap on the cheek also, but unlike Marie-Thérèse, she did not allow her lips to touch Étienne's flesh. Jérôme, in his plain, starched coat, shook hands. Nathalie, another *petite main*, had flared her smock to accent her waist. She maintained her distance as Étienne kissed, making it clear his lips should not touch her. Around their necks, the staff toted brown pochettes, clutches for scissors, needles, and thread. Étienne and Didier had similar coats and bags, but neither wore them. The sewing hands continued to the dressmaking workshop. Laurentine ducked into the sales *salon*.

« The collection, » Didier said. « We never settled on the name. The printer is waiting. »

Spring 2003. Nameless, thus far.

« It is not your problem, Didier. Let the marketing people do it. I should give you ready-to-wear, Didier. The fickle American consumer kills us ... »

« Étienne, a name, » Didier said. « I will take ready-to-wear, but... »

Étienne peered at his second-in-command.

« You look awful, » Didier said.

On the jet, Étienne never slept. Combine that with the car accident and his weekend in the emergency room with his almost-miscarrying wife, Étienne retained his just-discharged-from-the-hospital pallor. Plaster accessorized it perfectly.

« You need to be more careful, » Didier said.

« You sound like my wife, » Étienne said. « What about 'candy shop?' »

Didier cringed.

« From the designer who sleeps with 15-year-old virgin models, » Didier said.

Only Didier could say that without repercussions. Army buddies earned special privileges.

« You know that's not the kind of man I am, » Étienne said.

Didier shrugged. "What I know doesn't matter. The gossip matters in this business. »

« Then 'white nights' would be equally bad, » Étienne said.

Didier arranged his hands on his hips.

« Name, » he demanded.

« I have a staff for this. Ask Alain or René or Solange, » he returned.

Étienne hobbled toward the stairs. His leg ached, but that's what he got for walking on it. Didier followed. As Étienne hauled his leg to the next step, simplicity struck.

« Fresh blossoms, » Étienne said.

Didier stroked his cheek as he considered it.

« That cries for a perfume. Do you have plans for a scent? » Didier asked.

« No, » Étienne said, climbing.

« Something light, fresh, floral — »

« Didier, I have business problems as it is. I do not need a perfume. Perfumes can kill a house. I told my wife I would not get into perfume, I tell you — »

« People love perfume, » Didier interrupted. « Perfume made Chanel. »

« And destroyed her when her business partner sued for the rights. Don't you have work to do? » Étienne snapped.

Didier retreated down the stairs. Sabine, the head secretary, intercepted Étienne as he reached the second floor. She clutched a clipboard to her chest, wrinkling a d'Amille jacket too big for her frame. He kissed her cheeks. She reciprocated.

« Someone must alter that, » Étienne said as he picked at her sleeve.

« What's wrong? » she said sheepishly.

He tugged it.

« Your sleeve should not touch your thumb, » Étienne said.

He grabbed the fabric at her side.

« This should drape with your curves. It falls square. »

« It does? » she said.

« I don't have time, so if Jérôme has a free moment ... »

She tapped the clipboard with manicured fingernails.

« Italy called, » she said. « Problem with the sample handbag. »

He answered her questions while he approached his other support staff. Everyone murmured greetings as the ritual kissing commenced. Sabine continued.

« Before they left the office last night, » Sabine said. "New York asked for fabric I'm not sure we have. »

« Holiday? » Étienne asked.

Sabine nodded. "Adelaide said Bergdorf Goodman might cancel. »

The room hushed.

« It is a risk we take, » he said.

Clatter resumed.

« Mme. Coulombe d'Amille called, » Sabine said.

« My grandmother? »

« Mme. Bônot has a broken zipper. »

Étienne sighed. His father had done alterations for Mme. Bônot.

« We scheduled her for quarter-to-ten, » Sabine continued.

Étienne trudged downstairs. At precisely 9:55 a.m., Laurentine escorted two elderly women into the small dressmaking workroom where Marie-Thérèse and Nathalie embroidered a custom wedding gown. Étienne's grandmother, whom he recognized by her bonnet and the lace shawl over the shoulders of her dark dress, shook her cane at him as they entered.

« Little Devil, » she said. « You do have a gift for getting in the shit. »
Étienne embraced her, her long gray braid swayed with her movement.
Their lips touched.

« And Basilie? » his grandmother asked.

« Still in the United States, Mémère, » he replied.

Mémère clucked. Étienne reached for Mme. Bônot's shoulders and kissed
her cheeks. The old woman offered him an ancient skirt, circa 1975. She
arranged herself in a nearby chair. Étienne leaned against the table as he
carefully removed the old zipper. Mémère lingered beside him, her eyes
squinting at Étienne's handiwork.

« And the baby? » his grandmother asked.

Étienne stopped. Laurentine brought coffee, which Mme. Bônot sipped and
Mémère refused. Mme. Bônot had an eagerness in her eyes that prompted
Étienne to whisper.

« Fine, » Étienne said.

Laurentine scurried from the room.

« The doctor has suggested pelvic rest, » Étienne said even quieter.

« An American doctor, isn't it? » Mémère said. « You need to get that girl
home, to France, because for an industrialized nation those Americans have
some ridiculous ideas. »

Jérôme brought a zipper and a spool of thread. Turning the skirt wrong side
up, Étienne opened the zipper and pinned it. He basted small stitches close to
the teeth. Jérôme and Mémère stared at Étienne's hands. Jérôme hid his eyes
whenever he noticed Étienne watching, but Mémère did not flinch. Étienne,
while normally ambidextrous with a needle, needed his left-handed man to
compensate for the cast.

« I need Denis, » Étienne told Jérôme, « and get an iron and a press cloth. »

Mémère retrieved her pipe from the pocket of her dress. She set it between
her lips. Étienne's eyes widened. His hands trembled against the wool skirt.

« Mémère, you're not going to light that? I've got a silk gown over there! »

She pushed her body forward against the cane and glared at him with
Basque blue eyes.

« Étienne, I'm going outside. »

He exhaled in relief. She patted his shoulder and kissed his cheek as she
strolled past.

« Pelvic rest, » she muttered. « Absurd. Exercise is good for the baby. »

Étienne smirked. Denis came and affixed the opposite side of the fastener.
While Étienne pressed the skirt, Mme. Bônot updated him on the neighborhood activities. Upon finishing, Étienne hung the skirt in a garment bag.
Mme. Bônot opened her purse, giving Étienne thirty-two francs, the same
price from twenty years ago. The old woman left and Jérôme shook his head.

« You lose money when she comes in, » Jérôme said.

« I'm surprised my grandmother lets me take Mme. Bônot's money at all, »
he answered.

Étienne yawned. As much as he craved a nap, he had work to do. He headed out the workshop door. Étienne reached for Mme. Bônot's empty cup and wondered if Laurentine had more coffee brewing. Mémère returned. Étienne wallowed in the scent of tobacco that surrounded his grandmother. Étienne pushed the hair from his face.

« If you got a haircut, it wouldn't be in your eyes, » Mémère said.

« Then I'd look like Papa, » he replied.

She turned, blocking his exit and meeting his eyes.

« Yes, » Mémère said. « True. Though you are too thin. Your father was never that thin. Come home. Now that the old cow has gone ... »

« Mémère! Zélie may be far from perfect but I can't leave her in the United States, pregnant and alone. She hasn't decided how she feels about all this ... »

« Not Basilie, you ninny. Madame Bonot. And I meant lunch. We'll have *bayonne* and *reblochon*, and your mother's leftover fish soup. It's not my *ttoro*, but... »

« Oh. I can't, grandmother, » Étienne said. « I am submerged in work. »

« You sound like them, » she replied with a hearty emphasis on that last word.

He knew what she meant. She hated Americans. Mémère warned that nothing good ever happened in New York and pointed to the Sept. 11 attacks as proof. New York, and the gun-toting Americans, would kill Étienne for his sneakers even though he didn't own sneakers.

« You're becoming a Yankee, » she said.

Étienne couldn't argue with his grandmother. He did have an incredible amount of work to do, but she didn't care. She didn't care about the upcoming ready-to-wear show. She didn't care about gaining *haute couture* clearance. If he mentioned it, she would remind him that his family had custom-made clothes since before the upper echelon of *couturiers* existed. That her father had earned the designation and it added nothing to his business. That his father had no interest in women's clothes. It didn't matter that he wasn't his father. This was a family business.

« Your mother would like to see you, » Mémère said. « She's worried. »

« My mother is always worried, » Étienne replied.

« And is that wrong? »

Mémère rapped her knuckles against the cast on Étienne's wrist.

« You come home for lunch, » Mémère said. « I can't stay. I have lace to finish. My boss is a real dirtbag. Is that the dress? »

Mémère tilted her head toward the wedding dress. Étienne nodded.

« A dirtbag, eh? Then tell him off. Don't you have some fancy title? » Étienne said.

« Vice president, » she replied, « in charge of bossing everybody around."

« Technically, it's vice president in charge of the creative department and quality, » he reminded her.

She shrugged. Mémère joined Marie-Thérèse and Nathalie around the wedding gown. Mémère placed her long, curled fingers against the armscye.

« And she wants lace sleeves? » Mémère asked.

« Yes, » Étienne confirmed.

« I can do that, » Mémère said, « but then, so can you. Let's go home. »

Étienne obeyed. He hailed a taxi to the neighborhood in the eighth *arrondissement* where his great-grandmother, Mémère and his deceased grandfather had purchased a building in 1935. His father had grown up in the apartment over the d'Amille Fine Tailoring workshop, the same workshop where he had died.

« You're quiet, my devil, » his grandmother said as the taxi wove through crowded streets.

« Thinking, » he said, gazing halfheartedly at the storefronts of the Champs-Elysée.

« What happened? » she asked. « The last time we talked ... Well, she was healthy and you didn't have any broken bones. I'm told that *ParisMatch* keeps telephoning your office for confirmation of some scandal. What's going on, boy? »

« I miss how my private life used to be private, » he replied.

The car turned off the main road.

« Mémère, if it happens again, Zélie will leave me, » he said.

« So it's a woman. »

Étienne scowled in his grandmother's direction.

« No, » he said. « Yes. But that's not what scares me. If anything happens to that baby — »

Her fingers squeezed his good hand.

« It won't, » she insisted.

He used his broken arm to push the hair from his face.

« I hope you're right, » Étienne said. He peered to the floor, talking to the gleam in the leather of his Ferragamos. « I find out in the emergency room that she'd lied to me. She had a miscarriage I never knew about. »

« You wouldn't understand, Étienne, » Mémère said.

« No? » he said. « Maybe I never carried a child inside me, but I've suffered too. If it weren't for you ... »

« It's hard, » Mémère said. « It happened to me. Babies die. Grown children die. You never get over it. But you are far from innocent. You never told her what we did. »

He shook his head.

« That's not all, Mémère, » Étienne continued. « She's never well when she's pregnant. And we'd already had some problems. Nothing serious. Then — »

« Look at me, boy, » Mémère interrupted.

He did.

« We haven't had a conversation this convoluted in thirty years, » she said as the taxi double-parked. « Who did you fuck now? »

« Mémère! » he yelled sharply.

They exited the taxi and Étienne offered a crisp set of Euros to the driver. Étienne's face grew hot. His limbs under the casts turned slick with sweat. Mémère stepped to the sidewalk.

« Basilie found out about Adelaide, » Mémère said plainly.

His tongue stuck to the roof of his mouth.

« How did you know? » he finally uttered.

« I'm your grandmother, » she said. « I know more about your dirty deeds than you think. As soon as you figured out what it was for — »

« Mémère, » Étienne said, holding up his hand.

« That girl was trouble since the day you found her in that airport. You met your match. »

« Wait a minute, » Étienne said. « Do you think we had an affair? »

« I'm not naïve like your mother, boy, » she replied. « You're young. You're rich. You've always been a whore. »

« Mémère! »

« A man in your place is entitled to a mistress. »

Étienne rose his hand to his forehead and hit himself in the temple with his cast.

« You think ... » he paused. « She's my mistress? »

« Isn't she? »

« No! »

« But you've slept with her. »

« It looks that way, » he admitted.

« Looks that way? » she repeated. « Did you or didn't you? You never looked. You touched. »

« I touched, » he said. « But I was very drunk. And I didn't know what I was doing. And it was when Zélie left me. »

She laughed, blatantly, loud, resounding.

« I'm serious, Mémé, » he said. « I don't remember it. »

She leveled her blue eyes against his, locking their pupils.

« You've been faithful, » Mémère decided. « All these years. »

Étienne nodded.

« And you, and Adelaide, in the absence of the woman of the house, who had gone off and filed for divorce ... »

« I slept with her after drinking a bottle of Chartreuse. »

« Chartreuse? »

Étienne nodded.

« A bottle? »

Étienne nodded again.

« A whole bottle? »

Étienne shrugged. « I don't remember the details. »

« I'm not surprised. That's drunk, » Mémère replied. « And you managed to take a tumble? Most men wouldn't have had full cooperation. You sure she's telling the truth? »

« Alcohol has never impeded me in that regard. »

« A bottle of Chartreuse? »

He nodded. « I blacked out so badly I don't even remember the next day. »

« That's drunk, » Mémère said.

« She was fifteen, Mémère. A virgin. She says she took advantage of me. »

« That's a new one, » Mémère said. « Like I said, you sure have a gift for getting yourself in the shit. I wouldn't mention this to your mother. »

« She might be able to pray for me, » Étienne remarked.

« Yes, » Mémère said. « Someone should. She'll pray for you anyway so don't distress her. »

Mémère got her pipe, puckered her lips around it, and lit it. « We'll talk more later. »

They mounted the narrow stairs in anticipation of ham, cheese and leftover fish soup. Maman opened the door, wiping her hands on her thin gingham apron. She seized Étienne and kissed his cheeks, his lips and then his forehead. The smell of yeast and butter consumed the apartment, mixing with his grandmother's smoke. Maman led them to the sunshine-filled kitchen, her tiny realm. The metal cabinets clanged as she set the table. Mémère took her regular seat and focused on her smoking. Maman, her blue eyes gleaming, brought Étienne hot chocolate in a breakfast bowl and a warm brioche, dripping with French triple-cream butter. Maman sat gingerly in the empty chair, her wide smile emphasizing the lines around her mouth and lifting the sag in her cheeks.

« What happened to your arm and your leg? » Maman asked.

« The accident? » Étienne said. « Zélie suggested marital counseling. I got upset and drove too fast in the rain. I totaled my car. That's it. »

Mémère snickered. Ripping the roll with his hands, Étienne dipped it is his chocolate.

« Edmond called, » Maman said. « He said you seemed anxious. »

« I'm fine, Maman. I'd like to rest. »

Étienne finished his brioche and placed his dishes in the sink. He kissed Maman's forehead. He hopped past the kitchen cabinets and into the floral-papered hallway, limping to the room he occupied after his father died, the same room his father shared with Étienne's Uncle Gaston, who died in Algeria, and Étienne's Jewish Uncle Josse/Jean-Victoire. A photo of the three of them hung on the wall, an old black and white shot, taken in the early 1950s. Reclining on one of the twin beds, he fell asleep within seconds.

He woke when Maman touched his face. They returned to the kitchen where Étienne helped with dinner. Mémère volunteered to go to the butcher for a fresh rabbit. Étienne attempted to cut the potatoes, but he couldn't hold them with his plastered arm. Mémère finished the job. Maman gave him the leeks. Étienne baked a batch of rabbit *pâté* and turned to the *Roquefort* sauce. As dinner cooked, Étienne poured *kirs*.

Edmond arrived shortly before seven, toting white wine. He stood slightly shorter than Étienne and had Mémère's gentle blue eyes. An old man's concerned expression passed between them.

« Why do you wish to see me so badly? » Edmond asked.

Étienne placed his wine glass on the table, his hand tightly on the stem.

« I have ruined everything, » he said.

Edmond raised his eyebrows and rolled his eyes.

« Why don't I believe you? » Edmond responded.

« I'm serious. »

« Étienne, you think everything is serious. »

Edmond enjoyed a slow drink of wine.

« Zélie almost lost the baby, » Étienne whispered. He motioned to Mémère who scurried into the kitchen to distract Maman. « Edmond, have you ever cheated? »

« Yeah, » Edmond said. « I had a lover, when the girls were young. Who is it, Étienne? A model? A celebrity? An old flame? Like Arlette! Revisiting your first? I choose Arlette. »

« Adelaide, Edmond. »

A pensive flash struck Edmond's face. Maman centered the chicken on the table.

« Chicken looks great, Ma, » Edmond said.

Edmond spread *pâté* on his bread. He made agreeable noises and smacked his lips.

« What is this? » Edmond asked.

« Rabbit, » Étienne replied.

« Since when does Ma cook rabbit? »

« She doesn't, » Étienne said. « I needed something to do. »

Mémère appeared with soup. Maman folded her apron over the chair and asked Étienne to say grace. He did. Maman and Edmond crossed themselves. Étienne hesitated, then moved his hand. Mémère rolled her eyes. The basket of rolls headed around the table.

« This is great, » Edmond mumbled.

It was the first time Étienne had ever heard his brother talk with a mouthful.

« Thank you, » Maman said. « Étienne helped. »

Étienne whispered into his brother's ear. « I had to make sure she didn't overcook it. »

« He's rich and he cooks! » Edmond exclaimed.

Mémère offered berries *gratin* for dessert. Étienne glanced at his watch. It was nearly nine-thirty. Maman excused herself to do the dishes. Mémère poured more wine.

« So, that is what is troubling you? » Edmond asked.

Étienne nodded. « Among other things. »

Mémère set her glass on the table. « The girl was fifteen and a virgin. Chose our little devil to relieve herself of her innocence. »

« The *pâté* isn't the only hot rabbit, » Edmond said. « There was a day any girl could seduce Étienne. I often wondered if you limited yourself to girls. »

« Neither of you are helping, » Étienne said.

« Look — you took more than your fair share of virgins, » Edmond said. « Now you are troubled that one took you? Let it go. »

Mémère cackled. They sipped their wine. Étienne sighed. The doorbell rang. Edmond answered it. J.P., Étienne's old friend from their youth in the twentieth *arrondissement*, burst into the room, embracing Étienne's brother and waving a newspaper. Laughter and kidding ensued, until finally J.P. spread the British rag on the dining room table.

« Étienne, your past haunts you, » J.P. said.

Étienne peered. The black-and-white photograph from early 1977, a couple months before he turned eighteen, featured him with the dreadlocks that infuriated his father and tight black pants, chains from his neck to his waist, red suspenders and a vest he had stolen from Papa. Arlette stood beside him in these massive black boots that didn't even fit her and a pleated skirt. The photographer hadn't included it in the photograph, but they were standing on a small stage. Ghislaine sat on the edge. She wore a torn black mini-dress and chains that circled from her neck to her waist. Her hand reached to the front of his pants, while his arm rested on Arlette's shoulder. He had a beer in his other hand.

« That was our first performance, » Étienne said.

« This is why you failed your college entrance exams, » Edmond remarked.

« Is that Ghislaine? » J.P. asked. « You never said she was into chains. »

« We were a punk band, » Étienne said.

« Wait, » J.P. said. « You really were in a band? »

« Yeah, » Étienne said. « I invited you to our shows. I played drums. »

« He does play drums, » Edmond verified.

« All these years, I thought it was a code phrase for, you know, girls, » J.P. said.

« Geep, when I was with a girl, I told you I had plans with a girl. »

Étienne crumbled the newspaper into a ball and shoved in his pocket.

« Let's go, » he said, dangling keys. « We'll get the DB5 and meet Evel. Who's driving? »

« The Aston Martin? » J.P. asked.

« Be safe, boys, » Mémère called after them.

Edmond swiped the keys. Three grown men crammed into Edmond's crusty green Citroën AX for the ride to the garage. Edmond pulled his car beside the Aston Martin. In both cars, Étienne was relegated to the backseat. They met Evel at a trendy cabaret in the hazy area between Montmartre and Pigalle. They shared a bottle of rum.

Dark-haired Evel dug out photographs of his latest baby, the motorcycle he entered in the Tourist Trophy. The conversation slid from motorcycles to cars to women to Étienne's issues.

« I'm innocent, » Étienne insisted.

His brother snorted. J.P. stifled laughter.

« How many people here have covered for Étienne's so-called innocence? » J.P. asked.

J.P. and Edmond raised their hands, then clinked their glasses.

« Your mom always thought our geometry teacher was keeping us both after school for tutoring, » J.P. said.

« Madame might have liked that. She certainly helped me master my forms and my angles. »

« You didn't need any help with those angles, » J.P. replied.

« That's one proof I managed on my own, » Étienne said.

« I shoved your ass in the shower when you were hung over before Mass, » Edmond added.

« Don't forget I took the blame for your acid, » Étienne replied, clapping his good hand from open to closed to tell his brother to shut up.

« No one would have believed it was mine, » Edmond said, hand flying across the top of his head.

J.P. suggested they walk to the seedier Pigalle, but Étienne knew even admiring girls would invite trouble.

« We are too old for such nonsense, » Étienne said.

« Never, » J.P. responded.

« I'm not, » Evel said.

« We are married, » Edmond added.

« I'm not so sure, anymore, » Étienne said.

« I'm not, » Evel repeated.

Étienne's lips turned devilishly and he took his brother's arm.

« Arlette! » he exclaimed.

Edmond shrugged and paid the bill with Étienne's credit card. Sometime after midnight, they made their way to 7 Lézards on Ile St. Louis. When they entered the *cave de jazz* (the others practically carrying Étienne across the stairs), the rich tones of Arlette's voice faltered and recovered. The men claimed the last small table in the room with a bottle of wine and some cocktail chasers. Étienne plopped into his chair. Stunning Arlette in her red silk evening gown leaned to the pianist. Her long, straight hair blocked their conversation, but Étienne knew it without hearing the words. She wanted him to play their song.

Before she had a chance to sing it, another woman crossed the room and squeezed into their table. At first Étienne didn't recognize her, despite the familiar angles of the face and cute eggplant nose, because of the an Audrey Hepburn style haircut that trotted the line between gamin and princess. The big brown eyes, if paler, and the shape of the face, if plumper, could have easily belonged to his wife. Her middle sister, the girl with whom he'd won dozens of ballroom dancing trophies, had joined them.

« Hello, Claire, » Étienne said as Edmond had already risen to offer her kisses.

« Greetings, gentlemen. Edmond, Evel, Geep, Étienne, » she said, baptizing their cheeks with her lips.

« What are you doing here? » Étienne asked.

« Basilie was worried, » Claire explained. « I called to see if Arlette was performing tonight. When I found out she was, I figured it was only a matter of time until you turned up. »

« Marital espionage, » Étienne replied. « So you'll join us? Have a drink? » Edmond passed her the bottle of wine.

« Of course, » she said.

On stage, Arlette, vibrant in the spotlight despite nearing fifty years old, finished her first set with "You're so Vain," the same song she had sung the night she and Étienne met. The night she had stripped him of his virginity. The crowd politely applauded, but Étienne's entourage went wild. Arlette sashayed to them. Her right shoulder glittered with the crystals on the thin strap, the other hid beneath a silk sash circling her body across the waist and abdomen. The red dress flattered her, as Étienne intended when he constructed it.

« Good evening, everyone, » she said, *bisou*ing them and saving Étienne for last.

Her lips dampened his cheeks. He returned the kisses. She extended her hand toward what looked like an empty chair, but a woman returning from the toilets beat her to it. Instead, Arlette draped herself across Étienne's lap. He welcomed her, placing his good hand against her thigh and keeping his cast from the delicate silk.

« Arlette, you know the guys? Guys? Do you all know Arlette? » Étienne asked.

« You don't spend time with Étienne and not know the illustrious Arlette, » J.P. answered, his brown eyes twinkling.

« You remember Claire? » Étienne asked.

« Of course, » Arlette said. « I've seen the two of you tango. »

A twist of Arlette's lips teased a smile might follow. She tapped the plaster on his wrist.

« What happened? » she asked.

« Car accident, » he replied. « Don't fret. What do you have planned for your next set? »

« Some Gréco, » Arlette said.

« Really? Or is that because I'm here? » Étienne responded.

Edmond got her a bottle of water from the bar. She amused the group with her sordid observations of Paris nightlife until she had to return to the stage. When she left, the warmth went with her, Étienne's body cold from her absence. She resumed her performance with « *Si Tu t'imagines.* » Claire slid her chair closer to him. Her leg brushed against his under the small table.

« When Arlette opens her mouth, » J.P. said to Edmond, « he drools like a teenager. »

« Our relationship ended thirty years ago, » Étienne replied. « Why can't I appreciate her? »

Claire's hand rested on his knee, not moving, not exploring, merely sitting.

« Appreciate ? » Edmond responded. « Is that what it's called ? My first love won't speak to me. Étienne's sits on his lap. I hate my brother. Where are your hands ? Keep them on the table where I can see them. »

« Hey, Claire, » Evel said. « Where are your hands ? »

« Nowhere they haven't been before, » she responded.

Étienne's spirits had lifted enough that the women looked too good. Between Arlette on the stage and Claire leaning more and more against him as she drank, Étienne needed to disconnect from the females of his youth and Bacchus' delights. He suggested they go home. They staggered across the Pont Marie and the Quai d'Anjou, even Claire. Étienne struggled with his balance, his keys, and his liquor. Edmond held him in the doorway as the group effort placed the key in the knob. They entered the house, tangled and tripping in the darkness. J.P. laughed and crashed to the floor. Étienne wished he had struck the lights, because a familiar scent surrounded him. A voice called.

« Étienne, where have you been ? »

Étienne sobered significantly. The scent was Chanel No. 5.

« Zélie ? »

« You have some explaining to do. I think you are here, alone, an invalid. In reality, you are carousing. »

A click and a blinding flood of light.

« Oh, Edmond, » Zélie said. « J.P., Evel ? Claire ! I didn't know... »

Edmond raised his hand.

« I will show myself to the guest room, » he said.

« Yes, of course, » Zélie said. « You know where to find everything ? »

« All I need is a bed or the floor, » Edmond replied as he groped the banister.

J.P. crawled to one sofa and Evel collapsed on the other. Étienne hung on a table while Claire, who had imbibed the least, propped him up from behind.

« Claire ! I asked you to check on him and you're partying with him ? »

« Sorry, » she muttered.

« What are you doing here ? » Étienne asked.

« Étienne, you drunk, » she responded. « I was thinking, about us, what has happened. It doesn't matter, any of it, because I can't exist without you. When did I lose sight of that ? »

« About ten years ago, » Étienne replied. « I've been a jerk, Zélie. I swear I shall never look at another woman again. »

« Are you having elective eye surgery ? » Zélie quipped.

From the couch, J.P. snickered.

« Shut up, Geep, » Étienne and Zélie said in unison.

CHAPTER TWENTY-FIVE

Adelaide curled the comforter into a rosette as the James Bond theme erupted in her bedroom. After ten minutes, she silenced the ringer and laid the phone aside. She had ignored "Jack and Diane" earlier. She wouldn't answer James Bond either.

This whole week, teenagers had swarmed the office and Adelaide put them to work. Becky coordinated fabric and supplies. John alerted the press. Joey constructed a runway in an up-and-coming hip-hop club. By the end of the week, Adelaide and Marcy modeled the freshest ensembles in Manhattan for an audience of twenty-five journalists, including an assistant editor (at least not an editorial assistant!) from *Women's Wear Daily*, and six photographers.

James Bond resurfaces now. She could have used his help when Taneisha's best friend had to ease the sleeves on her jacket, like Adelaide had any idea how. When Étienne did it, they just matched. She never realized how impossible it was. But she did it. She basted and eased and gathered and tweaked until it worked.

The screen on the phone glowed. Her hand dropped the blanket and edged toward it. Then she stopped herself. James Bond had not called since he left abruptly Tuesday with Rich Girl following via Air France on Wednesday. He could wait until the official work week, tomorrow. 9 a.m. She tossed the phone onto the nightstand. The cat jumped onto the bed. Zut placed her front paws on Adelaide's thighs and stretched her nose to her owner's. The cat's eyes twinkled.

"Answer it," the cat suggested.

A whisper inside her head concurred. Adelaide glanced to her shoulder, where a fluorescent shadow hovered. She threw the covers off the bed and slammed her feet to the floor. Once again, the glow of the phone attracted her. Adelaide seized it, her jerky hand spilling a full ashtray. She had emptied it before she went to bed. She set the phone down, reaching for cigarettes instead. The cat shook her head. The phone glowed again. She answered.

« *Mon chou?* »

Cheeriness lined the syllables. Though French inflections always sounded cheery. Even when she got her ass reamed in French, it sounded cheery.

« *Ouias, chef,*" she said.

"We talk. You are in *Pennsylvanie?* I come."

The heaviness in her shoulders quadrupled. Her hand slunk toward the cigarettes.

"Et, I'm sorry — "

She lifted the box, surprised at its lightness. The phone went dead. Shaking the cigarette box, Adelaide showered specks of tobacco across her sheets. Empty. It was full when she woke. Adelaide set the phone down. No wonder her throat hurt.

She soccer-kicked a pair of jeans. Adelaide pulled her nightgown over her head. She stepped into her closet. Scoop-neck tank with pleats, Spring 2002, Étienne; blouse with short sleeves and rear vent, Fall 2001, Étienne; bias-cut, diagonal stripe, one-shoulder baby doll dress, Spring 2002, Didier; super-tailored sundress, Spring 2001, Étienne … Adelaide closed the door. She grabbed an old camisole from her bureau. Target, high school, Fall 1995.

Coffee first, fashion second. With a big, black cup of coffee, she wandered to the atrium balcony. She sunk into the Adirondack chair, sipped her brew, and followed the flight of the last butterflies. One tumbled toward the water-fall, wings slowing as it got caught in the spray, and it whirled into the current with other dead butterflies. She closed her eyes, leaned her head against the chair, and locked her fingers around the mug. When her coffee had gone cold, Étienne thumped into the room, dragging his broken leg.

« *Bonjour,* » Étienne said.

« *Bonjour, chef,* » Adelaide replied.

He *bisoued* her. Étienne leaned against the banister. He offered Adelaide a DVD case. She quickly identified Sean Connery. Zut approached, rubbing against Étienne's good leg until he lifted her. He rested her on his shoulder.

"*Goldfinger,*" she said.

"I thought we would watch it."

He set the cat on the floor. Adelaide traced the golden woman.

"Sure," she replied.

"Addy," Étienne said, "I have good news, *je pense.*"

She put the movie on the floor.

« *J'espère,* » he said with a heavy sigh.

« *Quoi de neuf?* » she replied.

"I am promoting you," he said.

"To what?" Adelaide responded

"Vice president of North American operations," Étienne said. "Zélie made the title. I wanted 'Chairman of Creative Operations.' It is a better... how do you say... *acronyme?*"

"COCO," Adelaide said.

"You will head the New York office," he said.

"A bribe?"

"No," Étienne answered. "I need to go home."

"And I stay behind?"

He bent his finger and ran it along her jaw. He kissed her cheeks, left-right-left-right.

"And Bas?" Adelaide asked.

"Will join me," he said. "With the baby, she prefers the French soil."

"You're exiling me," she replied.

« *Non, certainement pas,* » Étienne responded.

Adelaide closed her eyes to fight the tears. She breathed slowly to keep her voice steady. She crossed the balcony, wanting to escape.

"If you're uncomfortable, fire me," she suggested. "I'll find another job."

Étienne took one large hop. He pushed her hair behind her ears and set his forehead against hers. His long bangs teased her face.

"Please," she choked. "Don't leave me."

His lips pressed against hers for a fleeting second.

"You do not make me uncomfortable," Étienne said.

He turned and went to the opposite end of the balcony.

« *Jamais,* » he said.

"Take me with you," she said.

"The New York office needs an American," he said.

"Pick someone else."

"Who?" Étienne asked.

"Anyone," she replied. "John. Not me. I need you."

« *Non,* » Étienne said.

"Telling me is just a formality," Adelaide said. "I don't really have a say."

A butterfly crossed between them.

"What if I quit?" Adelaide asked.

"Where would you go?"

"Home," she said.

To open a chocolate shop, she yearned to tell him. The butterfly dipped. It would die like the others. In this fake garden. Not the real world. She stepped into the bedroom.

« *Mon petit chou,* » he called.

Adelaide paused. Étienne brushed the hair from his face.

"I understand," he told her. "I do not like but I understand."

"And Bas?"

"She must let it go. You are too important."

"To the company," Adelaide said. "And you're returning to France."

Étienne nodded.

"This afternoon, though," Étienne said, "we have a party."

« *Une fête? Pas encore,* » she protested.

She'd hit her quota of Étienne's lavish get-togethers. Adelaide dropped onto the bed and stared at the ceiling.

« *Peut-être,* » Étienne said as he placed his hand on her knee, "if I treated you as the woman instead of the child, *peut-être* it would be different, *n'est-ce pas?*"

"It would be different, Et, but it wouldn't be easier. It wouldn't be better."

Adelaide went to her apartment. Without much thought, she took a rayon-acetate dress (Spring 2001, Étienne) from her closet. Then, she checked her cellular for messages, and saw none she wished to retrieve (only Jay and Marcy). Adelaide went to the guest room for the movie. She stared at it for a moment and then she took it downstairs.

Debussy played in the ballroom. Laughter chased it. Étienne and Basilie danced awkwardly amid Étienne's broken limbs. They kissed, a slow and leisurely kiss, light yet long. The heaviness that had rested in Adelaide's shoulders and neck now weighted her heart.

Basilie grabbed Adelaide's hands and *bisou*ed her, which Adelaide reciprocated. Adelaide clung to the clumsy silence. Bas's lips parted. The light from the glass prisms in the chandelier reflected the sparkle of a small diamond in an aged gold setting against her slender ringfinger. Adelaide looked quizzically to Étienne, then to Basilie.

"Your wedding ring," Adelaide said.

Basilie nodded and stretched her fingers.

"You kept it," Adelaide said.

Basilie shook her head.

"He did," Basilie revealed. "I threw it at him when I left, but he kept it."

Étienne pressed his fingers into Basilie's waist, leaned his chin on her shoulder from behind, and kissed her neck.

« *Mais oui.* It belonged to *Mémère.* She would kill me if it left the family. »

Adelaide looked to the movie and to Étienne. She wished she could splash across the floor, under the door, and continue down the street like a wave.

"Why are you wearing it?" Adelaide asked Basilie.

"I think I'm going to marry him," she said, beaming. "Once he proves he can behave."

Adelaide peered at Étienne, the hurt deepening.

"You couldn't tell me?" she screeched.

Étienne's face fell. He frowned. He reached toward her. She stepped backward out of the room. Flinging the movie at them, she raced upstairs. She wanted to share Étienne's happiness, but she had lost her best friend.

CHAPTER TWENTY-SIX

For the party, Étienne gave her a blouson with floral embroidery. As if Adelaide would forget everything because of a new dress. She had to accept her place as COCO and as something Étienne could dress. The heat of the oyster Dupioni silk roasted her. She couldn't complain because then she'd have to endure one of Étienne's lectures that began with "when I did my service, which was mandatory in my day..." and lead to descriptions of full battle gear in the desert when the temperatures reached 110 degrees in the shade and sucking on pebbles when they ran out of water. White crêpe paper broke off the walls. The guests had returned to the city when the sun set. Even the hosts left early. This situation blowed.

Adelaide paid the caterer. She forged Étienne's name so well even he couldn't tell the difference. Marcy and Liz lingered. She didn't understand why her friends hadn't abdicated to the Big Apple like everyone else. Adelaide doused her diet Coke with Jack Daniels. They found her by the liquor cabinet. Liz, God love her and her Armani — one shoulder, baggy *à la* eighties-retro with shiny parachute pants — had scarcely spoken, while Marcy hadn't stopped prattling.

"Sheena E. called," Adelaide quipped. "She is so pissed you stole her outfit."

Hurt lined Liz's face, but she hid it and stepped closer to Marcy.

"You look fabulous," Marcy said. "Until you see the pain in your eyes. Quit, Addy. Go make your chocolates. Forget Étienne d'Amille."

"I'm writing my resignation," Adelaide admitted, "in my head."

Her purse reverberated with Salt N Pepa's "Big Shot." Adelaide pulled out her cell.

"It's Taneisha. I should take this," she said to Marcy.

Adelaide noticed bite-size Milky Ways in her clutch.

"Hello?"

Adelaide downed the contents of her glass. Taneisha thanked Adelaide for the great week. She had compiled a portfolio for her interview at Pratt. Adelaide rolled her eyes at Marcy and Liz. Cell phone under her ear, Adelaide's fingers crept into the purse and peeled the wrapper of a Milky Way. When Marcy wasn't watching, Adelaide popped the chocolate into her mouth. Liz saw, but Liz wouldn't do anything.

"You're not listening," Taneisha said.

"Sorry," Adelaide said between mouthfuls of caramel and nougat. "Look, I got to go."

She pushed the phone into her purse and Marcy zeroed in on her moving jaw.

"What are you eating?" Marcy asked.

"A Milky Way."

"Now?"

"It's one bite. Do you know what I ate today?" Adelaide snapped. "A handful of grapes, a dice-size cube of cheese, and a green salad with exactly four calories of dressing."

"Let her go, Mar," Liz said.

"That's why we smoke," Marcy retorted.

"I have to cut back," Adelaide snarled. "I'm close to two packs a day."

Marcy set her hand against Adelaide's arm. She meant the gesture as reassuring, but Adelaide resented it. She imagined the ocean at high tide, and Marcy's arm a shell in the sand. Marcy's arm dropped.

"He prances in, offers me a promotion, and dresses me like a freakin' bride for this stupid engagement party," Adelaide said.

She refilled her drink.

"The Bergdorf Goodman blouses shipped, with approval. The teens had a great time. The staff brainstormed for the next collection. So, I can do the job," Adelaide said.

"But you don't want to," Liz reminded her.

"No," she said, forcing herself to keep her shoes on. "Especially now. I do it for him. It's how I can please him. He's the only man on earth who doesn't come on to me, and he's pissed because of something I did when I was fifteen."

"This will blow over," Marcy said. "Come back to the city with us."

"I have work to do," Adelaide said.

"Please, we're worried," Marcy said.

"I'm a big girl."

Adelaide walked her friends to their rental car. She got another diet Coke from the kitchen and cut a big slice from the three-tier wedding cake. She plopped into a chair. Adelaide savored the buttercream icing and followed it with more Tennessee whiskey and diet. She sat there, mesmerized, high on sugar and low on alcohol, soothed by cigarettes. She stood, but couldn't balance in her six-inch Valentino sandals. Like she needed to be six-foot five.

She staggered to her briefcase for her laptop, cracking her head against the doorway. People must have been midgets in the 1700s, she thought. When she finally settled at the dining room table, she realized she forgot her glasses. She didn't want to trek to her purse again. She relied on her typing skills to compose the most succinct sentences she could. She fought the urge to slip into *franglais*.

"I hereby tender my resignation. I have my own dreams that I will never achieve in the fashion industry. *À bientôt.*"

She directed it to the printer in Basilie's den, two rooms away. She clicked out of the word processing software, nothing but the d'Amille logo and her own photograph on the screen. She gripped her JD and diet coke and stared at her platform Valentino shoes. Sweat doused the expensive silk of her dress. The air conditioning didn't help. Make-up seeped into her pores. She'd have to do a mask tonight, maybe exfoliate. The cat jumped into her lap and purred. Adelaide grumbled at the girl on the computer screen.

That girl didn't have a hair out of place. She had the perfect smile. Hell, she had her boobs taped to keep them exactly where the photographer wanted. That girl wore a short skirt, thigh-high brown leather boots and a cropped plaid jacket, in fuchsia and brown, with brown suede trim. Where she was going in such an outfit, Adelaide couldn't guess.

She scratched the cat between the ears. Étienne didn't have houseplants in the dining room so slimy, drunk Adelaide closed the laptop while reciting her mantra, hoping her emotions wouldn't fry the machine.

"Big penis. Big penis."

"Am I interrupting something?" Galen asked.

Startled, Adelaide knocked the Jack Daniels off the table. Galen's hand darted toward it. His fingers clutched the bottle's neck. A fine spray of whiskey jostled from the rim, but Galen's swift action kept it from over-turning. The cat puffed as she poised herself between them.

"Who got married?" he asked.

Adelaide nearly toppled on the platform shoes.

"What do you want?" she said, lowering into her seat. Adelaide extended her hand, expecting Galen to return the bottle. He shook his head.

"You don't need this," he said.

"Galen, give me the bottle and go," she said. "You've gotten your revenge."

Adelaide gazed at his hands. No sign of the stab wound she'd given him less than two weeks ago.

"There's not even a mark," she said.

"I don't want revenge," he said.

He put the bottle on the table. The cat showed her fangs.

"Can you do something with her?" Galen asked.

"Don't," the cat said.

Adelaide wouldn't send her only ally from the room. She opened her mouth to tell him where to go, but before she got one syllable out, he interrupted.

"The cat," he said, peering into Adelaide's pupils. "Lock her up."

Her brain expanded against her skull. Agony roared. She gripped her temples. Galen repeated his command. Adelaide fell to her knees, sweat and tears coating her face as she struggled. She wiped her cheeks with her hands, and discovered blood on her fingers.

"The only way to release the pain is to do what I say," Galen said.

The cat wailed, hissing and clawing. Adelaide crawled, following the noise, unable to open her eyes from her migraine. Adelaide grabbed the cat. Zut kicked. Adelaide flung her into the porch. Relief washed over her as she locked the door. She rose to her feet.

"You want it," she said. "The power. It's your last chance. I'm due for my period."

Galen nodded. "You shouldn't drink. It makes you unstable."

"Unstable?" she said quietly, tears flowing freely. "I've played along with Kait's 'big penis' meditation. I've tried to control it. I've tried to use it. I'm just hurting people."

His hands circled her. He searched her eyes.

"Why me? I just want to go home and make chocolate. That's all."

She reached for her cigarettes.

"I can make that happen," Galen said. "Give it to me."

Galen lit her cigarette. Adelaide puffed. Something buzzed in her ear. The fairy.

"Étienne won't talk to me," she said. "I almost burned their house down. I almost killed their baby."

"It's not your fault," Galen said as he lit his own cigarette.

The scent of cloves enveloped her. He hooked his fingers under her chin and kissed her. Shivers consumed Adelaide. Goose pimples rose across her flesh. He brought a large silver chalice to the table and set a small mortar and pestle beside it. He dropped leaves into the bowl. His wrist twisted, easily pulverizing the greenery. He chanted something in Irish and ignited the damp contents of the mortar. The smell turned Adelaide's stomach. He rested the pestle on the table. Adelaide returned her seat, next to the laptop. She took the pestle. She read it.

Her touch to the pestle quickly brought a vision of Meadhbh into her mind, splitting Adelaide's drunkenness into clarity. Zut yowled mournfully from the porch. Adelaide gasped. Her sister had mentioned an Irish branch of the family. Adelaide woke her laptop. She couldn't find the file without her glasses. Adelaide went to her briefcase and dug them out. She opened her sister's genealogy research. Galen seethed at her flickering screen.

"What are you doing?" he asked.

She held up her hand, almost ready to explain but something made her stop. Her sister's words haunted her.

"We were pagans... Our ancestors never set foot in church."

If you traced the Larkins back to England, Adelaide realized, the maternal side existed throughout Britain and Ireland where in the 17th and 18th century the women served as midwives.

"Meadhbh Bean Mhic Crabháin, youngest sister from the clan..."

Adelaide scanned the chart for the nearest last name in this mess, belonging to middle sister Margaret who married Kermit Anderson, but the surname for the healers had disappeared. Adelaide returned to Meadhbh.

"Born in 1580, died in 1610 in Athy-on-Barrow, after a fire."

Galen had Meadhbh's tarot cards. He had her mortar and pestle. She closed the laptop, without exiting the file. She'd read it later. Adelaide finished her cigarette. Zut clawed at the screen door. Meadhbh was Kait's mother, and Kait and Adelaide were related.

"What were you doing?"

"Nothing," she said.

From his pocket, Galen pulled two small vials. His hand pressed against her forehead. She slid her chair away from him. He stopped her. He opened the first container and brought minty liquid to her lips.

"What is it?" she asked.

"Something to subdue your powers," he explained. "So you won't hurt anyone."

Adelaide didn't trust his tight pupils and foamy irises. She closed her eyes as she oscillated between the instincts to run or to surrender.

"Drink," he said.

Galen offered her the vial. She cradled it. Once she started this, he would finish it. No turning back. No second chances. Did she really want her powers gone? Kait appeared in the doorway. Briefly, she and Adelaide made eye contact.

"Addy, no!"

Adelaide gulped the vial like a shot. It tasted like peppermint schnapps. Her navel stung. Galen stroked her face. He grinned like the Cheshire cat.

"Take a deep breath," he commanded.

Adelaide pulled air into her lungs. The expansion of her chest spread warmth. Kait screamed and lunged toward Galen.

"Damn you! She was figuring it out!"

Kait grabbed his head and shook it.

"I don't want it, Kait," Adelaide said.

"Hold your breath," Galen said.

He placed a cold hand against her chest. His other arm elbowed Kait. The heat ascended toward and into him. Adelaide grew lightheaded. She worried she might pass out. She willed herself to move but all she did was shake. Numbness followed. Kait chanted wildly, her arms turned up toward the ceiling.

"I feel funny," Adelaide said.

"It's the alcohol," Galen said. "This could kill you."

"I won't let him," Kait said as she slid across the hardwood floor and came between them.

The tears commenced. Adelaide's heart rate soared. The numbness expanded. She begged her body to flee, but nothing happened.

"You're kidding right?" Adelaide asked.

"No, if you pass out," he answered, "I don't know if I could revive you."

Numbness spread into her shoulders.

"I don't want to die," she said. "Kait, help me."

"You smoke, drink, and hardly eat, but you don't want to die," Galen said.

He held the chalice now. Adelaide lost feeling in her arms. She couldn't move her fingers or her hands.

"Please, Galen, I don't want to die."

"I don't care," he said. "We're going to fill Kait's cup."

One hand on the chalice, his other reached forward and snatched Kait's necklace.

"No!" Kait screamed.

Galen elevated the chalice with both hands over his head, and he thrust it downward onto Kait's skull. She hit the floor. Galen slipped the necklace in his pocket. Kait used Galen's legs to pull herself toward a standing position. Galen placed the chalice on Adelaide's chest and secured her arms around it. He backhanded Kait across the face and slammed his knee into her chin. She toppled backwards. A golden bolt sprang from Galen's hand, striking her forehead with a splitting sound.

"Don't get up again," Galen warned.

He placed his palm against Kait's temple and her body vibrated violently, arms thrashing. Her eyes closed.

"Stop!" Adelaide yelled. "She's not involved in this."

Kait stopped shaking. Galen removed his hand from her face and turned to Adelaide.

"This is all about her," Galen replied.

He scooped Adelaide into his arms, carrying her and the chalice to Étienne's room. In the master bathroom, he laid her on the floor. He lifted her arms, removing her arms from her sleeves, and pushed her dress down to her waist.

"Why are we in Étienne's bathroom?" she asked.

"Give me the power, and we'll sober you up with a nice bath."

"Why did you take her necklace?"

"It takes two things to be a guardian, the cup and the enchanted totem. The cup entitles you to the job. The necklace makes you invulnerable."

"Why did you need to knock her out if your plan is to save me?"

"I don't care what happens to you."

She wanted to watch him, but her head wouldn't rotate.

"Kait. We're distant relatives from like four hundred years ago," Adelaide said.

"I don't care about family."

A lid popped. She lay paralyzed so she couldn't turn to see what it was to or what was in it. A ring spun toward her. Galen's wet hands massaged her shoulders with sweet and spicy oil.

"What is that?" Adelaide asked.

"What we used to keep the fairies away."

"Because even though Kait couldn't stop you, the fairy won't let you do this."

Galen kneaded her muscles, arms then hands. He tossed the Valentino sandals into Étienne's bedroom. Slipping his hands under her skirt, he massaged her legs and feet. Galen's fingers circled her forehead. He mumbled. The world blurred into various colors. Her searing cheeks welcomed his cool hand.

"Now," Galen said, propping her face so their eyes met, "this is the part where you give."

"I can't... do anything," she said.

She could barely manage the words. One of Galen's hand supported her head and the other pushed against her bare chest.

"Imagine the power leaving you, flowing like water."

She did. His hand burned. Power connected them. Her body churned. A river of magic sputtered from some spot deep with her and rushed into Galen's hot hand. It flowed, and lapped, and rushed... Water flowing down-hill, until only a puddle remained. Drop by drop, Galen sucked that puddle away and it dripped from his other hand into the chalice.

Galen dropped her. He exploded with color, streaks of motion spinning like the lights on a Ferris wheel. Suddenly, Adelaide rubbed her eyes, and the lights disappeared. She pulled a deep breath into herself and her body responded with an unfamiliar weightlessness. She could move! She hadn't died! She scrambled to her feet. She adjusted her dress to cover herself. She soared across the bedroom, craving a chocolate bar, as Galen snatched her and flung her into the tub.

"Let's not forget your bath," he said.

Adelaide scratched with her nails, elbowed him in the cheeks, and pounded his shins with her feet. He laughed and slammed a knee into her stomach. One leg spanned the tub as his hand twisted her dress. He squeezed her arm, so tight her hand tingled with lack of circulation. He pushed her, wedging her head under the faucet and pinning her.

"Galen?" she said, desperate for her voice to remain steady. "You're leaving, right? You have the power."

He wanted to toy with her. She cringed. He wouldn't be the first man to do so.

"Take what you want and go," Adelaide said, as she had a million times before.

She forced herself to relax. She didn't want to fight. That would spur his anger. If she played along, he wouldn't hurt her. Kait staggered into the bath-room, blood streaming across her face in a thin line.

"Lughaidh," she said. "Neferkaba would like to see you."

Adelaide shoved Galen but hit her head on the spigot.

"Why do you care so much?" Galen asked. "Why do you do so much to protect her? To save this?"

He pointed to the chalice, his body pushed against Adelaide.

"What was inside Adelaide is all I have left of my mother, Galen. I don't have a grave to visit. I never said goodbye. Instead, I have watched her power pass from generation to generation. I didn't want to lose it. Just like I never wanted to lose you."

He jabbed his elbow into Adelaide.

"The number three is sacred," he said.

He held up his thumb.

"Your power," Galen said. "Got that."

He added his index finger.

"Your blood," Galen said.

His middle finger rose.

"What do you suppose makes three?"

Adelaide swallowed. She bit her lip. She didn't want to cry, not in front of him.

"Sex?" she whispered.

"No, Lughaidh, no!"

Galen cackled.

"Don't flatter yourself. Sex makes magic. You have none. Why would I sleep with you?"

Adelaide exhaled. Now two men on earth didn't want to sleep with her. Did that mean her luck would change?

Kait's arms motioned in sweeping configurations as she screamed for Neferkaba, or even for her peer, the fire guardian. She called Gaelic words that Adelaide didn't recognize. Lights and strange silhouettes came into the bathroom.

"You're too late, Kait," Galen said.

Galen showed Adelaide a knife. It glimmered, as he set it under her wrist and rocked the blade as he sliced toward her elbow.

"Number three," Galen explained, "is your life."

Adelaide screamed as she bled into the bath. Kait grabbed her arm, the blue light quickly working to heal. Galen seized her neck and throttled her. Kait's face turned purple and Adelaide closed her eyes.

CHAPTER TWENTY-SEVEN

Kait slammed Galen's hands away in a move that was half-magic, half-martial arts. She fell to the floor, choking, gasping, arms gesturing as she screamed at him but the words did not form in her wounded throat. He fastened her necklace around his neck. He crouched beside the tub and drug his fingers through the bloodied water, placing his wet hand against Adelaide's forehead as if checking her for a fever. A collection of stars, as small as specks of dust, exploded from her body. They collided with his arm, zapping him as they passed.

"She's dead," Galen said.

He rose. Kait ran for the chalice. Extending his arm, Galen knocked her to the floor. He picked up the chalice as she climbed to her feet. He walked to the wall between the windows of the bedroom where Étienne had his little work-space. Kait followed, her body clouded with maroon tufts of anger. She chanted again, but this time her voice could not be deciphered. Galen ignored her and set the chalice on a nearby table. He lifted a wedding portrait of Étienne and Basilie from its perch. He smashed it over Kait's head and left it on the threshold of the bathroom door. Kait tripped. He reached for the chalice.

"Put the cup down," she said clearly.

"You healed yourself," he said.

"You took my invulnerability, but you didn't take my magick."

"And if I have this," he said, shaking the chalice. "I'm the guardian."

"You don't know what to do with what's in that cup," she said. "It's dangerous."

Galen went to his backpack and retrieved Adelaide's tattered copy of *The Little Prince*. He tossed it on the floor. He swung the sack over his shoulder.

"You have violated the temperance of what we do," Kait said. "Only when the power cannot be controlled or surrendered do we kill, but you have taken her power and then killed her. I feel Neferkaba's displeasure."

The backpack slid from Galen's shoulder. He shrugged to inch it into place. His grip on the chalice loosened and to keep from dropping it, he plunged the fingers of his other hand against the rim of the cup. A chill coursed through him, dampening the heightened alertness that came from the magick. His arm froze. He could not unfold his fingers.

"Shit!" Kait screamed.

Galen could no longer focus on the room around him. Kait, the bathroom, and the sewing workshop swam with color: the bold blue of the shower tile, the rainbow range of Étienne's fabrics, the pale purple-raspberry red of the bedroom walls. The intensity nauseated him. The colors twisted and faded until they appeared like film washed out by a bright white light.

If a shadow could burn white, that's what Galen saw, the shape of a woman in gleaming white with hands like copper the only confirmation of a body beneath that glimmering presence. It had to be Neferkaba.

Kait had said that when Neferkaba donned the sacred veil, her skin acquired an opalescence and transparency that transformed her into sunlight incarnate. No one could stare into her eyes, to do so, even for a guardian, would evoke eternal blindness. Galen doubted any truth behind the custom, but he valued his vision and his immortality too much to test it. He wondered if exploring Neferkaba's gaze would transfer her power or perhaps reveal secrets like the so-called Tree of Good and Evil in the Garden of Eden. If Galen believed in God, he would label Neferkaba "Eve," the woman who knew too much and might control the downfall of man.

"You are not the Guardian of the West, yet you wear her totem," the woman said, mildly offering an upraised palm toward the pendant at Galen's throat.

"Great Spirit Guardian," Galen said. "You have felt my offering."

"Your offering?" she said. "The young witch did not deserve to die and you claim her blood an offering? I am not some primitive beast, my nameless impersonator."

"I am Lughaidh Mac Meadhbh."

"You do not belong here."

Neferkaba spread her arms and drew them above her head with her palms upstretched.

"I call the quarters," she said simply into the white emptiness around them.

The ground below them blended into everything else, but Galen's feet believed it stone. Others appeared. Galen noticed Kait first, kneeling before Neferkaba, her forehead to her knee. Glimmering fish scales covered her body from breasts to toes, clinging to her like a sequined dress. Galen crossed his hands in front of his chest. The other guardians stood behind them, the heat of Neferkaba's presence washing across all of them.

"I call the North Guardian, Protector of the power of Earth," Neferkaba said.

"I am here, Spirit Guardian," came the reply.

Galen had heard Kait's stories so he knew them. Mathilda, her hourglass figure adorned with lush robes of leaves and grass and a crown of coins, approached Neferkaba and curtsied.

"And East? I call Air."

Benedict stepped before Neferkaba, bending his lithe body with the perfection of a ballerina to swirl his sword before her. He wore the wind itself, his masculinity hidden below a loincloth of fog. The eldest of the Elemental Guardians, Benedict had lived during the height of Roman influence.

"Present, Spirit Guardian," he said.

"South, I call Fire."

Tiny Jiang rushed forward, dropping to her knees and pressing her forehead to the stone. She had made flame itself into her dress, sizzling from her breasts to her thighs.

"I burn for you, Spirit Guardian."

Her feet fumbled as she rose from the gesture.

"West," Neferkaba snapped. "I call for my Water Guardian."

"I am here," Kait said without raising her head, "but I am without tools to fulfill the duties of my post."

"Where is your cup, my guardian? And your totem?" Neferkaba asked.

Kait's head lifted, sending a spray of red and orange curls across her shoulders.

"You have summoned the thief," Kait said. "My brother."

"A guardian serves until power fades and I chose a successor. You have served me well, Guardian of the West, protector of the power of water."

"Thank you," Kait said softly.

"Approach me, brother of Cacht Ni Crabháin, and plead your worthiness or I shall smite you. You have mastered no water power. Why have you done this?"

He stepped closer, fingering the shell and pearl pendant of Kait's necklace.

"She hadn't done her job. I did it for her," Galen said.

"Why?" Neferkaba asked.

"He who outsmarts the guardian can take his place."

"You have weakened the Guardian of the West and yet you cannot fill that role. You are a fire mage sullied by the water you have stolen."

"But I have weakened your water guardian."

"A gesture which angers me. Why have you undertaken this?"

"I have too much power to live as a man, but not enough to live as a god."

Neferkaba laughed, circling her belly with her arms. "Gods? We are slaves, not gods."

The necklace disappeared from between his fingers as the chalice dissipated from his hand. The cup reappeared in front of Kait.

"The Guardian of the West may resume her duties," said Neferkaba.

Kait slowly rose. She turned to Galen, her eyes squinting and her lips twisted in anger. She faced Neferkaba.

"Thank you," Kait said.

Neferkaba stepped nearer to Galen. Her presence burned, but not like the heat of the fire. The closer she came, something reached inside him as if probing his soul, layers peeled away and left him exposed. Neferkaba drew nearer. Her veil brushed against his shoulder. A piercing headache made him teeter.

"Your thoughts are impure," she said. "Selfish."

Neferkaba waited.

"Your punishments are one and the same. For your insolence, Lughaidh Mac Meadhbh, I bind you to the Guardian of the West until you heal your splintered water."

Kait's shoulders and face fell into a pout. Neferkaba retreated, and a refreshing breeze sailed through Galen's body. He exhaled, without really wanting too, as if the gail had hatched inside him and needed to exit. His stomach quivered. Neferkaba circled Kait. Kait's freckled body absorbed some of Neferkaba's glow. They stood together inside a bubble of light. Kait faced Neferkaba with straight posture and relaxed muscles and if Neferkaba's veil lifted, the two women would meet each other eye to eye. Kait smiled. Neferkaba continued to the front, taking her light and leaving Kait alone.

"I have spoken," Neferkaba said.

An odd thump surrounded him. Galen looked first to Kait and then to the others. The guardians had dropped to their knees in unison. A force tugged Galen to the ground. His knees hit with uncomfortable pressure. He gazed to Neferkaba, but Neferkaba no longer stood before them. The guardians rose. They surrounded him, but he could not get up. He looked to Kait. When he peered into her eyes, he did not find the rich green he expected, but instead he found the night sky twinkling with stars.

"Let's go," she said.

With that, his legs would bend and he scrambled to his feet.

"What was that? What did that mean? Her punishment?" he asked.

"You're my apprentice now," she said.

"I think not," he replied. "Now how do we leave this place?"

The other guardians worked to hide their smiles and failed.

"We leave when I say so," Kait replied. "First, you need to proclaim your allegiance before the others."

"Neferkaba left. I'm done."

"Swear, Lughaidh."

"No."

Jiang grabbed his shoulder. Galen's fire magic surged within his chest and burned toward the touch of the guardian.

"Swear, or Jiang will empty you."

"You can't be serious."

His shoulder exploded with heat. As it lessened, Galen couldn't focus. The blow had confused him. He fell to the ground.

"If you don't swear, this ends here. Jiang will take your fire and I'll take the water. And you'll die, like you should have died 400 years ago."

"What water?" Galen cried. "I don't have — "

"Go ahead, be stupid. Don't listen to us," Kait interrupted. "I wanted that power to stay with a mortal. Instead, I get to teach you to use it. Go ahead, give us a reason to take it away."

"I put it in the cup."

"But you screwed up, and Meadhbh's gift is not in the cup. It's in you."

"Your mother's magick?"

"Yes," she answered. "Will you swear?"

"I swear."

"You can't use magick against me in any way."

Galen wanted to scream at her, insult her. His cheeks burned. His eyes ached. He had no choice. He had no doubt that they would kill him.

"You can be my slave, Lughaidh, or you can go to Hell," Kait said.

He could swear allegiance now and scheme his way out of this later.

"I proclaim my allegiance to you, Kait."

"Are your intentions pure?" she asked.

"My life is in your hands."

He kissed her hand.

"Neferkaba has humbled you and spared you," Kait said. "I guess I'm glad."

CHAPTER TWENTY-EIGHT

The skyscrapers crawled by as Zélie fought traffic, pedestrians, buses, and taxis. No one could tell Zélie the pointlessness of driving in Manhattan.

"You really think we should wait?" Étienne inquired as they stopped for the fourth time this block.

"Yes," Zélie answered.

"But a year?" he asked. "Why can't we bring her to Paris and let her do it? Why New York first?"

"If we transfer her to Paris too soon, she'll run to you for everything," Zélie said. "Plus, she and Didier need time to learn to get along. You need time, too. And you need someone to run the New York office."

The car rolled a few meters.

"Perhaps," he said, "it is too soon."

"For what?" Zélie asked.

"For me to step down," Étienne said. "To give Adelaide *prêt-à-porter* and Didier *couture*."

"We agreed," she replied firmly. "I quit, you quit."

"But I keep my *haute couture* clients, design a little? My family's business, Zélie. You'll walk away from your career?" he asked.

"Everyone doubts my maternal instincts. Do you?" she inquired.

The car stopped again.

"Do we have the assets to do this? To stop working?" Étienne asked.

"What do you think?" she responded.

Étienne considered it.

"I don't know," he answered. "How much money do we have?"

Zélie's laughter filled the car.

"You have no idea," she said.

He shook his head. "How much?"

"That depends," she said.

"If I went to the bank right now, what could I get?"

"Depends which bank," she answered.

Étienne slammed his head against the window. She double-parked in front of his office. He unfastened his seatbelt, kissed her, and reached for the door handle.

"Étienne."

He looked to her.

"You had a net income of about a million last year. Your net worth is about fifty million, depending on the market."

"Humph," he said, surprised at his own lucrativeness. "And you?"

"Net? Eighty-nine million, " she said.

He couldn't fathom those figures.

"Francs? Euros?" he asked.

"U.S. dollars," she replied.

More laughter ensued. The Mercedes pulled away, a glimmer of gold against a dreary Manhattan skyline. He went into the office. Fatigue consumed him. He hadn't slept well. He had bizarre nightmares of blood. They stopped around midnight. The dreamless sleep that followed troubled him just as much. He hoisted his leg toward the stairs, his cast landing with a kaboom. John raced down the hall and jumped onto the landing, peering at him as though he had hoped to see someone else.

"He's alone, Seema," John hollered.

Étienne froze.

"Looking for someone?" he asked.

"Yes," John replied with a forced smile. "Adelaide."

"Where is she?" Étienne asked.

"Normally I'd say she overslept but..."

"But?"

"She missed her fitting for de la Renta. Again," John said.

Étienne pulled his curls back.

"Help me," Étienne said as he released one hand from his skull.

John hustled down the stairs.

"Seema!" Étienne screamed.

Seema darted to him.

"Get Oscar on the phone," he directed.

Étienne and John teetered upstairs.

"John," Étienne said, setting his good hand against the young man's tie. "I need you to go into Adelaide's desk. She keeps a spare key. Go to her apartment."

John nodded.

"Mr. d'Amille, Oscar de la Renta on line one," Seema called.

Adelaide didn't behave like this; she didn't miss bookings, she sure as hell didn't miss fittings. Could this be her way of getting even?

" Oscar..." Étienne grabbed the first phone in the first office.

Étienne wasn't listening.

"I know it's nearly one, she must be stuck in traffic. It's my fault, Oscar..."

As soon as he hung up the phone, he burst into his own office.

"We overreact, yes, Seema?" Étienne asked.

"She's been in the office at eight a.m. while you were gone," the secretary answered.

A few minutes later, the phone rang.

"Chez d'Amille, Mr. d'Amille's office."

Étienne rubbed his temple.

"Yes, John... See you soon."

Seema hung up.

"She's not there. He said he'd check for the cat..."

"*Merci.* I will find her."

Étienne opened his cell and dialed his wife.

What, Étienne? » Zélie screamed. « I'm not even to work yet. »

« Come for me, » he said. « Adelaide is not here. »

« She's a big girl, Étienne. »

« Come for me or I will take a cab to Pennsylvania, » he said, raising his voice.

« What's wrong? » Zélie asked. « You never yell at me. »

« I hope nothing. »

The next couple hours blurred into a mishmash of bad songs on the radio, Zélie's mindless talk, and Étienne's impatience. When they pulled into the driveway, Adelaide's CLK sat where it had the previous day. The back door stood ajar. Étienne retrieved his cellular from his pocket.

« Étienne, this isn't right, » Zélie said.

He passed her the phone. She called the state police. It would be an hour before anyone arrived. He stepped into the entry. Nothing seemed amiss. He scanned the kitchen, waving Zélie into the house. They made their way into the dining room, which remained exactly as it had the day earlier. The caterer's cart with remaining tiers of cake waited beside Adelaide's computer.

A bloodcurdling feline scream roared. The sound cut Étienne's spine. Zut dangled from the screen door. He opened the door and Zut bolted upstairs. Étienne and Zélie crept toward the cat.

« *Ecoute-toi,* » she directed.

He listened.

"There's water running," she continued.

Zélie extended the cellular like a sword. They opened their bedroom door.

"Adelaide," he called. "*Mon petit chou?*"

They kept walking.

"This isn't funny," he said.

Zélie stopped. She lifted a picture frame, gripping it by the support. She slowly rotated it. It was their wedding portrait with youthful smiles and bad circa 1980 hair. The glass was broken.

"Adelaide," he called again.

Pages torn from a book lined the floor. He kicked them with his good leg, *Le Petit Prince*. Water spilled over the tub, heading for the drain of the walk-in shower. Étienne stepped around a puddle.

"Adelaide," he said.

He continued. Zélie touched his elbow. She pointed with the phone.

"Don't get your cast wet," she said.

Étienne leaned against the cold sink as he passed, then the toilet. He hoped for a logical explanation. Nothing bad could happen to her. Étienne hopped over the water, pounding against the bathroom tiles. He steeled himself as he peered around the wall.

Orange-blond hair fanned on the water, away from gaping vacant eyes. One arm dangled over the tub. A jagged cut opened her vein from the braided chains on her wrist to the flesh by her elbow. Dried blood marred the skin. Sunken blood discolored the bottom of her arm. Her body buoyed, the wet, stained white silk of her blouson clinging to it.

Zut rushed past him. She trotted to her owner's side and licked her arm. The cat moaned. She stood on her rear legs. Étienne pulled his head inside the shower stall. He placed his palms firmly against the tile, waited, rested. She couldn't... She didn't... He set his head against the wall. His heart throbbed so strong, so loudly. His breath got caught inside of him and he couldn't remember how to exhale. He shifted his weight. His bare toes grew wet. *Merde!* Étienne coughed. Zélie walked into the bathroom. He moved from the wall as heaviness consumed his chest, as if someone had lowered a slab of marble against him.

"Zélie," he said, intending to warn her, but he couldn't get out any more syllables.

Étienne shifted into the center of the stall, his feet centimeters away from the drain gurgling with excess water. He glimpsed Adelaide's body again, the cold emptiness of her face. The weight in his chest crushed him. Pain jolted into his jaw. He stumbled.

"Zélie," Étienne repeated.

He clutched at the excruciating pressure in his chest, rubbing at the ache. He fell into shower. His head landed below the hot water knob. He sat in the puddle. He closed his eyes, forced himself to breathe. Sweat lined his cold flesh.

"Need..." he muttered.

Did she hear him? The word took more effort than anticipated. He opened his eyes. Zélie stared at Adelaide.

« *Hou hou* ... » he whispered.

He wanted to stand. He needed his medicine. He prayed the pressure would dissipate enough for him to crawl.

"Zay," he said, impressed with the volume of the syllable. "Lee."

If she didn't snap out of it soon... Perhaps there would be two corpses here. His heart screamed in another burst of pain. Zélie's head rolled slowly toward him. His posture, his hand on his chest. She blinked. Her eyes popped and she leapt into action.

Dieu merci, Étienne thought.

"Your tablets!"

She darted toward him.

"Are they in your pocket?" she said as she grabbed his shirt.

« *Non,* » Étienne whispered.

"No?" she replied. "Why not?"

His lightheadedness increased. Zélie unbuttoned his collar. She rocketed to her feet. She disappeared and next something banged. She flung everything from the cabinet.

« *Voici, je les ai,* » she yelled.

She slid into the shower as she struggled with the cap.

"Fucking childproof caps!" she exclaimed.

Please don't let that be my epitaph, he thought. His nitro didn't have a childproof cap. His head swirled. Zélie fought the bottle. His cellular teetered on her arm. Zélie finally wrestled the cap open, while the phone flew into the water. Zélie tapped out a pill and placed it under his tongue. She watched him, her gaze never faltering.

"I need you," Zélie said. "I won't be anything without you."

Call the ambulance, he thought willing her to read his mind. The pressure in his chest subsided enough to relieve his troubled breathing. He opened his mouth and it didn't feel like someone had broken his jaw.

"Hospital," he said.

Zélie grabbed the cellular. Water dripped from it. She dialed anyway.

"Hello?" she said.

She had tears in her eyes.

"The phone is dead, " she said.

« *Sans fil,* » Étienne reminded her.

"Yes, the cordless. By the bed. Don't move. Don't pass out. How are you feeling?"

« *Bien,* » he said.

The symptoms had faded, except for a funny headache. Zélie rose, then folded his fingers around the open nitroglycerin container. Zélie left the bathroom.

"Étienne," she yelled. "What's our house number?"

He told her, ridiculously slowly.

"Ad..." Étienne said.

"There appears to be a dead body in the bathtub," she added, a brief silence then, "of course I know who she is."

Étienne closed his eyes. He couldn't take much more of this.

« Don't pass out, » Zélie screamed in French.

"No," he answered staidly. "Staying calm. Having a heart attack... Can I take more?"

Zélie shrugged. She hung up the phone.

"Do they help?" she asked.

"I do not know," he answered.

He didn't want to tell her no. She knew that nitro wouldn't help a real heart attack. His chest felt tight. Sweat lingered on his flesh. Zélie sat next to him on the floor.

"Is this how my father died?" he asked.

"You aren't dying, Étienne."

"Maybe," he said.

"No," she said, touching his face. "I won't let you."

"Why, Zélie? Why? Why did she kill herself?"

"I don't know, Étienne. Try not to upset yourself."

"Pray with me."

They recited the rosary as they waited. A siren blared. Voices called from downstairs. Zélie beckoned them. Two men came into the room with a stretcher. Étienne recognized one from his car accident. The EMT slapped a blood pressure cuff on his arm.

"How bad?" Étienne asked.

Zélie returned to Étienne. The EMT flashed a bright light in his eyes. Étienne squinted but the EMT held his eyelids. The other guy had his fingers on Adelaide's wrist.

"This girl's dead," he said.

"You're not having much luck, are you?" the EMT said.

"No," Étienne said as the men helped him onto the stretcher. "I am not."

ABOUT THE AUTHOR

The beauty of words has infiltrated the life of Angel Ackerman for her entire life — from reading *Green Eggs and Ham* thousands of times to writing groundbreaking poems titled "My mom wears flip-flops" in Mrs. Sanders' second-grade class. She started the *Fashion and Fiends* series at the age of 16 and rewrote the novel *Manipulations* at least ten times before declaring this version "the one" in 2016.

Angel spent 15 years as a print journalist, specializing in weekly newspapers where reporters learned to write about every topic and take their own photographs. With the decline of print media, Angel explored the non-profit sector where she worked in public relations, program design, social media, grant writing and development.

Although now separated, Angel enjoyed a 20-year marriage to poet Darrell Parry who proved pivotal to bringing Angel's fiction writing career to fruition. Angel and Darrell both have disabilities. Angel has mild cerebral palsy which she has embarked on a journey to understand more. Darrell has a club hand. They have an able-bodied teen daughter, Eva, who keeps bringing home strays — leaving them with a current count of four cats, one pit bull/black lab/mastiff puppy, one goffin cockatoo, one parakeet and seven foster cats from their volunteer work with Feline Urban Rescue and Rehab.

Angel holds a bachelor's degree in English Language and Literature and French from Moravian College, a bachelor's in International Affairs (with honors) from Lafayette College, and initiated a master's degree in World History at West Chester University. Her academic interests include French post-colonial Africa, Muslim relations, and the politics of miscegenation. She hopes to revisit her honors thesis which looked at the stereotypes of Muslims in France and how they continue the thought process of the colonial era.

In addition to Lehigh Valley, Pa., newspapers, Angel has been published in *Ten Word Stories* by *Dime Show Review*, *Rum Punch Press*, *StepAway Magazine*, two volumes of *The SAGE Encyclopedia*, and did book reviews for *Hippocampus Magazine* and *Journal of Global South Studies*. She occasionally writes for the horror website Crash Palace Productions.

When not examining the world with a post-colonial critical theorist's eye, Angel loves to travel and study foreign languages. She has visited Canada, France, Tunisia, Somalia, Djibouti, Yemen and various parts of Russia (trekking to Siberia for pizza). Read more of her escapades at AngelAckerman.com and follow her on YouTube, LinkedIn and Instagram.

Coming in late November:

Book Two of the *Fashion and Fiends* Series

COURTING APPERATIONS

World famous fashion designer Étienne d'Amille knows he should be grateful. He's survived several personal tragedies and almost died. He and his ex-wife, Zélie, will welcome their first born child into the world after 20 years of infertility. But grief has crippled Étienne. And when he's just about to crack — he discovers his house is haunted and the ghost stuck there begs him to free it before familiar supernatural creatures kill them all.

Coming Early 2022

Book Three of the *Fashion and Fiends* Series

RECOVERY

Jacqueline Saint-Ebene left her career as a gynecologist and joined the military, never expecting to find her pregnant, stroke-victim sister and world famous brother-in-law at the center of a decades-old mystery. Jacqueline's universe of perpetual culture clashes faces personal, ethical and professional challenges as the answers appear other-worldly. When the science of medicine meets superstition and olde worlde beliefs, can the two be reconciled into modern society?

sneak peek ...

Courting
Apperations

Book Two of the Fashion and Fiends Series

by Angel Ackerman

CHAPTER ONE

É tienne d'Amille clung to the steering wheel of his wife's Mercedes, his fingers' grip stretching the leather of his favorite driving gloves. The keys laid in his lap as he surveyed the parking lot from his rearview mirror. The typical array of dusty pickup trucks, Chevrolets and Fords surrounded him except for one gleaming black sports car with white racing stripes.

A Dodge Viper. His eyes remained nailed to the spot. Or, how did the Americans put it? Glued. Glued to the spot. The heavy emptiness inside him since September now ached, even worse than inside the house.

He couldn't sleep inside the house. He hadn't gone into the bathroom where Adelaide committed suicide, where he had his heart attack, but yet his wife slept in the next room. He couldn't. But then, these days he barely slept anywhere... Not in Paris, not in Manhattan and certainly not here in rural Pennsylvania.

He thought he would sneak to the bar, have a beer, and go home. This tiny town had a population of 400 people and in that respect, it reminded him of the French countryside. Not much to do and not much there. This particular hamlet had one option at this advanced hour of the night: a bar *péquenot*... peasant? Redneck? He hadn't expected to find anyone he knew, or anyone who knew him, let alone the Viper.

Galen's Viper. The aspiring photographer had dated Adelaide. She was completely infatuated with him. Étienne hadn't heard of him or seen him since her death. Of course, Étienne hadn't been in the United States... His gaze shifted from the reflection of the parking lot onto his own eyes, their color partially hidden by his blond bangs. He brushed the curls from his face, touching the wrinkles in his forehead that had grown deeper in recent months. He took the keys from his lap and climbed from the car, his left leg protesting as he stood. He retrieved his cane. The golden S600 chirped as he locked it with the fob and slipped the keys into his pocket. He slowly approached the bar, the gravel crunchy and uneven under his feet.

The door led to a smoky stairwell that climbed toward the cracking billiard balls and blaring country music. Étienne emerged from the entry to find two men in black motorcycle jackets playing pool, a twenty-something in a ratty flannel pounding a video poker machine and a half-full bar. Slurred vocabulary, a product of collective drunkenness, transformed the normally harsh English into a cacophony of trumpeting elephants. He scanned the figures on the barstools.

Étienne slid between two women close to his age, somewhere in the forties, one with teased bangs and one plain brunette, both with plunging sweaters and less than firm cleavage.

"Pardon," he said to the first, regretting the sing-song syllables. Then, with flatter intonations more akin to American English, he translated the phrase: "Pardon me."

The same tall, lanky bleached blond female bartender with bad teeth that had served him during the summer visit noticed him now.

"What can I get you?" she asked.

Chicken flesh rose across his arms. He hadn't found Galen but something told him that Galen had spotted him. A draft crossed his neck, which between the cashmere coat and scarf should have been impossible.

"A beer, please," he said softly.

The bartender did nothing. Étienne glanced to the taps and to the cooler. What kind of beer? Her eyebrows raised and she waited. He stood there, dumbstruck, unable to remember the names of American beer. They all tasted like donkey's piss, so what did it matter?

"Bof," he muttered. He wanted a 'Yuengling' but the word got tangled in his tongue. 'Rolling Rock' would fare no better. So he ordered a Miller, which, based on the combination of eye twitches from the bartender, sounded like 'Mee-yer' or worse, 'Mee-yeah.'

"MEEL-ler," he repeated, in the same way he would correct someone's pronunciation of his family name, "da MEEL."

"Bottle or draft?" the bartender quizzed.

"Bottle," he replied. "Give me brandy, French, if you have, and the drinks for the ladies."

"French brandy," the bartender muttered under her breath as she walked to the cooler.

The distance between him and his neighbors suddenly closed, at which point he cleared his throat and hoped they would return to their original slouch over the bar. They didn't. He removed his billfold from his interior pocket and pulled free a twenty. The bartender returned with a bottle, a glass and a shot. Étienne delicately tugged his gloves from his fingers and placed them in his pocket. He set the brandy, shot glass and all, in the glass and poured the beer over it. He rested his cane on his wrist, beer bottle in one hand and glass in the other, as he moved awkwardly to a booth. Étienne stripped off his winter wear, arranging it nicely on the seat before settling against the vinyl cushion.

His hands circled the drink, but he didn't bring it to his lips. He looked into it, his bangs falling over his forehead. Étienne hadn't imbibed alcohol in six months. The doctors discouraged it with his blood pressure medication. After the last few days... He lifted the glass.

"Well, well, well," Galen's voice boomed. "Look what the cat dragged in."

Étienne lowered the untouched beer as Galen slid into the opposite side of the booth. Boyishly handsome with bronze skin and hazel eyes, a broad build, and auburn hair... Galen possessed a figure that Étienne would love to feature in front of the camera instead of behind it. It would never happen. Though *un bel homme* or 'a beautiful man,' Galen was too short for high fashion.

"You look like shit, Étienne. What's with the cane?"

"Galen," Étienne said, rising with an outstretched hand. His leg chastised him.

Étienne, though he hadn't attended Mass since Christmas, whispered an internal prayer asking the Mother to guide him with any questions Galen might have regarding Adelaide's death. Galen ignored Étienne's gesture and slammed a glass of golden liquor against the table.

"How are you?" Étienne said. He sat.

"Better than you, apparently, old man."

Étienne's chicken flesh prickled and he shivered.

"Did you have need of something?" Étienne asked.

"Nope," he said, gulping his drink.

Something orange flickered from the cuff on Galen's wrist.

"What would I need?" Galen said.

At first Étienne thought maybe Galen had a stray thread on his sleeve, but it moved. The color splashed across his arm like a flame.

"Galen? There is something on your arm. Were you smoking because..."

The photographer leaned across the table, heat scorched Étienne. Étienne pulled his torso back, throwing his spine against the booth.

"You know what I would like?" Galen said. "An explanation. I was seeing this really nice girl, and she started avoiding me. Then *People* magazine calls me... Me ... and asks me if I have more pictures of Adelaide Pitney because she committed suicide. Nobody told me. I heard from some jackass at *People*."

Étienne could almost taste the beer in front of him. He wrapped his fingers around it. The bubbles tickled his nose as he rehearsed the English for how he wanted to apologize. He exhaled slowly as rose his gaze toward the young man. Fire surrounded Galen's head. It exploded from his neck, danced across his cheeks and surged over his eyes. Étienne jumped.

"You're on fire!" Étienne exclaimed in French.

The beer tumbled. A strange bellow escaped Étienne's lips as he slammed into the wooden booth. His beer glass landed on the floor and rolled toward the bar. The clatter distracted Étienne until the familiar pain shot through his chest. He gasped and threw his hand against his ribs.

"I'm on fire?" Galen repeated calmly in English. "As in 'I'm on a hot streak'?"

The flames licked Galen's flesh, receding from his skull and eventually dying under the collar of his shirt. The pain in Étienne's chest receded. The bartender tossed a kitchen towel at them. Étienne mopped the beer and shot confused glances at Galen.

"Non," Étienne said. "Must be the light. It is nothing."

Étienne moved toward Galen, dabbing the towel, seeking the cause of mysterious burning.

"Must be nice," Galen continued. "Your collections sold like crazy. You're engaged, a baby on the way."

"Engaged to my ex-wife," Étienne clarified. "And men my age don't want the babies —"

"At least it's your ex-wife. What if it was somebody else? With your history..."

Étienne froze. The flames flickered with renewed intensity.

"What do you say?" Étienne replied. He switched to French knowing Galen understood the language. "Do you think I have mistresses? That I cheat?"

Galen's lips straightened and curled as a strange pink swirled inside his irises, like the fire in an opal. In the distance, something dripped with a deafening ferocity. Étienne searched for the source of the noise with his peripheral vision, afraid to look away from Galen.

"Oh, Étienne, the whole world knows about you and Adelaide. Rumors say it's why she killed herself," Galen chuckled. "The tabloids got the gist of your up-and-coming days and what you did when Adelaide was an innocent teenager."

The flames sizzled. The dripping quickened. Fire and rain. Galen's face glowed red in a mask of fire.

"*Non*," Étienne said. "I did not. I would not. You believe *les ragots*."

"The gossip?" Galen replied. "I believe that's the word you're missing."

Crushing consumed Étienne's chest as the pain erupted with renewed tenacity. His shaking fingers fumbled for the nitroglycerin on the keychain. He got the pill into his mouth, closing his eyes as it disintegrated.

"She told me," Galen said. "She told me exactly how you touched her."

"Non," Étienne insisted.

Étienne's chest loosened. He opened his eyes to a film of water covering Galen's skin and no more fire.

"I have no memory of doing anything with her," Étienne said.

"She said you had the softest hands of anyone she had ever met," Galen said.

He grabbed Étienne's fingers. Étienne's flesh gleamed positively white next to the rich hue of Galen's even in the dusky light. Étienne jerked free.

"They're not," Galen responded.

"I have not done the sewing. The silks ... require..."

Droplets from Galen's skin trickled across Étienne's palm. He wiped them on the damp towel.

"Excuse me," he told Galen.

Étienne returned the towel to the bartender and hobbled to the restroom without his cane. Étienne pushed inside the swinging saloon doors. The room washed in and out of shadow from the single dangling bulb. He loosened the tap with a paper towel and washed his hands. The hair on his neck curled tighter. He checked the mirror. He found nothing but himself, thinner and more haggard than he liked, but himself nonetheless.

The walls of the bathroom shrank. The flow from the spigot surged. The water ricocheted from the basin onto his shirt and slacks. Brutal cold filled the room followed by vanilla scent. While he fought with the taps, something darted across the room and touched his back. The lingering aroma heightened, melding with notes of rose, anise, ginger. His knees buckled. Gaultier Classique, Adelaide's perfume. He gazed again to the mirror, where he discovered the hazy silhouette of a tall woman.

Étienne squeezed his eyes closed. Opening them again, he confirmed his vision amid a sea of black spots. Adelaide stood behind him, her unmistakable curves, her strawberry blond locks framing her heart-shaped face and her blue eyes gleaming like lapis lazuli. The water now overflowed the basin. Étienne cursed his lack of sleep and indulged his heavy heart. A tear welled in his eye. He turned, ready to face the reality behind him and discard the reflection. He stepped onto thick boots and walked directly into Galen.

How did Galen manage to sneak up on him? The hallucination must have distracted him. Étienne glanced over his shoulder at the mirror. Adelaide stood there, exactly where Galen should be, but no Galen. Étienne pivoted.

Now Galen had disappeared, leaving Adelaide in the middle of the bathroom with water circling her Christian Louboutin pumps. She wore a flawless suit in official Chez d'Amille off-white. The pencil skirt fell almost to her knee, a coin pocket on the left hip. The unfastened waist-length jacket showed a ribbed orangish-salmon turtleneck that perfectly matched her hair. Grief finally had driven him to madness, Étienne thought. He could never again mock his mother for imagining the ghost of his father...

"You have to stop blaming yourself, Et," the phantom said.

Only Adelaide called him 'Et.' His grandmother would blame this experience on heartsickness. His mother would say that Adelaide had found him. The world hushed, even the rushing water. Adelaide placed her warm hands on his face, her long, pale fingers stroking his cheeks. Her body leaned against him.

Intense pain racked the muscles of his neck. A killer headache hit him as Adelaide's trademark 'Woodland Rose' lips fell against his in a chaste peck. He closed his eyes. Real or imagined, Étienne didn't want this to end. Her lips dampened one cheek, then the other. Painless pressure slammed into Étienne's chest. He could die like this, another heart attack, but he didn't care. He wrapped his arms around her.

Étienne returned the familiar kisses. Left cheek, then right, then ... a resounding ache erupted in his skull as some force knocked him to the floor, his head striking the overflowing sink along the way. He landed in a puddle against the wall.

"What the fuck are you doing?" Galen screamed.

The saloon doors opened. A second man stepped inside, a burly figure heading for the urinal. Étienne tried to focus on the newcomer's face, but he couldn't see. Galen crouched before Étienne, arms balanced across his knees.

"Did you strike me in the eye with your fist?" Étienne asked in French.

Étienne shook as Galen pulled him to his feet. Another man entered the restroom, this one older with strength in his face. The water now flooded from the bathroom.

"What's going on in here?" the man asked.

The guy at the urinal shrugged. "I don't know, Jack, looks like these two had a fight."

"This is my bar," Jack replied, turning to Galen and Étienne. "I want you out."

Galen laughed, and it echoed. His arm lashed out, smashing the stern bar owner in the face. A second blow headed for Étienne, but Étienne managed to duck, at least enough so it landed against his jaw and not his eye. A salty, metallic flavor filled his mouth as Étienne bit his cheek.

"I'm calling the cops," Jack said, walking from the bathroom rubbing his chin.

The guy at the urinal zipped his pants and left abruptly. Étienne slipped around Galen, hoping to sneak out, but Galen grabbed his shirt.

"I am sorry," Étienne said in French. "Sorry no one told you that she killed herself. It was a bad time. It is still a bad time."

"Why did you kiss me?" Galen asked.

"It doesn't matter."

Galen clenched his fingers into a fist.

"I think it does," Galen said.

Étienne cast his eyes to the floor and mumbled. "I imagined her."

"Adelaide," Galen added.

Étienne nodded. Galen released him. The scream of sirens cut through the walls, and Galen disappeared. Étienne poked his head out the door, wondering where Galen went. The sirens grew louder. Étienne limped to his table, still searching for Galen. He got his cane, his coat and his scarf. He placed a twenty on the table as a generous tip. How did Galen leave so quickly? Étienne fumbled to button his coat. A cop barreled through the front door.

"The one guy's gone," Étienne heard Jack yell, "but the French guy's still here."

Merde, Étienne thought. How do they always manage to label him 'The French Guy'? He didn't even talk to anybody but the bartender and Galen. Étienne crept toward the stairwell. The cop circled the bar and walked toward him. Étienne pretended not to notice.

"Hey, buddy," the cop called.

Could Étienne feign complete ignorance of the English language? Partial ignorance? He continued toward the stairwell, until the cop blocked him.

"You look rough," the cop said.

"Comment, *flic? Est-ce que vous me dites?*" Étienne replied.

Hopefully, the cop didn't speak French. '*Flic*' wasn't the worst thing to call a cop, but it didn't exactly endear respect.

"Your face. It looks rough. You got blood on your lip."

"My face?" Étienne repeated.

"Yeah," the cop said. "You start something?"

"Do I look the one that starts the something?" Étienne replied. "Blow him with my cane, *n'est-ce pas?*"

"What happened? Why did he hit you?"

Étienne said the only thing he could: "A woman."

"Jack says he's not gonna press charges, as long as you and your friend stay out of his bar."

"And this ambiance will be missing to me..." Étienne remarked.

The cop's face remained blank.

"If I say yes, you will permit me to go?" Étienne asked.

"Yeah."

"Oui, oui, yes, I stay out."

The cop stepped aside. Étienne did not stop until he reached the car. He set his cane in the back and collapsed in the driver's seat. With the excitement done, and the cop maintaining vigilance from his cruiser along the street, Étienne's face throbbed with renewed rawness. He started the car and wondered how he would ever explain this to Zélie...